Praise for HIGH STRANGENESS

"HIGH STRANGENESS indeed! Alison Drake knows about the terror of the sudden confrontation with the unknown, a terror that is even greater when the unknown is not 'out there,' but within ourselves: in our brains, our souls, in human relationships, in everyday actions. She has captured that terrible force, harnessed it, and translated it into a haunting story that takes us beyond the edge of madness and threatens reality itself."

JACQUES VALLEE

HIGH STRANGENESS

Alison Drake

BALLANTINE BOOKS • NEW YORK

Copyright © 1992 by Alison Drake

All rights reserved under International and Pan-American Copyright Conventions. Published in the United States of America by Ballantine Books, a division of Random House, Inc., New York, and simultaneously in Canada by Random House of Canada Limited, Toronto.

Library of Congress Catalog Card Number: 92-90621

ISBN 0-345-35779-5

Manufactured in the United States of America

First Edition: November 1992

For Linda Griffin and Renie Wiley,
who have always understood;
and for Patti Cannon Scott
and Lorraine Renouf Sneider,
the best of the Caracas crew

High strangeness: any event or experience related to UFOs that is above and beyond the usual strangeness associated with the phenomena.

Special thanks to my editor, Joe Blades,
for all his support;
to Jim Moseley for an insider's view;
and to my husband, Rob, my first reader always

Part One

FLIGHT

"There has been no evidence indicating that sightings categorized as 'unidentified' are extraterrestrial vehicles."

—Project Blue Book

"Keep your eyes
on the skies."

—Betty Hill

I

(1)

The car whipped through the warm, oily darkness, up and down hills, around bends as sharp as broken bones. She gripped the steering wheel and leaned into it, trying to see the next twist. But the headlights were no better than candles against the blackness.

The tires shrieked. The car's rear end fishtailed. She didn't slow down, couldn't. They were back there somewhere, seeking her, coming for her beneath the ebony skin of a sky where stars bulged like luminous pimples. But they wouldn't find her, wouldn't catch her or trick her again. She was a moon in hiding.

The humid air rushed through the open windows, mixing with the stink of blood. It was everywhere, on her hands and clothes, in her hair, seeping from the seats and the windshield, a stigmata. She couldn't remember where it had come from and she couldn't escape it. The odor clung to her, covered her.

Her hands climbed around the steering wheel, twisting it as the road twisted. The headlights bounced off giant mushrooms festooned in streamers of moss. As she neared them, she saw that they were trees, of course, trees whose name she couldn't remember. And the moss, what was it about the moss? *It speaks in tongues.* . . . Who had said that to her? Who?

The road angled steeply upward again. She anxiously

scanned the sky for the moon. Hidden, it was her consort, her confidant; exposed, it was her betrayer. Which would it be this time?

She glanced in the rearview mirror. Unrelieved darkness stretched behind her, a black continent. But she knew it was a trick, a mask, a lie. They were still after her, racing to claim her as if she were an invaluable heirloom or the artifact of some ancient civilization. She chewed at her lower lip, pressed the gas pedal to the floor, begged the car to move faster, faster, please.

The moon remained concealed and the growth of trees thickened, crowding the road and the sky until only a narrow band of stars was visible. A highway of stars that shimmered like Popsicles, close enough to lick. She recognized these stars, this sky, this Band-Aid of a road, but she couldn't place the details in any context, couldn't connect them to one another. They were like names of people whose faces she had forgotten.

Near the top of the hill the headlights washed across a lopsided wooden sign coming up on her right. Beyond it, nearly obscured by a web of hanging moss, yawned the mouth of a dirt road. Her hands remembered it and turned the wheel sharply, suddenly. The car bounced like a beach ball over ruts, potholes, ditches. Gravel pinged against the doors. Dust flew through the open windows and settled on the dash, the seat, her skin. She coughed, downshifted, tapped the brake. The trees closed in, the stars vanished. The road dipped down, down through the trees, spiraling, coiling, choked by underbrush until it simply ended.

It didn't matter. She knew the way now, knew it as though a map had unfolded inside her, the place marked with a large black X that shouted: *Here, this way, quick.*

Branches clawed at the car as she dodged trees and bushes. Shadows congealed until they assumed shape and depth and loomed in the dark like buildings in a city that remained just out of reach. Panic seized her, turned her inside out like shirt, a sock, a ruined shoe. She wept and laughed until the sounds were identical and knew that what they said about her was true. She was deranged. There was no safe place in the woods, there was blood on her hands, she had seen lights in the sky, she had died and been reborn and didn't know her name.

Then she saw it, a flash of glass, and laughed out loud. Since the little house was there, tucked away in the huge mushroom trees, then she wasn't crazy, was she? The tires crunched over fallen branches, brush, weeds. She drove under the moss; it whispered across the roof of the car. The moss was real. The house was real.

She stopped at the side of it, left the headlights on, climbed out. What now? What was she supposed to do now? Her hands saved her. They remembered where she was, what to do. They pulled moss from the nearest trees and draped it over the hood, the roof, the trunk, rendering the car as invisible as the moon.

When she was finished, she turned off the headlights, grabbed her bundle from the passenger seat, removed the keys, and locked the doors. She lit the candle that she'd carried in her bundle, held it up like a staff, a sword, and made her way toward the front door.

Weeds grew from the cracks in the sidewalk. Lizards skittered away through the tall grass. An owl hooted. The night was alive with noises that were, in some odd way, familiar to her.

The door was locked, but again her hands remembered what her mind did not: She reached into a flowerpot filled with weeds and dug around until she found a key. It was badly rusted, but it worked. The door creaked as it swung open and stale air washed over her, warm as the sea. She stepped inside quickly. After locking the door, she held the candle high so she could see.

A vaulted ceiling, exposed beams, a fireplace with a chimney. It seemed that she should remember these details, but she didn't. The few pieces of furniture were covered with white sheets. Dead bugs littered the floor. The lights didn't work. The air smelled of dust, secrets, regrets.

She hurried around, opening windows that still had

screens, tearing the sheets from the old chairs, the couch, a rocking chair, waiting for a surge of memories that would fix this place within the context of the life she couldn't recall. But only her hands and the motions of her body possessed any certainty at all.

In the hallway mirror, she gazed at the woman in the glass, a tall, thin stranger holding her candle like the Statue of Liberty held her torch. *Free me*, she thought at the reflection. *Give me back my memories.* But the stranger had nothing to say to her. The stranger had blood on her clothes. Madness shadowed the blue of her eyes.

"Get lost," she whispered to the stranger, and the woman in the mirror turned away.

She fixed the candle in a pool of wax on the stone of the fireplace and stripped off her bloodstained clothes. She wrapped herself up in one of the dusty sheets, a Roman in a toga, an impostor at a costume ball.

She retrieved the candle, hastened to the kitchen, dropped the soiled clothes in the sink. She let the water run until the dust had cleared, then filled the sink and left the clothes to soak. Tomorrow she would find soap and wash them. She would hang them in the sun to dry. They would absorb the scent of trees and earth, water and sky, scents that would obliterate the sharp, metallic odor of the blood.

Whose blood?

Where?

I killed him.

The thought slammed into her. She grabbed on to the edge of the sink to steady herself. When her knees had hardened again, when she could feel her legs, she backed away from the clothes, the water, the sink, and tore into the front room where she had left her bundle. She cradled it like an infant in the crook of her arm and moved toward the stairs. Up there, on the second floor, she would be safe. She didn't question how she knew this; she simply did. It was like the memory in her hands, pure, undiluted.

But as she climbed the stairs, her eyes fastened on the landing window just in front of her, a huge rectangle of glass that was uncovered, naked, pale with starlight. The sight of it terrified her. She didn't think she could move past it. She began to tremble and tugged the sheet more tightly around her shoulders and arms. The window, something about the window. She almost seized it, an elusive memory of brilliant lights, a sea of light.

Then the memory was gone and she stumbled up the stairs, weeping, the emptiness of her womb like a terrible penance for a sin she couldn't recall. She passed the first room, stopped in the doorway of the second. Here, the bed was made and thick curtains covered the windows. She melted wax onto an empty saucer and twisted the candle into it until it stuck. She set it on the nightstand next to a small lamp.

It was a child's lamp, with a teddy bear sitting on a wooden base and a dusty, faded shade covering him like an umbrella. She touched the teddy's black button eyes, his floppy ears, his funny ball of a tail. His mouth, no longer than a dash, seemed to smile at her. The pinched tightness returned to her chest. Her eyes filled with tears again. She didn't know why she had chosen this room over the others, but what did it matter? The mattress was soft, the sheets were damp from the humidity, the pillows welcomed her.

Her head sank into a nest of feathers. She drew the sheet up over her, hugged her bundle against her. The windows were shut and covered and she couldn't hear a sound. Not the wind, not the insects that were surely buzzing against the glass, not even the house. She felt small, compact, secure.

Then the candle hissed, a viper inches from her head, and she started to shake again, to weep again. She didn't know how long the attack lasted—and that's what it was, an attack, an assault, a violation—but after a while it passed.

Exhaustion settled through her and she closed her eyes. Her last thoughts were of blood and *them*, of windows exploding with light, of deserted roads begging for dawn, of mushroom trees, and of moss that spoke in tongues when the wind swept through it.

(2)

Evan Nate stood in a corner of the greenhouse behind his home near Homestead Air Force Base. He was watching a large tropical spider put the finishing touches on a web she had spun between two of his papaya trees. This particular variety was a *Nephili madagascariensis*, a virtual giant that could grasp a human hand with its outstretched legs. Although it wasn't native to Florida, it survived here quite well. Especially in the greenhouse, where the temperature was maintained between eighty and eighty-five degrees.

The web had been constructed with more than one kind of thread. The center, the spider's lookout where she would sit motionless in wait of a prey, consisted of dry threads produced by a pair of bottle-shaped glands. Other dry threads radiated from this, spokes that extended to the rim of the web. Attached to the spokes were sticky threads, produced by two different pairs of glands, which filled the space between hub and rim. These were known as the *trapping spirals* and were coated with a secretion from the glue glands. Once secreted, the substance contracted and formed small beads, or *birdlime*, in which insects got caught.

One would suppose, Nate thought, that the spider herself would become caught. But she gripped only the dry threads as she maneuvered around the web, adroitly avoiding any contact with the sticky spiral. She was a marvelously tactile creature, a fact that never ceased to fascinate him. By keeping one leg on a spoke or on a specially constructed *telegraph wire*, for instance, she could tell when a prey had flown into the web simply by the vibration of the thread.

If the prey didn't move, she located its position by plucking each thread with astonishing speed. Then she immediately secured her victim in a cocoon of very fine silk threads secreted by yet another gland and bit it several times to paralyze or kill it. Once the insect was completely helpless, she released it from the web and carried it to the lookout center, where it was hung by a short thread. There, she injected peptic juices into her victim and sucked them up later when all the nutrients were dissolved. The exterior skeletons were then tossed out of the web.

Spiders were an example of Nature at her most efficient best. And since this pretty lady had chosen his greenhouse for her web, he would reward her with a tidbit for breakfast. Something that would entice her to stick around and do what pesticides had failed to do.

Nate studied the glass aquariums lined up on the counter to his left. Each contained a particular species of bug that had given him trouble here in the greenhouse. Fire ants, caterpillars with a fondness for periwinkles and orchids, roaches that feasted on virtually anything, snails that had decimated his last crop of mangoes, bugs that flew, that crawled, that burrowed.

From time to time he tried different poisons on them— granules, pellets, sprays—and kept meticulous notes on what each experiment yielded. So far, though, he hadn't found any single poison that was unilaterally efficient. But he would, sooner or later he would.

As Nate leaned close to the aquarium that held the ants, his reflection was trapped briefly in the glass: bald head, gray eyes as hard and round as marbles, a mouth more suited for a woman's face, the hawk nose he had always hated, and the creases. The creases of time, of five and a half decades. *You're getting up there*, he thought.

He tapped the glass wall; the fire ants swarmed through the intricate tunnels of their mounds, scurried across the inner walls. Busy busy busy. He'd stumbled into a fire ant nest years ago and before those nasty fuckers were finished with him, his feet had swollen to twice their normal size and he'd nearly died of anaphylactic shock.

From a drawer, he brought out a long metal instrument with a blunted end. He stuck a folded strip of very sticky tape to the end, then slipped the device through the trapdoor in the aquarium's lid. Seconds later, he pulled it out, a fire ant squirming valiantly against the tape, and walked over to the web. With a second instrument that resembled a pair of elongated tweezers he extricated the tape with the ant still on it, then touched it to the birdlime in the web. The spider, instantly alerted by the vibrations, raced toward the fire ant.

Nate smiled as he watched, anticipating the instant when the spider would pounce. But the spectacle was spoiled by the peal of the phone, a sharp, irritating noise that seemed to echo within the walls of the greenhouse. Even if he ignored it, if he let his wife or daughter pick up in the house, the caller would eventually track him down. They always did.

"Nate here."

"Colonel, sorry to, uh, disturb you at this hour."

"I was up." He moved toward the web, the telephone line stretching. "What is it, Doctor?"

"We have a, uh, problem here."

Yes, of course. His callers always had problems that he was supposed to solve. "What sort of problem?" He watched the spider wrapping the fire ant in a neat, silken cocoon.

"One of our patients has escaped and killed Vance Liscomb and an attendant in the process."

Liscomb. Christ. He squeezed the bridge of his nose, suddenly conscious of a debilitating fatigue that nibbled at the edge of his awareness. "And just what do you expect me to do about it, Dr. Winthrop? Revive him? Bring him back from the dead?"

"Uh, no, sir, I thought you might want to know."

"Yes, yes, of course. Thank you for telling me. I'll take care of things from here."

"But that isn't all."

Winthrop's hesitation didn't bode well. "Yes? Go on, what else?" He watched the spider carrying her treasure to the center of the web, watched her biting it, injecting it with peptic juices. Digested alive, he thought. "Dr. Winthrop? Are you still there?"

"Yes, sir, yes, I am. The, uh, patient was Margaret Wickerd."

Nate shut his eyes and dozens of details crowded his head, each one shouting, demanding his immediate attention with the crassness of shoppers at the return counter the day after

Christmas. Liscomb, Margaret Wickerd, who else? Who? "Have the police been called?"

"Yes, sir."

He was surrounded by inept fools. "You should have called me first, Dr. Winthrop."

"I . . . I wasn't here when it happened. Dr. Treak found the bodies and under the circumstances, well . . . I mean, there was a nurse who saw the bodies and a couple of the patients and well, what else could she do, Colonel?"

His head pounded. He stared at the spider, who had returned to the center of her web, waiting again. The cocoon that held the fire ant dangled nearby like some tiny, pale lantern. Such marvelous efficiency, he thought wistfully, and he was surrounded by incompetents.

"Is there anything I should do, Colonel?"

He almost laughed. "You've already done it, Doctor. Say as little as possible and I'll be in touch."

Nate disconnected, then stood there with his hand on the receiver, his eyes fixed on the web. Do nothing for now, he thought. Do nothing and wait, like the spider.

2

(1)

The atrium at the side of the lighthouse was as lush and crowded as a rain forest. When Aline parted the dense growth with her hands, her fingers vanished beneath leaves of ivy a foot wide, her feet were hidden by a dome of bougainvillea bursting with crimson buds, and a tall stalk of pampas grass tickled her nose.

"Boo," she whispered. "You in here?" She placed a plate of raw fish on one of the circular stones in the footpath. "Chow time, little guy."

Leaves rustled and the screech owl's head poked through them. He hopped over to her, barely visible in the dim wash of starlight in the predawn sky. He stood just seven inches high from his eartufts to his feet, with reddish brown feathers streaked here and there with darker brown, like chocolate-swirl cookies. She and Kincaid had christened him Boo, short for *buho*, the Spanish word for owl.

They had found him a month ago, on their first night in the lighthouse. He had hopped out of the weeds around dusk, a scrawny little fellow with a broken left wing and grass in his feathers, easily tempted by the raw fish Aline had left on the front porch for him. Within a few days he'd allowed her to get close enough to touch him and at the end of the week the vet had driven out to the lighthouse to take a look at him.

The verdict on the wing wasn't good. Two bones were broken, a large and a small. The vet set the first, said the other would mend on its own, but that the owl probably wouldn't fly again. And if he couldn't fly, his diet would be restricted to whatever rodents, frogs, and insects he could catch on his own. The vet suggested a zoo; Aline balked and decided to keep him.

In the weeks since, Boo had flourished in the atrium. The fence that separated it from the yard provided protection during the day when he slept. At night, he simply ducked under it and ventured into the woods around the lighthouse. The splint was gone from his wing now, but he still hadn't flown and she continued to feed him.

He held each chunk of fish with his claws and tore off pieces with his sharp beak. Now and then he looked away from the fish, as if seeking the source of some small sound she couldn't hear. Since his eyes were nearly immovable, this required that he turn his head.

An owl's eyes were more forwardly directed than other birds', so their visual fields overlapped. This created a binocular span of sixty to seventy degrees, about a sixth of a circle. Some species of owls were able to turn their heads in a three-quarter circle or completely upside down, in a one eighty. But not this fellow. The most he could manage was a turn of about one fifty, roughly the angle of a shrink's couch, as Kincaid put it.

As soon as he'd finished eating, he hopped up close to Aline and touched his beak gently to her outstretched palm. He tapped it twice, his way of saying thanks for the chow, she supposed, then permitted her to inspect his wing. He knew the routine as well as she did by now.

Despite the vet's admonitions that Boo would probably tear off the splint within a day or two, the owl had proven him wrong. Perhaps at some rudimentary level he'd understood it might help him fly again. So he'd endured three weeks of the splint and for what? The wing remained limp and droopy. "Well, it looks better than it did yesterday, Boo."

He blinked, then vanished into the leaves. Aline went back inside, where Unojo and Wolfe glared at her, jealous spectators awaiting some of that raw beef, thank you very much. Kincaid's tabby cat and her skunk still hadn't adjusted to the new addition in the family and maintained a respectful distance.

But Wolfe also pouted and behaved as though she had betrayed him. After all, for years it had just been the two of them, sharing whatever a human and a skunk could share. Then suddenly his space had been violated by a cat, and just when he was getting accustomed to her, the owl had arrived. How could she blame him? So she tolerated his little fits of temper, the towels that he gnawed, the shoes that he urinated in.

"Don't worry, I've got leftovers for you guys, too." Unojo (Ewn-*oh*-ho was one of those Spanish words she always saw phonetically in her mind)—One Eye—rubbed up against her leg, but Wolfe growled and stamped his feet, sure signs that he intended to blast her. Never mind that he couldn't because he'd been de-scented; it was the threat that counted. His eight-inch tail flicked up, quivered, then he sauntered off, indignant.

"You're as bad as a two-year-old," she called after him.

He replied with another flick of his tail.

Aline picked up the cat and headed for the kitchen. Each of these animals had found her and Kincaid; the word had apparently spread that they were a couple of suckers for the orphaned, the injured, the down and out. Four years ago, when she lived alone at the south end of the island, Wolfe had appeared in her yard one day, huddled next to a rock. He'd been maybe a month old, if that, and no larger than the palm of her hand.

Unojo had jumped into Kincaid's car last May and settled into the passenger seat as if by invitation. The way he told the story, she was an enchanted cat, blinking at him with her weird eyes, one amber, the other the color of milk, just daring him to oust her.

And now the owl.

What next? A rabbit? A friendly iguana? One of the island's Florida panthers? She rather liked that idea: Aline

Scott as a naturalist, a Jane Goodall of Tango Key. During Kincaid's absences the animals would prowl the lighthouse at night; sentries, guardians, companions of her solitude.

This time Kincaid had been gone only three days but it seemed much longer, especially at night when the size of the lighthouse and its isolation were enhanced by the darkness. The place rose from the lip of a cliff on the western slope of Tango Key, a great bleached bone standing on end. Built between 1870 and 1872, it was a monolithic relic of the days when the island was a dark green pearl afloat in the Gulf Stream. Like most old buildings, its history was rich with superstitious lore.

She had heard many of the stories when she was a kid, tales whispered over campfires until they had assumed almost mythical proportions. The strange lights, the sounds from the glass beacon room at the top, the chill of the air around the old seamen's graveyard, the ghosts of pirates and fishermen roaming the darkened hallways. She wasn't immune to the mystique of things that went bump in the night, not then, not now. But so far nothing had bumped that couldn't be explained, which was disappointing. At the very least, she'd hoped for a benign ghost, a mischievous prankster as clever as a cat whose presence would compensate for the fact that she and Kincaid were now cash poor.

Strapped with double mortgages because her house in town still hadn't sold, their finances had never been worse. They lived on her income from the police department and used what he made on insurance investigations for emergencies. But the insurance biz was slow these days, which was why he'd taken a surveillance case in Miami.

Kincaid, naturally, hated surveillance cases nearly as much as he did insurance cases and was chafing for the freedom of *real* travel. To him that meant Asia or Australia, not Miami or Key West. Like a smoker who couldn't get through his morning coffee without a cigarette, he couldn't start the day without a map or a travel book in front of him.

But the bottom line, she thought, was that they were living together for the first time in the four years since they'd met and she wasn't convinced that the arrangement really suited either of them. Until now, they had shuffled back and forth between her place and his, with long gaps in between when Kincaid traveled and the relationship went on hold. There had been a separateness to their lives then that she liked. Now the way out was sealed. They shared the same bathroom.

In the kitchen, she started the coffee and chopped up leftover beef for Wolfe and Unojo. The sky to the west had lightened to violet. The turquoise waters of the Gulf shimmered in the mist, suggesting a submerged continent or a lost world. It was easy to imagine pirate ships churning through all that blue water two hundred years ago, plundering the coastal waters and the island in search of gold. It was easy, in fact, to imagine almost anything out there.

The phone rang, an intrusive noise that seemed to echo up through the lighthouse, bouncing against its thick walls like a ball defying gravity. It irritated her—the noise, the fact that it was just past six—and she was tempted to let the answering machine pick up. But it wouldn't be the department; this was her day off. So it had to be Kincaid, probably calling to let her know he would be in Miami longer than he'd expected.

"Hi, Ryan."

"Sorry to disappoint you, Al. It's Bernie."

Claudia Bernelli, her long-time partner and oldest friend, rarely rose before the sun or called before nine. The fact that she had done both didn't bode well for Aline's day off. "I'm free today, remember?"

"Tell it to the chief, Al. We've got a mess at the Wellness Center and he wants everyone over there pronto. I'm on my way out the door now."

The center was an exclusive clinic for mental patients at the northern end of the island. Aline thought of it as the sort of place that catered to the Zelda Fitzgeralds of the Nineties, rich, neurotic women with time on their hands. It had been built three years ago despite outraged protests by people who

lived and worked in Pirate's Cove, its nearest neighbor and
the wealthiest community on the island.

"You want to define mess?"

"An escapee who took down an orderly and one of the
shrinks."

Bye-bye, free day. "I'll meet you there in twenty minutes."

(2)

Tango Key measured eleven miles at its longest point and
seven at its widest. It was shaped like the head of a cat with
a few proportion problems: ears that were set too widely, a
jaw that was too rounded, a face that was much too long.

Pirate's Cove with its two-million-dollar marina occupied
the left ear and the other was a wilderness preserve. The cat's
mouth fell around Tango, the main town to the south, and its
nose and whiskers marked the location of the airport and the
beginning of the hills.

Thanks to the abundance of rain this year, the October
hills were a deep, emerald green. Dew glistened on the cushions of grass, the pink and lavender periwinkles, the wild
daisies, the pines, and the banyans. The air here possessed
an entirely different scent than it did where she lived. It was
sweeter, richer, more earthy.

This was the rural heart of the island, equidistant from
either town and sparsely populated. The homes scattered
through these hills belonged to snowbirds and to old-time
natives who continued to farm the same plots of land their
ancestors had tilled. Most of the papayas, mangoes, and gua-
vas grown here were sold to local markets in the keys and
were among the best Aline had ever tasted. But the heads of
pygmy lettuce, the sweet green beans, and the Tango County
citrus were now competing in the statewide market. Combined with the fish industry and tourism, the island's econ-

omy was booming. And nowhere was it more evident than in Pirate's Cove.

The town had thrived for two hundred years and its history was everywhere: in the names of things (Doubloon Drive, Treasure Mall, Pieces of Eight Theatre), in the logos that graced store windows (full-masted ships, anchors, mermaids), even in the color of street signs (gold). The tidy roads were packed with expensive boutiques, small parks, and homes that were uniformly large, gracious, and affordable only by millionaires.

The main road through town was already bustling. Pedestrians strolled the cobbled walks, exotic dogs strained at expensive leashes, cars that cost more than she made in a year idled at curbs and stoplights. Even if she could afford to live here, she probably wouldn't. She preferred the casual, laid-back life-style in the town of Tango. The gulf between the island's two main towns, however, wasn't simply a difference in life-styles and incomes. It was cultural, as though they were separate countries with unique languages and customs.

The Wellness Center appeared on her left two miles east of town. The iron gate was open and the guardhouse was empty, so she drove on through. And yes, it was impressive. Ten acres of landscaped grounds were intersected by footpaths, ponds, a bicycle trail. The lazy-S driveway curved past a water fountain to six wooden A-frames arranged in a half-moon. And all of it was surrounded by a white wall partially covered by ivy. It had the feel of a religious cloister. She expected to see nuns in habits, priests in robes, would-be saints awaiting canonization. Instead, ordinary-looking people were clustered in small groups near the driveway. She couldn't tell if they were patients or employees; none wore a uniform or a name tag.

Two police cruisers, the skeleton crew's forensics van, Chief Frederick's aging pickup, and Bernie's spiffy new Cherokee crowded the driveway. Aline parked her Honda on the grass and hurried toward the main building. No one stopped her, asked who she was, or questioned her right to be here.

The lobby reminded her of a seaside resort: Mexican tile floors, rattan furniture, throw rugs, soft music, cool, fragrant air. A profusion of plants basked in the early sunlight that streamed through the picture windows overlooking the Gulf. Tasteful paintings adorned the pastel walls. But the room was utterly deserted, its silence broken by the forlorn peal of a phone in some other part of the building.

She felt as though she had strolled onto a movie set where the plants were fake and the walls were made of cardboard. Any second now, the view of the Gulf would vanish like a mirage, the sunlight would wink out, and a director would rush out shouting: "Cut, cut, let's take it again."

She walked over to the reception counter, hoping to find a bell that she could ring, and caught sight of herself in the mirrored wall behind it. She looked as disheveled as she felt. Her cinnamon hair was loose and, thanks to the humidity, fell in a frizz halfway down her back. Her vibrant blue eyes were bloodshot from lack of sleep, her nose seemed pinched, too narrow, and her mouth was a shade too large for the rest of her face. But what the hell, she had terrific teeth.

She stood five foot eight in her bare feet, was slender but not skinny, and worked at maintaining curves in the right places. In all, she looked pretty good for a woman pushing forty, she thought. So why had she dreamed repeatedly last night that Kincaid had found a sweet young thing up there in Miami? Why had the dream driven her out of bed before the sun had risen? Was the approach of the big Four-O marked by sudden insecurities?

Her self-absorbed musing was interrupted by a woman who appeared in the mirror, a ghost in the reading area behind her. Aline turned to make sure the woman was real. She was, and she looked like a reject from a Tennessee Williams play: unruly red hair, skin that was pale, a body that was beanstalk thin. Dressed in white slacks and a white shirt, she fluttered about with a hummingbird's nervous energy, rifling through the neatly arranged magazines on a coffee table.

"Excuse me," Aline said, walking over to her.

The woman's head snapped up, her eyes narrowed with suspicion, and she flattened a magazine to her chest. "Who're you?"

"Detective Scott. Do you know where—"

"Through that door." She waved vaguely to the left. "The one that says EMPLOYEES ONLY. They're in the treatment room."

"Thanks."

"They won't find her, you know."

"Who?"

"Margaret. That *is* why you're here, isn't it? Because of Margaret? Of course it's why you're here. You're a cop, right? Unless your first name is Detective." She laughed. It eased the lines of suspicion at her mouth, the squint of her eyes, and returned youth to her face. Aline realized she was no older than her early thirties and quite pretty, like a woman on a cameo. "Oops, sorry." She giggled and covered her hand with her mouth. "I've got to stop doing that. Dr. Treak says it makes people uncomfortable. But then she also says Margaret killed Hugh and Dr. Liscomb and that's just not true. She adored Hugh and hated Liscomb as much as I do, but neither of us would *kill* him."

"You know her?"

"Sure." She pulled a pack of cigarettes from a pocket in her slacks, lit one, dropped her head back, and blew the smoke up into the air. "We roomed together until they separated us. They said we stirred up too much trouble."

A muscle now ticked wildly under her right eye and, as if this were some sort of signal to the rest of her body, she began to twitch and fidget. Her hands patted at her clothes, her hair, the magazine still clutched to her chest. Her shoulder hunched up and she rubbed her cheek against it. She shifted her weight from one foot to the other. Over and over again these mannerisms repeated themselves in precisely the same order, with the same rhythm, like some intricately choreographed dance. Only the tick under her eye remained constant.

"How long did you room together?"

"I don't remember exactly." Twitch, twitch. "Well, let me see. Margaret had been here for six months and I guess we roomed together for about half that. Yeah, about half." She turned her head to the side, blew smoke toward the light streaming through the window. "Then Liscomb started in with the machine."

"What machine?"

She looked at Aline, the twitching worse now. "The Zapper. That's what Margaret and I call it. Zap, zap, and you can't remember the things you knew yesterday. Zap again and your address vanishes. Another zap and you can't remember if you've ever been married or if you have kids or a family and sometimes you can't even remember your own name."

Her voice trailed off, and for fifteen or twenty seconds, she didn't speak, didn't blink, didn't move at all. Even the twitching had stopped. It was as if some neural plug had been pulled, leaving only the hollow husk of the woman's body. Aline didn't know whether to speak to her, to sit her in a chair, or to call for help. Before she had to decide, the woman twitched to life again like a puppet, settled on the couch with her magazine, and paged through it with the indifference of a woman under a hair dryer at the beauty shop.

"Uh, excuse me," Aline said. "You were saying something about the Zapper."

The woman raised her eyes; they were completely blank.

"We were talking about Margaret," Aline went on.

"Ssshh." The woman held a finger to her mouth. "Margaret was bad. I can't talk about Margaret if I want to get out of here." Then she bowed her head and returned to her magazine.

"Hey, Al." Bernie breezed through the front door, as thin and quick as a coed, her fingers stabbing at her short blonde hair. She had obviously dressed hastily: jeans, high-tops, a cotton shirt, and none of her customary jewelry. A cigarette burned between her fingers. "Where've you been, anyway?"

"Right here, trying to figure out where to go."

"Well, c'mon." She took Aline by the arm and led her

away from the woman on the couch. "There're some things you need to see."

"Give me some background first. What the hell's going on?"

Whispering now: "A fruitcake named Margaret Wickerd killed her shrink and one of the orderlies when she was brought in for electroshock treatment around four this morning." They were already moving toward the door marked EMPLOYEES ONLY. "She was supposedly going to be moved to a facility in Miami if this series of treatments didn't work. Anyway, she killed them and split in the security guard's car. Apparently no one knew about it until the bodies were found shortly after five."

"Where was the car?"

"Just outside the gate. The guard had fallen asleep."

"What was she being treated for?"

Bernie smirked. "You'll love this. She claimed that eight months ago she was abducted by little gray men who performed medical experiments on her and caused her to have a miscarriage. She became severely depressed and her husband committed her two months later."

"Little gray men?"

Bernie looked at her. "Yeah, you know, Al, little gray spacemen with big, black bug eyes."

Aline laughed. "C'mon."

"I knew you'd like it."

The door opened and a short, plump woman strode through. Her skin was very pale, as though she rarely saw the sun. Her mahogany hair, frosted with gray, bumped against her jaw when she moved her head. She wore a blue print cotton dress that enhanced the odd blue of her eyes, tiny gold earrings shaped like roses, and a matching pendant that hung from a gold chain at her neck. Aline guessed she was in her late forties and pegged her for a doctor before she spoke.

"My secretary will print out a copy of Margaret's file that you can take with you, Detective Bernelli."

"Thanks, I appreciate it. This is Aline Scott. We'll be working together. Aline, Nina Treak."

Her smile didn't touch her eyes as she extended her hand. Her grip was firm and brief. "Nice to meet you, Detective Scott. Give me just a moment, will you? Then I'll take you both back to the treatment room."

Aline glanced at Bernie, brows lifting. Bernie shrugged, indicating that the verdict on Treak wasn't in yet. She strode over to the woman on the couch and said something to her that Aline couldn't hear. The woman shook her head, not looking at Treak. The doctor leaned closer to her, touched her arm, whispered. The woman stood and shuffled toward the front door, shoulders slumped, arms swinging loosely at her sides, everything about her now suggesting surrender. Treak gazed after her a moment, then returned to Aline and Bernie, her smile fixed in place, as before. "I'm afraid this has hit some of our patients extremely hard, especially those like Jean who were fond of Dr. Liscomb."

Interesting that the woman—Jean—had said the exact opposite, Aline thought. "Did she know Margaret?"

"We have only thirty patients, Detective Scott. They all know each other."

The evasion annoyed her, but she kept her mouth shut and followed the two other women through the door. Little gray men with dark bug eyes. Yeah, the day was off to a fine start.

3

(1)

The room was a perfect square, twelve by twelve. Everything in it was a cool, coral pink, including the bed that dominated its center and the straitjacket that hung limply over one side.

On the floor to the right of the table was a man with a syringe embedded in his neck. Strands of his thinning white hair clung to his forehead like the fine threads of a spider's web. Blood had seeped onto the collar of his white shirt and shouted with the exuberance of a telltale lipstick stain. About six feet away lay a younger man whose throat had been slashed. His blood had turned the pink carpet around him a dark red. A scalpel stuck out of the wall closest to him.

Aline was struck immediately by the perfection of the scene—the bodies here, one of the weapons there, the cool pink background, the pristine condition of everything else in the room. She glanced at Treak, who was already watching her intently, as if measuring her against something, and gestured at the man with the syringe in his neck. "Dr. Liscomb?"

"Yes. Vance Liscomb." She seemed relieved to speak. "And the other man is Hugh Franks, one of the orderlies. Nothing has been touched in here since the bodies were found this morning."

"Who found them?"

"I did. When I work days, I'm usually the first one here in the morning and I relieve the physician who is on duty at night. I checked the clipboard where we post medications and treatments; Margaret's name was the most recent entry. I contacted her residence counselor to make sure she wasn't in her room and then called the police.''

"How often was she given electroshock?''

"She had six treatments the first two weeks she was with us. She improved so dramatically, she became a trustee two months later. As a patient improves, he or she advances through each of our five residences, and with each move, there is greater freedom. A trustee has the most freedom and is allowed to leave the center and go into town to shop, see a movie, whatever, and is eventually allowed to go home for weekends.''

"How long was Margaret a trustee?'' Bernie asked.

"Up until six weeks or so ago, when she and another patient got into an argument that precipitated a sequence of violent episodes. Dr. Liscomb removed her from trustee status, put her in the second residence, and started the treatments again. Last night's would have been the fifth of eight.''

Aline crouched next to Liscomb's body and turned his head slightly so that she had a better view of the syringe. The plunger was depressed and the syringe was empty. "Are patients who are about to undergo electroshock sedated first?''

"Yes. We've been using Seconal. And according to the medication post, which I gave to Chief Frederick, that's what was in the syringe.''

Aline stood. "I didn't realize electroshock was still used.''

"For patients who are severely depressed, Detective Scott, it's sometimes the only thing that works.''

"It apparently wasn't working on her.''

"Quite possibly because she had stopped taking her medication.''

"How many psychiatrists are there on staff?''

"With Vance gone, there're just Tyler—that's Dr. Winthrop—who's our director, and myself full-time. We have two other part-timers. There are also six psychiatric nurses, six house counselors, five orderlies, and two cooks. Let's talk in my office, shall we? We'll be more comfortable.''

Her furtive glance at Liscomb as they left was strained and pinched, as though his murder were an irritant, a gross inconvenience. It wouldn't take much to dislike this woman, Aline thought.

"Does Dr. Liscomb have any family?"

"Two grown children who live up north. I've already notified them. Hugh was married. I haven't been able to get in touch with his wife."

"We'll do it," Aline said.

Treak's office was spacious and comfortable: polished pine floors, a Persian carpet that marked the sitting area, a breathtaking view of the Gulf. Framed degrees and awards adorned one of the walls; another was solid books, medical tomes from the look of them. The room had a masculine feel to it, and except for the professional credentials, it contained nothing personal.

Treak buzzed her secretary and asked her if she'd printed out Margaret Wickerd's medical records, then the three of them settled in the sitting area with weak coffee in Styrofoam cups. Aline's preliminary questions about electroshock seemed to annoy Treak; her manner became somewhat defensive.

"The proper name is electroconvulsive shock therapy—ECT—and with most patients, it's administered three times a week for two to six weeks. It involves a brief passage of about a hundred and fifty volts between two electrodes placed on the patient's temples. The current inhibits glucose and oxygenation, which causes convulsions and immediate loss of consciousness. No one really knows why it works, but there's no question that it does."

"What medication was she on?" Bernie asked.

"Thorazine. Like I mentioned earlier, we suspect she may have stopped taking her medication several weeks ago. It's usually dispensed by the house counselors and taken in their presence, but . . ." She shrugged. "These things happen from time to time. And it would explain the violent episodes."

"What sort of violence?" Aline asked.

"It's in the medical records, Detective Scott."

"I'd rather hear it from you."

Her aggrieved sigh made it clear that she was a busy, busy woman and would like to wind this up as soon as possible. "Violence toward others precipitated by what you or I would consider trivial incidents. In one instance, another patient inadvertently sat where she'd been sitting in the cafeteria. Margaret grabbed the woman by the hair and shoved her out of the chair. A fight broke out. That sort of thing."

"What's the monthly fee here, Dr. Treak?"

Without blinking an eye, she said, "Twenty-five hundred a month."

"Does insurance cover Margaret's bills?"

Treak's smile smacked of condescension. "You obviously haven't kept abreast of developments in health care, Detective Scott. During the 1980s, insurance policies offered quite liberal psychiatric benefits. Then as employers began to feel the sting of escalating costs, policies began to limit stays in psychiatric hospitals to a matter of weeks instead of months. And suddenly the facilities that had been reaping enormous insurance profits were competing madly for patients. Our center is an answer to that dilemma.

"Our full-time staff is small, we limit the number of patients, and we take only those patients who can afford to be here. That means no one is discharged just because their insurance runs out. The average stay is about three months; with some patients, like Margaret, the stay is longer, from six months to a year. So to answer your question, no, insurance wasn't paying for Margaret's bills. Her husband was."

"She was admitted for depression, is that correct?"

"Severe depression over a miscarriage. She was also somewhat delusional in that she claimed the miscarriage had been caused by her abduction by extraterrestrials." A smile touched Treak's constipated-looking mouth and she paused, letting the absurdity of the statement settle. "This was preceded by a stressful period in her marriage and the miscarriage simply made things worse."

"We'll need the husband's address and phone number," Bernie said.

"Certainly." She was already jotting it on a slip of paper, eager to end the interview. "He divides his time between Miami and Tango. I haven't contacted him yet. I wanted to speak to you people first."

"Any other family?" Aline asked.

"Just a younger sister. She owns a shop in town. I'll give you her address and phone number, too. Their ties to the island were the main reason they chose to commit Margaret here."

Aline frowned. "The sister and husband had her committed?"

"Well, technically, her husband did, but her sister had the legal right to contest it and didn't. Margaret was incapable of making any decisions for herself at the time." The phone buzzed and Treak answered it, listened, thanked the person on the other end, and hung up. "Margaret's file is ready. You can pick it up on your way out."

Aline smelled the approach of an abrupt dismissal. "We'll need a current picture of Margaret."

"Chief Frederick already has one."

"We'd like another."

"My secretary should have several more on file."

There was a quick rap at the door and a rather dignified-looking man in a shirt and tie poked his head into the room. "Excuse me, Nina. But there's a call for you. You can take it in my office."

"We were just leaving," Aline said.

"Detectives Scott and Bernelli, this is Dr. Winthrop, our director."

His smile was all teeth, and what fine teeth they were, Aline thought, small, white, and square. His voice was New England crisp, boarding schools and old money, and she couldn't imagine this guy as her shrink or anyone else's. He escorted them from Treak's office, saying all the right things about what a tragedy this was and how the clinic was at fault and if there was anything he could do, anything at all, to make their investigation easier, they had only to ask.

So Aline asked. "There's a red-headed patient named Jean who roomed with Margaret Wickerd. I'd like to talk to her."

"Jean . . . Jean." He rubbed his jaw. "A redhead. Oh, right, of course. Jean Mancino. When would you like to speak to her, Detective Bernelli?"

"Scott," corrected Aline.

"Forgive me. I'm terrible with names, Detective Scott. I'm afraid she just left with one of the counselors on an outing with some of the other patients. This has upset everyone and we thought it best to divert the patients for the day."

"How about tomorrow?"

"Just give me a call and we'll arrange something."

They had reached the secretarial pool, where Winthrop left them and they picked up Margaret Wickerd's medical file. It was a relief to step outside. "Remind me to never lose my marbles, Al," whispered Bernie.

"You get a load of her Rolex?"

"With nearly a million bucks a year generated here, it wouldn't surprise me if she's wearing gold underwear. You smell something funny around here?"

"Don't you?"

Bernie grinned. "Just making sure we're on the same wavelength, Al. C'mon, let's find Bill."

Bill Prentiss was Bernie's husband and the local coroner. He was leaning against the forensics van and scribbling on a clipboard, a slender, handsome man who, at the moment, looked like an actor down on his luck. Whenever he was agitated or fully absorbed in something, he ran his hand over his curly dark hair again and again, which he was doing now.

Aline had known Prentiss all of her life. They were born thirty seconds apart in the Tango hospital, where their mothers had shared a room in the maternity ward. They'd gone through elementary school and high school together and he had been her first lover. When the affair had ended, they'd remained close, and now he was the brother she'd never had whose opinion she trusted implicitly.

"You're going to go bald if you keep doing that to your hair," Bernie remarked.

He glanced up from the clipboard, a wry smile easing the fatigue in his face. "Thank you, Nurse Claudia. You two interested in a preliminary observation?"

"Jesus, from the man who never says a word till the autopsy's done? You bet," Aline replied.

"Two things I don't like. First, the orderly. Hugh, that's his name, right?"

"Was," Bernie corrected.

"Whatever. The slash at his throat is consistent with what you find when the wound is inflicted from behind."

"So?" Aline said.

Prentiss patted the air with his hands. "Hold your horses, Al. Let me finish. Okay, the shrink. His neck is broken. The easiest way to break a man's neck is from behind."

"So?" Aline repeated.

"I'll show you. Come here for a second, Bernie. Stand with your back to me. Yeah, like that. Okay, Bernie is the shrink. I come up behind her, right? I grab her around the throat, jerk her head back, snap her neck in the process, then plunge the syringe into her throat."

"Yeah," Bernie grumbled. "And you weigh one seventy to my one ten."

"Exactly my point." He bussed her on the crown of her head and released her. "I helped lift both of those men. Liscomb is as solid as a block of goddamn concrete. I'd guess he weighs one ninety or two hundred pounds. But according to the stats on the back of the picture Dr. Treak gave to the chief, Margaret Wickerd weighs a hundred and fifteen."

Bernie fixed a hand to her narrow hip. "Uh-oh, Al. I hear echoes of women as the weaker sex in this observation."

"Hey, he outweighed her by at least seventy-five pounds. I'm not saying it's impossible that she broke his neck or slit the orderly's throat, just that it's damn unlikely. Not unless she knew karate or judo or something. Otherwise, either guy would have overpowered her. Also, her height is listed as five foot eight; the shrink is six foot one, the orderly is an even six feet. So in addition to their weights, there's the height detail. She would have to reach up to do what she supposedly did to either of those men.''

"She might have been standing on something," Aline said.

Bernie made a face. "Shit, she'd just been brought in to be zapped.''

"She could've killed one of them first, then waited for the next guy to come into the room," Aline said.

"Possible," Prentiss conceded. "But think about how that room looked when you first saw it.''

"Arranged," Aline and Bernie said simultaneously.

Prentiss smiled. "Very good, ladies. Now think about this. The normal procedure for electroshock includes sedation, and as far as I know, sedation usually occurs before you get to where you're going.''

Neither Aline nor Bernie said anything, and Prentiss smiled again. "I rest my case.''

"Case?" echoed Chief Frederick as he joined them. "What case?''

"A theory," Prentiss said, and told him.

Gene Frederick was a thin, intense man with hair the white of Ivory soap, who looked as hot-tempered and demanding as he often was. When Aline had started in the department seven years ago, he'd been chief of homicide. Now he was chief of police, directly below the mayor in the island hierarchy. In her mind's eye, though, he was still about thirty, her father's fishing buddy who had raced up to the house on Saturday mornings, the back of his truck loaded with gear.

"Keep the theory to yourselves," Frederick said softly when Prentiss had finished.

"He's got a point, though," Bernie said.

"Of course he's got a goddamn point, Claudia. But this isn't the place to talk about it. Right now, our job is to contact everyone on this island who Margaret Wickerd knows or has ever known. I want the sister's house watched in case she goes there. Same with the husband. And I want a full report on this center—who owns it, where these psychiatrists worked before they came here, what their specialties are, what they've published. The whole nine yards.'' He uttered this in the same soft voice, as though he believed microphones were hidden in the trees and buried in the gravel where they stood. ''And I want it yesterday.''

''Jesus, Chief, you need some coffee,'' Bernie muttered, then clicked her heels, saluted, and sauntered off.

''When's Ryan due back?'' Frederick asked Aline.

''Tomorrow or the next day.''

''Tell him to call me. There's an opening for the security guard job and Ryan's going to apply for it.''

''Not for minimum wage he isn't,'' Prentiss said drolly.

''Leave Ryan to me, Bill.''

''I'm just telling you like it is.'' Prentiss shut the doors to the van and started to the front. ''You always underpay him, Gene.''

''Don't expect your wife home for dinner,'' Frederick called after him.

Without turning, Prentiss shot him the bird. Frederick chuckled. ''That boy spends too much time with the dead.''

''Well, you know what Dad used to say about coroners, Gene. It's bad luck to piss them off.''

Frederick flipped the huge ash from the end of his cigar. ''Yeah? And when did he say that?''

''When Bill left Tango for medical school.''

As Prentiss cranked up the van, Aline and Frederick moved off to one side. ''And what do you think he'd say about a woman who claims she was kidnapped by little gray men, Aline?''

It was not a frivolous question. Frederick was rarely frivolous. ''I don't think little gray men were something he thought about.''

''Hell, there wasn't much he *didn't* think about.'' Frederick shook his head and gazed after the van. ''We started fishing together thirty years ago this month, you realize that? He and your mom had just added a second room to the bookstore and things were going real well for them.

''I remember how he'd sit in the boat for hours at a time

with his pole balanced between his knees and his nose in a book. Heavy stuff: religion and physics and psychology. And then the weird shit: dowsing and ESP, spooks and UFOs. He was looking for something, Aline, a connection.''

Her parents had died twelve years ago, within six months of each other, her mother first, from a brain embolism, and her father from a broken heart. Twelve years, she thought, but the rawness of the emotion that squeezed at her throat said it was yesterday.

''And?'' She had never heard this particular story and wondered what Frederick was working up to.

Frederick dropped his cigar in the gravel, crushed it with the heel of his shoe, then picked it up and slipped it into his pocket to finish later. He slipped on his sunglasses, and they started toward his pickup, her question suspended in the early morning heat.

''Four or five months before your mother died, we were out fishing one night in the glades on the north side. It was a real clear night, hot, but no mosquitoes, probably around midnight or one. We saw a light. It was brighter and closer than any stars and it was, uh, moving.''

Like the other stories about her parents that Frederick had shared with her over the years, this one imbued her with an odd levity and warmth. She felt as she had several years ago when she'd discovered a packet of love letters her parents had exchanged before they'd married.

''Moving how?''

''Erratically. One second it'd hover about a hundred yards above the trees, not making a sound, and the next second it'd shoot off at a ninety-degree angle, then sweep into complicated loops. It lasted . . . oh, I don't know, maybe thirty seconds, then it just . . . winked out.''

''What'd Dad say?''

Frederick smiled and leaned against the door of the pickup, rubbing the back of his neck. ''He told me to keep my mouth shut and write down everything I'd seen. He did the same, then we compared notes. They were damn close, but there were some important differences. Your father heard noises;

I didn't. He saw a large, pulsating white light with a runner of soft blue lights beneath it; I saw a single pulsating light that was sometimes white, sometimes blue. I thought the experience lasted no more than thirty seconds; he thought it was two or three minutes. I said the light winked out, just vanished. He was convinced it plunged deep into the glades. We argued about it. He wanted to go look for it, I said no way.''

"Did he?"

"Sure enough. He took me back to my car, then went in alone. He didn't find anything." Frederick shrugged. "I guess what I'm trying to say, Aline, is that I learned something that night about perspective. Everything is a matter of perspective. I know what I saw, your father knew what he'd seen. Even though the two versions differed and even though most people would argue that we'd seen a weather satellite or Venus or whatever, it doesn't mean the experience wasn't real.

"So now we've got a killer on our hands who was committed because she believes her abduction by little gray guys was responsible for her miscarriage. Maybe she's crazy. Maybe she isn't. The point is that she *believes* it and my gut says that's where we should start trying to unravel this thing. It isn't as simple as a woman killing two men during an escape."

It was just like Frederick to expand the horizons of a case rather than to pursue the more traditional route of seeking a simple answer. He didn't inhabit a black-and-white world of either/or; he never had. "You telling me to pursue the weird, huh, Gene?"

He smiled. "Something like that." He climbed into his pickup and shut the door. "Tell Ryan to call."

"Yeah, I will."

As the pickup crawled down the driveway, the tightness in her throat eased. Her father had never told her about any of that and probably hadn't even divulged it to her mother. The incident hinted at a layer of life that had existed separately from the family, a kind of secret life, a quest for connections between the odd and the prosaic. She could easily imagine him returning alone to the glades on the strength of nothing more than his belief. The saw grass had rustled as he passed through it, the briny odor of water and mud and darkness had clung to the air, stars had danced against the obsidian sky, and— What? How far into the glades had he gone? How long had it taken him? Where in the glades had this happened?

It suddenly seemed vital that she get more details from Frederick. She wanted to reconstruct the journey and understand what it had been like for her father that night nearly thirteen years ago. And she would go through the boxes of her parents' belongings again to see if he'd mentioned it anywhere: the scrapbooks, journals, and mementos that comprised the colorful mosaic of her family history. A history, she thought, that would end with her, an only child without heirs.

Who is now pushing forty.

What a morbid fact, she thought, and hurried off to find Bernie.

4

(1)

When the Super Cub crossed the state just south of Homestead Air Force Base, winds were eleven knots out of the east, the ceiling was eleven thousand feet, and visibility was ten miles. With the tail wind, Kincaid figured they would be on Tango within twenty minutes if Ferret didn't puke or lunge for the yoke.

He'd been hunkered down in his seat since they'd left Pembroke Pines Airport just north of Miami and hadn't risen since. His baseball cap was pulled low over his eyes, his arms hugged his chest, and it was anyone's guess what he was thinking. Although he was terrified of flying, he'd bought the Cub primarily to get to and from Miami, the hub of his lucrative and complex bookie network. Kincaid didn't know what tips the Miami jai alai had yielded this time; he hadn't asked. He never did. He just followed Ferret's advice when he placed his bets and if they panned out, which they frequently did, great. And if not, well, better luck next time.

"How much longer, Ryan?" Ferret asked over the racket of the engine.

"Twenty minutes, more or less."

Ferret flicked back his cap and glanced over at him, lips drawn away from his teeth in a grimace that completed his resemblance to the rodent he was nicknamed after. "Which? More or less?"

"Less."

"Are we over water yet?"

"No."

"Can you see the bridge to Tango?"

"No."

"Is everything working?"

"Relax, Ferret. The plane's doing fine."

Better than fine. The craft was a beauty. The Super Cub, built in 1979, was a variant of the original Piper Cub developed in 1932 from an even earlier prototype, the Taylor J-2 Cub. Its previous owner, a collector on Tango who had filed Chapter 11 and sold it to Ferret for a song, had maintained the craft in mint condition. He'd added a new and more powerful engine and twelve grand worth of instruments that would enable a pilot to navigate in the dead of night in zero visibility. But Ferret wasn't interested in any of that. All he cared about was whether the plane would get him where he was going and home again in one piece.

"Hey, you can look now," Kincaid said. "Tango Bridge coming up on the right."

"I don't want to look, Ryan." He jerked the cap over his eyes again. "You look. Tell me how the traffic is."

"Light. Morning rush hour is long gone."

"No accidents on the bridge?"

"Nope, all clear."

"Can you see the ferry?"

Kincaid scanned the turquoise waters and spotted the ferry at the Key West dock, right where it was supposed to be. "Got it in sight."

The ferry had been around since the last century, when it had been Tango's only connection with Key West and the mainland. Once a month a mailman had ridden his horse on board and made the twenty-minute crossing. Then he'd spent the next two days traveling the Old Post Road, which circumnavigated the island, delivering mail to the three or four hundred inhabitants.

Now, Kincaid thought, the year-round population stood at about five thousand, a figure that tripled during the tourist season. Land that had once sold for a hundred an acre and included a home now brought in an average of a quarter of a million, the highest in the state. Gasoline was almost fifty cents a gallon higher on Tango than on the mainland, clothes and food cost fifteen percent more, and property taxes were grounds for revolt.

But Kincaid had lived on the island for twenty-five years and couldn't conceive of any other place as home. The air was virtually pollution free, the wilderness preserve was vast, and the topography was as diverse as anything in the entire state. Beaches, marshes, hills, lakes, even a lagoon.

For him, Tango was that rarest of jewels, a place that changed but not so much that his personal history was ever effaced or lost. He had survived two marriages on this island, the ups and downs of several careers, and four years with Aline.

He throttled back as he approached the island's eastern shore and turned slightly south. Ferret detected the change in the engine's power and was instantly alert for bad news. "Is there a problem?"

"Christ, Ferret. Everything's fine. Really." He got on the radio and notified Tango Tower of his approach, then began his descent to a thousand feet. Ferret gradually straightened and dared a look out the side window.

"Is that TP&L's lake?" he asked.

TP&L was Tango Power and Light, and yes, it was their lake, all right, prime fishing spot and home to dozens of seaplanes. The airport lay just to the south, a dark stain flattened against the top of a shallow hill. The four runways, shooting from a circular hub like spokes in a giant wheel, weren't long enough yet to accommodate commercial jets. But sooner or later the airport-expansion issue would be voted in and some new tax scheme would be dreamed up to pay for it. Tango Air, which operated twin-engine puddle jumpers from the island to Marathon and Miami, would probably be driven out of business, the surrounding hills would be bulldozed, and wildlife would die off or be moved to zoos. All for that great bitch called progress.

As he swung into the traffic pattern, the wind buffeted the

wings and Ferret said, "Hey, Ryan, if the engine quit now, could you land without killing us?"

"No."

Ferret went rigid in his seat. "You're joking, aren't you?"

"Yeah." Kincaid laughed.

"Very funny."

He turned onto the final approach. Ferret fell silent, gripped the edges of his seat, and pressed back into it, a man preparing for impact. He didn't relax until the plane was taxiing toward the tie-down area at the far end of the airport.

"I think you'd better sign up for a fear-of-flying course, Ferret."

He gave an indignant snort. "You know I detest group activities, Ryan."

"Go through hypnosis."

"No way."

"Then learn to fly. Confront the fear. You've got the plane, all you need is an instructor."

He brightened. "You teach me, Ryan."

"Uh-uh. I don't instruct my friends."

"You taught Sweet Pea how to fly."

Sweet Pea was Aline. "That was different."

"Why?"

"She wasn't scared shitless every time she got near a plane."

"I'm not scared shitless, Ryan. I'm just a bit apprehensive, that's all."

"Sure. That's why your face is green." He slipped into the Cub's tie-down spot and killed the engine. "I'll recommend an instructor."

"I don't want someone else." He was pouting like a kid now. "I trust you, Ryan. I'll pay you twice what you usually get."

"Uh-uh."

"You need the money, Ryan."

"I just finished a job."

They were striding toward the terminal building now, the island's Mutt and Jeff. Kincaid, who stood six four, was a full foot taller than Ferret, had light hair to his dark, and sported a beard. Though they were roughly the same age, in their early forties, Kincaid looked it and Ferret didn't. His appearance, in fact, didn't seem to have changed one iota in the twenty-five years since they'd met. It was as if Ferret, like some enchanted prince in a fairy tale, wasn't governed by the same laws that ruled other men.

"You hated that job," Ferret said.

"It paid well."

"Okay, look, we'll make a fair exchange. You teach me how to fly and for as many weeks as it takes I'll guarantee you wins of a minimum of a thousand bucks on any bet you place. If a tip doesn't pan out, I take the loss."

Given Ferret's past record, how could he refuse an offer like that? "I'll absorb my own losses."

"Okay."

"And there're two conditions."

"Shoot."

"When we're in the air, I'm in charge."

"I'm not an asshole, Ryan. What's the second condition?"

They stopped at Kincaid's Saab. "We're both free to call off the deal at any time."

"Fair enough. C'mon, I'll spring for breakfast or lunch or whatever at Lester's." Then he flashed that rodent grin and ducked into the car.

(2)

Aline had spent most of the day before wading through Margaret Wickerd's medical records and waiting for calls that weren't returned. Tyler Winthrop was always "in a meeting"; Peter Wickerd, Margaret's husband, was away on business; Julie Ames, Margaret's sister, was "tied up with customers"; and Bill Prentiss, who was usually conscientious about returning calls, was "with a patient."

She'd finally knocked off around three and on her way home had swung by the dead orderly's home to speak to his wife, Heather. According to her sister, though, Heather had already heard the news from Dr. Treak and was sleeping off a sedative her doctor had given her. Aline had offered her condolences and left her card, asking that Heather call her in the next few days.

She'd gone to bed obscenely early and had slept straight for ten hours. Now, her optimism restored, she was ready to do battle with the people who hadn't returned her calls. There was nothing that irritated her more than being ignored.

It was just past ten and business as usual along the Tango boardwalk. The shops were open, the cafés bustled with business, and the hardcore sunbathers were already on the beach, soaking up skin cancer.

The original boardwalk, built by the Flamingo Hotel in 1836, was a mile-long structure that ran parallel to a white Gulf beach. Constructed of the same pine that grew on the island, it was reserved for guests of the hotel. But in 1837, it and the Flamingo were destroyed in a hurricane when five miles of beach washed away. The hotel was rebuilt farther inland and the boardwalk was reconstructed on wooden pilings, extended another three miles, and became part of the public beach.

In 1948, a hurricane packing 140-mile-an-hour winds snapped the pilings like toothpicks. The boardwalk was again rebuilt, this time on concrete pilings a foot thick that were fortified with steel. All new buildings along its perimeter were constructed of reinforced concrete, had triple-strength cypress doors, and were equipped with hurricane shutters. These structures were the only ones to survive Hurricane Donna in 1960 and Cleo three years later.

But in the nearly three decades since, the number of shops and cafés had proliferated like rabbits and hurricanes had grown considerably stronger. She didn't think the boardwalk or anything on it would survive a category-five storm, with winds greater than 155 miles an hour and a storm surge higher than eighteen feet. And it wouldn't surprise her if the shop that Margaret Wickerd's sister owned was among the first casualties.

Julie's Curios looked as though it had been slapped together from spare driftwood and stained glass made by an aspiring artist stoned on speed. The roof tilted downward on the right, the lettering on the glass had a distinctive upward slope, and the heavy front door was hung crookedly.

It wasn't much better inside. The narrow aisles made it difficult to move around without bumping into one of the crowded shelves. There didn't seem to be any particular order or theme to the merchandise. A lovely antique rocker stood next to a tacky ceramic cat; a wooden bird cage hung from a light fixture; delicate china bowls that bore the chips and nicks of advanced age occupied a shelf with plastic drinking glasses.

The shop was longer than it was wide, and the deeper into it she ventured, the weirder it got. Fake flowers, dusty books that smelled as ancient as they looked, haphazard stacks of *Scribner's Magazine* and *Life*, a genuine bureau from fifteenth-century Spain. *Curios* apparently encompassed anything and everything.

It was the kind of store that appealed to the pack rat in Aline, a place that enticed you to browse, touch, perhaps even bargain for the objects you coveted. She couldn't recall having noticed it before, but she rarely came down here anymore. When the tourists were absent, the teenagers filled the gap, claiming the boardwalk with their skateboards, their bikes, and their boom boxes, and they were sufficient reason to stay away.

A white-haired woman was at the register, ringing up a sale and chattering nonstop about the heat, the traffic, the advent of the tourist season. She was the prototypical grandmother, exactly the sort of person who might own a store like this. But she was too old to be Margaret's sister.

"Excuse me," Aline said when the customer had left. "Is Julie Ames in?"

"She's with a client, ma'am. Can I help you with something?"

"How much longer is she going to be?"

"Well, that's hard to say. These things can take anywhere

from twenty minutes to two hours. If you'd like to make an appointment for—''

"I'd like to see her now." Aline didn't have the vaguest idea what the woman meant by "these things," and she wasn't about to wait for two hours or come back later to find out. She flashed her badge. "I phoned yesterday."

"Oh, my. Yes. Detective Scott. Right. She was very busy yesterday. Just a minute." She vanished through a side door behind the counter and reappeared a few minutes later. "Come through here, please."

She unlatched a swinging wooden gate and Aline followed her into a room that was smaller and even more crowded than the first. A hobbit room, a little warren. The air was redolent with the scent of cinnamon from a burning candle. Sunlight poured through the windows and spilled across a wooden table as messy as Aline's desk at home. A thin woman in a long skirt stood outlined in a wedge of light at the rear door, her back to Aline as she spoke to someone Aline couldn't see.

"Come on now, don't be like that. In or out, you can't have it both ways . . . okay, good girl." She shut the door as a fluffy white Persian strolled in and frowned when she saw Aline. She was an attractive woman with short blonde hair but missed being pretty by a long shot. Her face was too long, too angular, too sharp. The only softness was in her eyes, blue pools so pale, they looked almost silver. Aline guessed she was in her mid-thirties.

"Yes. I'd—"

"Funny, I had the impression you were male." She shrugged and smoothed a palm over her flowered skirt, the sort of style that had been favored at rock concerts in the Sixties. "Your energy is male. Well, anyway." She gestured toward a chair at the front of her desk. "Just move that stuff to the floor and make yourself comfortable. Would you like coffee or anything, Detective?"

"No, thanks. I'd like to—"

But she interrupted Aline again as she settled in the wicker chair behind her desk. "I already know about my sister. Dr.

Treak phoned me yesterday. I always felt that Thorazine wasn't going to do the trick forever. Anyway, I don't think there's much I can tell you that you can't get from Dr. Treak. I've hardly seen Maggie at all since she was institutionalized.''

She made *institutionalized* sound dirty, uglier than it was.

''Have you heard from her since she escaped?''

''No.'' She lit a Marlboro with a quick, graceful flourish of her hand, then set it in an ashtray and picked up a deck of cards. They were the size of ordinary playing cards, but she handled them the way a priest might a chalice. ''Since I was partially responsible for her commitment, I'm probably the last person she'd call.''

''Tarot cards?'' Aline asked.

''No. I designed these myself. They're better than Tarot.'' Julie shuffled the cards and gazed at her with eyes that waited, that seemed to be calculating and plotting some secret strategy whose content Aline couldn't fathom.

''I understand her miscarriage was what led to her breakdown.''

''Look, Detective Scott. There's something you have to understand about my sister.'' She took another puff on the cigarette, then stabbed it out. ''Her paintings weren't selling. She and Pete were living most of the time in Miami, a city she detested. She was at a point in her life where nothing seemed to be working for her and the smallest thing would set her off. We all knew it and were treading eggshells around her. Once a month or so she'd take off for a few days and not bother telling anyone where she was going. Her behavior was real weird *before* the miscarriage and just got worse afterward.''

''In her medical records, her profession was referred to as illustrator.''

''Well, yes, that's how she made her living, as a free-lance illustrator. Book covers, magazine covers, brochures. Did real well at it, too, over a hundred thousand a year. But she wanted to be a *real* artist.'' Julie smiled and sat forward. ''Now I ask you, Detective, just what the hell does that mean? Starving in between sales?''

She slipped the top card off the deck and turned it over. It depicted a lovely young woman kneeling in front of a pond and studying her own reflection. "This is Maggie. Her eyes were always turned inward, analyzing, tearing things apart, then putting them back together again in new ways. It's part of what made her such a brilliant illustrator but so difficult to get close to. Personally, I think she used the miscarriage as an excuse for a breakdown so Pete wouldn't leave her."

"They were having problems?"

"*She* had the problems and drove Pete away with her bullshit. She drove me away. She talked herself into being crazy, Detective Scott. You can do that just as easily as you can talk your body out of being sick."

She turned over the next card. It was a repeat of the first except that now there was a shadow behind the woman. "Yup. Here I am," Julie said. "Living in the shadow of Maggie's histrionics." She quickly set down the third and fourth cards. Two men. The first man stood on a hill in the moonlight, arms outstretched as if reaching to embrace the sky. "There's Pete. It typifies him exactly."

The fourth card showed a man in a rowboat on a body of water, a miner's light attached to his head. "And this has got to be Dr. Liscomb, the guy who illuminated the waters of her subconscious. How's that for psychobabble, Detective?" She sat back with a sigh. "I don't know what else to tell you about her."

"Tell me about her alleged abduction."

"ETs." Her brows lifted into small, fussy peaks. "I can't tell you how sick I got of hearing about the goddamn ETs. But Pete's to blame for that one. Aliens are his passion."

"I don't understand."

"No one does." She laughed, a full, throaty sound. "Probably not even Pete. But that's what he does, okay?"

He investigated aliens? Was there a word for that? Something simple like schoolteacher or architect or attorney? "That's how he makes his living?"

"I guess Dr. Treak didn't talk to you much about Pete, huh. Probably because she doesn't know what to make of him.'' She turned over a fifth card, a woman running in a forest with a white wolf. She frowned as she studied it, then looked up at Aline without commenting on it and shuffled the deck some more as she continued. ''Pete was an amateur magician who made a lot of money as a real estate developer. He got bored with real estate, turned to the magic full-time, then realized he could duplicate so-called psychic events through magic and became a professional debunker.''

She smiled and leaned forward slightly, light from the window cupping a side of her face. ''In other words, he's a watchdog who investigates anything that reeks of the Strange and the Weird, Detective Scott. UFOs, ESP, spoon bending, psychics, all of it.'' She tapped the fifth card. ''I think you're the lady here with the white wolf. It symbolizes the enormous power of intuition. Since the woman and the wolf are companions in this picture, it means you're attuned to your own intuitive capacity.''

Now she drew a sixth card from the center of the deck. A man with a gun. ''Interesting. The Hunter. See how he's facing the other cards? It means he's in the near future, approaching us.''

''Does Pete also debunk card readers?''

She laughed. ''Hell, I'm family and small potatoes to boot. Besides, he pretends that facet of my personality doesn't exist. To him, the shop makes me a respectable businesswoman.'' She shuffled the deck again. ''But I think his investigation of UFOs is what got Maggie started on all this. So I blame Pete to some extent.''

Aline was missing something here. ''I don't understand.''

''I'm no shrink, okay? But the way I see it, Maggie knew that by claiming she'd been abducted and blaming her miscarriage on it, she would get Pete's attention. And she definitely did. In some ways, I guess she and Pete were never closer than when he was researching the details of her, uh, experience.''

''How far along was she when she miscarried?''

''Supposedly nine weeks. She said her extreme fear is what made her miscarry.'' She shrugged. ''Who knows for sure.''

"But the miscarriage didn't push her over the edge."

Julie shook her head. "No, the final straw was when Pete told her he didn't believe she'd been abducted. I don't know if he ever really believed it. But by then she'd started attending this abductee group and was really immersed in the delusion."

"Where did the group meet?"

"Sometimes here, sometimes in Key West. The people come from all over the keys."

"Is there anyone in the group she'd turn to for help?"

Julie shrugged. "I don't know. I hope not. They're all a bunch of weirdos who feed one another's delusions."

"Is there anyone she was close to?"

"Not really. Most of her friends in the Miami art community had backed off when she started getting manic."

"Who can put me in touch with this abductee group?"

Julie set the deck on the table and shook her head. "It's a waste of time, but what the hell, it's your time. The guy in charge is Sam Newman. Before he got involved in this UFO stuff, he was a physicist with a reputation. Now he's the brunt of bad jokes in scientific circles and makes a real comfortable living writing about all this. He's—" A knock at the door interrupted her. "Yeah, Mimi, what is it?"

The woman with white hair poked her head into the room. "You taking any more appointments today?"

"That depends on Detective Scott, I guess." Julie looked pointedly at Aline.

"I'm just about done."

"Five minutes, Mimi."

Mimi shut the door and Julie finished her thought about Newman. "He's got a place somewhere in the hills. I don't know the exact address, but he's in the book."

"When I called Mr. Wickerd's Miami number, his housekeeper said he's out of town. Do you have any idea when he'll be back?"

"Tomorrow sometime."

"Then you've spoken to him since Margaret's escape?"

"No, I just know when he'll be back."

"Do you have a forwarding number?"

"Nope. Tap the deck, Detective Scott, then pick a card, any card. Let's see what the outcome of all this is going to be."

"I'll pass."

Julie shrugged, scooped up the cards, stacked them in the deck, and stood. "If I hear from Maggie, I'll let you know, Detective Scott. But don't hold your breath."

"I'll be in touch." *And watching your ass.*

(3)

Lester's Bar was strictly a neighborhood hangout that tourists rarely found. That alone, thought Kincaid, made the place unique. But it also had the coldest and cheapest draft beer on the island, good food, and existed in a kind of time warp where nothing dated beyond 1960.

The counter was lined with twirling stools that went back to the bar's days as a soda fountain. The movie posters on the walls attested to Lester Senior's love of Alfred Hitchcock. At one end of the bar, large glass jars were filled with beef jerky and hard-boiled eggs floating in vinegar. Every time Kincaid was in here, he felt like a teenager again.

They were at their usual booth at the back, sitting with Bino, Ferret's longtime sidekick and business partner. He was an albino, a stick of a man with soft pink eyes like a rabbit's that were usually hidden behind dark shades, as they were now. He was poring over lists of jai alai players and racing forms for Calder Race Course. Now and then he grunted or scribbled something next to one of the names, then passed the list or form on to Ferret for his perusal. The exchange was their way of processing information, like two computers connected by modem. But damned if Kincaid knew how it worked.

"Okay, Ryan," said Ferret, glancing up from one of the lists. "I think six hundred on Pretty Girl in Calder's second race is a good bet. All she has to do is come in first, second, or third for you to win."

"When do you need the cash?"

Ferret slipped off his Ben Franklin specs, folded them, slipped them in his shirt pocket. "This is for Saturday's race, so tomorrow morning would be fine." His small dark eyes watched someone behind Kincaid, and as he waved, his mouth swung into that weird rodent grin. "Do tell. Claudia Bernelli. I haven't seen you in a coon's age."

"Hey, boys." Her wide taffy eyes fixed on Kincaid. "You just get back?"

He nodded.

"Then I guess you haven't talk to Al yet."

"Nope." He wondered why she asked. When it came to Bernelli, he was never sure which way the wind was blowing. "Why? What's up?"

"Plenty." She scooted into the booth, lit a cigarette, and started talking.

"Peter Wickerd's an asshole," Ferret said with undisguised contempt.

Bernelli nodded. "You know him?"

"Not anymore. He used to place bets with me but lost a bundle on horses I told him not to play. He also tried to discredit a friend of mine who writes about UFOs. Sam Newman. You met him, Ryan. At my place, remember?"

"Sure." Kincaid had first met Newman several years ago at one of Ferret's rare parties. Over drinks on the terrace they had talked about UFOs. It wasn't *what* Newman had said that had impressed him, but the fact that he was a voice of reason in a field riddled with weirdos and fanatics. "It was around the time he'd started working with that group of abductees."

"Alleged abductees," corrected Bernelli. "I just talked to Al a while ago, and according to Wickerd's sister, she was a member of the group for a while."

"And Pete knew it?" Ferret exclaimed.

Bernie nodded. As she told them about Aline's conversation with Margaret's sister, her hands moved about; it made her silver bracelets dance down her arm. She fussed with them, spun them with a finger, removed one, slipped it back on. When she wasn't fiddling with the bracelets, she smoked or tapped her peach-colored nails against the table. She was forever in motion, Kincaid noted, and difficult to follow, a puzzle of metabolic consumption. It was this quality that had doomed their brief affair years ago, before he'd met Aline. She'd never quite forgiven the breach, although she would be the last to admit it.

"Listen, Ryan," she said, her voice softer now, "there's something screwy going on at this clinic and the chief thinks you're the guy to look at it from the inside."

"From the inside." Kincaid laughed. "I suppose that means I have to commit myself."

"Don't knock it, Ryan. You might learn something about yourself," Ferret said.

Bino and Bernelli snickered.

"I don't think commitment is what the chief's got in mind," Bernelli said, still smiling. "The security guard was fired over all this and Gene seems to think he can slide you into the spot. But when you talk to him, don't tell him you already talked to me." She pushed up from the table. "You know how he likes to give you the rundown himself. And Bill already set him straight on your fee."

Kincaid chuckled. His fee for free-lance jobs for the department was usually a point over which he and Frederick haggled just as a matter of principle. He would ask high, Frederick would counteroffer, and they would settle somewhere in between. It made the chief feel he had won something and provided Kincaid with income between insurance jobs. "Thanks for the tip, Bernie."

Her mouth slipped upward in a slightly mocking grin. "I hope you can handle weird shit like little gray men, Ryan." Then she waved and was gone.

"I get the impression sometimes that she really doesn't like you too much," Bino remarked.

"Thank you for that sage observation, Bino," mumbled Kincaid, and got up to call Frederick.

5

(1)

To Aline, the Tango Key Library was one of perhaps half a dozen buildings that embodied the island's history.

The original structure, built in 1823 by the island's first postmaster, had been a tiny one-story house that stood next to a crooked barn. It had been surrounded by a wilderness of pine and banyans that stretched from coast to coast over the Tango hills. By 1905, when Henry Flagler had bought the place, small settlements had broken up the terrain and wagon trails branched inland from the Old Post Road, making travel much easier.

Flagler had razed the barn, added a second floor to the house, refurbished it, then never lived in it. Five years later he sold it to Tango County and it was converted into a library. Today the building was listed in the National Registry of Historic Places, had a gabled roof, a wraparound porch on the first floor, and several smaller terraces on the second. It reminded Aline of a house in a fairy tale: the decorative gingerbread wood, the sagging beams on the front porch, the tall, narrow windows.

Aline's destination was an office on the second floor, where Meg Mallory, the head librarian, hid out when she wasn't cruising the stacks in search of some obscure bit of information. She was at her cluttered desk typing furiously on the computer keyboard, her bifocals balanced precariously at the tip of her nose. She was a seventy-five-year-old grandmother who didn't look a day over sixty. Like Aline, she was a fritter, the Tango equivalent of a Key West conch, born and raised on the island. A native.

"Hey, lady, can you spare me five?"

Meg chuckled without glancing up. "Clear off that chair, Aline, and grab yourself a mug of coffee. I'm almost finished here. Where's your other half, anyway?"

"In Miami on a surveillance job."

"Miami, huh? Ryan must be strapped for cash if he's in Miami instead of Nepal."

"It's called a double mortgage, Meg. My place still hasn't sold."

"Oh, it will, it will. Everything I've heard says the market on Tango is turning up again." She finished typing, swirled in her chair, and pulled a bulging envelope from the top drawer. She slid it across the desk to Aline. "I included the major articles that Liscomb and Treak have authored, their official bios, press coverage on the opening of the clinic, anything I thought would be helpful. The clinic, incidentally, is one of a dozen around the country owned by a private company called Whole Health. It sprang up in the mid-Eighties and basically, its policy focuses on easing patients back into society. None of its clinics has more than forty residents. Its board of directors reads like a Who's Who in the mental health field."

"Have any complaints been filed against the company?"

"Not that I could find. Did you talk to the security guard, Jay Paulson?"

"The chief did. Why?"

"Well, he blew in here late yesterday afternoon looking for a job. His big concern is that stolen Firebird. It was a gift from his folks when he graduated from college last June. I think he's afraid his old man is going to get all over him. Anyway, what I wanted to tell you was that he said he *did* fall asleep on the job, but he thinks it's because his tea was drugged."

"I don't think he mentioned anything about tea to the chief."

"He says that when he worked the graveyard shift, Margaret occasionally brought him something cold to drink from the kitchen. The night she escaped, she'd brought him tea and he let it sit around for a long time before he drank it."

Aline wondered if Margaret had been stashing away her Thorazine for just such an occasion. "Did he say anything else?"

"No, that was about it. So tell me about Margaret Wickerd."

As Aline talked, she realized how foolish the story sounded when it was told aloud. Aliens. Abductions. Medical experiments conducted inside a flying saucer. But Meg wasn't laughing. She didn't even look amused.

"Ever heard the name Betty Hill?" she asked when Aline was finished.

"The name seems familiar. Does she live on Tango?"

Meg laughed. "No, in Exeter, New Hampshire. In 1961, she and her husband, Barney, were supposedly abducted by aliens who performed experiments on them. The story came out over a period of months when Barney started suffering from insomnia and anxiety and sought medical help. He—"

Aline snapped her fingers. *"The Interrupted Journey."*

"Right, that was one of the books. The other was *The Incident at Exeter*. In the last decade, the abduction issue has surged in popularity, thanks in large part to *Communion*. Did you read it?"

"I started it, but you know how I am, Meg. Books like that give me the creeps. Ryan gave me a blow-by-blow description when he breezed through it, though."

"Well, I think you should read it and some of the other books I've listed here." She slid a piece of scratch paper across the desk. "And definitely talk to Sam Newman. You won't find a more rational voice in the UFO field."

"I'd love to talk to him, but no one answers the phone at his place and his address isn't listed. The only thing the post office has on him is a box number."

"That means he's probably working on deadline." Meg scribbled something on another piece of scratch paper.

"Here're the directions to his place. Tell him I gave them to you. And if you want a general roundup of what's going on in ufology these days, talk to a guy named Joe Mahoney. He puts out a real informal newsletter called *Saucer Slurs* and knows everyone who's anyone in the field. He lives in town. I included his address, too."

Aline wondered if there was anyone on the island who Meg didn't know. "So does this mean UFOs are one of your secret passions?"

Her laughter deepened the creases at the corners of her eyes. "Not so secret really. I just keep tabs on the sightings and whatnot on Tango for historical purposes. Who saw what when. That kind of thing."

"Have there been a lot of sightings on Tango?"

"A fair share. Probably four hundred or so in the sixteen years since I've been keeping records. Most have been nocturnal sightings, and of those I figure ninety or ninety-five percent have been planes or stars or satellites."

"And the rest?"

Meg shrugged. "No telling. Maybe the real thing, maybe something else. I don't investigate, Aline. I just keep the records." She leaned forward and lowered her voice. "You have a few more minutes?"

"You bet."

"Good. Let's make this private." She got up and shut the door, then returned to the desk with a mug of fresh coffee. "This psychiatrist, Vance Liscomb, was not just one of your run-of-the-mill shrinks, Aline. Before he started at the clinic three years ago, he was in private practice in Washington, D.C., where he was also a psychiatric consultant to the Department of Defense. Twenty years on their payroll as a part-timer.

"In the early Seventies, he pioneered one of the early studies on Vietnam POWs. He worked with the Iranian hostages in 1979 and with some of the Mideast hostages. He wrote extensively about his findings in professional journals and, from what I can gather, was considered one of the foremost experts on this kind of insidious brainwashing."

"And Treak?"

"Pretty bright lady. In addition to her medical degree in psychiatry, she has an advanced degree in computer science. Her psychiatric publications are minimal; she's best known for her expertise in the computer area."

"What kind of expertise?"

"Among other things, she writes about microchips, in particular the transistor component in microchips."

"You've lost me."

Meg crossed her legs at the knees and sipped her coffee. "A microchip," she explained, "is an integrated circuit that contains thousands of electronic components crowded onto a sliver of silicon less than one centimeter square. These components are connected to things like memory cells and logic gates, standard equipment on computers and calculators. In each microchip, there's a transistor that switches the current off or on. Anyway, Treak's contention is that modified versions of these transistors can be used to control aggressive behavior in criminals."

A fine Orwellian concept, Aline thought. "How?"

"By implanting a transmitter in the pituitary gland. When stimulated, it would cause the gland to release a flood of endorphins, the body's own morphine, thus subduing the aggressive behavior. The transmitter would be inserted through the sinus cavity in a procedure similar to the way some pituitary tumors are removed."

"Jesus. Has this actually been done?"

"Well, at the time that Treak wrote the article, it had only been tried on animals, with mixed results. So I searched the recent medical literature and found several experiments with human volunteers. The most promising was conducted four years ago, with six volunteers—four men and two women—who were doing time in maximum-security state prisons for violent crimes. With them, the transmitter was stimulated by electroshock but in a much higher dosage than what's used in electroconvulsive therapy."

"What were the results?"

"Aggressive tendencies in three of the volunteers were significantly reduced. The other three didn't seem to show

much change at all. But in both groups there was considerable short-term memory loss, which may have been associated with the ECT. Two of the patients suffered from
hallucinations that lasted as long as two weeks after the electrical stimulation. The experiment was conducted at the University of Miami and Treak and Liscomb were in charge of
it. She was on the medical faculty at the U. of M. at the time
and he was still a consultant with the DOD.

"What's especially interesting is that a lot of the UFO
literature—whether it's from the nutty fringe faction or from
respected researchers—mentions medical experiments conducted on the abductees. One of the most common is the
insertion of a tiny device through the nostril. Under hypnotic
regression, abductees have often referred to it as a *transmitter* that enables the aliens to keep tabs on them."

Aline knew what Meg was implying but couldn't quite
grasp the absurdity of this erudite grandmother talking with
a perfectly straight face about little gray men inserting inter-
galactic probes into the sinus cavities of their human victims.
"You believe all this shit?" she blurted out.

Meg shrugged. "What I believe or don't believe doesn't
make any difference. The fact is that some very bright people
believe it and there seem to be some rather odd parallels
between Treak's experiments and what these aliens supposedly do." She smiled. "That in itself would probably qualify
as high strangeness."

"I definitely agree with the strangeness part."

Meg smiled. "That's an actual term in ufology for an event
or experience that is strange above and beyond the usual
strangeness in the UFO field."

Oh, hey, how simple.

Aline left shortly afterward, thinking about microchips,
transistors, the DOD, electroshock, a missing woman, and
two dead men. She found herself watching the sky, as though
a part of her expected something to materialize against the
canvas of blue. She moved the pieces around in her head,
arranged and rearranged them, and saw that the suggestion
of a pattern existed, but a pattern of what?

Had Liscomb been violent at one time? Had he volunteered for Treak's little group? Had he been part of some DOD experiment? How were the pieces connected? Even if she knew the answers, what would they tell her? Suppose an image was hidden within the pattern that she couldn't detect? Something subliminal, like a suggestion threaded through the pleasant music on a self-hypnosis tape. There but not there.

The truth, Aline thought, was that she was out of her element and her ignorance might prevent her from recognizing an answer that she needed. In that sense, the murder of two people she'd never met had suddenly become quite personal.

(2)

Yesterday she had stayed inside, exploring the house, plundering its secrets. She had found food (canned goods, pasta, bottled water, juice); clothes in an upstairs bureau that fit her; an attic filled with old things: blankets, dusty furniture, boxes of toys, two hurricane lanterns that she'd lit as soon as the sun had set.

She had slept deeply, without dreams, and had awakened this morning with a ravenous hunger and a sense of purpose. To clean the house, to explore the area outside, to take inventory of her food supply. And she would not try to figure anything out.

When she walked outside, her shadow on the crumbling walk was long and narrow, suggesting that it was midmorning. But she couldn't be sure. Life at the clinic had stunted her sense of time, she wore no watch, and there wasn't a clock in the house. And yet, the air tasted of morning, sweet and hopeful. Ten, she thought. She would assume that it was around ten.

By the time she finished her search, the sun had moved to the other side of the house, her shadow was short and plump, and the air was warm, still, breathless. Details like date and time, though, no longer seemed as important as they had earlier; her discoveries had liberated her. She'd found a toolshed behind the house and a generator that worked, that would give her light at night. Real light. Electric light.

On the gas stove in the kitchen, she fixed a plate of pasta smothered in canned ravioli and a mug of instant coffee. A while later she devoured two tins of tuna fish, spearing the chunks straight out of the cans with a tarnished fork. Then she decided not to eat anything else until she'd taken inventory of the food and estimated how long it would last.

She listed everything on a scratch pad that had been in a kitchen drawer and posted it on the empty refrigerator, where she could see it. Whenever she used an item, she crossed it off. She guessed she had enough food for a week or ten days, depending, of course, on how much she ate.

And when the food runs out? What then?

She didn't know. She wouldn't think about it. She wouldn't think about any of it. She would sweep, mop, scrub, clean. Movement was the answer. Movement was always the answer. As long as she moved, the past could not catch up to her. She had learned this on her walks at the center, walks that were urged as part of her therapy, as though the act of walking could somehow deliver her from madness.

So she immersed herself in chores, moving through the rooms as though she owned them. And she did. For now she did. It made no difference who had lived here or why the house was abandoned. She lived here now. This was her house and she wanted it clean, wanted it perfect for— *Who? For what?*

A terrible pressure built at the back of her skull. Names slammed against the wall in her mind, shrieking for release, and with it, a suggestion of faces, features superimposed over one another, noses poking from mouths, eyes growing from foreheads. There were memories attached to them, memories that terrified her. She didn't want to remember. She craved this anonymity, this absence of history. It was as if she were newly born from second to second and floated on the surface of light, her past as unformed as her future.

A breeze kicked up. It took the edge off the heat and stirred up the dust she had swept into neat little piles. She began to sneeze and walked outside for fresh air. Shadows had lengthened. The Spanish moss whispered in a language she couldn't understand. Dead leaves and twigs snapped and crunched under her shoes as she approached the car.

Some of the moss had slipped away, exposing paint and chrome and glass. They were portals to the past: She remembered that the car had belonged to a security guard at the clinic. She didn't know its make or model but had watched it arrive on innumerable evenings, a dark, powerful vehicle that the guard always parked in the same place, just outside the gate. She remembered seeing him stash the keys in the overhead visor and realized her escape plan had begun to take shape then. This was after the treatments had started for the second time, but she couldn't recall exactly when. Days ago? Weeks? Months? Did it matter?

Yes, yes, of course it mattered. But not right now. What mattered were the problems the car presented. A, B, C, problems that could be listed that easily. A: If she drove it into town, it might be recognized. B: If she got rid of it, how would she get into town? C: If she kept it, what good would it do her?

The rusted old bike in the toolshed would get her into town if she needed to make the trip, but how far was it? Another portal popped open; she saw herself walking and biking the distance from the clinic to town during that brief period when she was trusted. But the exact mileage escaped her. Was it 1.4? Or maybe 2.3? Hadn't the digits added up to five? She had a vague recollection of herself pedaling down a hill as she repeated the sum of the numbers to herself over and over again, memorizing it.

Her memory had been clear then, but she had been fortifying herself for a time when it wouldn't be, walling off certain memories so that the treatment wouldn't touch them. And yet today she didn't even know her name. Like the distance to town, her name had been torn away by the treatments. It was an echo she couldn't hear, a sound she couldn't form.

She brushed her hands over the car's roof, its hood, its trunk. The moss slipped to the ground. The door creaked when she opened it. A stink rushed at her, of heat, old food, beer. But where was the blood? She knew there had been blood in here when she arrived, blood on the upholstery, on her hands, on her clothes, but no trace of it remained. Now she saw only the mess: crinkled wrappers, butts spilling from an ashtray, empty beer cans on the floor in the backseat.

Maybe she'd imagined the blood.

Yet, there had been blood on her clothes, hadn't there? She was sure of it but couldn't confirm it now because her clothes were clean. No stains on them at all.

She crouched and peered under the driver's seat. She found a pack of unopened Winstons and two cans of unopened Coors. She unlocked the glove compartment. The wallet inside contained $228, three credit cards, and a driver's license in the name of Jay Paulson. He'd been born twenty-two years ago in Gainesville, Florida, and looked like an ex-jock. She was sorry about the car and the money, but she had to look out for herself, didn't she? She had needed the car and now she needed the money.

She stuffed the bills into a pocket of her jeans, kept the cigarettes, then locked the wallet in the glove compartment again and checked the trunk. A beach towel, a beach chair, two bags filled with old paperbacks, a spare tire. She slammed the lid and leaned against it, pressing the heels of her hands against her eyes. Get rid of the car? Keep it? What, dear God, what?

Nothing, do nothing now, she thought, and felt instantly better.

She glanced toward the house, decided not to return to it just yet, and began walking through the woods. Up one slope and down another, up and down, threading her way through brush and stickers until she reached the dirt road that led to the highway. Now and then she stopped to rest, to wipe her face with the tail of her shirt. Once, she paused next to a tree into which a heart had been carved. Inside it were the initials MS. She slipped her fingers into the grooves of the *M*, aware of some shift within herself, and wondered if her name started with *M*. Mary, Marie, Margaret, Maude, Micki, Marge, Marianne, Marion . . .

Mag-gie, Mag-gie, ready or not, here I come. . . .

Was that her name? Maggie? Frowning, she moved away from the trees and turned slowly in the road, peering back toward the house. The house was no longer visible. But a young girl was racing down the middle of the road calling: *Mag-gie, Mag-gie* in a singsong voice that lifted up through the branches and the heat.

"Hey!" she shouted. "Hey!" But the little girl didn't turn around. She just kept on running, running, her fists balled at her sides, the pink bow in her hair fluttering.

The woman sprinted after her, shouting again, but the girl was beginning to fade, to *fade*, for God's sake. By the time she reached the spot where she'd last seen the child, she was gone. Breathing hard, sweating from the exertion, she dropped to the ground, looking for the child's footprints. But the only prints were her own, headed for the highway. "But I saw her," she whispered.

Of course you did," Dr. Liscomb replied in his calm, maddening voice. *Of course you did, Margaret.*

"Margaret." The name rolled off her tongue with a familiarity that made her ache all over inside. "Margaret, Margaret, Margaret." She began to laugh and rock and repeated her name again and again. Then she tore it down into syllables, *Mar-ga-ret*, and put them together in new ways: Ga-mar-ret, Ret-mar-ga, Ga-ret-mar, Ret-ga-mar.

Elated, she leaped up and sprinted back to the tree, to the carved initials. If *M* stood for Margaret, then what did the *S* stand for? Had she carved these initials? When? And if *S* was the first letter of her last name, why had she enclosed them in a heart?

Margaret pressed her palm over the heart, as if it would yield its secrets through the magic of her touch. She tried very hard to remember herself standing here beneath the thick, sagging branches of the mushroom trees, carving initials into the trunk. But she couldn't. Dismayed, she let her hand slip from the heart. Maybe the initials had nothing at all to do with her. But then why had she turned down this road? Why had her hands known where the key to the house was hidden? Why did the clothes in the drawers and the shoes in the closet fit her? Why?

She began to weep and wrapped her arms around the tree trunk, hugging it, her cheek pressed to the carved heart, Dr. Liscomb's voice in her ear whispering: *You are many steps from well, Margaret. But we're going to make the journey back together.*

Liscomb, who was dead.

Liscomb, whom she had killed.

She couldn't remember doing it, couldn't recall the precise moment of his death, but she was responsible, wasn't she? And what about Hugh? It seemed that he had been there when it happened, but she couldn't place him anywhere in the room. Had anyone else been present? It seemed so, but she wasn't certain. Maybe she'd only imagined that Hugh had been there, just as she had imagined the little girl with the pink bow in her hair.

But she hadn't imagined stealing the security guard's car or speeding along that dark road or swerving in here. *Here.* The dirt under her feet, the scent of pine in the air, her arms embracing the thick, cool trunk of the mushroom tree: These things were real. And her name, she had her name now. Margaret.

"Margaret," she whispered.

It wasn't much, but it was a start.

(3)

Evan Nate flew from Homestead Air Force Base to Key West and rented a car at the airport. He drove into town, wending up and down the narrow, mostly one-way streets until he arrived at the dock on the west side of town.

The line for the next ferry to Tango was long, but not as long as it would be by Thanksgiving weekend and definitely not long enough to discourage him from riding it. He pulled

in behind a van, turned off the engine, got out, quickly
scanned the crowd. No telling which car the congressman
would be in. That green Seville? That black Chrysler? Maybe
a foreign job, a VW, a Toyota. He might even be on foot;
there was just no telling.

One thing was certain: Henry Sheen didn't share Nate's
love for the ferry.

It was one of the few frivolous treats that Nate allowed
himself, like a cigar or a glass of Dom Pérignon after dinner.
It also connected him to the past, to the early years of his
daughter's life when she'd called him Daddy and believed he
could walk on water. The years that had passed too quickly.
A blur, he thought, it was all a blur frozen in his memory's
snapshots.

There: his daughter beside him at the railing clutching his
hand as the sea breeze blew through her hair. And there: his
wife on her other side smiling at him over their daughter's
head. Those kinds of memories. A sense of union, of bond-
ing. Irreplaceable. And somehow it had gotten lost in the
shuffle of the intervening years.

Now his daughter, Beth, was thirty-three, a refugee of two
marriages and several alcohol and drug rehab centers, a miserable, bitter young woman living at home in between dead-
end jobs. His wife had her charities and social functions and
the company of other officers' wives, a life with which she
was quite comfortable and to which he was incidental. After
thirty-five years his marriage was a cliché.

He, of course, had his greenhouse, his twenty acres outside of Homestead, his hideaway on Tango, and his work.
He'd always had his work. It was his balm, his passion, his
connection to a world that was larger than himself. Yes, there
were problems, particularly with this project. But there had
been problems before and there would be problems again.
This, too, would pass, he thought, touching the small black
device hooked to his belt. It would. It had to.

He was sitting at a table on deck, sipping a beer, when a
man straddled the stool across from him. Khaki baseball cap,

khaki slacks, pale blue shirt with pink flamingoes on it, khaki
windbreaker, dark shades.

"Let me guess," Nate said. "Jimmy Buffet? Ollie North
on vacation?"

"Tom Tourist from Cleveland."

"You don't look well, Henry."

"On a calm day, I can take maybe five minutes on a boat,
Evan. In case you haven't noticed, the sea is *not* calm today."

The sea, Nate thought, had less to do with it than the
chemo he was taking for pancreatic cancer. But you didn't
talk about it with Henry Sheen, the venerable congressman
from Palm Beach, the shoo-in for the seat his old man had
vacated eighteen years ago. Sheen the Dean. That's how he
was known on the Hill. He was the man who pulled more
strings than a kid at Christmas. Need that bill passed? Talk
it over with The Dean. Need votes on the new budget? Get
The Dean on your side. Nate's association with the man went
back before Congress, before Sheen had inhabited the governor's mansion in Tallahassee, before any of that. Thirty
years ago they had flown together in Vietnam.

We're getting old, Henry.

"So let's make it snappy, Evan." Sheen whipped off the
cap and ran his palm over wisps of gray hair that, before
chemo, had been thick. "I've got to catch an evening plane
back to D.C. What's going on?"

"We've got a problem."

"You want to be a bit more specific?"

"The Lost Pleiade, Henry."

His pallor, the way his mouth suddenly drooped at the
corners, the way he tilted his sunglasses back onto his head:
Nate now had his full attention. "Go on."

Nate explained; Sheen rubbed his pale hands over his face
and sighed. "Jesus, that woman's been more trouble than
she's worth, Evan."

"I agree."

His hands dropped to the table, then curled around the can
of Coke in front of him. "At least we agree on something.
What do you propose to do about it?"

"The only thing I can do. But I have to find her first."

"Then do it." Sheen raised the can of Coke to his mouth.

"That shit will rust your insides, Henry."

"And no telling what that shit will do to you." He gestured toward Nate's Corona. "What is it that you need?"

"For starters, I need that agent from the Bureau."

"Jones, John Jones?"

"Yes. I need him to come in and take over the local yokel investigation. I need him and however many guys they can spare at the Miami office to look for this woman, Henry, because if the cops find her first, we're fucked. All of us. And that's it in a nutshell."

Sheen slapped the cap back on his head, removed his shades, and rubbed his eyes. For a moment there in the sunlight, Sheen looked old—not aging, not just getting there, but *old*. The deepening creases at the corners of his eyes, his pallor, the tissue-thin texture of his skin, his thinning hair, even his hands, curled like claws around that damnable can of Coke. And it scared him. Sheen was fifty-nine, only two years older than Nate himself.

"Is it worth it, Evan?" he asked softly. "Do you honestly think the Lost Pleiade is worth it?"

It was a lament, not a question, the haunting song that bound them more deeply than Nam, than politics, more deeply than the nearly three decades they had known each other. Yeah, it was worth the secrecy, the deception, the millions spent, the blood that had been spilled, yes, Christ, yes. It was worth it. "I wouldn't be here if I didn't think it was," he replied.

Sheen smiled sadly, nodding to himself like the weak and frail man that he was. "Whatever you need, you'll have," he said, and pushed himself up from the table with visible effort. "It'll take time, but you'll have it."

Nate watched him walk away, walk toward the stairs that led to the lower deck, then raised his beer to his mouth and polished it off. Sheen, he thought, was a rarity in politics, a marvel of quiet efficiency. Like the spider in the greenhouse.

6

(1)

Gene Frederick had assured Kincaid that the security job at the clinic was his and the hiring process was merely a formality. *Fifteen minutes tops, Ryan.* But it took two long and excruciating hours.

He was photographed and fingerprinted and interviewed by the head honcho. He was measured for a uniform, shoes, and a hat. He was forced to sit through a boring recitation of company policies and benefits by the personnel director, a plump blonde with a beehive hairdo that had gone out with *Leave It to Beaver* and *The Ed Sullivan Show*.

And at a quarter of five he was sent on his way with a nightstick and a badge that identified him as Ray Rourke. He was supposed to report to work tomorrow night at nine-thirty, half an hour early, for a brief orientation with Dr. Treak. None of this was exactly what he'd had in mind when he'd called Frederick from Lester's.

But Frederick hadn't dickered about his fee this time. That meant the heat was on from the mayor's office to wrap things up fast. After all, the tourist season was right around the corner. The mayor had undoubtedly delivered the message himself in that slow, good-ole-boy drawl.

Y'all know as well as Ah do, Gene, how these snowbirds get turned off by these unpleasant things. . . . And never you mind if they come from someplace like Houston where mur-

der's the number-one recreation. That don't count worth a hill of beans. Tango is where they play.

Yes, sir, Mr. Mayor. Playing here was definitely more important than living here.

He took a shortcut through the hills to the Tango hospital in the hopes that he could catch Bill Prentiss before he left for the day. The volunteer at the front desk didn't know if Prentiss was still around or not but directed him to the morgue, where Prentiss did his autopsies and hid out when he didn't want to be bothered.

Kincaid rode a freight elevator to the bowels of the building and moved through the eerie twilight of clanking pipes and cold concrete walls. The air down here smelled the way he imagined a coffin would smell, of earth and dripping water, of tight, dark spaces. It was no small miracle, he decided, that Prentiss had turned out to be a rather normal human being.

The door to the morgue was unlocked and the air inside reeked of Pine Sol and Clorox, scents that didn't entirely conceal the stink of death. Prentiss, gowned and masked in surgical greens, was busy at the autopsy table, speaking softly into a mike suspended above him. The bright light by which he worked buzzed and clicked, white noise that seemed to flow over and around the monotone of his voice.

When he stopped talking, he hummed or whistled to himself, snatches from Broadway musicals, old Beatles tunes, bars from a children's song. The choice didn't seem to matter; the point was to fill the silence.

"The Whistling Coroner: there's got to be a story in that," Kincaid remarked as he shut the door.

Prentiss laughed and turned off the mike. "Bernie says it's the ghoul in my personality. Three days in Miami and you miss all the action, Ryan."

"So Bernie told me. I ran into her at Lester's."

"And the chief's already grabbed you, right?"

"I start at the clinic tomorrow night."

"He give you any shit about your fee?"

"Not this time. It's too close to snowbird season."

"You don't have to stand over there, you know. This guy isn't going to suddenly sit up and howl."

Kincaid approached the aluminum table and watched Prentiss closing the incision that ran from the man's throat to his pubic bone. "Is this one of the guys from the clinic?"

"Yeah, the doc. Vance Liscomb." The irreverence disappeared from his voice; it meant Prentiss had discovered something in the autopsy that disturbed him. And that bothered Kincaid; there was rarely anything in an autopsy that troubled Prentiss. "They found him with a syringe in his carotid and a broken neck. I don't know what killed him first, the broken neck or the anaphylactic shock from the Seconal in the syringe."

"An allergy to a barbituate? Is that possible?"

"People can be allergic to anything. Hell, I'm allergic to codeine and it's something you're not even supposed to be allergic to."

"Is Seconal used to sedate patients before electroshock?"

"Sodium Pentothal is more common, although any barbituate will do. But we're assuming he was going to give it to Margaret Wickerd before administering shock treatment and I'm not so sure that's what happened. I'm not convinced that Margaret was anywhere near that treatment room, Ryan, and if she was, why wasn't she already sedated?"

He stabbed a thumb toward the body bag on a gurney against the wall. "Take a look at that guy over there." Kincaid walked over and unzipped the bag, and Prentiss stood beside him, gesturing like a conductor. "His throat was slit by someone standing behind him. Although it's entirely possible that a person shorter than he was could do it, the individual would have to be strong enough to overpower him. Margaret Wickerd weighs a hundred and fifteen pounds and stands five foot eight. So unless she's proficient in the martial arts, I just can't see it."

"Who was killed first?"

"Based on the serotonin levels in the blood, I'd have to say the attendant was first. Liscomb died fifteen or twenty minutes later."

Kincaid zipped the body bag shut and returned to the table, careful not to touch anything. "That's quite a while if the woman was in the room the entire time."

"Yeah, it is. But right now it's all speculation, anyway, because I can't prove anything."

Prentiss unraveled a black hose that was connected to the spigot in a nearby sink and proceeded to wash down the body and the table. There was something terribly impersonal about it, Kincaid thought, as though the body was no more than a slab of bloody beef. Cremation was looking better all the time.

"But since we're speculating," Prentiss went on, "I've got a couple of other weird bits to share with you."

There it was again, Kincaid thought. That difference in tone. He'd known Prentiss nearly as long as he'd lived on Tango and he wasn't a man who spooked easily. But he was spooked now, spooked enough to speak softly and carefully.

"Someone broke in here last night. It's not too hard to do. There's just a dead bolt on the door. Nothing's missing, but a couple of the body drawers weren't closed tightly and my files were fucked up. For some reason, I'd left Liscomb and the orderly in the morgue on the second floor rather than bringing them down here when I left yesterday afternoon." He paused, turned off the water, drew a plastic sheet over Liscomb's body. "I realize it sounds paranoid, Ryan, but I think whoever broke in was looking for the next thing I'm going to show you."

"Did you report it?"

"No." Quick, flat, and unequivocal. He snapped off his latex gloves, mask, gown, and scrubbed up. "Since there are some things about these two homicides that bother me, I decided to take a series of X-rays just to be sure I didn't miss anything in the autopsies. I found something in Liscomb's head."

Prentiss dried his hands, then they went into the adjoining room, a makeshift office with a computer, a few file cabinets, and several pieces of sophisticated equipment on carts whose purpose Kincaid could only guess. A dozen X-rays hung from clips against a large panel of light. Prentiss tapped the third X-ray from the left.

"What you're looking at here, Ryan, is the part of the brain known as the *between brain*. It's the region deep in the forebrain, between the brainstem and the cerebral hemispheres. And right here"—he pointed with a pen—"is the hypothalamus. It weighs a quarter of an ounce and isn't much bigger than the tip of my thumb. For its size, it performs more tasks than any other part of the brain and controls things like thirst, appetite, body temp, sexual behavior, fear, sleep, and aggression. It also controls the pituitary gland." The pen moved a fraction of an inch, to an area directly under the hypothalamus. "See it there?"

Kincaid nodded; it looked like a tiny worm with a bulge at one end. "So?"

"What do you see here?" With the pen, Prentiss touched a black line that might have been a hairline fracture except that it was inside the brain.

"A defect on the X-ray?"

"That's exactly what I thought. But it's not a defect. Just to be sure, I did an ultrasound scan." He walked over to the computer, tapped several keys, and, a moment later, brought up an image similar to what was on the X-ray but in greater detail.

"It looks like a straight pin or something."

"Or something. Yeah, you've got that right." From a pocket in his jeans, Prentiss brought out a small plastic bottle. He snapped off the cap, tapped it against the edge of his palm, and a dark sliver slipped out. "I pulled this from Liscomb's left nostril. I messed up his sinuses pretty bad, but it was worth it."

"What the hell is it?"

"Beats the shit outta me, Ryan. I think it's silicon, but that's all I can tell you." He put it back into the bottle. "Considering the break-in last night, I'd rather not keep it here tonight. How about if you give it to Aline to lock up at the station? Then tomorrow I'd like to show it to the pathologist in Key West and see if he's got any ideas.

"This isn't going in my report. I'll tell Frederick about it, but I'm not putting it in writing. Frederick would probably disagree, but there's something not quite right at that clinic. The place hasn't sat well with me since I drove in there two days ago, and this hasn't improved my opinion. You'll see what I mean. It's in the patients' faces, in Nina Treak's attitude, it's in the fucking air, Ryan. I can't explain it." He slipped the sliver back into the bottle, capped it, and handed it to Kincaid. "Tell Aline I'll pick it up tomorrow."

When he and Prentiss walked outside ten minutes later, the sun had slipped behind the trees and the sky to the east was already violet. Birds swooped through the waning light. Distantly, he heard the drone of rush-hour traffic on the Old Post Road. He knew it was his imagination, but it seemed he could feel the shape of the silicon sliver against his thigh.

(2)

As the crow flew, the distance from the hospital to the lighthouse was two miles. But crows hadn't built the island's roads, Kincaid thought, and the two-lane highway cut back and forth through the hills in a chain of jagged Zs.

Traffic was moderate. Most of the commuters were headed in the opposite direction, east to the bridge or to the interstate that cut the island in half from north to south. But the dark van behind him had been there since he'd left the hospital, its speed as steady as the passage of time. The front of it was shaped like a bullet, and through the tinted windows he could make out two people in the front seat.

He couldn't recall having seen the van in the hospital lot when he and Prentiss had left the building. But he probably wouldn't have noticed it even if it had been there because he hadn't been looking for it. Besides, it didn't stand out in any way; it was just an ordinary van, a Toyota, a Ford, something similar. He had no reason to think it was tailing him, but that was exactly what he thought.

Kincaid slowed and so did the van, remaining three to four car-lengths back. When he turned into the next bend, he lost sight of it. He accelerated, flicked on the headlights, and glanced in the rearview mirror as the road straightened again. The van appeared moments later, keeping pace with him, its headlights still off.

If Miami's newest road game had migrated to Tango, then any second now the van would draw up alongside him and the driver would motion wildly toward the back of the Saab, indicating a flat or a fire or fuel pouring from the gas tank. Then he would stop to see what the problem was and the van's occupants would jump him.

In one such incident, a British couple had just left the Miami airport in their Hertz rental when a passing motorist on the interstate had shouted that their car was on fire. The driver had stopped, was shot, killed, and robbed, and his wife was critically injured.

These days, paranoia was justified. So at the next sharp turn he killed his headlights, swerved across the left lane, and drove into the pines. It wasn't quite dark yet. Twilight clung to the air and seeped through the branches like some ancient balm against the night. But he didn't think his Saab would be visible from the road. He exited quickly and sprinted to the edge of the trees to await the van. It materialized right on schedule, its headlights still off, its speed holding at about fifty. It was a new Ford, gray with black stripes around the middle. He couldn't read the numbers on the license plate but saw it well enough to determine that it wasn't a Florida plate.

After it passed, Kincaid waited ten minutes, long enough for the men to realize he'd given them the slip. When they didn't return, he walked back to the Saab and jotted down everything he remembered about the van. In the old days, the days before he'd turned forty, he'd rarely taken notes. Now he did it routinely. Although the clarity and sharpness of his memory was unchanged, it took him longer to retrieve information now than it had twenty years ago. Writing things down helped to fix information in his mind and provided him with a continuous personal record on his cases. A record, he thought, from which he could reconstruct every case he'd had in the last three years, if he had to.

It was dark when he swung onto the road, and for the final home stretch, he didn't see another car. The trees ended just short of the cliff on which the lighthouse sat. Against the dark sky, where only a few stars glistened, the lighthouse resembled a tower in a Shakespearean play where the forces of good and evil were constantly pitted against each other. Since the place wasn't blazing with lights, he knew that Aline wasn't home yet. But he didn't doubt that the windows had burned like carnival lights in his absence.

He pressed the button on the remote-control box that controlled the iron gate and drove through, leaving the gate open for Aline. The sprinklers were on, water whirling like mindless ballerinas in the glare of the headlights. He parked in front, retrieved his bag from the trunk, and unlocked the front door.

Usually the cat or the skunk or both scampered into the hall as soon as a key was turned in the lock. But neither of them appeared. They were probably irritated that no one was home to feed them and had split through the swinging panel in the utility-room door to scrounge on their own. Kincaid left his bag at the bottom of the stairs and headed for the kitchen. He stopped in the doorway, frowning, looking around slowly.

Something was different about the room, but what? The chairs at the tile breakfast table were pushed in, the usual things were arranged on the counter, the blinds hadn't been pulled across the picture window. Everything just as it should be.

Except for the desk. It was a shiny black structure built into the wall on his right by the previous owner, and the place where Aline often dumped her paperwork. On any given day, it was buried under haphazard stacks of books, bills, notebooks, pens, pet food, and whatever else she'd dropped on it. By mutual agreement, it was her space, her black hole. But now the books were neatly piled here, the notebooks there, the pens and pencils were gone, and all the drawers were shut. If she had cleaned house in his absence, the surface of the desk would be absolutely clear and the drawers would hold the chaos. She wouldn't just straighten; it wasn't in her nature.

Someone had been in here, searching her belongings.

He checked the windows in the front room; none had been jimmied. But the lock on the atrium's sliding glass door had been sprung when the door was lifted off the track. The wooden gate that separated the atrium from the side yard stood ajar, swinging in the breeze that skipped up over the edge of the cliff. Nothing too complicated to figure on this one, he thought.

He stepped carefully through the profusion of plants, just in case Boo was hidden in them, and stopped at the gate. The wind gasped at his legs. Directly in front of him was the sloping expanse of pines and banyans that stretched south and east to the six-foot wall that marked the end of the property. Beyond it lay the woods and the old seamen's graveyard. And just off to his right he glimpsed movement, a man fleeing into the trees.

Kincaid tore after him, cutting a jagged path through plants and shrubbery. His arms pumped hard at his sides, but he wasn't fast enough. He hadn't been running since they'd moved into the lighthouse and he felt it in his lungs, in the tight burning in his muscles, saw it in the distance the man maintained.

He was tall, thin, and fleet and sprinted through the darkness as though he commanded it and the terrain over which he moved. Weeds and drooping branches parted for him like the Red Sea and fought Kincaid at every step. Then the guy stumbled, fell to one knee, scrambled up again. But it gave Kincaid the advantage he needed.

In a burst of speed, he closed the gap between them and tackled the bastard. His head snapped back, he went down with a grunt, and they rolled fast and furiously down the incline toward the wall. Kincaid struck it first, struck it hard on his right side, head, shoulder, hip. Air rushed from his lungs, stars exploded like firecrackers inside his eyes, his muscles went slack, and the man was suddenly scrambling up the wall like a monkey.

Kincaid leaped up, the ground tilting beneath him, and lunged. His hands closed around an ankle and he jerked it hard, but the man twisted, kicked out with his other foot, and the toe of his shoe sank into the fleshy underside of Kincaid's jaw. He stumbled back, blood filling his mouth, the man's shoe in his hands, and hit the ground. The interloper vanished over the wall.

He pushed up, blood oozing from his chin. His skull felt as though it had been squeezed as flat as a dime. He weaved back toward the lighthouse, the shoe clutched in his hand.

In the half-bath on the first floor, he tended to his jaw, which wasn't as bad as it looked, then examined his prize. It was a well-worn black New Balance running shoe with red laces, a size nine and a half and an E width.

He put the shoe and the plastic bottle that contained the silicon sliver in the safe in the den. They'd had it installed in the closet floor after they'd moved in, eight feet deep in the foundation and secure enough to withstand anything short of a nuclear blast.

As he was replacing the lid, the doorbell rang and Unojo scampered out from under the bed and raced into the hall ahead of him. She stopped just short of the door and sat back on her haunches, blocking his way. "That's it?" he asked. "That's all you've got to say about the intruder? Feed me before you open the door, Ryan?" She peered at him with her single good eye and meowed. He picked her up as the bell rang again and opened the door.

Two men stood side by side on the unlit stoop. Behind them was the Ford van that had followed him earlier, with a third man leaning against its front fender. The trio wore identical black suits and black hats with wide brims pulled low over their foreheads, casting their faces into shadow.

Hats. Kincaid couldn't remember the last time he'd seen

anyone on Tango wearing a hat. "Help you with something?"

The taller man moved his head slightly. In the wash of light from the hallway, his features seemed vaguely Oriental, but he spoke with no discernible accent. "Is Ryan Kincaid in?"

"No, he isn't." Unojo leaped out of his arms with a hiss and ran off. The air seemed unpleasantly heavy, as though the barometric pressure had suddenly risen, prefacing a thunderstorm. But the sky was clear. "I'm his brother. Can I help you boys with something?"

"His car is here," observed the shorter man.

"I drive it when he's off the island. I don't believe I caught your name."

The man glanced quickly at his companion, who said, "We're with Air Force Intelligence."

Yeah, and I'm Arsenio Hall.

"We'd like to talk to him when he gets back. Do you know when that will be?"

"You have ID?"

The man ignored the question. "When will he be back?"

"I don't know. Why don't you leave a number so he can call you?"

"We'll call him," the taller man replied, and he and his companion walked back to the van; the third member of the trio was already behind the steering wheel.

Kincaid stood in the doorway, waiting for the van to turn around so he could see the license plate this time. But the driver simply put the vehicle in reverse and backed out onto the road, where it nearly collided with Aline's Honda as she barreled out of the hills. She hit the horn and the van lurched forward and shot south.

She swung into the driveway and got out of her car, one hand on her hip, the other gesturing in the direction the van had gone. "Who the hell was that?"

"Three men in black." He strode quickly past her and shut the gate. "Did you see the license plate?"

"I didn't even see the van until the last second. Another

inch and the turkey would have taken off my front bumper. What'd they want?''

"To talk to Ryan Kincaid. They said they were Air Force Intelligence.''

A corner of her mouth dimpled as she grinned. "Yeah? What'd you do, Ryan? Fly over restricted air space or something?''

"Or something." He slipped an arm around her slender waist and hugged her hello. His face burrowed into her hair, which flowed over her shoulders, a whiskey river. It always astonished him that she rarely felt or looked the same to him after an absence. It was as if the life she lived when he was gone changed her in some vital, invisible way. Now he would spend days or weeks discovering her again. "Let's talk about it over dinner.''

She leaned back in his arms and touched a fingertip to the Band-Aid under his chin. "Is that part of this story or did some sweet young thing in Miami deck you, Ryan?''

"A sweet young thing.''

"Yeah?" They started walking toward the lighthouse. "And what'd she look like?''

"Tall, thin, dark. She wore black running shoes with red laces.''

Aline laughed. "Tacky. No socks? No garter belt and stockings?''

"Uh-uh.''

"So why'd she deck you?''

They stepped inside and Kincaid shut the door, locked it. "I was chasing her.''

"Ah, well. No wonder. A virgin. Serves you right for picking on virgins. They're nearly an extinct species, you know.''

"She'd gone through your things.''

"What things?''

"Your desk." He gestured toward it and her eyes followed. "He got in through the atrium." He told her what had happened as they stood in the kitchen doorway, the dark pressing up against the windows that surrounded them.

(3)

The wind prowled the lighthouse, an invisible beast that had sprung from the sea. Now and then a gust shook the panes of glass in the den so hard they rattled. The big grandfather clock in the corner ticked ticked ticked. She felt absurdly grateful that she didn't have to spend the night alone here, roaming the lighthouse like a possessed witch, tempted in her solitude to unlock the safe again and again to have a look at the shoe with the red laces, at the silicon sliver that had been lodged in Liscomb's brain, to speculate about its similarity to Nina Treak's experiment on a group of aggressive criminals.

Nearly forty and still afraid of the dark. But in all fairness to herself, her fear was quite selective. When she leaned her head back against the rocker in which she sat and closed her eyes, she saw little gray men at the foot of her bed. The Grays, as they were known in UFO lore. And waiting in the hallway were the men in black, who, according to the lore, often appeared to witnesses or researchers during UFO flaps and claimed to be from a government agency. *We want your photos, your evidence; we want your silence.*

MIBs, as they were commonly known, were actually an ancient phenomenon. During the Middle Ages, they were blamed for acts of vampirism, and like their modern counterparts, they sometimes spoke with accents and had vaguely Oriental features. In the fairy lore of Celtic countries, one type of fairy was the size of a normal man who looked quite human and wore black clothing. In ancient Oriental beliefs, there was an underground city ruled by the King of the World who maintained his power through emissaries on the surface who dressed in black robes and suits.

Contemporary MIBs seemed to follow a particular pattern of behavior. They sometimes posed as salesmen or Seventh-Day Adventists; often drove dark cars (black Cadillacs were popular); intimidated people involved in encounters by threatening them to remain silent about what they'd experienced; followed witnesses and researchers; knew intimate details of their lives.

Some MIB episodes included other curious and bizarre phenomena as well, like harassing phone calls by ''electroniclike voices'' and homes buzzed by black, unmarked helicopters. These MIBs of the air had been identified at various times as Bell-47s, Chinooks, and Hueys. Military aircraft. To some researchers, the choppers were proof of the government's involvement, and to others, they were illusions created by advanced beings to muddle the truth about UFOs.

Laughable in daylight, Aline thought, opening her eyes. But not at night. Even though she believed there was something rational and earthbound behind all of this, the stories alone possessed a certain elemental power.

''Hey,'' Kincaid said. ''Did you know there's a ghost-ship legend in Chile?''

He had lifted up on an elbow, his finger marking the page in one of the books he'd picked up in Miami: *Chiloé: La Isla Encantada*. The only time Kincaid read books in Spanish was when he was preparing for a trip. So it was fair to deduce that his next destination would be the island of Chiloé. She was almost afraid to ask when he was leaving because she knew she wasn't going to like the answer.

I'll be leaving in a few weeks. You coming? It'll only be for six months.

''Al?''

She blinked and his face swam back into focus. The sandy beard, the lean, roguish face, the interminable twinkle in his eyes. ''I heard you. A ghost ship. So exactly where is this island?''

''Off the southwest coast of Chile. It's huge compared to Tango, thirty miles wide and a hundred and fifty miles long. There're two main towns and you get there either by ferry or by plane.'' He walked over to the tremendous world map that covered one wall of the den. ''C'mere, look.''

The island was the first in an archipelago that followed the long, gradual curve of the lower third of Chile. Kincaid ran his finger along the coast of the island. ''The ship, the *Ca-*

leuche, has supposedly sailed these waters since the 1500s.
But to a lot of the locals, it's not just a legend. They believe
it's real.''

The triple-masted ship, he said, was most frequently
sighted as it entered the shallow, unnavigable waters of the
Rio Pudeto. It was supposedly manned by a crew of *brujos*—
sorcerers—who were the ultimate shape shifters, capable of
transforming their shapes at will. Like the little gray men in
ufology, these mariners abducted islanders who, upon their
return, realized they were 'missing time' and remembered
nothing of the experience. They often had physical scars they
couldn't explain.

''It's starting to sound familiar, isn't it,'' Kincaid remarked.

''Very. What else?''

''A man in black parallel. Quite often, people who have
sighted the ship or are involved in the investigation of a sighting are visited by a man or a trio of men dressed in black.
They usually deliver a vague threat about maintaining secrecy.''

He flopped back onto the couch and rested his bare feet
against the coffee table. ''Even the arguments and theories
about the nature of the *Caleuche* are identical to those about
what UFOs are: that it's superstition; an archetype of the
collective mind of the islanders; evidence of interdimen-
sional travel; a myth that's still evolving; that it's exactly what
it seems to be.''

Few things, she thought, were ever exactly as they appeared to be.

''In fact, the only theory about UFOs that doesn't also
pertain to the *Caleuche* has to do with the government.
There's never been the equivalent of a Project Blue Book
about the ship. There are no secret documents, no rumors
of a disinformation campaign, no *official* verdict about what
the ship is or isn't.''

''Probably because the Chilean government has other
things to worry about: coups, runaway inflation, political
subversives. And just for the record, Ryan, it sounds like

you've already made up your mind that all this UFO stuff is a government conspiracy.''

"I think the government's a convenient scapegoat.''

This from the man who had definite opinions about government, few of them good. "Well, frankly, I think they're behind the whole thing. I just don't know the details yet.''

"I didn't say they aren't involved, Aline. They might be, particularly in this case, given Liscomb's connection to the Department of Defense. The government might be just one facet of the whole. Maybe a foreign government's behind it.''

"Russians?" Aline smiled as she said it. "C'mon, Ryan. I think the Russians have more to worry about these days than UFOs.''

"Look, the question isn't whether ETs are zipping around screwing up NORAD computers and abducting people. It isn't that simple. People are experiencing *something* and there are definite patterns to what they're experiencing.''

"But. . . ?''

He sat forward. "Think about this. Chiloé is populated by unsophisticated people; most of them are fishermen. There isn't much tourism. Televisions are a rare commodity. Probably the only communion these people know about is the Sunday wafer at church. So how the hell can there be parallels to MIBs?''

"Coincidence?''

He made a face. "Dirty word, Al.''

"Okay, so MIBs are as common a folktale as UFOs. Maybe Carl Jung was right about UFOs as an archetype.''

"And suppose someone has figured out how to capitalize on that?''

"In what way?" She stared out the window at a star-studded sky as benign as a ladybug. "And for what reason?''

"I don't know. I'm just speculating.''

Speculation. It was all speculation. How many galaxies were there like this one? How many with planets that could support life? How many light-years would it take to get to Alpha Centauri? Why would the government even bother with a disinformation campaign if that was, indeed, what this was?

The phone on the desk rang. Considering the time, it was probably someone selling something—home security, life insurance, panty hose. If not that, then a personal call for her; Kincaid wasn't a phone person. His clients, in fact, always reached an answering machine at Ferret's place, where he also received his mail. It was one of the many small precautions he took so that his business would not be compromised because he lived with a cop. Except for his name on the mortgage, there was no traceable evidence that he lived here. Not a good metaphor for a long-term relationship, she thought, and picked up the receiver.

"Aline Scott, please," said a man's voice.

"Speaking."

"Detective Scott, this is Peter Wickerd."

"Oh, Mr. Wickerd. Your housekeeper said you weren't going to be back until tomorrow sometime."

"I'm catching a flight out of Newark late tonight. How about if we meet tomorrow morning around nine at the Tango Café?"

"That'd be fine. I guess you've spoken to the clinic?"

"Yes, earlier. I'll do whatever I can to help you people find my wife, Ms. Scott. She's a very sick woman."

The way he said it irritated Aline. "Is there anyone she was close to before she was committed who she might go to for help, Mr. Wickerd?"

"No, no, not anyone I can think of offhand."

"What about somebody in the abduction group she was attending?"

His voice tightened. "I doubt it, I sincerely doubt it. She hasn't seen any of those people in months. But we'll talk about that tomorrow, Ms. Scott. Nine, the Tango Café."

"Just a min—"

But the line was already dead.

Part Two

PATTERNS

"I believe that the UFO phenomena represent evidence for other dimensions beyond spacetime; the UFOs may not come from ordinary space, but from a multiverse which is all around us. . . ."
—Jacques Vallee,
from *Dimensions:*
A Casebook of Alien Contact

7

(1)

Margaret awakened in a room filled with light. It baked her pupils, blinding her to the voice that seemed to come from inside it.

Do not be afraid. We will not hurt you.

Abject terror flooded through her. She screamed and tried to escape the light but couldn't. Her body was paralyzed; her head wouldn't move.

Why do you scream? Are we causing you pain?

Pain, yes, the pain burned up through her nose and blazed in her skull until it felt hollow. Then the pain was gone. *Is that better?* the voice asked, touching her forehead with something cool and light.

She begged the voice not to hurt her baby but knew it was too late for that: the baby was gone, the walls of her womb had collapsed, she was bleeding. She wrenched free of the restraints that had held her and bolted upright in bed, blinking against the blades of light that lanced through the window, her heart pounding, her T-shirt soaked with perspiration. She threw off the sheet and stumbled down the hall to the bathroom, through the still thickness of the air.

The voice hurt me. Stuck something in my nose, took my baby.

She collapsed against the edge of the sink, alternately sobbing and laughing until she was unable to do either. Her knees buckled and she crumpled to the floor, clutching her knees against her, rocking, murmuring words that comforted her but had no meaning.

After a while, she pulled herself up and pressed a wet towel against her face. *My baby's gone.* Nothing connected with this thought except the voice, the voice she had dreamed that was not a dream. When she removed the towel from her face, there was blood on it.

She looked at herself in the mirror, the stranger with the wild black hair, the haunted blue eyes, the gaunt face that might have been pretty once. And as she watched, a drop of blood bloomed at the curve of her nostril, a delicate rose. And then another and another. Something was in there, inside her nose, she could feel it, a slight pressure, an intrusion. Panicked, she tilted her head back, trying to see up inside the nostril, but she couldn't.

She wet a towel, sat on the toilet seat, dropped her head back, and pressed the towel to her nose. Pressure would stop the bleeding. *Please don't bleed please Jesus God please.*

She heard water dripping. She heard the generator pumping electricity into the lights that had burned all night so she could sleep. She heard the frenzied beat of her heart as she sat there, waiting for the blood to stop.

When it did, she moved closer to the mirror and attempted to look up inside her nostril again. *Nothing. Nothing to see.*

She touched it with her fingertip, probing at the opening. It wasn't sensitive, didn't feel unusual in any way. Was she prone to nosebleeds? Had she scratched the inside of the nostril when she was thrashing about during the dream? Perhaps . . . She threw down the towel, disgusted with herself, and hastened back to the warm bedroom. She jerked the curtains open the rest of the way, admitting the full light, then unlocked and raised the windows. A warm breeze stirred through the trees. Shadows eddied across the front yard. It felt like late morning and she was starved.

Breakfast. Then she would decide what to do about the car and she wouldn't think about the blood, the dream, the voice, her baby. She discovered that she was good at that, at not thinking, at sealing certain details in a back room in her mind.

Details like why the clothes and the shoes she'd found here fit her. Or why she'd turned down the dirt road to this place to begin with. Details like that.

After she showered in the downstairs bathroom and put on a clean pair of shorts and a cotton shirt, she turned off the generator and puttered around the kitchen, opening cans, boiling water for pasta. But this time she made a clam sauce to go over it, and although it wasn't bad, it wasn't enough. She wished for fresh mushrooms, chopped walnuts, spices, herbs, real coffee, fruit. The list was endless.

One trip into town. That was all she needed. Maybe she wouldn't even have to go all the way into town. There would surely be a market somewhere close by. But the police would be looking for the car by now, wouldn't they? If she was stopped, if she was recognized . . . Perhaps they believed she'd left the island. If so, they would be watching the bridge, the main roads. If she disguised herself, if she was careful . . . *If.*

Margaret pushed back suddenly from the table and went through the kitchen drawers, looking for the scissors she had seen. Goodbye, hair. Goodbye, Margaret. Goodbye, goodbye.

The blades were rusted and not very sharp, but they would do. She brushed her hair away from her face, drew a comb straight down the middle, gathered half of it to the left side, and cut just below the ear. She repeated this on the right side, then brushed her hair again, fluffing it with her fingers. Hardly professional, but it changed her appearance drastically. Her jaw looked wider now, her face fuller; her mouth belonged to someone else.

She experimented in front of the mirror—with sunglasses, makeup, a red bandanna. And then she was ready. From her bag, she brought out the wad of money she'd taken from the security guard's wallet. She counted out four twenties and two tens, divided the bills between her pockets, and walked outside to the toolshed behind the house.

There were many things inside, most of them useless. But the rusted bike with the rusted basket on the back of it would be her backup. She wheeled it out to the car, emptied the trunk so the bike fit. Then she slipped behind the wheel before she could change her mind and started the car.

It was 2.2 miles to the end of the dirt road. She hesitated at the end of it. No traffic, just sun and blue sky and the mushroom trees lining the far side like foot soldiers. Do it, she thought, and pressed down on the accelerator.

The road followed the edge of a cliff. Through the trees she saw the sudden precipitous drop and the glimmering blue waters beyond it. If she decided to get rid of the car, this would be the place to do it. She would simply drive it over the side, and if it didn't explode, it would sink. Then she would bike back to the house. If the police discovered the car, they would believe she had perished in the crash.

It would work, wouldn't it?

The road dipped. Margaret tapped the brake and downshifted. A car sped up behind her, tailing her so closely she could barely breathe. She saw another car behind it and a third car burst from the blue space in front of her. She slowed. The cars passed and she was alone on the road again, alone and weak with relief.

Houses and turnoffs appeared. She took a narrow gravel road that led inland, where the deep lush green rose into hills. She passed a lake, heard a plane overhead. She was now nearly seven miles from her refuge; just ahead on her right she spotted an outdoor market. The lot was crowded, but that was fine; her car would be one among many.

She parked at the end closest to the road, next to a large sign that said TANGO PRODUCE. She knew this place. She had come here in her old life, her life before the clinic when she and Pete were happy, before he betrayed her.

Pete. And with that name she remembered another. Julie. Pete and Julie, two peas in a pod. Her husband, her sister, her jailers.

The memories hurt and she shoved them aside.

As she stepped out of the car, she started to freeze up. So

many people. They strolled among the wooden bins of fruits and vegetables, touching, inspecting, choosing. *I'm just another customer*, she thought, and forced herself to walk into the crowd, to pick up one of the plastic baskets. No one looked at her. No one paid any attention to her at all.

She moved among the bins, filling her basket with gleaming red apples, bananas, ripe gold papayas, strawberries, radishes and beans and small potatoes the color of rust. Her mouth watered. The voices of the people around her soothed her, rushed over her like water over stones. But it was the smell of the air, rich and earthy, that triggered the memory of a man's hand at her elbow, his mouth against her hair as he whispered to her.

I can't stand sharing you with all these people, Magpie. Let's get outta here.

She seized the memory, tried to enlarge it. She could see his hand against her skin, could remember the way her heart quickened at his touch, but she couldn't find his face. Pete? Was it Pete? She didn't think so, yet she couldn't find the man's name.

She didn't realize she'd stopped in the middle of an aisle until someone bumped into her from behind. She moved hastily aside, her head throbbing, and made her way toward the cash register. Had she drawn attention to herself by stopping? Were people staring at her now? Whispering things about her?

She got in line, kept her eyes down. Hurry, she thought at the cashier, please hurry.

The man who waited on her barely glanced at her. Another man bagged her purchases. She paid, pocketed her change, rushed away. She put the groceries in the backseat, got in, shut the door, locked it, sat there staring at her legs.

That day, the day she'd been with the man whose face she couldn't remember, she'd worn a skirt. It had been hiked up on her legs and the man's hand had idled against her thigh. She saw it clearly now, the short, square nails, the long fingers, the pair of freckles just above the knuckle on his index finger. His thumb moved lazily against her skin, inscribing some secret message.

She, laughing—she heard it, a trill that was almost musical—moved closer to him and drew her leg up against her, heel hooked on the edge of the seat, an invitation he accepted. She wasn't wearing panties and he teased her as he drove, strummed her with those long, practiced fingers as though she were a sitar.

The warm wind had blown through the car. She remembered this vividly, the scent of the wind, the hills, the richness of everything. She remembered how her hips moved in response to the exquisite pressure of his fingers and how sunlight streamed through the windshield and how she looked down once at herself, at his hand moving under her skirt as though it were a small, burrowing animal. When they were deep in the hills, he suddenly swerved off the road and into the trees.

Then her memory skipped ahead, into leaves and cool green shadows, where she was hugging the trunk of a pine and he was behind her, inside her, one hand gripping her at the hip, the other flat against her belly, holding her, and she was whispering, Oh God oh God, as though God might deliver her.

Margaret sped out of the lot and into the hills, her body burning with the memory, the phantom pressure, her head in an uproar. The next thing she knew, she was standing under a cold shower in the house, but it didn't help, the burning was still there, the pressure, the smell of the wind, the sound of his voice, the terrible need.

She slammed her hands against the faucet, turning off the water, and grabbed the towel. But her skin was drawn into tight, sharp peaks, so sensitized that the touch of the terry cloth was more than she could bear. She dropped to her knees and rubbed her hands over her breasts, her belly, between her thighs, sobbing at her depravity until she lay on her side on the floor of the shower, twitching like a dying frog, the man's face exhumed.

(2)

He was late. Wickerd was late and that was one point against him already. Two points, Aline thought, if she included the crack about his wife being a very sick woman.

Granted, Margaret Wickerd's medical records indicated it was true. But Aline had an innate distrust of shrinks and of Nina Treak in particular. Besides, there had been something distinctly distasteful about the way Wickerd had uttered it like a judgment, a pronouncement of guilt.

"A very sick woman . . . "

Aline sipped her coffee and gazed out into the busy street. Sunlight glinted off the hoods of passing cars and burned away the details of the park on the other side of the street. She remembered sitting in this same booth one morning this past May, waiting for Kincaid to show. A different case and a different life for both of them.

Kincaid had just returned from a long jaunt to the Orient only to find that good ole dependable Aline had gotten tired of waiting around and had started seeing a local attorney. Bad judgment on her part. The attorney had had big problems that had nearly cost her her life. But had he not entered the picture, she and Kincaid probably wouldn't have reconciled and bought the lighthouse.

But what difference had the commitment made? The prospect of Kincaid's next trip, to Chile, loomed like a blight in the not so distant future. And after Chile there would be China or the Congo or some other far-flung spot he simply had to see. What was wrong with California? The Carolinas? Even the Caribbean?

For most people, travel was a diversion, a hobby, a two-week trip tacked on to paid holidays; it was incidental to the rest of their lives. But it was Kincaid's passion, the heart of who and what he was, and that wouldn't change. So if the relationship was ever going to move beyond where it was now, *she* would have to change. To rearrange her priorities.

"Dark musings?" asked a familiar voice.

She laughed as Ferret bussed her on the cheek and joined her on the other side of the table. "Puzzled musings."

"Life, death, love, all that?"

"Right. So how was Miami, Ferret?"

"Good, except for the plane trip. Did Ryan tell you he's going to teach me how to fly?"

"He mentioned it."

Ferret sat forward, his lips pulling away from his teeth in a way that chilled her despite all the years she'd known him. "Come clean, Sweet Pea. What did he really say?"

"That he's not looking forward to it."

He sat back, deflated. "I knew it. I knew he'd say something like that."

"Don't feel bad, Ferret. He said the same thing to me when he was my instructor."

He signaled the waitress for coffee, and when it came, he wrapped his skeletal fingers around it as if to warm them. "Who're you meeting here, anyway?"

"Peter Wickerd."

Ferret made a face. "Not my favorite person."

"So Ryan said."

They talked for a while—about the Wickerds, the case— and the hands of the clock on the wall inched toward nine-thirty. She thought of the pile of folders and papers on her desk, of the mayor breathing down Frederick's neck for a quick and tidy resolution. "Do me a favor, Ferret, will you? Ryan said you know Sam Newman. Could you give him a call and tell him it's important that I see him?"

He grinned. "Already done, Sweet Pea. Nine-thirty tonight. His place."

The man who moves mountains, she thought. "He ever talk to you about this abduction stuff?"

He sipped from the mug, nodding. "Sure."

"And? You think it's real?"

"I guess that depends on how you define real."

"You know what I mean."

"I don't think about it one way or another. I don't think about it at all. Don't like to." He leaned toward her again.

"Frankly, Aline, the very idea of ETs whizzing around spying on us, nabbing us, well, I don't like it. It makes me feel like I'm seven years old again, huddled in bed and waiting for the bogeyman to step out of the closet, you know?"

Yes, she knew. Even though she didn't subscribe to a belief in flying saucers, the mere possibility made her feel diminished, insignificant, powerless, the way she imagined an ant might feel as it peered up at the sole of the shoe that was about to crush it. An atavistic fear.

"Time for me to vacate," Ferret said suddenly, and tilted his head toward the window. "Here comes your boy."

Wickerd looked nothing like she'd imagined from his voice. He was at least a half-foot shorter than Kincaid, with longish blonde hair and the tan of an aging beach boy. He was dressed like a man on the make: white designer slacks, Italian sandals without socks, a pastel shirt unbuttoned halfway down his chest, several gold chains tangled in the mat of hair.

"Have fun, Sweet Pea," Ferret said, and slipped away, headed for the rear exit so he wouldn't have to pass Wickerd.

He paused in the door, removed his sunglasses with a practiced snap of his wrist, looked around like a celebrity hoping to be recognized by the fans. Aline waved him over. He apologized profusely for being late, his alarm hadn't gone off, and he certainly appreciated her waiting.

Despite last night's remark about his wife being a very sick woman, he came across as a solicitous, concerned husband whose wife's breakdown was a tragedy with which he had learned to live. But his act was too slick. This was a man, after all, who had made a great deal of money peddling illusion.

"I got the impression from your wife's medical records, Mr. Wickerd, that her breakdown was actually triggered by your reaction to her supposed abduction."

His smile slipped a notch. "I was never convinced that there was any abduction. And her breakdown wasn't a sudden event. My wife has always been an intense, emotional woman and very ambitious. Professionally, things hadn't been going well for her for some time and that was probably the biggest factor in her breakdown. Her state of mind deteriorated rapidly from the time she believed she'd miscarried until she came here.''

''So you don't think she had a miscarriage?''

''I'm not even convinced that she was pregnant. She wanted children in the worst way and had already had one hysterical pregnancy. But she was so distraught over what had happened, I gave her the benefit of the doubt.''

How generous of you, Aline thought. ''When did she first tell you about her experience?''

''Several days afterward. I wasn't on the island the night it happened.''

''When did you last see her, Mr. Wickerd?''

He rubbed his long hands together. ''Maybe two months ago, maybe longer, I'm not sure. It was after she'd started the treatments again.''

''The electroshock, you mean.'' *Let's not be antiseptic about it, guy. Call it by its real name, its ugly name.*

''Yes. I thought my visiting her would just make things worse. We hadn't been getting along very well.''

Aline nodded. ''This must have been difficult for you professionally.''

He stirred cream into the mug of coffee the waitress had brought him and didn't look at her. ''Somewhat, yes.''

''The wife of a well-known and ambitious debunker claiming she'd been abducted by aliens: that might even be cause enough to have her committed, Mr. Wickerd. I mean, a lunatic raves and who cares? Who listens?''

His head snapped up. Anger flashed in his eyes. ''I resent what you're implying, Ms. Scott.''

''Detective Scott,'' she said with a benign smile, and dropped a dollar on the table. ''And since I had to spend thirty minutes waiting for you, I'm afraid I've got to split. Be talking to you, Mr. Wickerd.''

(3)

Margaret sat on the floor in the front room downstairs, the windows open, uncovered, the afternoon sunlight and the heat spilling over her in equal measures. She was studying the items that had been in her bag: a key (to her room at the clinic), her pretty comb edged in mother-of-pearl, a pack of Kleenex with Wellness Center printed across the front of it, her leather wallet, and a plastic card.

She picked up the card, sensing it was important. It wasn't a credit card, it was . . . What? The word was poised at the tip of her tongue, but she couldn't seize it. It rhymed with something. Art? Yes, that seemed right. Lark? Bark? Mart? Start? *Smart.*

A SmartCard. She laughed aloud as another window flew open in her mind. This was the card she hated. Its microchip contained a PROM—Programmable Read-Only Memory— and the data on it could not be changed, Nina Treak had told her.

The chip's microprocessor controlled access to the memory, which had three zones. The open zone held her vital statistics and her medical history. The working zone could only be accessed by someone who knew the password (Treak, Liscomb, others?) and kept track of the purchases she made at the clinic—meals other than those served in the cafeteria, toiletries bought at the pharmacy, paperback books purchased from the newsstand. The secret zone, which contained the password, couldn't be accessed.

There seemed to be something about the card she wasn't remembering, something vital, its connection to something else. She pressed the card tightly between her palms, as if her hands could squeeze out its secrets, but it yielded nothing. Well, never mind. Sooner or later she would exhume it from her ruined memories, just as she had the face of her lover. She slipped it into her shirt pocket, arranged everything else in the bag, and stepped outside.

Do it now or wait until dark? Shadows swam thickly against

the sidewalk and floated in the dirty windows; in the other direction lay the dense woods. She couldn't imagine trudging through there in the dark. It would have to be now.

Now, while it was still light, she thought, walking over to the car. Now. But how far should she drive before she ditched it? Two miles? Four? Five? How far was far enough?

If the car didn't explode and was found, there would not be a body. They would think she had either been thrown out of the vehicle and killed when it hurled off the cliff or that the whole thing had been staged. If they believed the latter, they would search the woods. If they searched long and hard and deep enough, they would eventually find the house. So would five miles be enough?

She released the emergency brake, then she drove, drove through the trees, weaving around them, dodging clumps of scrub brush. Light filtered through the thick branches. Sometimes it was pale and chalky and sometimes it was gold, God's light, imbued with magic and power. Birds trilled. The breeze grew stronger.

There were no cars on the highway. The mushroom trees whose name she couldn't recall loomed on her left, a wall of green. Now and then she caught glimmers of blue, commas of water. The needle on the gas gauge brushed empty: there would be no explosion. It would be for the best, wouldn't it? This way the car might not be discovered for a while. She imagined time passing, days melting into night and day and night again as waves broke on the rocks below, as wind strummed the trees on the cliff.

Perhaps a lone fisherman would come across the car, submerged beneath the turquoise shoals. Perhaps someone collecting shells on the beach would spot it first. Perhaps the car wouldn't sink at all because the tide was low. Perhaps maybe what if . . . There was no end to it. No end to the speculation, the second-guessing, the whims of destiny.

When she was 2.8 miles from the house, a car whizzed toward her in the other lane—and then past. At four miles, a car sped around her. At 4.6 miles, the trees on her left suddenly parted and the wind howled through the opening. Here, she thought. Right here. This was the place.

She pulled off the road and hurried to the lip of the cliff. The wind whined at her ankles, tore her hair away from her face, burned her eyes until they watered. Two hundred feet below waves crashed over giant rocks and foamed against a prayer rug of sand. Beyond this lay a continent of ever-darkening blues that extended to the horizon, where water and sky merged.

The sun was absent from this half of sky. Did that mean she was facing west in the morning or east in the afternoon? Clouds were stacked against the horizon, peaking in thunderheads that she associated with afternoon and deep summer. But the association might be flawed. Many of her associations were defective. That was part of her illness, part of the pattern that Liscomb and Treak and their goddamn drugs were supposedly attempting to break.

Instead they had nearly broken her.

House. What do you associate with house, Margaret?

. . . trap

Child?

. . . pain

Love?

. . . illusion

Art?

. . . salvation

Sex?

. . . passion

Treak's voice. Treak's presence. Treak, freak, seek, leak, beak, geek. Treak the Geek. She laughed. It was a grotesque sound, shrill, chopped-up. She rubbed her hand over her mouth and stepped back quickly. She removed the bike from the trunk, wheeled it into the brush a safe distance away, extended the rusted kickstand with her foot.

Her courage ebbed as she started back to the car, but she didn't hesitate. She locked her purse in the glove compartment, lowered the windows, pulled onto the road, and drove a mile in the direction where the clinic lay. Then she swung around in the middle of the road, floored the accelerator, and took off. Just short of the opening in the trees, she swerved and slammed on the brakes.

The tires screeched against the pavement, hit the dirt on the shoulder, and the engine died. She started it again, backed up, saw the telling black marks on the road, turned sharply, and headed in the opposite direction again. She didn't go as far this time, just half a mile, then she swung around and headed for the cliff once more. Now, as the car gathered speed, she touched her door handle, readying herself.

The speedometer needle hit thirty-five, thirty-eight, forty; she was exactly even with the trees. She swerved the steering wheel violently, jerked up on the handle, then threw herself out as the door swung open. She struck the dirt on her left side, rolled, scrambled to her feet in time to see the car vanishing over the brink of the cliff.

She ran toward the edge and watched as the car plunged soundlessly through the hot blue air. It crashed nose first, then the rear end slammed down against the water and the car began to sink. She watched it, a vanishing dark fish. The water crept up over the trunk, the rear windshield, the roof. Its nose seemed to struggle valiantly to remain above the surface for a moment, but then its own weight dragged it under.

Margaret stumbled away, her heart drumming, the heat pressing against the top of her head like giant hands, waves of sweat washing across her back. Moments later she pedaled madly down the side of the road, fear knotted in her chest.

8

(1)

Col. Evan Nate's hideaway backed up to twelve acres of citrus groves that had been bringing in a tidy sum every year for the last fifteen. Revenue that he tucked away for his retirement, for his daughter, for additions to the greenhouse, money that paid the wages of people like Paul Sapizzo.

Nate disliked Sapizzo, disliked his mixed blood, the surly set of his mouth, his black leather, his sinewy leanness. He especially disliked him now, as he sat at the kitchen table in the apartment over Nate's garage, trying to explain how he'd fucked up. But the beauty of men like this was that they didn't pretend to be something they weren't. And if they were grateful, Nate thought, and Sapizzo definitely was, they could be made to do almost anything, as Sapizzo had and would.

"So I get into the morgue, right?" He rolled the end of his cigarette in an empty matchbox he was using as an ashtray and knocked off the ash. "And I, like, you know, go through the body drawers just like you told me to do and nothin', sir, nothin'."

"No bodies at all?"

"No, sir." He combed his long fingers back through his thick black hair. Nate had been bald so long, he'd forgotten what it felt like for his head not to be exposed. "None."

"So you left?"

"Yes, sir." Sapizzo squinted his hooded eyes as smoke wafted toward him. Nate wondered if women found him attractive. All that hair. That powerful body. "And yesterday afternoon, late, I was at the hospital, waitin' to see if the bodies were goin' to be taken into Key West. That's when they transport the bodies from the morgue, see. But they didn't. The bodies were never moved."

"Not that you saw."

"Right. But the coroner left with this other fellow and I decided to check him out, find out who he was, and—"

"Were you alone?"

"Had my two buddies with me. We were doin' the men in black routine, sir."

Christ. "I didn't tell you to do that, Paul."

"Well, no, sir, but I thought—"

"I don't pay you to *think*. I pay you to follow orders."

Sapizzo's face took on the stricken expression of a young boy who has been reprimanded by his father. "I'm sorry, Colonel, but I—"

Nate waved the apology aside. He was pacing back and forth across the width of the tiny kitchen. A messy kitchen. When his daughter had lived here one summer, the place hadn't been this messy, had it? There hadn't been dirty dishes stacked in the sink, had there? Or clothes draped over the backs of the chairs? Or red stains on the stove? But the comparison was unjust: Sapizzo had been dealt his cards in life and Beth had been dealt hers. A continent separated them.

"So what did you and your buddies do?"

"Followed this dude. Got his plate number. Ran a make on it."

"How?"

"We, uh, were drivin' the van, sir."

Terrific.

"His name's Kincaid, Ryan Kincaid. No address. But later, as we were comin' out of the hills, we spotted his car in front of the lighthouse. So we, uh, you know . . ."

"Did your routine."

"Yes, sir."

Shit for brains. Nate walked back to the table, stopped in front of it, noticed the way Sapizzo sat back a little, as if in anticipation of a fist in the mouth. "What I want you to do, Paul, is find out where the bodies are, if something was taken out of Dr. Liscomb's nostrils, and if so, to get that something. Do you think you can do that, Paul?"

"Yes, sir. Definitely. You bet, sir. No problem."

"I'll be staying in the main house for a while."

"You got some broken sprinkler heads in the yard, sir."

"Fix them. That's your job." *Your cover, Paul, got it?*

"Yes, sir."

Sir sir sir: the word echoed endlessly in Nate's skull as he walked back to the house. *Sir sir.* He headed straight for the wet bar in the living room and poured himself two fingers of cognac. It burned a bright path down his gullet and chased away the dying echo of Sapizzo's voice. *Sir.*

Too many screwups, he thought as he went into the kitchen to fix a bite to eat. Liscomb's death, Margaret's escape, Winthrop calling the cops first, Sapizzo playing MIB. A rather distasteful and problematic pattern had emerged that he hadn't anticipated. He knew as well as anyone that once a pattern had been created, it had a tendency to reproduce itself; it was as true of his marriage as it was of this project. Unfortunately, he didn't know what to do about it that he hadn't already done.

He watched several ants wander aimlessly across the kitchen counter, oblivious to one another in their quest for food. He tracked one with his index finger, intending to squash it, then reconsidered and dropped a pinch of sugar onto the counter. In moments, more ants appeared from under the window over the sink. There were perhaps a dozen now, but they still functioned independently, each following its own peculiar rhythm. At some point, though, a critical number would be reached and the ants would fall into communal synchrony. They would begin to self-organize into a working society, each assuming its particular role within the larger framework.

The same rule applied to man—from his most sophisticated activities to his most mundane. Right now, for instance, the homicide investigation was fragmented, with each of the players following a highly individualized course. But sooner or later, as the layers of the case were peeled away, as the facts were culled, that would change.

And that worried him deeply.

(2)

Dead Man's Bluff was one of the high points on Tango. On a clear day, you could see Key West from its summit. But Aline's destination lay several hundred feet below it, a tiny cove reached by a twisting dirt road.

Her aging Honda complained during the entire descent, but it got her to the narrow strip of sand in one piece. A Zodiac raft was beached on the sand, and some thirty feet from shore was a car embedded in a foot of water. The area was illuminated by the bright lights of a tow truck and two police cars. Gene Frederick and one of the night-shift patrolmen were rocking the car, loosening it from the sand, while another man shouted directions to the tow-truck driver. The truck's wheels spun, then caught, and the car made a loud sucking sound and began to move toward shore.

It was the security guard's missing Firebird, all right, and it had certainly seen better days, Aline thought as she walked around it. The front windshield had shattered, the back window was a spider's web of cracks, the driver's door hung by a single hinge, the headlights were smashed, the front bumper was mangled, the body was gouged.

"High tide peaked around two this afternoon," Frederick said as he joined her. "So it's possible she got thrown from the car and her body washed out to sea. Or . . ."

"She just got rid of the car and wants us to think she died in the accident," Aline finished for him.

"Which means she might still be on the island."

"I wouldn't be if I were she."

"You would if you had a place to hide, Aline. Think about

it. Right now she's safer on the island than she would be if she tried to leave. The Key West PD is checking cars on its side of the bridge and we've got six men checking around the clock on this side." He shook his head. "My gut says she's still on Tango."

"Someone broke into the lighthouse last night and made off with Margaret's medical file, Gene."

"Why didn't you tell me this earlier today?"

"Gene, you were, uh, in a meeting all morning with the mayor and I was out of the office most of the afternoon."

"Oh. Yeah. Well, anyway. Is that all they got?"

"As far as I can tell." She gave him Kincaid's description of the man he'd chased, which was vague enough to fit half the male populace on Tango, then told him about the three men in black.

"Air Force Intelligence, huh? From where? Homestead?"

"It's the closest. Assuming that's what they actually were."

Frederick rubbed his jaw, then pulled a stogy from his shirt pocket and lit it. "So they didn't show him ID?"

"No."

"And he didn't get a plate number?"

"Nope."

"Then we've got nothing."

"How about a break-in to the morgue at the hospital the night before last and a silicon sliver removed from Dr. Liscomb's pituitary gland? Would that qualify as *something*, Gene?"

"It might."

"Bill Prentiss took it over to the coroner in Key West today to see if he can figure out what it might be." She told him about the experiment Treak and Liscomb had conducted at the University of Miami four years ago. Frederick's expression didn't change, but something in his eyes did. "Don't you think it's too similar to be coincidental?"

"Now you sound like your old man."

"Give me a straight answer, Gene."

"Liscomb was a shrink, not a convict."

"Maybe he was Treak's first volunteer."

"We need to know more about this sliver before we draw any conclusions or implicate Nina Treak. So for now let's check out the Firebird, huh?"

So much for support where it counted, she thought, and started searching the interior of the Firebird. She had to spring the lock on the glove compartment with a screwdriver, but it was worth the effort. Inside was a woman's purse, small, made of canvas, with several zippered compartments.

Aline carried it over to her car and emptied it on her front seat: a key with the number 10 on it, a comb with a mother-of-pearl handle, a soggy pack of Kleenex with Wellness Center printed on the front, and a small leather wallet that was as plain as the purse. It held six bucks and change and a business card with the center's address and phone number on it. That was it. No ID, no pictures, not even a scrap of paper. She unzipped the inner and outer pockets; they were empty.

Irritated, she turned the purse inside out, and the bottom of it, made of hard cardboard covered in fabric, came loose at one end. Aline peeled it back the rest of the way and a square of plastic tumbled out, the sort that usually held photos or credit cards. It had protected the scrap of paper inside from the water, so the four phone numbers on the back were legible.

"Goddamn trunk's empty." Frederick grumbled, scooting into the passenger seat.

"Take a look at this." She handed him the scrap of paper. "The second number belongs to Sam Newman, the guy in charge of the abductee group. I've got an appointment with him in a while."

He took the list of numbers and puffed on his cigar. "I'll run these down. Meanwhile, we've got the Wickerd home and Julie Ames's place under surveillance in case Margaret shows up."

"Yeah? And who's doing all this surveillance, Gene?"

He waved his cigar. "That's what the meeting was about this morning. The mayor allocated emergency funds for additional personnel."

The smoke stank up the inside of her car and she waved her hand dramatically in front of her face. "You mind?"

"Oh, sorry." He stabbed out the cigar in her ashtray and slipped it behind his ear like a pencil. "Keep an eye open and call me if anything comes up with Newman. Otherwise I'll talk to you tomorrow."

(3)

Kincaid pegged Tyler Winthrop as a man born to privilege. He possessed the cavalier countenance that was as much genetic as it was the right social circles and the right schools— Yale, Princeton, maybe Harvard. He was in his early fifties, with thick hair as white as the slacks and shirt he wore, and he pumped Kincaid's hand with all the spurious cheer of a politician on the campaign trail.

"Thanks for coming so early, Mr. Rourke. I know it was an inconvenience, but I certainly appreciate it. Please, have a seat." He gestured toward the Queen Anne chair in the sitting area of his huge office, where a tray with coffee and snacks occupied an ornately carved mahogany coffee table. Rather grandiose treatment for a security guard, Kincaid mused, but what the hell. The coffee smelled strong and he was hungry. "Did you have any trouble finding us?"

"None at all."

"Good, good." He poured coffee into a pair of blue china cups and told Kincaid to help himself to cream and sugar. "I always like to have a little chat with our employees when they start with us, just so they're clear on what we're about. I presume the security company gave you a copy of our rules and regulations?"

"Yes, they did." He hadn't read them. They were in his knapsack, which now rested on the floor against his chair.

"Do you have any questions about anything?"

"No, sir, not right now."

Winthrop shifted in his chair and lifted his cup with his pinky extended and slightly curled. He sipped delicately, then said, "As you undoubtedly know, Mr. Rourke, we had a rather unfortunate incident here and I hold your predecessor directly responsible."

"For the murders?"

"Well, no, not for the murders." His mouth pursed around the word as though he'd bitten into something distasteful. "For the patient's escape." He set down his cup, patted his midriff, smoothed a palm over his khaki slacks. "He should have been more careful about his car. He shouldn't have conversed with the patient as often as he did. And he definitely shouldn't have accepted anything she offered him to drink or to eat. In other words, Mr. Rourke, his comportment was dubious at best."

Translated: Keep your car out of sight; don't socialize with the patients; report any patient who gets too chummy. Uh-huh, Kincaid understood perfectly. And what a good thing it was that Winthrop believed he was just a security guard. "Yes, sir, I understand."

Winthrop's magnanimous smile was accompanied by nervous fidgeting: another pat at the midriff, another sip of coffee, another nibble at a cracker. "Good, good, I'm pleased we had this conversation, Mr. Rourke. And I trust that if you have any questions, anything at all, you'll speak to myself or Dr. Treak."

"I will, sir, count on it." He started to rise, but Winthrop wasn't finished yet.

"Just a few other things, Mr. Rourke. We have thirty patients here now. Eight of them are trustees. That means they're almost ready for release and have a great deal of freedom. They reside in the last house at the end of the driveway. In the house closest to this building are those patients who need us most. In between are the patients who are progressing. That's how we work here, Mr. Rourke. In steps. One step at a time. We are never sick; we are only several steps from wellness.

"Only the doors of the first house are locked at ten P.M.

The restrictions ease the farther from this building that you get. In the event that any patient is undergoing treatment, it usually takes place at night, when the other patients won't be disturbed, so don't be surprised if you see the orderlies escorting a patient to this building." He patted his midriff again, uncrossed his legs, crossed them once more. "You generally won't see any patients out walking after midnight, but if you do, that's fine. No need to notify us unless a patient seems inordinately interested in the gate.

"In the unlikely event that a patient becomes hostile or threatens you, the guardhouse is equipped with an alarm. There is also an intercom system to the front office that you are to use should we receive any visitors on your shift. Before the gate is opened, you need to see identification and obtain clearance from whoever is in charge. Any questions?"

"No, I don't think so."

"Good, good. Dr. Treak should be ready for you now." He walked Kincaid to the door and extended his hand. "It's been a real pleasure, Mr. O'Rourke."

"Rourke," Kincaid corrected, grasping his hand.

"Rourke, right, sorry." His laugh was quick and jolly. "I'm afraid my weakness is names. But I never forget a face, Mr. Rourke. Welcome to the Whole Health family."

Yes, welcome, welcome.

"And here comes Dr. Treak, right on schedule."

She was portly, tastefully dressed in pastels, and had vampire-pale skin as smooth as cream. There had probably been a time in Nina Treak's life when she was attractive, but that time was long past. Kincaid guessed she came from the opposite end of Winthrop's social scale. No privileged family, no ticket to Yale or Princeton or Harvard just because Daddy had gone there. None of that. Treak's story was in her face, in her straight, rigid posture, in the tightness of her smile, and it said she'd grown up dirt poor and had worked for every goddamn thing she had and she wasn't about to let anyone forget it.

And yet there was an appealing femininity about the way she dressed, in the unhurried efficiency of her movements, in her voice. It was low, husky, a scotch-and-soda voice that could address a crowd in whispers and hold their attention.

She gave him a quick tour of the building that included the treatment area. It resembled an emergency room in a hospital. But there was a conspicuous absence of patients and the nurse and the orderly on duty at the desk looked bored out of their minds. Kincaid noted the expensive computer system, the intercom speakers, and the layout of the area—exits, empty rooms, adjoining hallways.

"Every couple hours or so, it would be a good idea to make a circuit of the buildings," Treak said as they pushed through the double doors into the warm night air. "The door on the far side of the building is always unlocked and you can use the restroom on the first floor. Payday is Friday for the week you work. We don't hold back a week or anything like that. Any questions?"

"No."

"We've changed some of our policies since the murders, Mr. Rourke. We'll now have someone on duty throughout the night in the treatment area and both Dr. Winthrop and I will be residing here for the time being. I'm in the first residence and Dr. Winthrop is in the last one. You'll find our private numbers posted in the guardhouse." They stopped in front of it and Treak slipped a ring of keys from her pocket, unhooked one, unlocked the door, and handed the key to Kincaid. "Have a pleasant evening, Mr. Rourke."

With that, she strolled off.

The guardhouse was no larger than a bathroom. It had an air-conditioning unit that wheezed, a TV the size of a computer screen, two phones, and a panel of switches and dials with everything neatly labeled. He acquainted himself with what operated what, then opened his knapsack and studied his tools. First things first, he thought, and removed a device that detected electronic bugs.

The phones and the guardhouse turned up clean. He turned off the noisy air conditioner and propped open the door with a chair. The lights on the grounds were soft and unobtrusive, the fountain had been turned off, the silence was deep enough to hear the plants grow. Three A.M., he thought, that would be the time to poke around. The darkest hour.

Until then, he had plenty to keep him company. From his knapsack, he brought out *The South American Handbook*, the seminal guide to that continent, and the smaller volume about Chiloé.

He'd been to Chile once, shortly after he'd met Aline, and had made it to Punta Arenas, the southernmost city. But Chiloé would be his destination this time, and if the tides of fortune were willing, Aline would make the trip as well. Last night he had broached the subject for the first time, without coming right out and telling her about it. Half the battle was timing. He had to catch her when she was feeling good about things in general so her usual arguments—*I can't afford this, I can't get the time off work, I can't I can't*—wouldn't possess enough power to dissuade her.

Then he would have to present Chile like a travel agent selling a difficult destination: the excellent exchange rate, the beauty of the country, the scrumptious foods and wines, the congeniality of the people. She didn't dislike traveling; it simply wasn't the passion for her that it was for him. He would sell everything he owned just to spend a few months in a country of his choice and worry about putting his life back together when he returned. But Aline was far too practical for that. If she couldn't afford a trip, she stayed home, that was it.

Neither of them was going anywhere, though, until this job was tied up. And for some reason that he couldn't fathom, he felt there was something in the *Caleuche* tale that would help. Something connected, perhaps, to that silicon sliver Bill Prentiss had pulled from the shrink's sinus cavities. Something. But what?

(4)

Sam Newman's place was small and compact, an A-frame on stilts set back from the dirt road in a cluster of pines. Lights burned in the windows and their spill illuminated four cars in the driveway. She caught the faint strains of music as she pulled up at the curb and got out.

She walked among the cars, jotting down license plate numbers. Then she radioed the station and asked the dispatcher to run a make on them. "That's it, Al? Just names?" the dispatcher asked.

"Professions, addresses, phone numbers, whatever you can get, if it's not too much trouble."

"It'll take a while."

"No problem. I've got something to do. I'll radio back when I'm finished."

She was going to crash the party.

A woman in a wheelchair answered the door. She looked vaguely familiar, but Aline couldn't place her soft moon face. Her hair was very blonde, almost white, and she wore it in a single thick braid that rode over one shoulder. She didn't seem particularly happy about the noise, the company, any of it.

"Hi, come on in. They're on the porch." She shut the door and extended her hand. "You seem familiar to me, but I don't think we've met. I'm Helen Newman."

"Aline Scott."

Her smile, which was already strained, popped like a rubber band. "Detective Scott. The courthouse."

"Excuse me?"

"The courthouse. That's where I've seen you. I'm a family circuit-court judge."

"Judge Baltec." Who usually walked with a cane.

"My maiden name."

"I don't have too many dealings with the family court."

"Count your blessings. You've left a lot of messages on the machine."

"Four."

She shrugged. "Sam's bad about returning calls." She gestured toward the wide hallway behind her. "Through there and follow the music, Detective Scott. Only a few people in the group are here tonight, but it's enough to give you some idea of what it's about."

"Do they usually meet here?"

Her laugh was as dry as the wind in a drought. "Not when I have anything to say about it." She held up her hands as if fending off a blow. "This is strictly Sam's baby, Detective Scott. I'm just a neutral bystander."

"How often did Margaret Wickerd attend these meetings?"

"Margaret." She let out a soft, aggrieved sigh that made it clear she'd hoped to avoid this. "I'm not sure. You'll have to ask Sam."

"So you've met her?"

"Sure."

"And?"

"And what, Detective Scott?" She stroked the tip of her braid. "I already told you I'm not involved in Sam's research. It's fine that he makes a good living writing about UFOs, but frankly, I think most of it's a crock and he was better off as a physicist."

"Better off in what way?"

She rolled her hazel eyes. "Just what're you looking for, anyway? Information about Sam or about Margaret or about the field?"

"I guess all three."

Helen laughed again. "Yeah, well, Sam's the one to tell you about all three, Detective Scott. If you'll excuse me."

With that, she pushed a lever on the wheelchair and buzzed out of the room, the chip on her shoulder as solid as a block of cement. Aline wondered whether her attitude problem was the result of her handicap, her marriage, Margaret Wickerd, UFOs, the stress of court, or all of the above.

On the walls of the wide hallway were six framed book covers with Newton's name on them and numerous photo-

graphs. A plaque on the left wall identified the photos as
SITES and depicted hillsides and deserts, mesas and roads
where the land was scarred by patches of brown grass or no
grass at all.

The plaque on the right wall said PHYSICAL EVIDENCE.
These pictures were close-ups of people, of chests and backs
and limbs that bore cuts, burns, scars. At the end of the left
wall was a gallery of UFO lore: articles in various languages
on sightings and encounters; movie posters from *Close Encounters of the Third Kind*, *E.T.*, *The Day the Earth Stood
Still*; photos of Newton with people Aline recognized, thanks
to Meg's reading list. Some were researchers, others were
alleged contactees or abductees.

The music, a jazz piece by Antonio Carlos Jobim, was
coming from the comfortable family room at the end of the
hall. The French doors on the far side opened onto a spacious
screened porch crowded with potted plants. The four people
seated at the patio table fell silent as soon as Aline entered.

"Could, I, uh, help you with something?" Newman
asked, rising.

He looked exactly like the photos in his books and on the
walls, all brawn and muscle, as solid as a lumberjack, not at
all like her image of a physicist. His dark hair, like his beard,
was short and Brillo-pad curly, fading to gray at the temples.
His face wouldn't turn heads on a street, she thought, unless
you saw his remarkable eyes. Deeply set, Pacific blue, layered with emotion.

"Sorry to barge in like this, Mr. Newman. I'm Detective
Scott. We have an appointment at nine-thirty. About Margaret Wickerd?"

The name had a very definite effect on these people, just
as it had had on Helen. It seemed to possess a kind of elemental power, like a magical incantation, that dwarfed the
importance of whether the reaction was negative, as it had
been with Helen, or something else altogether, as it was here.
Ultimately, she thought, this might tell her more about Margaret Wickerd than anything else.

"Excuse me," Newton said to his guests. He and Aline

stepped inside and he shut the door behind them. He didn't try to contain his irritation at the interruption. "I'm afraid our meeting's going to run overtime, Detective Scott. Could this wait until tomorrow?"

"It's waited too long already. I've got an escaped mental patient who killed a psychiatrist and an orderly when she took off and who may still be on the island. I need answers. Tell me about Margaret's involvement in your abductee group."

"There isn't much to tell."

Of course not. There never was. "When did she join?"

He settled on the old couch with an air of cloying resignation and aimed a remote-control device at the stereo, turning it down. Aline claimed a nearby rocker.

"A week or so after her experience. She showed up at a seminar I was giving at the Flamingo Hotel."

"A seminar on abductions?"

"No, a seminar on physics for a group of graduate students. I recognized her as soon as she came in and knew it was going to mean trouble for me. Pete Wickerd and I have rarely agreed on anything. Have you talked to him?"

"Briefly."

"Anyway, she came to the next meeting and half a dozen after that, right up until Pete had her committed. Then when she was released for weekends during her good-behavior period, we saw her several more times. But it's been a while now." He paused, giving her a chance to reply, and when she didn't, he said: "Are you familiar with the subject?"

As though they were talking about life insurance. "UFOs, abductions, or Pete Wickerd?"

He smiled, he actually smiled, and she felt some of his hostility leak away. "All three, but I was referring specifically to abductions."

"Consider me a beginner."

Newman sat forward, suddenly in his element. "There's a pattern to these things. A kind of M.O. The classical abduction case usually occurs on a deserted road in a rural area and is prefaced by the sighting of a light or lights that move erratically. The car stalls, and the radio fills with static. Then suddenly the light's gone and the car works again, and the driver continues to wherever he's going. There're a lot of variations on that scenario, but that's basically what happens. The driver may or may not remember the sighting. But at some point, he realizes there's something screwy about the time involved, that he's missing time. Twenty minutes, two hours, three days, whatever. For some abductees, like Whitley Streiber, the abduction appears to be one in a series of abductions that go back to childhood.

"The driver might notice scars or burns on his body that he can't explain. Over a period of weeks or months, he might begin to experience insomnia, panic attacks, strange dreams. Eventually, he hopefully seeks professional help."

"In Margaret's medical records, it said that her experience happened at the north end of the island, on that dirt road that winds through part of the glades," Aline said. "Near Crystal Cavern."

His frown brought his thin brows together so that they looked as though they'd been penciled in. "That's marsh around there. All marsh."

"It's federal land, part of the wilderness preserve, and that hill you descend to get there is the top of Crystal Cavern."

"Oh, you mean the old mine."

"It hasn't been a mine since the mid-Fifties, when it was expanded and became a weather station. Now they mainly analyze satellite data on the Caribbean. The place has been off-limits since two kids were killed up there in a rock slide."

"Only a fritter would know that."

"Born and raised."

"How do you know Ferret?"

"I used to own Whitman's Bookstore. We ran a reading program for a while and Ferret was one of my first students and went on to become one of my best customers." His stab at congeniality was rather transparent and it irritated her. "So tell me about Margaret's abduction."

"It was February. She'd gone out there at sunset to take some pictures for a painting she was working on. Around seven, she started back into town. Ten minutes into the trip her car stalled. Then she saw a light moving low over the trees, coming toward her. That was all she consciously remembered.

"Next thing she knew, it was after midnight and she was driving in the direction from which she'd just come. There was a cut on her right calf that she didn't remember getting and she 'felt terrified' for no apparent reason. She drove home—"

"To Miami?"

"No, to the weekend place she and Pete have here. He was away at the time. She hurried around the house, locking the windows, pulling the curtains closed. Then she realized her period had started, which became a significant part of her story. If you've read her records, I guess you know that she was eight or nine weeks pregnant when this happened."

Aline nodded.

"What did Julie say about her sister's pregnancy?"

"Not much, except that she thinks aliens didn't have anything to do with Margaret losing the baby. Why?"

"I'm surprised she didn't mention that neither she nor Pete knew about the pregnancy."

"You mean Margaret hadn't told either of them?"

"That's the way I understand it. She and Julie haven't been close in years and Pete didn't want kids."

"How come you know so much about it?"

"Because it was relevant to the group discussion."

"Tell me about your standing battle with Peter Wickerd."

"Standing battle." He smiled again. "That describes it pretty well. It started a long time before Margaret's experience, although that didn't help things. Imagine it, Ms. Scott. Here he was, the debunker to beat all debunkers, and his own wife claimed she'd been abducted by aliens and she'd had a miscarriage as a result of it. It put him in one hell of a professional position. I think he hoped that if he humored her and made some pretense at investigating what had happened, she would keep quiet about it and the whole thing would blow over. But it didn't blow over. And when she joined the group, he started a smear campaign to discredit me.''

Funny, how the many versions of the truth had a game-show quality about them. ''You think she's crazy?''

''Absolutely not. I've got sixteen people in this abductee group, and have had as many as thirty-eight. If Margaret's crazy, then they all are and so am I for listening to them. She was depressed, but she wasn't crazy, and her condition sure as hell didn't warrant electroshock treatments. And I certainly don't believe she killed anyone. The only way Pete could save his professional credibility was by committing her.''

''Considering his attempt to discredit you, Mr. Newman, I hardly think you can be objective about his motives.'' She caught a glint of light against metal in the hallway and realized that Helen was there, trying to eavesdrop over the din of the music. ''How long's it been since you've seen Margaret?''

Newman looked uncomfortable now. ''Since her trustee status was rescinded. Nine or ten weeks, I guess.''

''That long?'' Treak had said six weeks.

''Maybe not. I honestly don't remember. When she came to the meetings, though, it posed considerable risk for her, since part of her treatment was to sever any ties with the group.''

''Did her husband find out?''

''You bet he did. And that's when the electroshock started up again.''

''Is there anyone you know of who she might turn to for help now?''

''No.''

''No one in the group?''

''No.''

Such emphatic denial. ''You seem real sure of that.''

''She would never jeopardize anyone in the group that way.''

''During that period when she was going home on week-ends, did she ever talk about the clinic or her treatment? Did she mention Dr. Liscomb?''

''No.''

It was a flat-out lie that poisoned his magnificent eyes. "What're you afraid of, Mr. Newman?"

Her bluntness caught him momentarily off guard, but he recovered with admirable aplomb. "People like you," he said softly. "You don't have the vaguest notion what any of this is about."

"That's what I'm trying to find out."

"No, I don't think so. You came here with your preconceived ideas and your badge, and frankly, Ms. Scott, I'm quite busy. Now if you'll excuse me, I'd like to get back to my guests."

He was already moving toward the door when Aline said, "Just one more question, Mr. Newman."

His face was like granite when he turned. "What?"

"Did you find anything at the site where Margaret had her sighting?"

"Yes. There was some physical evidence. Burn marks on the ground about thirty yards from where her car stalled. It's documented, Detective Scott."

"So then you plan to write about her case."

His spine snapped straight and passion sprang into his face. A darker Newman, she thought. The music stopped as he came over to her. His voice was dangerously soft. "You've got no idea what you're dealing with, so just back the hell off."

He was leaning into her personal space, close enough so that the blue of his eyes threatened to leap out at her. She had the urge to slam her hands against his chest and push him back. "Believe it or not, Mr. Newman, we're on the same side. Thanks for your time."

She spun around without giving him a chance to reply and wasn't surprised that his wife was no longer in the hallway. Eavesdroppers usually knew when to split.

She hoped they would have a better shot at things away from the watchful presence of his handicapped wife.

9

The peal of the phone eclipsed Nate's dream about his wife. His wife as she used to be. His wife before she was his wife, when she was the most sought-after young woman in Charleston. As he turned on the lamp, he remembered how the magnolias had bloomed the spring he'd met her.

"Yes?" he said.

"You always sound so hopeful when you answer the phone, Evan. I like that."

"Jesus, Henry, you know what time it is?"

"Damn straight. I ought to be in bed. I just wanted to let you know you've got Jones. The only thing he knows is what the Bureau and his babe tell him."

His babe: what an odd expression! Had his wife ever been his babe? Had his daughter ever been a man's *babe*? Just what did that mean exactly? Nate rubbed his eyes, wondering why he'd been dwelling so much lately on his wife and his daughter the way they used to be. It was the sort of thing a man diagnosed with a terminal disease might do. A man like Henry Sheen, for instance.

"Thanks, Henry, I appreciate it. How're you feeling?"

"Right about now I'm feeling real tired. But otherwise I'm okay. You know what they say, Evan, about the mean ones outliving everyone else."

Yes, he knew. But cancer didn't give a shit one way or the other. He gave Sheen an update. "I'll keep you posted."

"Do whatever it takes, Evan. Good night."

Whatever it takes. And just what was that, anyway? Time? More labyrinthian secrets? More complex disinformation schemes? More spilled blood? What? There were moments like now—yes, this was certainly one of those moments— when he regretted all of it. When he resented the task assigned to him and Sheen during the last presidency. When he wished that he was beyond the seduction of power.

But to be one of the few who possessed such a secret . . . It dizzied him.

He turned off the lamp, closed his eyes, but he couldn't sleep. His mind wandered into the future when Henry Sheen would be dead. What then? What would the protocol be? Who would replace him on the committee? With Sheen gone, he could count on only one other committee member to vote as he did. Jim "Jimbo" Booth. The other two, younger men who were new to the game and whose faces had changed over the years, could go either way. That meant the votes on major decisions would probably be two to two, deadlocked. And farther ahead, what would happen when Booth died? He was the oldest member of the committee, sixty-three, the money man. Although his health was good, you never knew. A vessel bursts in the brain, the heart gives out, cancer takes root: goodbye, Booth. Then he would stand alone.

And the truth was that he didn't want to stand alone. Not now and not in some yet undetermined moment of the future.

Nate threw off the sheet, swung his legs over the side of the bed. He needed to move, to get out of the house, to take a walk, a drive, anything. He dressed in the dark, got into his Avis rental car, and drove into the hills. The humid air, swollen with the scent of approaching rain, swept through the open windows, clearing his head. Sheen, Booth, and Nate. In Vietnam, they had been a trio of invincible pilots known as the Musketeers; now they were merely aging warriors who weren't even sure who the enemy was. The moral was clear, but he didn't dwell on it.

He turned onto the dirt road that led into the wilderness preserve. The headlights washed across pines and banyans and gumbo-limbos, pale spectators that had stood here since the beginning and would still be standing when he and Sheen and Booth were long gone.

The road curved, paralleling a ten-foot-high chain-link fence posted with signs that read NO TRESPASSING, PROPERTY OF U.S. GOVERNMENT. There were intruders from time to time, campers and hikers and teenagers in search of adventure, but they rarely stayed long. The area was too rocky and choked with weeds. Intruders who got to within five hundred feet of the concrete hangar were detected by the perimeter security and watched by cameras hidden under the hangar's eaves.

In the five years since the inception of Lost Pleiade, there had only been two instances where intruders had to be dealt with because they had presented a risk to the project. Excellent statistics by anyone's standards.

At the turn of the century, a hundred acres of this area had been a National Weather Bureau facility where balloons and box kites were released into the atmosphere to observe weather conditions. In 1935, it had come under the control of the U.S. Bureau of Mines. They had used the entrance to the cavern to dig a mine two hundred feet below the surface along an east–west axis. In 1954, the place officially became a weather research station. But unofficially the mine was expanded and converted into a bunker to house the top military personnel in South Florida.

Unlike some of its counterparts in Virginia, Colorado, and New Mexico, Crystal Cavern had never been intended to serve as an alternate capital in the event of a nuclear war. It wasn't large enough and was too far from D.C. It had merely been one of a number of smaller intelligence centers where several dozen people could live for as long as a year if it ever came to that.

For decades, in fact, the center's ubiquitous eyes had been focused on Castro ninety miles to the south and to the Caribbean nations beyond it. From the early seventies until 1984, when the center was under Nate's tutelage, it became the most efficient intelligence network for the Caribbean.

Then, due to the vagaries of the political beast, the center's responsibilities were usurped and divided among other military installations in South Florida. Nate was transferred to Homestead, the center's staff was stripped to a skeleton crew of three men, and that was how it had remained until the birth of the Lost Pleiades project.

Nate stopped in front of the gate, unlocked it, drove through, stopped again, locked it again. There was no road beyond this point, nothing to indicate that a road had ever existed here. But if you followed a route directly northeast, you wouldn't encounter rocks or gullies or fallen trees. You wouldn't hit discarded beer cans or empty bottles. Everything but the weeds was cleared periodically by the twelve employees who worked in the center, rotating by the week: seven days on, seven off, week after week. Men and women with top security clearances who were handpicked by him or Sheen or Booth.

Nate watched the compass on the dash and drove through the woods. He tried not to think about Liscomb, but he couldn't think of anything else. Liscomb was to blame for this mess. Liscomb with his shrewd brilliance, his smooth talk; Liscomb, who believed he could brainwash anyone, given the time and the tools. Nate had never liked the man; there were others who would have served their purpose better. But Booth had wanted him, had believed he was the right man for the job, and because Booth was the money man, Liscomb had been voted in.

It was the only time Sheen had voted against him, the only time Nate had stood alone among the five. Never mind that Sheen now regretted his vote, anguished over it, and did everything within his power to compensate for it. Never mind any of that. It didn't change the fact that Nate was the Humpty-Dumpty doctor who would have to patch things back together again.

A little more than a mile in, Nate turned sharply south, and a quarter of a mile later he stopped in front of the hangar. As hangars went, this one was quite small and looked like a weathered artifact of another era. Constructed of reinforced concrete, it had been painted to blend with the landscape. There were no windows and the door was steel and electronically controlled. But it served its purpose.

He got out of his car, the engine still idling, the headlights illuminating the steel door. He removed a plastic card from his wallet, pressed it against a barely visible seam near the left side of the door, and a moment later it slid open. He hurried back to his car and drove inside.

The door whispered shut behind him.

The interior looked like a small parking garage. And not a well-lit garage at that. Nate pulled in next to a red Porsche Carrera. He glanced down the line of cars as he climbed out and smiled to himself. The men and women who worked here were well paid; besides the Carrera that Bullwinkle drove, there were a BMW, a Mercedes, a Corvette, and a Land Rover. The other cars were ordinary family cars. Only Morales drove a piece of shit, a rusted-out Pontiac with a noisy muffler. And that bothered Nate, as though the car's neglect were indicative of some flaw in Morales himself, an observation that both Sheen and Booth had dismissed as paranoid.

He walked quickly to the column of concrete that rose through the middle of the hangar. He inserted his plastic card in the slot. When the front of the column slid open, Nate stepped inside the elevator, his heart already drumming in anticipation.

(2)

By one A.M., the sky was clouding over and the air was oppressively warm, still, and smelled of rain. Nothing stirred. Lights burned in the windows of the main building, but the residences, Kincaid thought, were as dark as they were going to get.

So far, there hadn't been much of a routine to observe

here. No one had arrived at or left the clinic. He'd seen a dozen people out and about, but it was impossible to tell whether they were patients or employees. No one wore white uniforms. For that matter, the only uniform he'd seen was his own.

Around eleven, Treak had strode next door with the casual, unhurried air of a woman window-shopping. Thirty minutes later Winthrop had left the main building swinging his briefcase and tugging at his tie, a commuter anxious to get home, kick off his shoes, and have a drink.

Now it was Kincaid's turn. He locked the door of the guardhouse and headed out for his rounds. His first walk, down to the last residence and back, had taken him seven minutes. Then, like now, there was nothing to see. Insects and moths fluttered in the dim glow of the lights that illuminated the sidewalks, the fountain, the beds of flowers. Snails inched across his path. He heard an occasional car somewhere beyond the confines of the clinic and once, the distant bark of a lonely dog. But mostly this was a world wrapped up in the sort of silence that made him feel like the last man alive on the entire planet.

When he reached the sixth building, he ducked around the side and followed the wall to the back. He could hear waves breaking on the rocks some fifty feet below with a steady, maddening rhythm. An island, a wall, a cliff, a nuthouse: the perfect prison.

He walked along the wall until he came to a padlocked gate. Beyond it, the cliff jutted out, forming a wide tongue of land that had been turned into a screened deck with tables and benches. Through it he could see the sky and the dark Gulf waters. Lightning seared a bank of clouds stacked against the horizon. Higher up, the moon struggled to show itself and lost the battle.

He watched the lights of a plane cruising at about two thousand feet, too distant for him to hear it. He envied the pilot, sealed up in the noisy quiet of the cockpit, instruments glowing, his destination as irrelevant as the place where his journey had begun. In the air, the only thing that mattered was your location at any given moment. Things were simple in the air. If you did A, then B or C resulted. There were rarely such guarantees on the ground.

Kincaid sensed rather than heard someone behind him and glanced around. A woman was moving toward him on feet of silk that seemed barely to touch the ground. In the spill of light from between the buildings, the diaphanous fabric of her dress was as transparent as glass. He could see the dark shape of her legs and thighs. Her wild, uncombed hair was like a thick web slivered with ice.

As she neared, he saw that her hair was a deep copper and her dress was sleeveless, scooped low in the front, revealing the swell of her ample breasts. She was barefoot. She looked like a simple peasant girl, thin and delicate and not quite right in the head.

"Evening," he said, trying to sound official.

She didn't appear to have heard him. She stopped at the gate and her long, pale fingers closed around the metal slats. "You think it's them?" she asked.

"Excuse me?"

Without looking at him, she raised her right arm and pointed; it wasn't clear whether she was gesturing toward the few glimmering stars or the lights, which were now turning their way. "They come from the Pleiades, you know." She laughed softly, gaily, and looked at him, a corner of her mouth dimpling. "I suppose you think it's an airplane."

Since even a fruitcake could prove to be a source of information, Kincaid repressed an urge to be flippant. "What makes you think it isn't?"

She turned her face out to sea again. "You look at an ink blot and see a flower. I look at the same ink blot and see another world. Which of us is right?"

"Both."

"And neither. The ink blot has its own perception of itself." She shrugged and her arms dropped to her sides, her hands seeking the hip pockets in her dress. "I say they're from the Pleiades, because that's what Margaret believes, but they might be from Sirius or Pluto. Who's to say, really?"

He didn't give a shit where they came from; she'd said the magic word. Margaret. "Who's Margaret?"

"A friend." She made a half-turn and raised her arm again, pointing to the clouded sky. "Right about there is where the Pleiades are."

Fruitcake or not, she was right about the location. The Pleiades were a cluster of nearly three hundred known stars in the Taurus constellation, four hundred light-years from the Earth's sun. In the fall, they rose to the east in the evening sky.

"You been a security guard long?" she asked, abruptly changing the subject.

"Long enough."

"It's quite a distance."

It took him a moment to realize she was talking about the Pleiades again. "Yeah, a little farther than a trip to Pizza Hut."

She giggled into her hand, a sound as girlish and silly as the gesture. "I suppose you're wondering how they get here, right?"

"It crossed my mind."

"They know how to fold space."

Like folding a napkin, he thought, and leaned against the wall, watching her, not quite sure what to make of her. She was still gazing out at the sky, the sea. The odor of rain was heavier now and a slight breeze stirred her hair. "If they know how to do that, then why bother abducting people?"

Her smile touched only a corner of her mouth. "Yeah, it makes you wonder, doesn't it." She wedged her feet between the bars and Kincaid winced, certain she was going to shake them or scream or both. "Personally, I don't know if I buy the ET theory. It seems just as possible that they're from our own future. Or from another dimension. Or maybe they're totally symbolic or related to consciousness in a way we don't understand yet. Or maybe they belong to our government. Now that's a thought, isn't it."

She was beginning to sound less crazy. Kincaid turned, watching the lights again. They appeared to be rising but were drawing no closer to the island. "You married?" she asked, changing the subject again.

"Yes." It seemed the safest answer. "You?"

"Nope." Then, with barely a pause for breath, she leaped back to the stars again. "In the myth about the Pleiades, they were the seven daughters of Atlas and half-sisters of the Hyades who were placed in the heavens to save them from Orion, who was hunting them. One of them remains hidden, either from grief or shame."

"The Lost Pleiade."

"Right. But I don't think it's shame or grief that keeps her hidden. It's fear. I don't know if Margaret really bought the ET theory, either. Her opinion changed every day. It depended on how much medication they were giving her." She stepped down from the gate and rubbed her hands over her arms and began to twitch, physical equivalents of a stutter. "It depended on who she'd seen, Liscomb or Treak, and whether she'd been zapped. Her story was never the same after she'd been zapped. Variables," she added with a sigh. "They're so important in the overall scheme of things. Like in a marriage. So many variables in a marriage, don't you think?"

She dropped her head back, the twitches worsening as she watched the plane climbing into the clouds, where it vanished. "Bye-bye," she said softly, waving at the sky, then glanced at Kincaid. "They fired Jay Paulson, huh?"

Another quick twitch, but he was getting used to it now. "Yes."

"Margaret stole his car when she escaped."

"So I understand."

"Then you already know who Margaret is."

Not so crazy, he decided. Just shrewd. "I was told she killed her shrink and an attendant during her escape."

"I don't think so." She gave a small, self-conscious laugh. "Not that anyone listens to me."

"I'm listening."

The dimple punctuated a corner of her mouth as she smiled

again. She was no longer twitching. "Yeah, you are. How come? You one of Winthrop's spies?"

"He has spies?"

She made an impatient gesture with her hand. "Oh, sure. That's how it is here. If I tell my house counselor I dreamed about cutting my stepfather up into little pieces, then Winthrop hears about it and Treak—or Liscomb when he was alive—brings it up in our next session. If I deny that I had the dream, they increase my medication so I don't dream at all. It's a terrible thing, not to dream."

"So why do you think Margaret didn't kill anyone?"

She rubbed the back of her hand across her mouth and anxiously scanned the rear windows of the nearest buildings. Then her eyes returned to Kincaid's face, scrutinizing him with an unapologetic openness he found vaguely discomfiting. "Why should I tell you anything? Winthrop probably hired you to talk to me, to find out what I know."

"You found me, not the other way around. I don't even know your name."

"That's true, isn't it." She moved slowly forward now, her fingertips trailing across the wall, and Kincaid fell into step beside her. When she spoke, her voice dropped to a whisper. "Hugh Franks, the attendant, and Maggie were good friends. He used to bring her stuff from the outside and even passed messages sometimes to that abduction group she'd belonged to. So Hugh is the last person she would have killed. She hated Liscomb, was terrified of him, but she wouldn't kill him unless it was self-defense."

"Maybe that's exactly what it was."

"Maybe." She sounded doubtful. "But then who killed Hugh?"

"You're the expert."

She stopped at a spot in the wall where they were shielded from the closest building by a tremendous banyan draped in Spanish moss. "I think it's possible that Liscomb killed Hugh because he was trying to protect Maggie or something. During the two weeks before she escaped, they really overdid it on the treatments. The most they ever do is three times a week, but Maggie was getting zapped every day.''

"How do you know that?''

"Hugh told me. He was real upset about it but didn't know who he could go to. He needed this job. They said that the security guard fell asleep and that's how Maggie escaped, but I think Maggie drugged his tea with pills that Hugh provided.''

A blood test would have solved this, Kincaid thought. But the guard had left the clinic before anyone in the department had known about the tea. "Did Hugh say anything else about it?''

"Yeah, he said the Lost Pleiade was to blame for everything, but he couldn't prove it, and I don't know what he was talking about. You have any kids?''

There it was again, Kincaid thought. The sudden switch to something else. "No. You?''

"Nope.'' She laughed self-consciously. "No time. I've been too busy cracking up.''

"How long have you been here?''

"Since it opened.''

Interesting that Treak hadn't mentioned that at least one patient had exceeded the one-year maximum stay. "I thought this place was short-term.''

"It is, but I like it okay here. I've been in and out of institutions for fourteen years and this is the nicest one yet. This is the one that prepares you for life in the world again. But, frankly, I'm not too interested in going back into the world. I know the ropes in here. There isn't much to worry about and my trust pays the bills. And right now I can come and go pretty much as I please, so all in all, it's not bad.''

She paused, her smile quick and bright. "But tomorrow I might change my mind. I already spend several nights a week at the San Ignacio Church in El Pueblito. I'm close to one of the nuns there. She was a friend of my mother's; she's kind of like my aunt. I do work at the convent. Treak likes that. I think she thinks it puts her closer to God or something.''

Kincaid nudged her back on track again by asking if Margaret had gotten any visitors. "Just her husband and her sister, but she refused to speak to them when they were here, so they didn't come too often."

"Why wouldn't she talk to them?"

"Well, Pete committed her and Julie didn't do anything to stop it, so why bother?" She uttered this as though the answer should have been perfectly obvious.

"She didn't have any friends?"

"Oh, she had plenty of friends. She was always getting letters from her artist friends in Miami. But outside of her family, she wasn't allowed to see the people she cared about. That's part of the treatment, see."

Kincaid started to reply, but she suddenly hushed him and pointed at a light that had come on in a first-floor window. "Treak's room," she whispered. "The bitch is having a bad night. I'd better head back. She'll be coming out soon for a walk."

"Wait. What's your name?"

"Jean."

Well, well, he thought. Jean Mancino. It had to be. How many other Jeans could there be who knew Margaret Wickerd? "I'm Ray."

The flash of her smile didn't disguise the twitches that had started up again, worse than before. She glanced nervously at the light in Treak's window. "I was wondering if you could do me a favor?"

"What?"

"There's this detective who was out here the other day. Scott, I think her name was. I should talk to her, but without anyone from the clinic present. Winthrop will get real uptight about it, so she shouldn't tell him she's coming. Just show up. Then he'll have to let her see me."

"Okay, I'll tell her."

"Thanks. Thanks a million."

She gave his arm a quick squeeze and hurried away as silently as she had approached. Kincaid headed in the opposite direction, thunder rolling through the dark, the breeze at his back. He emerged from between the first residence and the main building a few moments later. The sidewalk was clear, but a car stood outside the gate, headlights burning, engine idling.

Odd time for a visitor. He sprinted to the guardhouse and reached it just as the driver exited the Mazda Miata and came over to the gate.

"I thought I was going to have to honk for service," the man said good-naturedly.

"Sorry. I was doing the rounds. Your name, sir?"

"Wickerd. Pete Wickerd."

The Traveling Husband in the flesh. He looked pretty much as Aline had described him: the expensive clothes, the shirt unbuttoned halfway down his chest, the gold chains around his neck. Kincaid pegged him as obnoxious but basically harmless. "I'll need some ID, Mr. Wickerd. A license would be fine."

"No problem."

He passed it through the bars. Kincaid had yet to see a photo on a driver's license that wasn't a mug shot and Wickerd's was no exception. But he looked much more conventional in the picture—short hair, a coat and tie, show biz in the smile. And it was this face that Kincaid recognized, but he couldn't immediately place the memory. He noted the address (in the hills near Tango airport) and the age (forty-four), then passed the license back through the bars. "Is Dr. Winthrop expecting you?"

"He should be if he isn't."

Nothing like a solid answer. "This will just take a moment." Kincaid unlocked the guardhouse and punched out Winthrop's number. He picked up on the second ring; Kincaid heard the drone of a TV in the background. "Peter Wickerd to see you, Doctor. Should I send him through?"

He grumbled about the time but said he'd meet him in front of the main building. Kincaid hit the button for the gate and it rolled open, a noisy, antiquated jaw begging for a healthy dose of WD-40 lubricant. Wickerd's Miata whispered through, plum blue with smoky windows. A clap of thunder accompanied him to the front of the building, where he parked crookedly. He trotted up the steps but didn't try the door; he evidently already knew it was locked.

It started to rain as Wickerd waited on the stoop. He paced back and forth under the narrow overhang, hands deep in his pockets, shoulders hunched as though he might melt if the rain touched him. Kincaid suddenly remembered where he'd seen him before.

On a talk show a year or so ago, he and Sam Newman had shared the stage with three people who had had close encounters. Newman was pushing his newest book; Wickerd was simply pushing the opposing point of view. His tactics were so rude and unimpressive, Kincaid had promptly forgotten his name and couldn't recall the name of the show, even now. But he did remember the photos Wickerd had shown, of luminous disks and cigar-shaped objects hovering in skies that were crimson and violet and black. Photos, it turned out, that were faked, the result of darkroom magic.

Kincaid wondered what sort of magic Wickerd was going to conjure for Winthrop. Whatever it was, Aline would want to know about it, he decided, and picked up the phone to call her.

(3)

Nate's office on the second level of the complex wasn't large or lavish. But he felt at peace there. He supposed it had to do with all the earth that stood between him and the rest of the world, the tons of rock and dirt creating an impenetrable shield between him and the madness of life at the surface, the lunacy of politics.

Eighty feet above him was the computer room, a small gym, the kitchen and dining area. There was also an air shaft dug from the main tunnel to the surface where pumps and fans had been installed for air circulation. Below him on the third level were the heart and lungs of the complex: diesel engines that generated electricity; two septic tanks; and two ponds, one for drinking water and the other for the sprinkler system and for cooling the air pumped through the mainframe computer to keep it from overheating.

On the second level were two offices, including his own; six rooms with double bunks; two restrooms with three showers each. At the end of the hall were a pair of tunnels that led, via different routes, to the main cavern now known as Room 13.

Nate, stretched out on the couch next to his desk, shut his eyes and forced himself to wait a little longer. In Vietnam, he'd discovered that the anticipation of a bombing mission was almost as sweet as the moment when he dived out of the sky. It was the same with Room 13, the anticipation building until it was an exquisite pressure in his head. So he lay there and created a mental image of the main cavern, the twelve-foot ceiling, the natural rock walls, the soft lighting, the secret.

A rap at the door interrupted this rather pleasant exercise. "Yes, what is it?" he asked sharply.

"It's Morales, sir. You asked for the night's printouts."

Nate sat up and swung his legs over the side of the couch. "C'mon in."

Ricardo Morales didn't look Hispanic. He was sandy-haired, blue-eyed, built like a wrestler. His clothes suffered from the same neglect as his beat-up Pontiac: faded jeans that looked like a relic from the Sixties; an old work shirt; scuffed running shoes. His square jaw begged for a session with a razor. His appearance, like his goddamn car, also disturbed Nate.

And yet his patriotism was beyond question, wasn't it? He'd escaped Castro's nightmare as a youngster in 1959, fleeing with his family. He understood the cost of freedom and democracy, didn't he? He understood the necessity of secrecy, right? Yes, yes, of course he did.

"Thought you might like some coffee, too, sir." He held out a mug and Nate took it.

"Thanks. Any activity on the perimeter tonight?"

Morales passed him the computer sheets and shook his head. "Negligible, sir. A deer tripped the perimeter alarm before you arrived. Upstairs, computer number two went down for an hour or so. Dole fixed the problem. She says it's the hard drive."

"How many does that make?"

"Uh, six in the last year, sir."

"Any explanation?"

"Dole says we'd be better off buying Japanese drives."

Shit. Japanese hard drives, Japanese microchips, Japanese cars. Was there anything the Japanese *didn't* excel at? "We buy American, Morales. Make sure she knows it."

He smiled. "Oh, I think she knows it, sir. She's just hoping you'll change your mind."

"Fat chance. Anything new on the electronic networks?"

"Several interesting tidbits on Prodigy, sir. There was an alleged close encounter with the grays in Maine, which the usual groups are investigating. The individual involved is a reliable witness, a local cop with twenty years under his belt."

The grays, he thought, were old news. "Anything else?"

"The editor of a local UFO newsletter in Kansas says he's received a tip from a reliable source high in the government"—Morales grinned and crooked his index fingers, indicating quotes around the last phrase—"concerning new information about MJ-12."

"Like what?"

"He didn't say."

"You'd think people would come up with something new to puzzle over."

Morales chuckled. "I know what you mean, Colonel. You need anything else?"

"No. And thanks for the report."

When Morales had left, Nate lay back on the couch, vaguely irritated with the MJ-12 business. Operation Majestic Twelve supposedly had involved the retrieval of a UFO that had crashed in a remote region of New Mexico in July 1947. The most popular version of the story was that four small humanlike beings had apparently ejected from the craft before it exploded and were ferreted away to different locations for scientific study.

Nate doubted the story was true. What interested him most was the public's fixation on something that might or might not have happened nearly fifty years ago. It went back to his primary axiom: *Once a pattern has been created, it tends to reproduce itself.* And it had.

The most celebrated cases in the UFO world—MJ-12, the alleged abduction of Betty and Barney Hill, the Andreasson abductions, Whitley Strieber's intimate accounts in *Communion*—had fed the collective imagination and brought forth new stories, new encounters, new abductions, new investigations, new celebrities. The pattern had not only reproduced itself but had resulted in the emergence of new patterns.

A stone, he thought, was tossed into a pond. The ripples that emanated from it created other, more complex ripples that, somewhere beyond his capacity to perceive, were giving birth to worlds. It was the beauty and the puzzle of this process that sustained him and quelled his misgivings about the project.

By the time he finally got up and hurried through the tunnel toward Room 13, his anticipation burned inside him, a bright and hungry sun.

10

(1)

Aline stuck her head out of the window as Kincaid approached the Honda in a yellow rain slicker. "Hey, you look good in yellow, Ryan. Remind me to get you yellow underwear for Christmas or something."

He grinned. Rain dripped off the hood of the slicker onto his forehead and spilled to his nose. "Let's make this look legit. Show me your badge, then drive on through and I'll call Winthrop's office."

"Tell him I made a stink about being admitted but don't mention anything about Jean Mancino." She flashed her badge. "I'll spring that on him myself."

He stepped back and waved her through the open gate. The grounds no longer resembled a religious cloister. The silence, the absence of movement, the heaviness of the air lent an almost Gothic feel to the place, as though it were possessed by something sinister.

A nurse let her in the front door and took her to Winthrop's office without calling him first. She felt an immense satisfaction at the expression on his face, the sagging in his jowls, as if gravity was suddenly working against him. He rose quickly, covering his surprise with a smile, a cordial greeting, then turned to Peter Wickerd, who looked a bit wan, and said, "This is—"

"We've met. Hello, Mr. Wickerd." She deliberately turned her back on him and addressed Winthrop again. "You

were going to call me about a time when I could see Jean
Mancino. Since you didn't, I thought this would be a good
time, Dr. Winthrop.''

"Now?" The cords in his neck stood out. "It's two in the
morning."

"Which means she's here."

"Well, yes, but I can't very well—"

"Of course you can, Doctor. Now please have someone
wake Jean, will you?"

Aline couldn't tell if his helpless glance at Wickerd was a
supplication for interference or an apology. But several things
were abundantly clear. Dr. Winthrop didn't make decisions;
he was a gofer who was in over his head and Wickerd knew
it and wasn't about to intercede. He coughed, brushed at
something on his slacks, consulted his watch.

"I'll ring her residence counselor," Winthrop finally said,
shuffling toward the phone.

"And I'd better run along." Wickerd pushed to his feet,
smiling like a loan shark who knew when to exit. "Good to
see you again, Ms. Scott."

"We'll be talking soon, Mr. Wickerd."

He smiled as if at some private joke. "No doubt."

Wickerd left and Winthrop hung up the phone a moment
later. He stood behind his chair, his hands on the back of it
like a man from another era posing for a photograph. "I find
your coming here at this time of night highly irregular and I
intend to file an official complaint about it. I've cooperated
fully with the police."

He was beginning to sound like a New England stuffed
shirt. "I *am* the police."

"Well, yes, that's true, but . . ."

"And I don't think you've cooperated to the best of your
ability by any stretch of the imagination."

"Look here, young lady, I lost two of my best people
because of Mrs. Wickerd. The—"

"Then you might be interested in knowing that the results
of the autopsies suggest that Mrs. Wickerd may not be responsible for those murders. And I think the American Psy-

chiatric Association will find some of your procedures questionable.''

It was more than she'd intended to say, but it got a rise out of him. He marched out from behind his chair, color blazing in his cheeks, a man on the verge of apoplexy. ''Young lady, you barge into my clinic at two in the morning demanding to see a patient whom you could have seen anytime during normal hours. You make insinuations, you—''

''Oh, really, Tyler,'' snapped Nina Treak, materializing in the doorway with the silent stealth of a professional thief. ''She's just doing her job.'' She smiled pleasantly as Aline turned to look at her, smiled as if they were just two women who had met over a sales rack at Sears. ''Jean's out in the lobby, Ms. Scott. Would you like some coffee? Maybe something cold to drink?''

''No, thanks.''

''I wasn't aware that the autopsies had been completed,'' Treak went on. Despite her attempt to inject an air of normalcy into the situation, her smile was stiff and didn't touch her eyes. She wasn't at her best at this hour of the morning. Stripped of makeup and jewelry and wearing an olive green raincoat over baggy slacks, she looked like a dowdy housewife suffering from a mysterious ailment.

''The official word isn't in yet,'' Aline replied.

''Official, unofficial.'' She gave an impatient wave of her hand. ''The question, Ms. Scott, is who else could have killed Vance and Hugh?''

''That was precisely what I was wondering,'' Winthrop said, his voice still huffy.

Aline shrugged. ''As soon as I have an answer to that, you two will be the first to know.''

But Treak persisted. ''She and Vance and Hugh were the only people in the building.''

''But not the only people on the grounds.''

Treak's equanimity began to show strain. ''What you're suggesting is ludicrous.''

Interesting choice of words. Aline wondered what it would be like to face this woman as a patient here, knowing that she held the power to release you or keep you here for another six months. She thought of the experiment on violent criminals that Treak and Liscomb had engineered at the University of Miami. She thought of the silicon sliver Prentiss had removed from Liscomb's sinuses. She thought of Treak dressed in a white robe and passing judgment with just a flick of her finger—*This one goes up, that one goes down*—and knew that it was just that easy for her.

"I'm not suggesting anything, Dr. Treak. I'm just giving you the facts. You know, like Jack Webb. So if you'll excuse me, I think I'll talk to Jean Mancino now."

As she brushed past Treak, the skin on the back of her neck tightened, and she was suddenly grateful for the .38 in her purse. For the fact that she was a reasonably sane woman with a reasonably sane life who had never been in therapy and who, thanks to this brief exposure to psychiatry, never would be.

Then she was free of the office, of the warm, stifling air, and hurrled down the hall, her shoes squeaking against the slick, polished floors.

(2)

Despite what Kincaid had indicated, Jean Mancino didn't act as though she were eaten up with urgency to talk to Aline. She sat tensely at the edge of the couch, her slender legs crossed at the knees, her right foot tucked behind the calf of her left leg, and lit one cigarette after another. She answered questions readily enough but in quiet monosyllables that suggested she was afraid of being overheard.

"Would you rather talk some other time?" Aline asked finally.

"Oh, how rude of me," she said, twisting her cigarette into the soil of the nearest potted plant. "Smoking like a fiend and not offering you one. Here.'' She extended the pack of Larks. ''Help yourself.''

Aline started to say she didn't smoke but realized a piece of paper protruded from the cellophane wrapping on the cigarettes. She looked up at Jean, who mouthed *Take it*, so she did. She slipped the paper from the wrapping, pulled out a cigarette, passed the pack back to Jean.

''What time of the day is best for you?'' Aline asked.

Her twitching had worsened. ''Afternoon. If it's sunny, we can walk around outside. That'd be nice, don't you think? The grounds are so pretty when the sun shines.''

The double doors behind them swung open and Treak strolled out with an umbrella tucked under her arm and a polite smile fixed on her face. Aline got to her feet, but Treak patted the air with her hands. ''No need to hurry, Detective Scott.''

''We're finished for now. I can get the rest of what I need in a couple of days.''

''Good, good. Why don't you walk out with us, Jean?''

Treak unlocked the door and they stepped outside. The rain was still coming down and the crackle of thunder promised that it wasn't going to let up anytime soon. Jean flinched as lightning tore open the black sky on the other side of the gate; she slipped the hood of her raincoat over her head.

''You want me to walk you back to the house, Jean?'' Treak asked with an odd solicitousness.

''No, that's okay. It isn't far. Night, all.'' She darted out from under the protection of the awning and took off at a swift clip down the sidewalk.

''Lightning has unpleasant associations for Jean,'' Treak remarked, gazing after her. ''Did Dr. Winthrop tell you anything about her?''

''No.''

Treak fussed with the button on her umbrella. ''Fourteen years ago, she killed her stepfather and chopped him up into little pieces. Although she was only seventeen at the time, she was tried as an adult, her attorney pleaded insanity, and she was institutionalized. Her sentence ended five years ago."

"Why'd she kill him?"

"Abuse, but that didn't come out until she'd been in therapy for several years. She'd managed to create elaborate fictions in her own mind to cope with the abuse and had convinced herself that he was responsible for her mother's death, which was due to natural causes." Her umbrella popped open. "At any rate, we consider her one of our successes, although it's doubtful she'll ever lead a normal life on the outside."

"With job training, she might."

"Oh, it's not that. She has the money to survive, she's bright and attractive, but institutions are all she's known for fourteen years. She's like an inmate who can't make it outside the prison walls. If we release her, it will probably be to another institutional setting, into a local convent where a friend of her mother's is a nun."

They started down the steps to Aline's car, the rain drumming on top of the umbrella. "Why're you telling me all this, Dr. Treak?"

"Just to alert you that most of what Jean says is fiction. She believes whatever she tells people, so it's not lying, it's simply . . . well, a colorful fiction, her defense mechanism against unpleasant realities."

"Like the murders."

"And Margaret's escape."

"I'll need to get her official statement, so I'll be back tomorrow or the next day." Aline opened the door to her car and slid behind the wheel. "Thanks for your candidness."

"Of course."

Aline backed out of the space, swung around, and headed toward the guardhouse. *She's watching me.* She adjusted the rearview mirror and, sure enough, Treak was still huddled under her umbrella, as motionless as a tree. The guardrail went up as she approached it and she drove through without so much as a glance at Kincaid.

Once she was well beyond the clinic, she pulled to the

shoulder of the road and unfolded the slip of paper Jean had passed her. Printed on it was:

> *I'll call and maybe we can meet when I'm in town so we can speak more freely. In the meantime, ask Joe Mahoney about the Pleiades photos and sketches.*

Did she really want to bother with a woman who told "colorful fictions" and had chopped her stepfather into little pieces? It was entirely possible, though, that Treak had told her the story specifically to plant doubt about Jean's credibility, which was already questionable.

But Aline realized that of the two women, she was more suspicious of Treak. She'd found both men; she had probably known about her colleague's allergy to Seconal; and she had a possible motive, to silence Liscomb about something he'd known. The problem was that she wasn't tall enough to have slit Hugh's throat from behind him. But Liscomb had certainly been tall enough.

Maybe Margaret had already been on the table when Liscomb and Treak started arguing about something. Treak killed him with the Seconal intended for Margaret. Hugh heard the argument, came in to see what was going on, and Treak—what? Leaped out from behind the door and rode his back like a monkey while she tried to slit his throat?

She couldn't see it. What seemed more plausible, and fit with Prentiss's conclusion, was that Liscomb had killed Hugh first, perhaps because he was attempting to help Margaret escape, then he'd called Treak for help and she did him in. But even this scenario didn't feel quite right.

Something was missing. But she didn't know what it was. Not yet.

(3)

When the generator suddenly cut out, plunging the bedroom
into blackness, Margaret jerked instantly awake. Her heart
slammed up against the walls of her chest. Her eyes darted
about, seeking a familiar shape within the darkness. But it
was too deep, too pervasive, as though she'd come to inside
the belly of a whale. She strained to hear something other
than the panicked rush of blood in her veins and finally did—
rain, thunder, wind whipping through the trees.

She sat up, patted the nightstand until she found the candle
and matches she kept on it. The candle's pathetic little flame
hissed and flickered. She swung her legs over the side of the
bed and tried to avoid looking beyond the flame but couldn't.
A monstrous darkness yawned in the doorway. Shadows puddled thickly a foot from the bed. The chair where she'd draped
her jeans was invisible.

"Move it, just move it," she whispered.

As she stood, a boom of thunder shook the glass in the
windows. Almost immediately, lightning flashed, its brief
illumination filling the room like mercury. Its brilliance mesmerized her, impaled her, literally stole the air in her lungs.
She was suddenly flat on her back, unable to move, the sun
slicing into her eyes. Then the door at the back of her mind
blew open and images poured through her, pulsing, burning,
beating their hard, tight fists against the inside of her skull,
her nose, the backs of her eyes.

Margaret stumbled to her feet, gasping for air, shaking her
head, clawing at it, trying to focus on something in the room.
A chair, a door, the candle that had dropped. But the light
was everywhere, a continent erupting from the surface of the
sea, a god in turmoil. She fell to her knees and threw her
arms over her head, her face smashed against the floor. Beings emerged from the light. She heard their small, rustling
movements, like a swarm of insects flying through a field of
ruined corn. They spoke to her in dry, whistling voices,
touched her with their strange, dry hands, watched her with

huge black eyes that seemed to float free from the rest of them, dark ships in the light. Distantly, she heard screaming, a shrill, terrible sound, and knew it was coming from her.

And then she was running, running and stumbling into the yawning mouth of the doorway, the hall, the stairs. She tripped, her arms flew out, her hands flailed for something to grab on to. They found wood. Hard. Solid. The banister. Yes, the banister. Jesus, run, run, run.

The steps trembled with life, rose up, bit at her ankles, and then she was outside, on her knees, her face pressed into wet leaves, the rain pouring over her. She sobbed and gulped at the air, bits of leaves stuck to the corners of her mouth, on her tongue, against the roof of her mouth, but she didn't care, it didn't matter. The light was gone. Gone, and she was alive.

(4)

Sometime later, she entered the house again. Her vision was still fuzzy, her head ached, and memories bumped around in her skull like survivors of some terrible disaster at sea. But otherwise, there didn't seem to be any lingering effects of whatever had happened.

Drenched to the bone, she made her way into the kitchen and found the flashlight. The bright, narrow beam was as comforting as dry clothes, as powerful as God. It melted shadows, illuminated shapes that her imagination might otherwise seize upon and pervert. At the door of the living room, she paused, listening intently, the light jumping around like a flea. Nothing in here. Nothing but the furniture, which she had draped in white sheets again earlier today, returning the room to the way in which she'd found it. She moved cautiously up the stairs, one hand on the banister, the other clutching the flashlight. Hello, God, she thought at the light, hello, welcome, please stick around.

The bedroom was black: the candle she had dropped had

gone out. She picked it up, slipped it into the nightstand drawer, moved the beam of the flashlight from one end of the room to the other.

The curtains were shut.

The sheet was puddled on the floor next to the bed.

Her jeans were where she'd left them earlier.

Her purse was on the chair.

She was alone.

Shivering, she stripped off her wet T-shirt, pulled a clean one from a dresser drawer, tugged on her jeans. She made the bed and picked up, a vestige of life at the clinic. This habit of straightening a room before she left it had once elicited an observation from Liscomb that she seemed to be trying to obliterate traces of herself. It was probably the single most astute comment he'd ever made about her.

She remembered him clearly now, him and Treak and Winthrop, Hugh and Jean and others, names reattached to faces again. Some details were missing, though, and others were hopelessly mixed up, disjointed, unrooted in time, black pearls that drifted in some primal sea. And she still couldn't remember what had happened in the treatment room.

She knew that Hugh had helped her in some way, but had he come for her that night? Had Liscomb been waiting in the treatment room for her? Had Treak? Had Hugh been fired over her escape? Was she supposed to have driven to some prearranged place? And what was the Lost Pleiade? In the plural, it was a star system, yes, she certainly remembered that much of it, but its meaning in the singular was different. It was the name of something secret.

In the kitchen, she hooked her purse over the back of a chair, fixed a plate of fruit and a mug of tea, and sat at the table, next to the open window. The flashlight rested on the base, aimed at the ceiling. The wind moaned through the trees and blew through the screen. Now and then, she felt rain against the backs of her hands as she drew three circles on a piece of paper, one inside the other.

Within them, she arranged and rearranged objects that represented certain people. In the outermost circle, Liscomb was a can of beans, Hugh was the pepper shaker, Treak was a matchbox, Winthrop was a can of ravioli, Jean was the salt shaker. In the next circle were her husband, her sister, Sam Newman and the group. In the innermost, smallest circle was the experience months ago, the source from which everything else emanated. How many months ago? A year? More?

She placed her wedding ring in the center of that circle, then began moving objects around, seeking the connections, hoping something would jar loose the rest of her memories. She smoked several cigarettes from the pack she'd taken from under the seat in the guard's car, got up, moved more of the objects around, walked over to the front window.

The rain fell in a shimmering sheet, a translucent veil. The dark shapes of trees loomed against it, but nothing else. It was as if the world beyond the house had winked out and she was doomed to live out the rest of her life within these four walls, alone. She felt an acute, overwhelming sense of loneliness, a terrible hunger for the presence of another human being. For Sam. Yes, for Sam, the hunger was quite specific.

She knew now that she had seen him briefly during her last weekend as a trustee, seen him here, and it was here he had left her, bowing out of her life with nothing more than a note that said he loved her but . . .

The *but* was his wife.

She didn't know when this had happened, weeks or months ago, didn't know why they had met here, but remembered that Hugh had been their go-between, their liaison, their trusted friend.

Either Hugh or Sam could fill in the gaps in her memory, but then what? She was still an escaped mental patient and her shrink was dead and it was quite possible that she had killed him. You couldn't get any less credible than that.

As she was turning away from the window, a glimmer of light caught her eye. She rubbed her palm over the glass, saw it again, realized it was a car. And it was headed this way.

Margaret backed away from the window, her eyes fixed on the rain-smeared window. Then she spun around and moved swiftly through the kitchen. She swept the objects on the table into a paper bag, looked about frantically for a place to hide it, then decided to take it with her. She grabbed the flashlight, slung her purse over her shoulder, and charged for the stairs.

She pushed the paper bag to the end of a shelf in the bedroom closet, jerked her wet T-shirt off the back of a chair, shoved it into her purse, switched off her flashlight, peeked out from behind the curtain. The headlights were closer, bouncing in the wet dark. She guessed the car had left the dirt road and was now threading through the trees. Although the front door was locked, it wouldn't keep out anyone who wanted in.

She let the curtain drop back into place. Where to hide? The toolshed and the attic might be okay, but there was only one way in or out of both of them. Discovered, she would be trapped. Then she remembered something she had noticed her first day here, when she was cleaning, and hastened downstairs.

Margaret dropped to her knees in front of the fireplace, jerked open the rusted screen, shone the flashlight up the chimney. It was old, wonderfully old, wide enough for her, wide enough for Santa Claus. The narrow ledges of brick staggered along the inside were ideal footholds. But how long could she hide inside it without being detected? Minutes? Hours?

Do it, just do it, she thought, and opened the flue. The wind whistled through the chimney, creating an updraft. She ducked under the edge, straightened up inside the chimney, grasped on to the nearest jut, put some weight on it. It would hold. She stuck the flashlight in the waistband of her jeans but didn't turn it off. Not yet. She wanted to see where she was going. She hooked the strap of her purse over her head, then started to climb.

11

(1)

Trouble was waiting for Nate in front of his house when he drove up and its name was Tyler Winthrop. Or, as Sheen and Booth referred to him, Winthrop the Dewdrop.

He marched through the drizzle swinging his arms, his trench coat flapping at the knees, a little tin soldier with a bone to pick. Nate's annoyance was quick and sharp. Why now? Why had Winthrop arrived precisely now, just when his own demons were appeased and sleep was finally possible? Winthrop would kill that chance. He was such a tedious man. Had he become an elementary-school teacher or a children's librarian, he would be the type who would insist that you whisper at all times and please, grasp the railing as you climb the stairs. *I'm getting too old for this shit.*

"A little late for a visit, isn't it, Tyler?"

"I apologize for the hour, Colonel, but it's imperative that we talk."

Such New England propriety. But to his credit, Winthrop had always known where the lines were drawn, and he knew now that he had crossed one such line by coming here. "I think there's enough cognac left for two. Come on inside. You look like a wet poodle, Tyler."

He didn't take umbrage at the remark, nor did he laugh. He just nodded miserably. "It's been a bad night, Colonel."

Oh, but it hasn't, Tyler, it hasn't. It had turned out to be a very pleasant night. Until this second. "And why is that, Tyler?"

"I don't like the direction in which this homicide investigation is moving, Colonel." He wiped his wet shoes carefully and thoroughly on the mat at the front door. "I don't like it at all."

For the next twenty minutes, Nate heard more than he wanted to hear about Detective Scott and Nina Treak and Peter Wickerd. He listened while Winthrop wore a track in the living-room rug, moving in an erratic square that took him past the fireplace, the Oriental vase Nate's wife had bought on a trip to China, the rattan furniture, and back to the overstuffed reading chair where Nate sat. Winthrop gulped intermittently at his cognac, ran his hands repeatedly over his white hair, and finally stopped and looked at Nate with naked pleading. *Tell me what to do, Colonel*, shouted his sorry eyes.

"What's this patient's name again?" Nate asked.

"Jean Mancino."

"Do you think she knows anything about Margaret's whereabouts?"

"I don't think so. They just weren't that close anymore."

"But they were once?"

"They roomed together for a while shortly after Margaret was committed, but I don't think they were ever that close, Colonel. These people aren't really capable of closeness."

These people: the words rolled off his tongue with obvious distaste, as though mental patients formed some sort of subspecies. "Assuming they *are* capable of the same emotions as the rest of us," Nate said with a sarcasm that eluded Winthrop, "it's possible, isn't it, that Margaret might have confided in her?"

"I guess it's possible." Winthrop sank into a rattan chair. "But with all due respect, Colonel, you don't understand how electroshock affects memory. When they were rooming together, Margaret was undergoing intensive treatments. On top of it, Nina had already done the implant. That means a double-whammy of short-term memory loss. I'd be surprised if Margaret was able to remember her name or address or social-security number.''

''Why didn't you just return the detective's calls about seeing Jean, Tyler?''

''I was busy.''

Sure. Busy burying his head in the sand. Nate's patience snapped and he let Winthrop have it. ''You knew Hugh Franks and Margaret were friends, Tyler, but you didn't put a stop to it. You knew Margaret was chummy with the security guard, too, didn't you? And you didn't put a stop to that, either. You knew all along why Margaret was committed, the areas in which Vance and Nina specialized, you knew everything you had to know when you became director and now you come sniveling to me. Just what the fuck do you expect me to do, Tyler? Tell me.''

His heart pounded, his blood pressure soared. He glared at Winthrop, waiting for him to say something. Winthrop's expression was that of a man who was tottering at the lip of a precipice. Then his face crumbled like a stale cookie and he pressed his knuckles to his eyes and began to weep.

Weep, for Christ's sakes. And he wasn't quiet about it, either. His great, heaving sobs resounded in the quiet room. His shoulders shook. The whole thing embarrassed Nate, filled him with pathos. But, most of all, it made him realize that Sheen and Booth were right; Winthrop had outgrown his usefulness. He was a liability. His name was scrawled in red ink.

A waste of revenue, he heard Booth saying.

Dollars and cents. In the end, Nate thought wearily, the question of who would live and who would die was reduced to money. If a man presented a security risk, Nate was supposed to look at it in terms of how much it would cost the project to silence him. That was part of his job. The unpleasant but necessary part.

A delicate balance. If Winthrop was silenced outright, police suspicion and scrutiny of the clinic would increase. That might prove to be hazardous to everyone involved and thus, very expensive. So the best way to deal with him right now was to remove him physically from the situation. A vacation. A bereavement trip due to a family death. Something along those lines.

Then Treak would take over in his absence. She wasn't anywhere as easy to manipulate as Winthrop but could be made to cooperate through her ambition. Give her a lab filled with human guinea pigs and she was as happy as Clyde Barrow with a bank to rob. When the local cops were out of the picture, when the heat was off, Winthrop would meet with an accident.

An old script, really, one that had been enacted so frequently in Nate's career that he had lost count of the victims. They were pawns you sacrificed in the long journey toward the checkmate of your opponent's king, the weak ones in the political scheme of things.

"Tyler, I think you should take some time off." Nate strove for an avuncular tone as he patted Winthrop's shoulder. "Take the wife and kids to the Caribbean. It's beautiful in the Caribbean now."

He peered up at Nate with damp puppy-dog eyes, rubbed the back of his hand across his nose, sniffled. "We can't afford it."

No, of course not. His credit cards were charged to the hilt, his sons were in private school, his wife buzzed around in a Mercedes and designer clothes and enough weight in gold and diamonds to sink the goddamn *Titanic*. Nate knew. It was his business to know.

"Nonsense. The cruise industry is begging for business and fares have never been cheaper." Nate twirled his glass, watching the cognac swirl, a dark, seductive spout. A pattern. "I strongly urge you to take some time for yourself. Nina can handle things in your absence."

Still sniffling: "I . . . I don't know. I'll have to think about it."

He really didn't get it. *Do it or die, Tyler.*

"The problem, Colonel Nate, is the police. Good God, their allegations, their—"

"Don't concern yourself with it, Tyler. The important

thing is that Margaret Wickerd will be found, and after what she's done, no one will believe anything she says to the contrary."

Winthrop looked relieved, as though the fact that Nate had uttered this made it so. "She *is* quite demented, Colonel. I mean, really, kidnapped by aliens." He snickered like a kid who had found his old man's condoms. "It's like a tabloid story."

Not quite, Tyler, not quite.

"And the electroshock was certainly warranted; we didn't make any mistake in that regard. Severe depression, the extreme violence she displayed the day she was brought in . . ." He spoke as if to a jury of his peers. "I just don't see how anyone can fault us."

"You did what you deemed correct as a professional who is trained in these matters, Tyler. No one can fault you or your staff for that."

"You're right." He brightened. "You're absolutely right."

"Good, I'm glad we agree on that. Now why don't you drive back to the clinic, collect your things, and go sleep at home, Tyler. And tomorrow look into that trip to the Caribbean, will you?"

Nate stood in the doorway as Winthrop loped out into the drizzle to his car, and tried to imagine him making love to his wife. Did he grunt? Did he sweat? Did he worry about getting it in right? The notion of a naked Winthrop humping his wife or anyone else was so depressing, Nate shut the door.

Fatigue closed around him, a damp fist. He wanted desperately to recapture the euphoria he'd felt in the cavern. But the sensation eluded him. It was a light that shrinks and dims the farther you move from it in time and space, the afterimage of a flashbulb on the surface of the retina. Then even that was gone, gone out into the wet dark with Winthrop.

(2)

The instant the front door opened, Margaret felt it in the air in the chimney. When the door shut, she felt that, too.

She was about halfway up the chimney, arms and legs extended to either side of her, a crucified martyr. If she had to, she could scamper out through the top, and yet she was close enough to the floor to hear the shuffle of feet moving her way. She couldn't tell how many people there were.

The front door opened again, slammed shut. She heard more footfalls, then a woman's voice calling, "I didn't find anything outside."

Treak the Geek. Here. In my space. Here here here.

Her fingers tightened around the handholds.

Please, God. Are you listening, God? You up there?

In her mind, she followed Treak through the hall to the front room. "If she was here, the car would probably be outside," Treak said.

"Unless she got rid of it."

Pete. She would know his voice anywhere. She sucked in her breath and held it so she wouldn't scream or sob or explode with laughter. Pete & Treak, like a circus act. "She wouldn't have the presence of mind to get rid of it," Treak said. "She probably got off the island that first night."

"And went where?"

"Miami."

"She'd lost touch with everyone there."

"Oh, Christ, Pete. She's not going to go to anyone she knows for help, and that's assuming that she remembers enough to know who her friends are, which is doubtful. It's probably the only thing we've got going for us at this point. She's much more likely to be holed up in a motel room somewhere in Miami or the upper keys."

"I don't think so. She grew up here. Six years in this house, Nina. She'll remember this place if she hasn't already."

I lived here. The girl with the bow in her hair was my sister.

"Who else knows about it besides Julie?"

"I don't know. Maybe Sam and his group. It might have come up at one of the meetings, and if it did, then sooner or later the cops are going to hear about it, and if they get to her before we do, that's it."

Treak laughed then, a quick, full sound that seemed to echo inside the chimney, a mockery, a promise, a confirmation that her soul was just as black as Margaret had imagined. "You have an amazing capacity for drama, Peter."

"You're underestimating her."

"I know the facts. In the two weeks before she escaped, she had ten treatments, nearly twice the norm. And with each treatment the pituitary was stimulated and that, in turn, affected the hypothalamus. My guess is that about now, she's not at all clear on what's real and what isn't. She's probably relived the abduction, is terrified of the dark, can't put names with faces, and is incapable of making the most basic decision. Even if the police find her, she's going to sound completely delusional. If we're lucky, she'll kill herself."

"I don't predicate my life on luck."

"No, you predicate it on paranoia."

"Suppose the silicon chip jarred loose, Nina?"

"Even in the unlikely event that it did, so what? Her memory has already been affected and she couldn't get much more passive."

"If she's so passive, then how could she have killed Vance and Hugh?"

"You're mistaking passivity for an absence of self-preservation, Peter. And that's probably what it came down to for her. You know how much she hated the treatments."

"But—"

She cut him off. "I'm going to have a look around upstairs."

Margaret listened to Treak's retreating march across the old wooden floors, heard her clomp up the stairs.

If we're lucky . . .

Her left hand slipped; she grasped the jut of brick more tightly, and the muscles in her arms began to fuss and complain.

. . . she'll kill herself. . . .

A gust of wind blew rain and dirt into the chimney and it mixed with the old soot, tickling her nostrils, bringing tears to her eyes. She stifled a sneeze, begging him to leave the room. *Go on, Pete, get out, leave me alone.*

Instead, he walked toward the fireplace as though he could smell her. She tightened her grip on the holds, ready to climb, and stared at the darkness below her. The beam of his flashlight passed through it, then probed it like a long, pale finger. Adrenaline pumped through her, her muscles tightened, she began to perspire. Her right hand groped above her head for the next hold.

Five feet to the roof, she thought. Then she would shimmy over the edge at the back of the house, drop to the windowsill, leap the distance to the top of the generator, and jump to the ground. She would be in the trees before Pete ever made it to the back of the house.

The beam of light moved to the left.

Now he's crouching down . . .

Light inched up the left wall.

. . . about to duck his head under . . .

Margaret's right hand found the end of the flashlight tucked in her waistband. She was prepared to pull it out and let it drop the second his head appeared. But Treak saved her, Treak calling, "Hey, Pete, c'mere. I think you should see this."

See what? The bed that was made? The clothes in the bureau? Of course, she should have stripped the bed, hidden the clothes, gotten rid of the shoes. Even if they believed, as she had when she'd arrived, that the house was being used by vagrants, they would think differently if they found the fresh fruit she'd bought, the vegetables, the jugs of water. But she'd stashed these things in the toolshed and perhaps they wouldn't look out there.

Please don't look out there.

She followed the noise of Pete's receding footsteps. Hall. Stairs. Second floor. Then silence. The steady *drip drip drip* of water into the chimney became the persistent tick of a clock in her head. One minute passed. Two. After three minutes, she stopped counting the seconds and began to climb. Right hand, left, right foot groping, finding, pausing, left foot now. She stopped to catch her breath, to wipe her damp hands against her jeans, and heard a distant roll of thunder. The storm was moving out to sea.

She resumed climbing. Her progress seemed agonizingly slow; the opening at the top of the chimney was as elusive as the details of her life that she couldn't recall. Her left foot slipped once, knocking loose bits of brick that showered the fireplace. She froze, her heart pounding. But the beam of light didn't reappear. She heard no voices. She went on.

When her head finally poked through the hole, it seemed as though she had been inside the chimney most of her life, eating soot and dirt. Margaret pushed herself the rest of the way out and sat back on the edge of the chimney, dizzy with relief, grateful for the taste of fresh air, open space, freedom.

She placed the flashlight against her leg as she turned it on, checked the slope of the roof around her. Then she turned off the light and swung her legs over the side. She discovered that she was as surefooted as a goat, and it didn't take her long to reach a place in the roof where she could see the yard below. She flattened out on her stomach and peered down.

Two cars parked side by side: how chummy.

Waiting for them, she realized the night had turned cooler. Much cooler. She hoped there were warmer clothes somewhere in the house. She hoped she had the opportunity to go back inside the house. She hoped their bodies would just fold up like beach chairs and blow away in the next gust of wind.

The drone of their voices and the beams of their flashlights preceded their appearance. They were in no particular hurry, striding from the house to the cars with the easy gait of oppressors who knew they held most of the cards.

When Pete opened the door of his car, Margaret saw him clearly: the pale hair that brushed the collar of his shirt in back, the stylish white slacks, and a face that had once possessed the power to stop her heart. And there, Treak in her arrogant bones, her corpulent flesh, Treak sliding her fingers through her pretty hair. Margaret had once feared her as much as she had Liscomb. But no more.

As she watched them get into their respective vehicles, she realized that the only thing she feared anymore was the loss of the freedom she had gained during the last few days, however lonely and uncertain it was. No one would rob her of that again. She apparently knew something that threatened them, something they would kill her for. Information, a secret, perhaps the nature of the Lost Pleiade. She intended to find it—and then she would vindicate herself and avenge the months they had stolen from her.

Part Three

LABYRINTH

"The worldwide stories of the UFOs are . . . the symptom of a universally present psychic disposition."
            —Carl Jung,
                from *Memories, Dreams, and Reflections*

"For me, the conclusion is inescapable: They are already here."
                        —Budd Hopkins,
                            from *Missing Time*

12

(1)

When the doorbell at the lighthouse rang that morning, it was a quarter past seven on the nose. Tardiness had never been one of Bernie's faults, Aline thought.

She stood on the porch in dark tailored slacks and a red pullover sweater that looked more appropriate for Denmark in the dead of winter. Her blonde hair was partially hidden by a red kerchief tied at the back of her head; gold hoops dangled from her ears.

"Can you believe this shit, Al? An honest-to-Christ cold front and it's barely mid-October? Last night's low of forty-five broke a record set in 1956." She stepped past Aline and into the lighthouse. "It's enough to make me move to Cuba. I hope you've got coffee brewing."

"Sshh." Aline shut the door and they headed for the kitchen. "Ryan's asleep. The raucous night life at the clinic is killing him."

"Must be all those rendezvous with Jean."

"Very funny."

"That was a joke. What the hell's eating you?"

"Lack of sleep."

"No offense, but you couldn't pay me to stay alone in this place at night, not without a couple of Rottweilers for company. You really ought to consider getting a dog."

"I'm sure the skunk, the cat, and the owl would be real happy with a dog."

"Details," Bernie said with a wave of her hand, and they laughed and settled at the table with mugs of coffee. Bernie, whipping out her notepad, got right down to business. "I figure we can cover a lot of ground today if we keep to the schedule I put together."

A schedule from the woman who, before Bill Prentiss, had winced at the word. "Shoot."

"I finally got ahold of Heather Franks late yesterday afternoon."

The dead orderly's wife. "And?"

"She said we could drop by this morning before nine, when she goes to work. She's a social worker in Key West. I think she'll tell us whatever she knows, assuming she knows anything that we don't. She sounded scared."

"Of what?"

"I don't know. I didn't ask and she didn't say. When we leave there, we head over to the site where Margaret Wickerd's alleged abduction took place. At one, we call Bill. He should have heard you from the Key West corner by then about the silicon thing. You hear anything from Sam Newman?"

"Nope."

"Well, I heard from Joe Mahoney of *Saucer Slurs* fame. He called after you'd left the station yesterday afternoon. Turns out he and I went to the same elementary school in Miami, ten years apart, but what the hell, it's like a blood bond, huh? He's going to meet us at the site. He claims he's got photos of what the area looked like two days after Margaret's experience. I have the feeling he's got more than that."

"Let's hit it."

Bernie's Cherokee descended through the Tango hills with the easy certainty of a car born to these roads, this terrain. It didn't sputter from the cold, didn't stall at stoplights, didn't do any of the things Aline's aging Honda did, and yes, she was envious. She had forgotten what it was like to feel safe in a car.

These were the spoils, she thought, of marrying a doctor instead of moving in with a man who hadn't had a regular, normal job since—when? Just how long had Kincaid been a gumshoe, anyway? Fifteen years? Twenty? Well, it didn't matter. As her mother would have said, he had his good points and she wasn't so sure she'd want him to buy her a car, anyway.

"Where do you think the chief stands on this case, Al?" Bernie asked, lighting a cigarette.

"Hard to say." She wrinkled her nose as smoke drifted toward her and cracked her window, hoping Bernie would get the hint. If she did, she ignored it. "Sometimes I think he feels like we do about the clinic and other times . . ." She shrugged. "I just don't know. He's being real careful."

"Bill's spooked. I found him in his den last night looking at those X-rays he took of Liscomb's head."

"He brought them *home*?"

"Yeah. He keeps them in the safe. I guess it's better than his bringing a body home or something, but it gives me the creeps."

Aline had spent much of the last few nights afflicted with the Creeps. It was like some weird new strain of the flu that struck only after the sun had gone down. Even if you didn't believe in flying disks and little gray men, there was something unsettling about it all.

"Last night," Bernie went on, "I lay in bed for the longest time, trying to put myself in Margaret Wickerd's place. And frankly, Al, if we have to bring her in, I'm only going to do it to protect her. How do you, uh, feel about it?"

"Exactly the same."

Bernie looked relieved.

"Did you really think I'd feel otherwise?"

"No, but I figure it's best to be sure where your partner stands."

"It may not be where Gene stands."

Bernie dismissed that with a flick of her wrist. "Hell, he's not a partner. He's the boss. I don't expect to see eye to eye with the boss on much of anything."

Irreverence always came easier when you didn't need the job you had. Aline felt that sharp prick of envy again and wondered what she herself would do if it came right down to it. Would she carry out an order she believed was wrong just to keep her job or would she stand by her conviction?

The thought made her uneasy; the most she could hope for right now was that it wouldn't come to that.

(2)

Heather Franks was a small-boned, attractive woman with eyes the same lustrous black as her short, curly hair. Everything about her, from her clothes to her makeup, was as neat and precise as the rooms in which she lived. Not a woman given to hysteria, Aline thought.

They settled in an enclosed porch at the back of the house. Over cups of thick Cuban coffee, Heather talked at length about her husband's friendship with Margaret Wickerd. She made it clear right from the start that she didn't believe Margaret had killed him. "Some people you meet and you know immediately that they're capable of murder. It might take extreme conditions for that violence to manifest, but the capacity exists. Margaret isn't one of those people."

As a social worker, Heather Franks no doubt saw her share of lunatics: the bozo who bayed at a full moon; the crack mother who beat her kid and then told the doctor those bruises were from a fall down the stairs; the con with a hundred rackets. Aline decided that made her judgments about people credible enough.

"When did you meet her?" Aline asked.

"Several times at the clinic when I picked Hugh up from work, and one Saturday I ran into her and Jean at a café in the Cove. The three of us had lunch together. She was a trustee then and home for a weekend. Her husband wasn't around much during those weekends. They didn't get along, but you probably already know that."

"Was she still meeting with her abduction group?" Bernie asked.

"Erratically and always when Pete was off island. Hugh would notify Sam that she was going to be released on a particular weekend and he would pull the group together. They met here five or six times. I didn't mind, but I was worried that the clinic would find out and fire Hugh. But he felt that the group was a vital support for her and this whole field fascinated him. Then later on he became Sam and Maggie's go-between."

"In what way?" Bernie asked.

"Letters, places to meet, motels. That bothered me a lot."

"They were having an affair?" Aline exclaimed.

Heather looked surprised. "I'm sorry, I thought you knew. I assumed Jean probably knew and had told you."

Aline shook her head. "When did the affair begin?"

"I may be mistaken about this, but I think it started before she was supposedly abducted."

That changed the picture somewhat. *If* Margaret had been pregnant, the child might have been Newman's, which would explain why she hadn't rushed out to announce the news to her husband and her sister. "Did Pete know?"

"He eventually found out about it. For a while, Hugh believed that's what prompted him to commit her and what triggered his smear campaign against Sam."

A new twist on an old theme, Aline thought, and realized Newman's wife had probably known about it as well. It would explain why she'd hovered in the hall that night, eavesdropping. "Did he come to believe something else later on?"

A small frown burrowed between Heather's eyes. "Not exactly. I guess you could say his theory expanded." Although her voice remained soft, almost delicate, something new had crept into it. Fear. "You have to understand that during the last few months, Hugh became"—she paused, struggling to find the right word or phrase—"well, obsessed with the idea that Maggie was the focus of an experiment."

"An experiment," Bernie repeated.

Heather smiled and rubbed her palms over her skirt. "I know how it sounds. That was my reaction when he first brought it up. But I'm beginning to think he might have been right. He claimed that the clinic's parent organization, Whole Health, has been subsidized by the federal government for the last five or six years. I'm not sure which branch. I don't think Hugh even knew.''

"The Department of Defense?" Bernie asked.

"It could be. I just don't recall Hugh ever telling me specifically which branch.''

"How'd he find that out?" Aline asked.

"My guess is that it's somewhere in their computers. Hugh was pretty good with computers, and on the night shift, he had access to most of the clinic.''

"Is that all he said about it?" Aline asked.

"Pretty much. Whenever I questioned him, he refused to talk about it. He said I was better off not knowing anything. We had some terrible arguments over it. We were married nine years and up until then we'd shared everything.'' Her voice cracked a little and she paused and sipped her coffee. When she'd regained her composure, she went on.

"A couple of months ago, he started acting very . . . well, paranoid, that's the only way I can describe it. If I'd already left for work in the morning when he got home, he'd call me to make sure I'd gotten there okay. He had a security system installed in the house. And he bought a gun and insisted I learn how to use it.

"When he was working days and we were home together in the evening, he was real jumpy. He refused to answer the phone unless the machine got it first and he could identify the caller. He didn't sleep much. One night I woke up and found him out in the yard, digging under that tree.'' She motioned toward the huge mango tree in the backyard. "When I questioned him about it, he blew up and accused me of spying on him. The next night he was out there again, digging up whatever he'd buried.''

"He never told you what it was?" Bernie asked.

"No. But yesterday afternoon I was cleaning out his drawers and I found a key that looked like it might fit a safe-deposit box. So I went over to Island Bank and sure enough, he had a box. I found a will and some savings bonds and this." She pulled a folded envelope from her sweater pocket and slipped out a sheet of paper that had obviously been stapled to something else at one time. Typed in caps at the top of the sheet was THE LOST PLEIADE and below it was a list:

> - the hidden one
> - copy DOD memo, 02/87
> - nosebleeds: liscomb/maggie
>   (connection?)
> - R. Ricardo

"Who's R. Ricardo?" Bernie asked.

Heather Franks worried her lower lip. "All I know is that there's a guy who runs a charter fishing outfit down at the docks who knows something. He came by the house one night after I'd gone to bed and I overheard him and Hugh talking. The only thing Hugh would tell me about him was that his name was Ricky Ricardo."

Hey, that would stand up well in court, Aline thought. "What was stapled to this?"

"I don't know. That's all I found."

"Did Hugh have a copy of this Department of Defense memo?"

"No. Ricky Ricardo was supposed to get it for him." She nervously fingered a button on her red cardigan. "I've gotten three threatening calls since Hugh's death. It's always the same voice, a man's. He whispers. He . . . he says he wants back what Hugh took from him. And last night, after I talked to you, Detective Bernelli, I ran into Tango for some groceries and I was followed by a gray van."

Kincaid's men in black had been in a gray van. "It followed you to and from the store?"

She nodded. "It was parked at the back of the lot when I came out of the store. I never got a glimpse of the driver, and once I was inside the house, there was no sign of it."

Aline scribbled her home number and Bernie's at the bottom of her business card. "If you get any more calls, Mrs.

Franks, or see the van again, don't hesitate to call one of us."

"I'm not going to be here. My sister and I are flying up north tonight to see Hugh's family. I'll be gone a couple of weeks." She gave them a number where she could be reached and they left a few minutes later.

"The chief isn't going to go for this DOD connection without proof," Bernie said once they were in the Cherokee.

"I know." Aline smoothed the sheet of paper open against her leg and wondered if the silicon sliver Prentiss had retrieved from Liscomb's nostril would cause nosebleeds. "Right now, we don't even have just cause for getting a subpoena for their computer records."

Bernie lit a cigarette and cracked open her window. "I'm liking this less and less."

"Maybe we're wrong, Bernie. Maybe Margaret killed Hugh and Liscomb in a panic over the impending treatment. And since she was panicked, maybe Hugh's murder was an accident. Maybe she didn't realize what she was doing. Maybe she's psychotic. Maybe nothing's going on at that clinic. Christ, what the hell do we know?"

"I know you don't really believe that."

"No. But let's face it, our best lead in there is a nut who chopped up her stepfather. That's depressing."

"Aline, our best lead in there is Ryan."

"Who isn't a blabbermouth by any stretch of the imagination."

Bernie laughed. "Well, maybe not, but I think it's an encouraging sign that Frederick wanted him in there."

"The chief was just covering his ass."

And whose ass was Kincaid covering?

In their lives before she and Kincaid had bought the lighthouse, there were times when they'd worked the same case from different angles and she hadn't had the vaguest notion what he was up to. But that sort of separation wasn't as easy when your toothbrushes hung side by side and your underwear ended up in the same washer.

Though the possibility still existed that she might be compromised by knowing too much about some of the illegal tactics Kincaid employed, she didn't worry about it to the extent she once had. Seven years in law enforcement had taught her that sometimes it was necessary to bend the rules to find what you needed so that the person you were after didn't walk. Because if he walked, then sooner or later you would run into him again. Gene Frederick knew it as well as anyone and that was the real reason he kept hiring Kincaid.

Get the answers, Ryan. I don't care how you do it. Just don't tell me about it.

See no evil, hear no evil, speak no evil, and amen.

(3)

They left the highway just outside of Pirate's Cove and followed a narrow road down the north slope of the island. They passed the old turnoff for Crystal Cavern, passed old picnic tables, old campgrounds. Old, it was all old, and she was getting there as well.

The pavement didn't end so much as it simply gave away, as if the years of neglect had robbed it of the will to persevere. Pines flourished at either side, serrating the absolute blue of the sky like the mandibles of a giant jaw. They thinned gradually until, at sea level, they vanished altogether and the first rounded curves of the mangroves appeared.

The trees proliferated in the shoals of the marsh like giant weeds, their exuberant green leaves glistening in the morning light. Their strange, curved roots, stained red from the tannic acid in the water, looked like cages made of discolored bone worn smooth by time. Nowhere did the island seem more wild, more primal, to Aline than it did right here. It was as if the clock had stopped ticking when the pines disappeared and this entire marsh had existed unchanged for millennia.

Weeds and brush marched steadily inward, claiming more and more of the road until it was barely wide enough for one car. The abundance of rain this year had washed away much of the surface gravel that had elevated the road above the marsh, and in sections it dipped steeply into huge potholes. Nature had made it clear that the road was an intruder here.

Since the water was warmer than the air, tendrils of fog curled over it like steam rising from the surface of some giant teacup. Aline lowered her window, welcoming the warmer air. The rich, loamy scent was straight out of her childhood, lifted from those long Saturdays when she and Prentiss had explored the marsh in an old canoe.

Secret expeditions to look for dinosaurs, swamp monsters, lost treasures. Picnics on a spit of land hidden by saw grass, alligators sliding through twilit waters, blue herons lifting from treetops. She remembered all the magic and mystery of this place in one magnificent moment that collapsed when the road dipped and curved and she saw a car speeding toward them, a dark bullet just short of impact.

Bernie swerved and slammed on the brakes. Aline snapped forward then backward, as though her body were made of rubber. ''That asshole,'' Bernie spat, and leaped out of the car before Aline had even extricated herself from her seat belt. By the time she reached the black Impala that was angled with its nose inches from the marsh, Bernie and the driver were leaning against the back fender, yukking it up.

This guy had to be Joe Mahoney. He looked like an alien in disguise: pale face, bulging, thyroid eyes, all bones and sharp angles. Although his hair was white, his face was relatively unlined, except at the corners of his eyes where creases burst against the skin. He wore faded jeans, a flannel shirt, running shoes that had long since passed their prime, and a thin windbreaker with Mickey Mouse stitched on one of the pockets.

''Hi, hi, so nice to meet you,'' he said when Bernie introduced them, and pumped Aline's arm as if he hoped to draw water from it. ''Sorry about that.'' He gestured vaguely toward the Cherokee. ''I've got a heavy foot. There's hardly ever any traffic out here and I never expected you ladies would be early." His small dark eyes flicked to Bernie. "The spot's just up the road a piece."

Bernie retrieved the camera and some other equipment from the Cherokee while Mahoney got a briefcase from his Impala that was as worn as his running shoes. He swung it as they walked, swung it like a kid with a lunchbox, and chattered nonstop about the weather, the glades, and the good ole days before every jerk in the universe decided to become a UFO investigator. Were they familiar with the literature? he asked. Had they followed the controversies about MJ-12? About abductions? Had either of them ever had a sighting? No? Good, good, skeptics were so much more reasonable about things.

Listening to him wore her out and during much of the walk to the base of the hill Aline watched their shadows, three little pigs moving through the cool sunlight toward the lair of the big bad wolf. She noticed things about Mahoney, how his eyes kept scanning the sky, that he had feet like a clown that were much too large for the rest of him, that the laces on his running shoes were red, like the laces on the shoe Kincaid had pulled from the foot of the lighthouse intruder.

You wear a size nine and a half, E width, Mahoney? You interested in Margaret's medical records? Was there anyone on this island who *wasn't* interested?

At the base of the hill, the road widened and hammocks of dry land preceded the encroachment of the marsh. Mahoney led them through brush and under shawls of Spanish moss that hung from the branches of gumbo-limbo trees. He stopped in a circular area where the ground was discolored and scarred, with a scarcity of growth.

"Right here," Mahoney said. "This is where Margaret saw the light. You can see for yourself that the soil is a light grayish brown, compared to the rich black soil just beyond the burned area. I was here two days after her experience and everything within several feet of the area had already withered. Now it's eight months later and you can see for yourselves that hardly anything's growing here."

He set down his briefcase and scooped up a handful of the

grayish soil. "This soil is dry. It feels more like gravel. The blacker soil is soft, pliable, loamy. I collected samples of both and had them analyzed." He let the soil pour through his fingers, brushed his hands together. "Crystallographic and spectrographic analysis didn't show any significant difference between the two. But the blacker soil had to be heated to eight hundred degrees Fahrenheit before it was the same color as the gray stuff. That gives you some idea of the tremendous energy that was emitted here. By something."

Something. Yes, that was the heart of it, wasn't it? Something. Why couldn't someone she met just come out and say fine, okay, a spaceship did this. An alien craft. She wanted to hear from someone credible who had drawn a conclusion. *If you believe ETs did this, great. Tell me about it, guy. I promise I won't laugh.*

Aline crouched at the edge of the burned area and dug her fingers into the soil on either side of her. Mahoney was right about the differences in texture between the two.

"There's also an absence of insect life here," Mahoney went on. "And yet right here"—he moved under an overhang of branches in the unaffected area—"is an anthill."

She estimated that the circle had a radius of eight or nine feet. Not very big. Not as big as she imagined a disk would be. How about a hundred feet? Two hundred? Spielberg's vision. But just what was Spielberg's vision? Richard Dreyfuss acting like a man possessed in *Close Encounters*? Or some cute little alien bombed out of his mind in *E.T.*?

"How'd you hear about this so soon after it happened?" Aline asked.

"From Sam Newman. We came out here together that morning."

"Who told him?"

"Margaret."

"Why would she go to him?" *C'mon, Mahoney, spell it out for me.*

"Pete wasn't on the island and she knew Sam would at least take her seriously."

"Considering the bad blood between the two men, Mr. Mahoney, I find it odd that Margaret knew Sam at all."

"They were friends. Margaret had done some illustrations for one of Sam's books."

"So you didn't know they were having an affair, Mr. Mahoney?"

His brows lifted into odd, bushy peaks; smoke drifted from his nostrils. He reminded Aline of some odd creature from a Dr. Seuss book. "It's news to me. But it's not too surprising. I never really understood how she and Pete had gotten together in the first place."

"So Sam never discussed their relationship with you?" Bernie asked.

"No way. Sam keeps his personal life totally separate from everything else. At least with me."

"What's your opinion about what Margaret supposedly experienced?" Aline finally asked.

Mahoney lifted his right foot, crushed his cigarette against the sole of his shoe, then began to shred it. His smile as he looked up was almost sad. "Look, I've been involved in this field for twenty-three years. I've investigated cases that had all the markings of the real McCoy but turned out to be as phony as Monopoly money.

"I've interviewed dozens of people who've supposedly had encounters. I've visited sites in forty-two states and six foreign countries. I've seen classified government documents. I've talked to military people who swear they saw the crashed disk in Roswell, New Mexico. And you know what? The only thing I've decided is that *something*'s going on, but damned if I know what it is.

"Maybe it's a psychological aberration. Maybe it has to do with dimensions of reality we don't know anything about yet. Maybe it's extraterrestrial. Maybe it's some incredibly complex disinformation campaign by the government. Maybe what we're seeing is the evolution of a mythology. Maybe all or none of the above."

He shrugged and lit another cigarette and glanced skyward again. So did Bernie. So did Aline. She almost expected to see a disk the size of a football field hovering against the blue. But there were only clouds and, more distantly, a jet headed south from Miami. *I'm losing it.*

"Look," Mahoney went on. "All I know is that the ground here was baked and Margaret experienced something that Pete believed was a threat to his livelihood as a debunker and that's why he committed her. Beyond that, ladies, it's all up for grabs."

He snapped open his briefcase and removed a dozen 8 × 10 photographs of the burned area. He said they'd been taken over a series of months and showed the progressive destruction of the vegetation around the burned area. He gave Aline and Bernie a duplicate set of the photos. Aline asked if Newman had copies and Mahoney shook his head.

"He has his own." He was crouched in front of his briefcase again, rummaging through it. Aline, who was standing, gazed down at the bald spot at the back of his head, a small, singular UFO as smooth as bone. Definitely losing it, she thought.

"Is he writing about Margaret's experience?"

"Probably. It's what he does for a living."

"How about you? Does this go into your next newsletter?"

"Like it is now?" He laughed. "No way. *Saucer Slurs* is informal, okay? Lots of gossip, lots of rumors. But if there's a conclusion, a spacecraft, a dead ET . . . Well, that'd change the picture."

"So why're you so interested in Margaret Wickerd's medical records?" Aline blurted out.

His eyes narrowed. "Who said I was?"

"Just a lucky guess, Mr. Mahoney." She decided to let it pass, for now. But Mahoney didn't.

"Look, the only reason I might be interested in her records is to find out just how big a lie Pete perpetrated."

Aline changed the subject. "Do you know anything about the Pleiades drawings?"

He stood with two large envelopes in his hand and smiled. He held out the 11 × 14 envelope. "You must read minds,

Detective Scott. That's what these are. Drawings Margaret made after one of her hypnotic regressions. They're quite evocative.''

Evocative was the wrong adjective, Aline thought as she and Bernie leafed through them. The drawings that Margaret had rendered with such bold, certain strokes were grotesque, fascinating, compelling, strangely frightening. These faces, these figures, weren't from the cover of *Communion*; it was as if they'd been wrenched from the primal soup of man's distant past—or from the ruin of a devastated future.

''What I found particularly interesting about the adult figures is that they don't resemble any of the popular depictions. I've seen drawings of these figures maybe a dozen times and only within the last four or five years and only associated with cases that haven't been media-blitzed.''

''Is that significant?'' Aline asked.

The question seemed to surprise him. ''You bet it is. To my way of thinking, it means we're seeing the emergence of a new alien archetype or a clever campaign to inject new blood into an old controversy or hell, maybe a new species of ETs has suddenly become very interested in Earth. At any rate, it makes my job more interesting.'' He grinned and from the second envelope brought out two sheets of paper. ''But what's really fascinating is that this particular being was apparently around as long as five and a half years ago.''

He handed the sheets to Aline. One was a photocopy of a drawing that was nearly a duplicate of the adult figures Margaret had drawn. The other was a photocopy of a memo on Department of Defense stationery, dated February 4, 1987, and stamped RECEIVED a day later.

To: All committee members
From: Jim Booth

As per our conversation, put Project Lost Pleiade into effect immediately. Contact V. Liscomb about time frame. Submit list of media-visible investigators in field and possible locations, three or four to begin with, widely separated geographically and economically.

We've got about six million earmarked for the first year and if this goes the way I'm hoping, money will be the least of our worries. I'm looking at this as a long-term project—five years to launch, ten years max for results to manifest. Evan Nate will handle the fine details. Let's get moving. (See enclosures.)

"Who're Jim Booth and Evan Nate and what committee is he talking about?" Bernie asked.

Mahoney grinned and held up his index finger, as if testing the direction of the wind. "Interesting question, Claudia. I've got no idea who Booth is, but Nate is career air force, now stationed at Homestead. He was a decorated pilot in Vietnam, headed an intelligence center somewhere here in the keys, and rumors say he was also in charge of something called Project Bluebolt. Its purpose was supposedly the study of gravity and antigravity propulsion."

"How'd you get a copy of this?" Bernie asked.

"Four months or so ago, a guy showed up at my door one morning and asked if I was Joe Mahoney who published *Saucer Slurs*. Then he said he had something I might be able to use in the newsletter and was I interested?" Mahoney lit his umpteenth cigarette, snapped his briefcase shut, and stood again. "I asked him what it concerned and he said, 'Margaret Wickerd.' "

"Did this guy tell you his name?" Aline asked.

Mahoney smiled. "Yeah. That's the funny part. He said his name was Ricky Ricardo."

13

The Super Cub weaved across the tarmac like a drunk. "Rudder pedals, not the yoke," Kincaid snapped.

Ferret jerked his feet back from the rudder pedals and crossed his arms stubbornly at his chest. "It's unnatural to steer with your feet, Ryan."

Kincaid repressed a snide remark and took over, steering the Cub toward the tie-down area. They didn't speak as the Cub rolled onto the grassy tie-down area or as they secured the plane and walked toward the terminal. The last sixty minutes had been quite possibly the worst hour he'd ever spent in a plane. Teaching a friend to fly headed his list of Things to Avoid and he regretted having made an exception for Ferret.

Just overhead a tired Cessna slipped into the landing pattern dragging an advertising banner for Platinum's, a strip joint on the boardwalk. It would land, Kincaid thought, the banner would be removed and replaced with another. Then the Cessna would take off again, fly up and down the beach again, return to the terminal again. The pilot would change from week to week, the slogan on the banner would change, the weather would change. But the plane would continue to take off and fly and land, over and over until its metal corroded or its engine wore out. In the end, its life was as finite as his own. There was a moral in this about friendship and time, but he didn't want to think about it right now.

"Flying isn't going to work out for me, Ryan. I can't relax in a tin can at five thousand feet."

"You'd do better with another instructor."

"No, I don't think so."

"And it would help if you didn't just sit there and think about dying."

Ferret smoothed a hand over his black hair. "I don't do that, Ryan."

"Right."

"I don't."

"Okay, you don't."

They reached the terminal building. "How about some coffee?" Ferret asked.

"No, thanks. If you've got your logbook handy, I'll sign off for today's lesson."

Ferret handed over the logbook. "You're absolutely right, Ryan. I sit there and think about the plane nosediving through all that blue and see myself flattened back against the seat, watching the ground rush toward me. But this was only my third lesson. It takes some getting used to."

It was the closest thing to an apology that he was likely to hear from Ferret. He handed him the logbook. "Look, let's try two more lessons. If you don't feel any more comfortable by then, we'll shelve it."

Ferret flashed his rodent grin. "Thanks, I appreciate it. Your patience is admirable, Ryan. If I were you, I would have pushed me out of the plane."

"I considered it."

The little man laughed and the tension between them broke. "Yeah, I bet you did. You been to bed since you got off work?"

"A couple of hours. Why?"

"You don't get a night off?"

"Not till Sunday. You have something in mind?"

They started toward the parking lot. "Well, it's like this, Ryan. There're ten garages on Tango, counting mine, and the owners all know one another. So I sent Bino out on a scouting expedition for a gray Ford van with black stripes around the middle and a black and white license plate. Turns out that a buddy of mine at Jiffy Lube over in the Cove did an oil change on a van like that a couple weeks back. It was driven by a guy named Paul Sapizzo. The name struck a bell with Bino and he checked it out. Two years ago Sapizzo was busted for armed robbery in Palm Beach and got eight to ten, with a mandatory three for the weapon. Up until six months ago he was at Raiford.''

"And he only did eighteen months? How? Was he pardoned?"

"Nope. But the real question, Ryan, is what's he doing driving a van with federal plates registered to a colonel at Homestead Air Force Base?"

"You have an answer or is this Twenty Questions?"

"I have an address and figured we could dig up the answer."

Kincaid grinned. "I'll drive."

(2)

The Tango docks occupied a mile-long strip on the southwest side of the island. There were three warehouses, two seafood shops, a fishing pier with a small restaurant, a small marina for the pleasure-fishing and charter vessels, and two other piers strictly for unloading the six hundred pounds of fish that were brought in weekly. Even if you didn't know where the docks were, Aline thought, you could find them just by the odor.

The stink of fish didn't simply hang in the air; it clung to it, defining it, drawing the gulls and pelicans that swooped and shrieked overhead. Sandpipers hopped along the docks, and crows as black and shiny as coal cawed from perches on the wooden posts. Aline and Bernie passed heaps of silvery fish writhing on the docks for air, dying in the cool sunlight. Stray cats as skinny as string beans darted in and out of shadows. Men shouted in Spanish from open warehouse doors, reggae and salsa pumped from unseen radios, coils of rope lay against the docks like serpents.

Aline realized they were the only women in sight and it made her distinctly uncomfortable. It was as if they'd stumbled into a third-world country dressed in transparent short shorts and halter tops. She glanced at Bernie; her eyes were fixed straight ahead and she began to walk much faster, swinging her arms like a woman on a six-mile walkathon.

Aline sped up, too, puzzled by the sharp bursts of fear that hurried her along. After all, it was broad daylight. The marina was just ahead; she could see the little building, the tall, fancy boats, even a few tourists tossing food to the gulls. She looked back, almost expecting to see a throng of shirtless men following them, muscles rippling under their darkly tanned skins. But the path they had cut through the crowd was now closed off by nets and fish and the business of the sea. No one was shadowing them.

It occurred to her that this vague sense of peril, this weird uneasiness, didn't have anything to do with the men on the dock. It had been dogging her since this whole thing had started and had worsened since she'd seen Margaret Wickerd's drawings. Those images didn't just linger in her mind. They roamed. They haunted. They bumped up against atavistic fears of loss, of darkness, of the vast arena of the unknown. They made her feel small and stupid. She felt as if she'd lived her nearly forty years with blinders on, with an acute case of myopia, seeing only what fit into her tidy view of the universe.

Margaret believed she had seen these figures. Believed they had poked and prodded at her aboard some luminous sphere. But perhaps those figures and their little gray relatives with the black, wraparound eyes were the internal made manifest through some weird alchemy. Archetypal figures, a new species of demons or angels, the unsung players of an emerging religion. Or perhaps those grotesque and fascinating creatures were symptomatic of a mass derangement, an epidemic, an AIDS of the mind.

She glanced toward the sky and watched a gull in a freefall toward the water, spinning earthward against all the blue. A UFO in disguise, she thought, and turned away when Bernie called her name. They were in front of a building with a sign out front that read:

TANGO CHARTERS
INQUIRE INSIDE

Bernie, frowning slightly, was holding the door open. "You okay?"

"The stink of the fish is getting to me."

The shop seemed to carry everything related to the sea except for fish. Boat hardware, life rafts and preservers, freeze-dried food, ten-gallon drums, nautical books and charts, knapsacks and compasses. Business was surprisingly brisk and they had to wait several minutes at the desk before a young kid with a pierced ear and an island tan came over and asked if he could help them with something. His name tag read: HELLO, I'M GERALD.

"We're looking for a man named Ricky who runs a charter service here on the docks," Bernie said. "Know where we can find him?"

The kid's eyes connected briefly with Bernie's, darted to Aline's, then flickered away, restless flies in search of tastier morsels. "Nope."

He started to move away, but Aline snapped, "Hold on, Gerald," and slapped down her badge. "The sign outside says charters. Now where can we find Ricky Ricardo?"

"On the reruns of *I Love Lucy*?" He grinned as he said it, but when neither Aline nor Bernie laughed, the grin collapsed. "You can usually find him in slip number seven out there on the docks, but I haven't seen him in a while."

"Does he have a charter outfit?" Bernie asked.

"Uh, yes, ma'am. Morales Charters. You'll see the sign right out there. Slip seven, like I said."

"Morales?" Aline said. "Who's Morales? We're talking about Ricky Ricardo."

Gerald looked mighty uneasy now. "That's his, uh, real name. Ricardo Morales. He owns this shop, okay? And all I know is that when someone comes in here asking for Ricky, I'm supposed to say he's not here."

"Why's that, Gerald?"

"I don't know."

"So quite a few people come around asking for Ricky Ricardo?"

"No, ma'am, not really."

"How many have come around in . . . oh, say the last six or eight months, Gerald?"

He ran the back of his hand over his mouth; his eyes were now glued to the surface of the counter. "Well, there was a woman who came by a couple of times, but I don't know her name. Then there was this guy, Hugh Franks. Last time I saw him was ten days, two weeks ago, something like that. Mr. Morales was here that day and he and Mr. Franks went out on the boat for a while."

"What'd the woman look like?" Bernie asked.

Gerald shook his head. "I was just closing up that night, it was raining, all the lights on the dock were off, and I didn't get a good look at her."

"What's Mr. Morales's address?"

"I don't know."

"Don't know or aren't saying?" Aline shot back.

"Don't know. I swear. If there's a problem here at the store, I just leave him a note. Once a week or so he drops by, tends to business, then he's gone again."

"When's he supposed to drop by again?"

"He's overdue. I figure anytime now."

Aline pressed her business card into his hand. "Make sure he gets this, Gerald, and tell him if he doesn't give me a call, I'll be back with a warrant."

"Sure thing." He turned the card between his fingers. "I'll tell him."

"Good. Because I'm holding you responsible, Gerald. As soon as you see Morales again, call me."

"No problem."

They walked out to the marina pier, where slip number seven was as empty as a plundered tomb. The sign for Morales Charters announced that charters were available by the hour, the day, the week, the month. As they stood there with a breeze blowing the stink of fish their way, Bernie said, "You think the woman was Nina Treak?"

"Yeah."

"But what's the connection?"

"Heads we ask the lady herself." Aline dug a quarter out of her wallet and flipped it.

Heads it was.

(3)

The gray van seemed benign in the light of day. Coated in a skin of dust that nearly obscured its smoky windows, it was parked in the driveway of a lone farmhouse in the Tango hills.

From their vantage point on a wooded rise on the other side of the dirt road, Kincaid could see the citrus grove behind the house. It covered ten or fifteen acres and most of the trees were thick with fruit. Tall sprinklers rose between the trees every ten yards or so.

The place looked well tended: the lawn had been cut recently, the hibiscus hedges that bordered the house had been trimmed as neatly as a poodle, the sidewalk boasted a Chatahoochee finish. Off to the right was a screen that covered a patio and a swimming pool. To the left was a two-car garage with stairs at the side that led to what might be an apartment above it.

"Who owns the house?" Kincaid asked, leaning back against the trunk of the nearest pine.

"Colonel Nate. Sapizzo is apparently taking care of the

place. Bino saw him out here yesterday fixing sprinkler heads in the yard and patching up the screen.''

''Was he here alone?''

''Bino never saw anyone else. Around five, he came down those stairs at the side of the garage and split. Bino followed him to the Moose, where he met two other guys. When they stopped at a gas station, they went into the restroom one at a time and came out wearing dark clothes. Around dusk, he tailed them to a place in a middle-class neighborhood outside the Cove. This morning he went by the house to see if he could find out who lives there. The names on the box were Hugh and Heather Franks.''

''Got any idea how long he's been here?''

Ferret sat back on his heels in the grass. ''Yeah. The clerk at the garden shop just down the road runs at the mouth for fifty bucks a shot. He says Sapizzo started shopping there five or six months ago, which would make it around the same time he got sprung from Raiford. He charges whatever he needs to the colonel's account. The colonel and his wife only come out here on holidays. The grove is for his retirement. That information is courtesy of the clerk, so take it for what it's worth.''

''You know anything about this colonel?''

''Nope. Most of my contacts end at the gates of the military. But I'm working on it, Ryan.''

Kincaid picked up his binoculars from the ground and scanned the front of the house. Through one of the tall, arched windows he could see a slice of pine floor, the corner of a throw rug, a rattan coffee table, and a cushion of a rattan couch.

A man in jeans and a workshirt came around the side of the house pushing a lawn mower. He was about five foot ten, lean and sinewy, with short hair as black as boot polish. Even minus the black clothes and the hat, Kincaid recognized him. ''That's him.'' He passed Ferret the binoculars.

They watched him for fifteen or twenty minutes as he weeded and fertilized the lawn. He dug up a dying lemon tree, filled in the hole with some sod, but didn't have enough to finish the job. He crumpled the empty bag and tossed it on the porch, then got in the van and took off.

"How far is it to the gardening center, Ferret?"

"Far enough." He was already on his feet, making his way down the slope, and Kincaid sprinted after him.

Sapizzo had locked the house, but Kincaid found an open window in the utility room at the back. He popped off the screen and, once he was in, replaced it and moved quickly through the house while Ferret stood watch on the porch.

The air inside was still and cool. Sunlight streamed through the numerous tall windows. The furniture was either rattan or solid pine, with cushions that were the rich pastels of tropical fruit. There was a fireplace. A baby-grand Steinway. Expensive electronic equipment. A computerized security system. Gracious holiday living, Kincaid thought, and went into the paneled den.

A search of the magnificent rolltop desk yielded nothing of interest. He scanned the shelves of books. Military tomes far outnumbered any other single type, but otherwise the collection was about as eclectic as you could get outside of the public library. The filing cabinet contained old tax returns, family photos awaiting an album, little else.

He moved on through the house, noting that the computerized security system was backed up by the usual steel pins in the sliding glass doors and windows. There were lengths of wood to fit into the tracks of the glass doors so they couldn't be slid open if the pins were knocked free. In another home, such security consciousness would have prompted Kincaid to believe there was something more valuable in the house than expensive furnishings. But Nate was probably a military lifer and that changed all the rules.

He opened the closet. The wardrobe was minimal, with a distinct preference for uniforms and casual wear, laid-back island clothes. But at the back were three black suits, three pairs of black shoes, and three wide-brimmed black hats on one of the shelves.

Ferret's whistle cut through the silence like a blade, a warning that a car was coming. By the time Kincaid reached the front porch, the little man was halfway across the yard, his short arms pumping at his sides. Kincaid didn't hear or see a car, but he didn't doubt that Ferret had.

They scrambled up the hill and vanished into the trees just as a mail truck appeared. Right behind it was Sapizzo's gray van.

(4)

On this cool and sunny Friday afternoon, the grounds of the clinic weren't reminiscent of a religious cloister or a Gothic-novel locale. Today the place resembled the campus of an exclusive private school. People were out walking, riding bikes, playing volleyball, visiting with family and friends. The doors of the half-dozen buildings were thrown open to the beautiful weather. It was as if the clinic itself possessed some strange capacity for disguise, Aline thought.

An orderly directed them to the clinic gym, where Nina Treak was walking the treadmill and looked to be on the verge of cardiac arrest. She wore navy blue sweats and had a towel draped around her shoulders. Perspiration poured down the sides of her face. She didn't bother to disguise her obvious displeasure at seeing them.

"Couldn't this . . . have waited, ladies?"

When she breathed, it sounded like air being suctioned through a tunnel. "We won't take much of your time, Dr. Treak," said Aline. "We just want to ask you a couple more questions about Margaret."

She kept walking, hands on the railing on either side of the treadmill, a smug little smile altering the shape of her mouth. "I guess you haven't spoken to Mr. Jones yet."

"Jones?"

"Special Agent John Jones. In fact, I'll ring him for you." She stopped the treadmill and stepped down, wiping her face with the towel, then went over to the phone at the front counter.

"FBI?" Bernie whispered. "Since when are the goddamn feds involved in this?"

"Call Gene from a pay phone, Bernie, and find out what's going on. I'll meet you outside."

"Right."

She hurried off and Aline walked over to the counter, waiting for Treak to get off the phone. "Mr. Jones will meet you in the lobby," she said as she hung up. "Now, if you'll excuse me, I've got another ten minutes on the treadmill. Got to keep the heart and lungs pumping, you know."

"Actually, I have a question about a project you and Dr. Liscomb conducted at the University of Miami a few years back. The one about stemming aggression in violent criminals?"

Impatient now, Treak shifted her weight from one foot to the other. "What about it?"

"Dr. Liscomb was still a consultant to the Department of Defense at the time, right?"

"He was in private practice, Detective Scott. Excuse me," she said, and walked off toward the treadmill.

(5)

Special Agent Jones was dressed like a fed (dark suit and tie), wore his curly blonde hair like a fed (short short short), and spoke like a fed ("Nice to meet you, ma'am"). But he had the rugged, tanned face of a construction worker or a sailor and his body had a lean toughness to it that suggested a diet of raw spinach.

Once he'd shown her his badge, he got right to the point. "The Bureau will be handling this case from now on. Chief Frederick knows about it. I spent two hours with him this morning. So I suggest you speak to him, Detective Scott."

"Since when does the FBI butt in on local homicide investigations?"

"We're not butting in, ma'am." His polite smile deepened the creases at the corners of his eyes, giving him a somewhat sinister look. "We're taking over."

A precise man, this Jones. "On what grounds?"

"I'm just following orders, ma'am."

"Yeah, so do hit men."

His smile faded and something hard and implacable came into his eyes. This was not a man she would choose to meet on a lonely road at night. "I think you'd better make that call to headquarters, Detective Scott. There's a pay phone right out there." He pointed through the open doors, where Bernie was leaning against the Cherokee, smoking. "From now on, the clinic is off limits to your department."

"I don't take my orders from you, Jones," Aline snapped, and brushed past him.

Bernie was already inside the Cherokee when she reached it. "The coroner's office in Key West was broken into last night and the silicon sliver was stolen," she said without preface. "And that's only for starters, Al. The Tango PD struck out and the feds are up to bat with the bases loaded."

14

Margaret had found the key ring yesterday, in an aluminum box labeled TEA that was pushed to the back of a pantry shelf. It was shaped like a frog and had four keys on it. One was obviously a house key; the second looked as though it might also fit a door, but it was smaller, well worn; the third had the number 33 engraved on it and she didn't have any idea what it fit; the fourth was a car key.

Now, like yesterday, she studied the keys as she sat on the front step and waited for them to yield their secrets. A chilly breeze blew through the trees, fragmenting the sunlight that glinted from the metal. What car did this one fit? Whose car? Where was it? Why was the key here?

When she posed these questions in the deepest silence of her own mind, she could feel the answer moving toward her with the inexorable slowness of a heavy liquid. But it didn't reach her and she couldn't seize it. Not yet. She had learned, though, that if she had patience and prodded her memories gently, as she imagined the elderly often did, they sometimes returned to her whole, pristine, in great blocks of time. Then she had only to fit the blocks into the rest of her life, so that there appeared to be a sequence, January through March of this year, for instance, or June to September.

Sometimes, a certain odor released these blocks of memories. The scent of jasmine tea, which she'd discovered yesterday with the keys, had unearthed several scenes. In one,

Hugh Franks had pressed this key ring into her hand and whispered: *hide it*. In another, she and Sam Newman had sipped tea and toasted marshmallows in the fireplace in the front room. And in still another she had been in Treak's office on a hot afternoon when the air-conditioning at the clinic was on the blink.

Draw me a picture of what you saw that night, Margaret. And there was Treak's plump face, weirdly distorted in her memory as if seen through a beveled mirror or the fish-eye lens of a camera, her outstretched hand offering a drawing pad and a sharpened pencil with number-two lead. *Show me, Margaret.*

And, for a moment, she'd been tempted. The muscles in her hand had ached to take the pad, the pencil. The nerves in her fingers had shrieked to sketch, to draw, to render the geography of her memory in the most minute detail. But in the end she'd told Treak that she no longer knew how to draw.

Margaret set the keys down and picked up the small drawing pad and piece of charcoal she'd found in a kitchen drawer. She imagined herself walking in here from the highway and began to sketch what she would see from that perspective. The trees, the precipitous dips in the dirt road, the way it narrowed until it simply ended, and then the house. To the left of the house was a car partially shrouded in Spanish moss. She drew the back fender, the rear wheels, then stopped.

What color was the car? What make?

She shut her eyes. A mental hand pulled streamers of moss from the roof, the hood, the windows. She opened her eyes, stared at the page, and her physical hand moved the charcoal this way and that, faster and faster. The car emerged from the sea of her forgotten memories and took shape on the page. She finally held it at arm's length, studying it, and suddenly laughed.

The memory. The memory was there, somewhat fragmented and tarnished, but it existed.

The car was a Beetle, a VW Beetle, Woody Allen's find in *Sleeper*, the miracle car that always started. She'd bought it for six hundred bucks from a college student in Miami. She'd had it refurbished—rebuilt engine, new upholstery, a spiffy new paint job—then had zipped all over the island in it. Yes, it had always started, and yes, it had proven more dependable than most people she knew.

Pete, she recalled, had hated it, called it undignified, and bought her a BMW. But the Beamer had made her feel as though she should be wearing silks, gold, and diamonds when she was driving it. Inside the Beamer, she became Mrs. Wickerd; in the VW, she was Margaret Ames, her maiden name, the name that graced her illustrations. Which was, of course, why Pete had hated the VW.

But that night in the glades, she'd been driving the Beamer, and afterward, she refused to get in it again, so Pete had sold it and his own car and bought an identical pair of Mazda Miatas. *Be like me, Maggie*, he'd seemed to be saying. *Be like me*. She'd told him she didn't want the car; he'd replied that she was being *irrational*.

The word was important. Despite his preliminary investigation, despite his assurances that he believed her, *irrational* was the word he used in his worst moments. Her fears were *irrational*; her behavior was *irrational*; the things she said were *irrational*; her belief about what had happened to her was *irrational*; her attachment to the VW was *irrational*.

During those weeks and months, the car had become the symbol of her old self, a self that had diminished rapidly under Pete's insidious attacks. She had been afraid he would sell the car or abandon it somewhere or damage it, thus robbing her of what had become her most important symbol. So during a week that Pete was away, she'd rented a storage space on the outskirts of the Cove and stashed it there. Stall 33, the number on the small key.

She had also filed for divorce.

Then he'd returned to new locks on the doors and his belongings strewn across the front yard. He had made a scene and she'd gone outside with his hunting shotgun and told him to get the hell off her property. The cops had been called and she'd been hauled off like yesterday's garbage.

And what happened to my divorce petition?

The question hung in a corner of her mind like an old cobweb; she didn't know the answer and decided it wasn't important right now. She thought about the car instead, about driving it during those weekends when she was a trustee to meet Sam here or at motels, meetings that Hugh had often arranged. She remembered the softness of Sam's hands, the urgency of his mouth, remembered his need and her own. She remembered the loud ticking of clocks, marking time they didn't have. And between them were his wife and Pete and the clinic and Pete's smear campaign against Sam, a sticky maze that had finally trapped her like some helpless fly.

Margaret dropped the charcoal and rubbed the heel of her hand against the hard throb between her eyes. *Why did I marry him?* Presumably she had loved Pete at one time, but that emotion in terms of her marriage was dead; its corpse rotted inside her. The real question was why she'd stayed in the marriage despite the demise of love, the absence of commonalities, despite Pete's need to control. She suspected it had to do with Sam, with maintaining some sort of perverse balance between them—since he wouldn't leave his wife, she wouldn't leave Pete, either. Like that.

She looked down at the sketch pad. The car, the storage space, stall 33. Was the VW still there? She needed to see it, sit behind the steering wheel, feel the texture of the seats against her hands, needed to connect with this relic of who and what she'd been before the clinic.

Margaret went inside and dug the old phone book out of the pantry. There were two listings in the yellow pages for mini-storage units. She jotted down the address for the one in the Cove, then hurried into the hallway and stood in front of the mirror.

The woman gazing back at her looked far different from the stranger who had stood here the night she'd escaped from the clinic. Her hair was shorter, her cheeks weren't as gaunt, and the light had returned to her eyes. She would still be recognizable but probably not at a distance, not with sunglasses, lipstick, a scarf around her hair. Not in this navy blue windbreaker. Not if she acted as though she had every right to be wherever she was.

Margaret waggled her fingers at her reflection. "Bye-bye, y'all come back now, heah?"

Smiling to herself, she left the house.

(2)

Most of the road into town was a twisting descent through cool green shadows. Now and then, when the trees on her right thinned or vanished altogether, she glimpsed blue and felt the chill of the wind kicking in off the water. It tasted of salt and that peculiar wildness that only the sea possessed, a wildness that touched her and whispered to her as the bike flew downhill and the air whistled past her ears. She was free.

Margaret imagined herself living indefinitely in the house, in the woods that surrounded it. She would collect rainwater to drink, sneak to the market for supplies, start a garden, adopt an animal, grow old with the company of her repossessed memories. She would be written off as a casualty of the highways, killed when the security guard's car plunged over the edge of the cliff. Eventually, Pete would remarry, Sam might or might not leave his wife, and their lives would go on. As would hers, such as it would be.

There was a certain seduction in the idea of removing herself so utterly from the world of people. But it wasn't possible indefinitely, not on Tango, and she recognized it as the kind of dulled fantasy that Thorazine inspired. The passivity of a slug, she thought, and pedaled faster. Faster.

When she was within a quarter of a mile of the clinic, she veered down a narrow side road that twisted through a small park. She remembered walking here during those weekends when she was a trustee. But she could feel the clinic behind her, as though the air back there were heavier, denser. She saw it in her mind, a bird's-eye view: the tasteful buildings tucked away in the trees, the lovely grounds, the lip of the hill on which it sat, the wall that kept everyone inside a prisoner. A sourness coated the inside of her mouth; her heartbeat sped up.

Jean, she thought, alone in there, behind those walls, Jean, who had been a good friend to her.

Then she was on the outskirts of town. It was such a pretty little town, really, the streets laid out just so, flowers flourishing in front of the shops, the homes, the offices. The air reeked of money.

Margaret reached an intersection, hesitated, uncertain where to go. Left? Right? Straight ahead? But her hands saved her again. They turned the handlebars on the bike to the left and a quarter of a mile later she saw it. COVE STORAGE.

The place was deserted, the gate was open, and she sailed through. As far as she could see were rows of white concrete structures, rising from the black asphalt like long loaves of bread, ten stalls per row. Each was clearly numbered, as anonymous as a Swiss bank account. She stopped in front of stall 33, hopped off the bike, propped it up on the kickstand.

The lock clicked when she turned the key, a sharp, triumphant sound, and she raised the door. The VW was there, all right, exactly as she had drawn it, but it was black not yellow. She quickly pushed the bike inside, flicked on the light, shut the door.

She stood there biting her lower lip, worrying the key in her hand. She was suddenly certain that the car, the stall, this strange levity that was rushing through her were all drug-induced. A psychotropic hallucination. If she breathed too hard, moved too quickly, it would vanish and she would come to with Treak or Liscomb leaning over her, saying her name.

But when she finally moved, jerking forward like a puppet, the car remained. She rested her palm against the curve of the hood and blinked back tears. *Mine, this is mine, all mine.* It seemed she could feel her old self stirring beneath the cold metal, resurrected through the magic of her touch. *Hello, Maggie. Hello.*

Her fingers trailed over the hood, the roof. Her hand trembled as she opened the door. Stale odors poured out in an invisible cloud—old cigarettes and perfume, gasoline and highways—all of it preserved here in the cool darkness, a butterfly under glass.

Margaret slipped behind the steering wheel, worked the pedals with her feet, ran her hands over the strip of leather wound around the wheel. She punched buttons on the silent radio, loving the feel of them against her fingertips, cool and hard and fat, like unchewed Chiclets. She slipped the key in the ignition but didn't turn the engine on. Her hand moved over the dashboard, dropped to the gear shift. Her fingers curled over the knob that crowned it and lost memories raced through her, an electric current, a flash of images too quick to grasp, lightning in a blackened sky.

Glove compartment. She opened it. Inside was a sealed white envelope, that was all. She tore it open, unfolded the sheet of paper. Her heart seized up at the sight of her name at the top, his nickname for her. *Magpie,* written in black ink against the white of the paper, as though the choice of colors was itself a statement about the kind of world that was forever closed to Sam just by the nature of his work.

Magpie,

This is the only safe spot I could think of for a letter. If you find it, then at least you have some of your memories and that's more than I've hoped for.

Desperate to see you, I've started for the house several times but have always turned back. I suspect I'm under police scrutiny right now and I don't want to jeopardize you if the house is, indeed, where you've been hiding.

You've been charged with a double homicide: Liscomb and Hugh. But something apparently turned up in the autopsy that casts doubt on the charge. I don't know what; the police are being tight-lipped.

I've gotten several irate calls from Pete, demanding to know where you are. Then he stormed by here, hurling the usual accusations, and as soon as he'd left, Helen and I got into it. I told her I've seen an attorney and have started divorce proceedings. She reacted as I expected—a sudden migraine, pains in her legs, aches in her joints. I won't burden you with the details, but I want you to know I've moved out.

I'm staying at my mother's place until she gets down here for the winter. I've drawn a map below, in case you don't recall how to get here. It's secluded and if you came here at night, I think it would be safe enough for us to talk. We need to talk.

I've told the police virtually nothing for fear that Pete or Nina Treak would get wind of it. But the cop investigating the case, Aline Scott, is a friend of Ferret's (remember my mentioning him? The bookie?) so she can't be all bad. And maybe, just maybe, if we presented her with the facts (and I've pulled together more since we last saw each other), there might be a way out of this.

Please come, Magpie, if you can. Or call, 555-1977. I've missed you terribly these past months and feel so godawful responsible for what's happened. I'm sorry I abandoned you when you needed me most, but at the time it seemed that I would do you less harm by removing myself until I could straighten out my own life. I love you, Magpie. That has never changed.

                              Sam

She rested her head against the cool steering wheel, the sheet of paper still in her hand. She didn't want to move, to breathe too hard or hope too deeply for anything. Her sorrow for Hugh, her passion for Sam, her fear for herself—all of it congealed in the pit of her stomach like an undigested meal. The weight of it skewered her to the seat and made her feel huge, slovenly, unclean.

Tell me what you saw that night, Margaret, whispered Liscomb, as he pumped something into her veins. *Tell me what was done to you. Have these beings ever been back? Have you ever seen them again? Have you?*

She lifted her head from the steering wheel. Five hours of

missing time. Five hours that had divided her life neatly into Before and After. Margaret Wickerd, Maggie Ames, Magpie. These three women were now so separate, so isolated, she couldn't find the center of herself, couldn't get a handle on whoever she was. It was as if her identity had been blown to smithereens that night in the glades, the molecules scattered so far that there was no chance of slapping herself back together again. *Poof, you're gone.*

Which was exactly what someone had wanted, wasn't it? Pete, Treak, Liscomb, Winthrop, and who else? Who? And why? Pete and his blind ambition, Pete and his bitterness about her affair with the very man who symbolized everything he debunked. Okay, fine, she could maybe understand Pete's motives. But what about the others? How did the clinic figure in? Why did she feel certain that she had been manipulated and controlled?

Sam had facts, old and new. Sam had answers that she needed.

She climbed out of the car, jammed the bike in the backseat, hoisted the door of the stall. The bright, cool light assaulted her, and for an instant, it was the *other* light, sharp and blinding. Bile surged in her esophagus. Her muscles tightened into a stupefying paralysis. Her heart jerked around in her chest, squealing like a rat that has just ingested poison.

But it passed and she hastened back to the car, got in again, turned the key in the ignition. The engine cranked up with miraculous ease. She paused long enough to shut and lock the door of the stall. Then she was off, marveling that there were some things you never forgot. How to drive, to hope, to survive, to love.

(3)

She filled the tank with gas, and when she paid, the cashier barely glanced at her. Since a free car wash came with the purchase, she drove the VW through, then pulled up in front of the vacuum pump. The interior was no dirtier than the exterior had been, but this was a labor of love, of gratitude, and she relished the mundaneness of the task.

Yet she moved about with the nervous energy of a woman who is expecting company and isn't ready for them. Something nagged at her. Something about the car. She couldn't grasp it.

She shucked her windbreaker and tossed it in the back, then pushed the driver's seat forward and moved the vacuum hose across the floor. As she nudged it under the seat, it struck an object. She crouched, felt under the seat, and pulled out a gun.

It was heavy and cool in her hands. The safety catch was on. She realized that she knew what kind of gun it was (a .38); that it was loaded; and that she would find a box of ammunition under the passenger seat. She did. She quickly locked it and the box of ammunition in the glove compartment, returned the hose to the hook on the machine, and left.

She drove aimlessly for a long time, trying to remember how she'd come into possession of the gun, and let the car take her wherever it wanted to go. Into the hills. Down to the beach. Into the park. Over to the pier where the ferry docked and tourists got off in droves. South to the boardwalk. West to the dock where she bought a sandwich, a bottle of wine, some fresh fruit, a loaf of bread. She drove back across the island to the park she'd passed earlier. She nosed into a space under a banyan tree and ate her sandwich in the car while she watched a mother herd three children from the playground.

The sun sank behind the trees. She could no longer make out the details of the pay phone. Pools of shadows grew against the grass, the asphalt. A swing creaked in the breeze. It would be so easy, she thought. Drop in a quarter, dial seven numbers, and wait for the sound of his voice. But what would she say to him? *Hi, Sam. I'm on my way and I've got the wine.* Better to drop in unannounced, to have the advantage of surprise.

Margaret watched the wall of pines beyond the play-ground, dense, thick, a green that deepened with the dusk. She wondered whether her child had been a girl or a boy and how her life would have been if she had carried the baby to term.

Sam's baby.

On impulse, she unlocked the glove compartment and removed the gun. Her thumb made a slow passage down the barrel and up again. She smoked one of the cigarettes from the pack she'd found in the security guard's car lifetimes ago. She drew the smoke deeply into her lungs, then dropped her head back and let it escape from her lips in a cloud. All the while her thumb stroked the barrel of the .38. The breeze stopped and the stillness was like the dark, complete and perfect.

The temperature had dropped a few degrees when she finally got out of the car and walked over to the phone. She fed in a quarter. Just the sound of his voice, she thought. That was all. She punched out the numbers and turned so she could see the lot. Nothing moved out there. Nothing.

"Hello?"

He sounded close enough to touch, his voice clear but guarded, as though he expected a call he didn't want to take. Her fingers tightened on the receiver. Words tangled in her throat.

"Hello?"

She hung up but didn't remove her hand from the receiver. Suppose the note was a ruse to lure her to the house, where cops or Treak or someone else would be waiting for her? Suppose something vital about Sam had fallen through the cracks in her flawed memory? Perhaps his wife and her husband had nothing to do with why their relationship had ended. Perhaps, suppose, what if . . . She had to be sure she could trust him.

Margaret called the number again. He picked up on the first ring, his voice no longer guarded when he spoke. She swallowed hard. "Hello, Sam."

She heard him draw in his breath. "Are you okay?"

"For the moment. Is the phone safe?"

"I think so. And I'm alone. Jesus, Maggie. I've been so worried. Can you come here? Can we meet somewhere?"

"Are the police still watching you?"

"I don't think so. But they know I've moved. Maybe I should meet you somewhere."

"I'll call you back in an hour."

"Wait, Maggie."

"What?"

"How much do you remember?"

"Enough," she replied, and hung up.

(4)

She drove south again, thinking about the call, about Sam. An hour would give him sufficient time to contact the cops, Treak, or whoever, if he were so inclined. It would allow time for a setup, if that was what Sam was about. One hour.

When she realized she was near the boardwalk again, she turned up a narrow alley. The sunroof was still open and she could hear music from the boardwalk. It pumped through the stillness with the irritating certainty of a bully who knows he will always have an audience.

She parked behind her sister's shop, wondering exactly when she'd decided to come here. Before the call to Sam? Last night? Although the shop was closed, Julie's Toyota was still parked out back. She was probably inside with a client, in that back room with the soft light. She would be speaking quietly as she laid out her cards, her witch's magic.

Had she consulted her oracles before she'd agreed not to challenge Pete about the commitment? And what cards might she have drawn? The Sorceress, perhaps, as cold and detached as the moon. Or Death, the skeleton riding bareback and backward on his horse, mouthing his own foul name.

Hi, Jules. We're going to talk and you're going to keep your mouth shut. Got it?

The sight of the gun would silence her. Julie professed an intense hatred for weapons, for violence of any kind, and yet she'd allowed her to be hauled away, screaming, to a nuthouse and she had not intervened. Her brain had been fried, but Julie had called it a Treatment, using the professional jargon as effortlessly as someone who had been in the shrink biz for decades. Yes, Margaret understood her sister's penchant for nonviolence. Turn the other way, hide your eyes, stick cotton in your ears, and hope for the best.

Well, sorry, Jules, your best just isn't good enough this time.

Margaret tucked the gun in the waistband of her jeans. Annie Oakley stalking bad guys on a desert in the Southwest: it had come to this. A light burned in the back windows, against the drawn curtains. She listened at the door, heard the soft drone of voices, a quick, fluted laugh, then voices again, quiet and furtive.

She rapped at the door. No shadows moved across the curtains, no chair scraped across the concrete floor. She knocked again, waited again, then her hand closed over the knob and turned it. The door wasn't locked. Perhaps Julie was expecting a client.

Margaret stepped quickly into the room, shut the door, stood against it. The voices she'd heard came from the TV on a bookshelf near the window. Canned laughter fluttered through the scented air. Her sister's witch table was lying on its side, the Tarot cards were scattered across the floor, magazines were strewn about, a ceramic pot was in pieces, and clumps of the plant's soil trailed around the overturned table like an animal's droppings.

"Julie?" As she moved deeper into the room, her foot struck an empty bottle of Perrier. It rolled noisily and struck the toppled table. Her sister was on the other side of it, sprawled on her stomach, her left cheek flat against the floor, a hand lost under her chin. She might have been sleeping except for the pool of blood near her chin, leaking from an unseen wound.

For many seconds, Margaret didn't move. She couldn't wrench her gaze from her sister's face, the odd repose of her features, the utter peace in her open eyes, the way strands of her blonde hair feathered her forehead. She finally raised her head and stared at the TV, where a man was hunched over a bowl of cereal. He could have been speaking Swahili for all the sense his words made to her.

A pulse pounded at the backs of her eyes. She barely resisted the urge to flee. She pulled the table out of the way. Her knees cracked as she crouched beside the body and pulled air into her lungs, air that hissed against her clenched teeth. She set the gun down, turned Julie over. A piece of wire at her throat had sliced through the skin to her esophagus. Her head lolled. Blood stained the front of her blouse, was smeared across two of the pearly buttons, and streaked her mouth, elongating it into a funhouse grin, a petrified rictus.

"Aw, Jules," she whispered, her voice breaking, her fingers clenched against her thighs. "It wasn't supposed to be like this."

She finally reached out and shut her sister's eyes. The lids were cool and smooth, like glass, eerie to the touch, and she jerked her hand back. *I'm going to be blamed for this.* The thought came to her almost lazily, a phantom bird in a glide. *Framed.*

A surge of adrenaline shot her to her feet, the gun tight in her hand again, and she stumbled back, panicked, and didn't stop until she reached the door. She groped behind her for the knob, suddenly terrified that if she looked away from her sister's body, Julie would rise, would move, would speak in the garbled tongue of her fallen cards.

But in the end she had to look away and peer through the crack in the door. Outside, nothing had changed, except that it was darker. She glanced back once, her heart seizing up with regret for her sister's unlived life, for the harsh words between them that had never been taken back, then she left as furtively as she'd arrived.

15

(1)

On Saturday morning, the seventeenth of October, Kincaid drove straight to the park from work. It was just three blocks from the lighthouse and had the only flat jogging track at the northern end of the island. The two miles of hard-packed dirt wound like a large intestine around a playground and a pond shaped like Florida.

The flatness alone was enough to make it popular. But bright, efficient lighting was an additional bonus that made the track one of the busiest spots on Tango with the before-eight and the after-five huff-and-puff crowd.

These were the Cove Bizzos, the men and women who owned stores, businesses, property, the wheeler-dealers who formed links in a corporate chain that extended from Miami to New York to L.A. and places in between. From nine to five each day, they dressed fashionably, zipped around in expensive vehicles with cool, soft interiors, made deals on their car phones, barked instructions that their minions dutifully carried out. They bought and sold stocks, invested portfolios of other people's money, argued in courtrooms, consummated ambitions over lunches and dinners at the Flamingo Hotel. And before any of this transpired—or after—they donned designer jogging and workout clothes and headed out in pursuit of longevity and good health.

Or, at least, that was how Kincaid imagined it. But what the hell did he know? Even in the most conventional periods of his life, he had not been employed as a businessman by even the loosest interpretation of the word.

He stretched before he got on the track, thinking of how easily the lighthouse intruder had eluded him. The burning in his lungs, the aches in his legs, the sense that his knees were going to crumple. But in the days since, he'd recaptured his former speed and much of his old endurance. And now, after a boring and uneventful night at the clinic, he intended to try for at least one six-minute mile.

Half a mile down the track Gene Frederick appeared at his side decked out in a sweat suit that looked as incongruous on him as training pants on a German shepherd would. He was sweating copiously, struggling for breath; he'd never jogged a day in his life and had evidently been here for a while, carrying out the pretense. "Gotta talk . . . Slow down a little . . ."

"Want to stop?"

"No." The word escaped with a heavy puff.

"All those cigars, Gene."

"Smug bastard."

Kincaid slowed to a trot and Frederick looked relieved, if not overtly grateful. "I guess . . ." *Puff, puff.* "You know about the feds."

"Aline mentioned it right before I left for the clinic last night."

"That's not a good way . . ." *Puff.* ". . . to conduct a marriage, Ryan."

"We're not married."

"Christ . . . might as well be." Frederick glanced at him and Kincaid watched a bead of sweat slide down the side of his face. "Anyway, you know . . . what the hell I mean."

"Which is why you're going to let her take some of her accumulated leave when this is over, right, Gene?"

Frederick slowed to a walk, a hand pressed to his side, and Kincaid slowed as well. "Not for a trip to Hong Kong . . . in the middle of the goddamn tourist season."

"Who said anything about Hong Kong? Maybe it'll just be a long weekend to Daytona."

"Sure."

"Or a trip to Chile."

"Chile. Fine. And how long does she need to go to Chile, Ryan? Eight weeks? Ten?"

"She needs a raise and then, oh, about eight weeks."

"Shit." Frederick guffawed; he sounded as though he was choking. "Eight weeks."

"I'm close to something, Gene."

"What kind of something?"

"Col. Evan Nate, whose name popped up in that DOD memo."

"And just how close are you?"

"Close enough."

He smoothed a hand over his white hair, which was already plastered to his head. "You crack this without breaking too many rules, Ryan, and Aline gets eight weeks whenever she chooses, all at once and with pay."

"And a raise?"

"Christ, yes, and a raise."

Frederick gestured off to the right, to a nearby bench, and sank onto it. Then, in the quiet, dilatory voice of a man who knows he is up against something much larger than himself, he summarized the situation. The details weren't news; Kincaid had heard most of them from Aline last night before he'd gone to work. But for the first time, he understood Frederick's position in this case, the delicate balance he'd sought between instinct and evidence. A balance, he thought, that the feds' intervention had unhinged.

Frederick had no great love for feds and it didn't make any difference to him from which agency they hailed—FBI, CIA, NSA, IRS, take your pick. To him, they were all inept, meddling bureaucrats who pulled rank when it suited them. But Kincaid knew this wasn't just about a fed pulling rank and sensed he wasn't going to like where this was headed.

"This fed, John Jones, checked out down the line, Ryan. He produced a memo from his boss in the Miami office. I called the guy, asked him what the hell was going on. He said Vance Liscomb was involved in 'highly classified research' for the government, that some documents were missing from the clinic, and they had reason to believe Mrs. Wickerd had taken them. He told me to turn over our records to Jones and that was that.''

"What'd the mayor say?''

"He escorted Jones to my office, then sat there like a lobotomized patient. He's relieved.''

"And that's it? We're off the case?''

"Yes.''

"Did you tell Jones or the mayor what Bill pulled out of the shrink's nose?''

"Nope. And it isn't in the autopsy report, either.''

"And you're just closing the books on this one.''

"You got it.''

"Sure.''

A small smile crept across Frederick's mouth. "I can't have Aline or Bernie or anyone else in my department sneaking around and asking questions.''

"I'm not in your department.'' Frederick looked at him, his smile widening. "That's right. You aren't. Which is why we're going to outline your next moves, Ryan. And this, my friend, is between you and me. Not you, me, and Aline.''

"And if I get caught, I won't get any official help from you.''

"That's about the size of it, Ryan. But I know you won't get caught.''

Kincaid, who'd been sitting on the edge of the bench, pressed his palms to his thighs and stood. "Find some other sucker, Gene.''

"Nine weeks. I'll give her nine weeks off with pay.''

"Make it ten weeks whenever she wants it, another three grand for me if I find your answers, and we have a deal, Gene.''

Red spots of agitation colored his cheeks. "That's fucking highway robbery.''

"Not for answers. Not if it gives you leverage over the mayor.''

Frederick considered it, but not for long. "Okay, done. Now sit your ass down."

Light melted across the sky. A cool dampness seeped from the ground. Joggers moved past them. Kincaid wondered about these implacable pacts that existed between men, this sense of some tight club of unspoken power. Did something comparable exist between women? Did Aline and Bernie, for instance, share secrets that Aline hadn't shared with him? Perhaps it was a matter of semantics, of perspective, and whether something was a secret or merely private was a result of how each person filtered his or her experience of the world. Yes, perhaps it was nothing more than that.

Language.

Everything was how you phrased it. You kill a man, but in a court of law it might be manslaughter or first-degree murder. But the person you killed was still dead.

Language.

Later, as Kincaid drove back to the lighthouse, it nagged at him. This was not the sort of thing he had kept from Aline before. She would see through it. She would know. Somehow, she would know. Although the boundaries between the professional and the personal with them were clearly drawn, there were times when she held it against him. It wasn't something she would readily admit, but he knew it as well as she did.

We're not married.

You might as well be.

Wrong. You weren't married until you were married. He ought to know. Two trips down the aisle and ready for a third, if Aline ever said the word, which she probably wouldn't.

Not as long as she was a cop and he was a gumshoe. And that was really the bottom line, wasn't it?

(2)

Aline, under the intense scrutiny of the owl, the skunk, and the cat, sliced a fillet of grouper into chunks, which she divided into three even piles. Boo watched from his perch on the windowsill at the sink. Wolfe waited patiently at her left, and Unojo, mewing softly, slipped in between her legs, begging to be first.

"I hope you kids appreciate what a good deal you've got here." She put a pile of fish chunks in each of the two bowls and dropped a third on Boo's plate. "Just go ask any of your kind in the neighborhood how often they get fresh grouper for breakfast." Wolfe nipped at her heel as if to say: *Okay, enough of the lecture. Get the show on the road.*

"Yeah, yeah." She set the plate on the windowsill and the bowls on the floor and was promptly forgotten. "Such gratitude," she muttered.

"You talking to me?" Kincaid strolled into the kitchen. His hair, still damp from the shower, was almost the same color as the baggy warm-up pants that doubled for pajama bottoms. When he bothered to wear pajamas at all. He didn't look like a man with a secret, but she could smell it on him as surely as the aroma of soap. "Am I being chastised for something I don't know I've done?"

She laughed. "Talk about paranoid." Aline gestured toward the fish that was marinating in a bowl of something Kincaid had whipped up. "Is this going to marinate all day?"

"Patience, Al." He turned the fish over, stuck it in the fridge for lunch or dinner, took out eggs, bread, butter, several vegetables. "That's the secret of good cooking."

She leaned on the counter, watching as he began to orchestrate breakfast. Omelets. Bacon. Hash browns. She passed him a mug of fresh coffee and he held it up. "Toast."

"To the aliens, who seem to be winning this round."

"I thought the feds were winning this round."

"Same difference. Bernie called right before you got home. John Jones now has eight men stashed away at the

Flamingo Hotel, Ryan, not to mention the scores of blood-hounds who're checking every motel and rooming house on Tango and in Key West.''

''They seem pretty certain she's still on the island.''

''Yeah, that's what bothers me.''

''That they're so certain or that she might still be here?''

''Both.'' She sipped her coffee, watched Wolfe smack his lips as he finished the grouper. The owl hopped off the windowsill to the floor, wings fluttering but not flapping, and continued his hop to the open atrium door.

''I'd place bets that he's going to be flying before the feds find Margaret Wickerd,'' said Kincaid, who would place a bet on virtually anything.

''It sounds like a real long shot to me, unless you know something I don't.''

She'd given him the opening, but he didn't answer immediately. He hustled around, flipping the omelets, popping bread into the toaster. She realized he had already decided to share the secret, but it was now a question of how much he would tell her, how circumspect he would be.

''Have you found out anything else about that colonel Joe Mahoney told you about? The guy who's mentioned in the DOD memo?'' he asked.

''No. Why?''

''Well, he hired an ex-con named Paul Sapizzo to play man in black, Aline.''

''You have proof?''

''Not yet.''

The way he said that worried her. ''When?''

''In the next day or two.''

''How? No, never mind. Don't answer that.'' She already knew it involved something illicit that would cost her her badge if it ever came out that she'd known about it. And with the feds already involved in this, she thought, the less she knew, the better. ''Does Gene know?''

''His hands are tied. He wants proof. So I'm going to bring him proof.'' He slid an omelet onto one of the plates. ''Almost ready here.''

"Toast coming up." She slapped jelly onto hers, butter and jelly onto his. She listened to the tick of the clock on the wall, waited for what he wanted to say. Her nails drummed impatiently against the side of her glass. But there was no rushing him. "Should I guess?" she asked finally.

"Guess at what?"

"At whatever you're mulling over."

He scratched at his jaw and left behind a flake of egg in his beard, which Aline plucked out. Mama monkey, she thought.

"How do you think we'd do working together full-time?"

It wasn't the first time they'd talked about this, but it had been months since she'd heard him mention it in this particular tone of voice. "Okay, I guess."

"Now *that* sounds guarded."

"It isn't meant to." When he looked at her, it struck her that his eyes were a peculiar blue, pale at the rims, then deepening and brightening as the blue closed in on the pupils. Fathomless, like some bottomless lake. In the early days of their relationship, these eyes had possessed the power to literally weaken her knees. Hell, who was she kidding? They still did.

"You want to elaborate a little?" he asked.

"If I were going to quit my job and go into business with anyone, Ryan, it'd be you. But I don't think I'm geared the way you are in terms of money, all that insecurity of no regular paycheck. Besides, we'd have to sell my place first."

"Agreed. And that would be enough to set us up in business, tide us over for a while." They were at the table now. "How's your omelet?"

"Perfect. What about Chile? We couldn't afford to do both."

It was obvious this hadn't occurred to him. God forbid that Ryan Kincaid should ever have to forgo a trip for lack of funds. Somehow, he was always rescued at the last moment. This past summer, when the IRS had frozen his assets and billed him for ten grand in back taxes, he'd won seventy-five hundred at the track. It had forestalled the IRS long enough to sell his house, which had enabled them to pay the remaining tax bill and put a sizable down payment on the lighthouse. She guessed he had also stashed away part of it, enough for a ticket to Chile, but had never asked.

"Well, Chile will always be there," he replied after a few moments of pensive consideration.

"Such optimism," she said with a laugh.

He concentrated on breakfast. The silence was one of uneasy waiting, Kincaid biding his time. She gazed out the window, where they sky was blue and cloudless. "Are the Pleiades visible from Tango during October?" she asked finally.

"Not from this window, but probably from the front yard." Barely skipping a beat, he added: "We could work out of the lighthouse, Aline. It would give us a tax break on the mortgage."

"And three months into it, we might run out of money."

"We might. Or we might be making double what we both make now."

She brought the coffeepot over to the table, refilled their mugs. "Okay, Ryan. Convince me. List the advantages."

"You make your own hours."

Translated: You work all the time.

"No boss."

No benefits.

"You set your own fees."

No paid holidays.

"You take only the cases that interest you."

Assuming you have cases to begin with.

"Between us we have enough contacts to make a go of this."

Maybe.

"Look, Al, all I'm asking is that you think about it seriously, okay?"

"Fair enough." The phone rang. She started to push away from the table to answer it, then changed her mind. Let the machine get it. Every time the phone rang these days, it was bad news.

"Exactly my point," Kincaid said with a smug smile. "If we were in business for ourselves, you'd be leaping to answer that phone."

Her recorded message came on. "I don't see you jumping every time the phone rings."

"That's different."

"Sure."

The beep sounded. "Detective Scott, this is Jean Mancino. I said I'd call you, remember? Could you come by San Ignacio Church around eight tonight? Give me a call at 555-7445. Thanks."

"Maybe Jean finally got sprung," Aline remarked. "Treak had said they might give it a shot. Did you see her around last night?"

"Nope. And you're off the case, remember?"

She reached for the box of toothpicks, removed a bunch, separated them as she spoke. "Here's Jean, nut case." A lone toothpick in the center of the table. "Here's Treak, the shrink with secrets." A third toothpick joined the lineup. "Here's Margaret's husband, a professional debunker whose reputation was on the line." A fourth now. "Here's Newman, Margaret's lover, who, by the way, has moved out of his house and into his mother's winter home. Or so Frederick informed me." A fifth. "Julie, Margaret's sister, the lady who didn't contest the commitment." A sixth. "This is Ricardo Morales, alias Ricky Ricardo, mystery man who supplied the memo from the DOD."

"I know the players," he said.

"Let me finish, Ryan." She slapped down another toothpick. "This is your Colonel Nate and right next to him"—she ran out of toothpicks and slid a fork into the middle of the table—"is ex-con Paul Sapizzo, a.k.a. the man in black." She picked up a spoon, a knife, the sugar bowl, and the creamer. "And here we've got our two dead men, Special Agent Jones, and our missing lady. It's all connected, Ryan."

She was already halfway across the room, her mind racing, when Kincaid said: "The feds will fry you if they find out you're still noodling around, Al."

"Jones doesn't know about Jean." She smiled and added, "Or about you," and picked up the receiver.

(3)

Aline's office was shaped like an old-fashioned keyhole. The doorway was the narrowest part, with the room gradually expanding until it curved to a window that jutted out over the street two stories below and offered a magnificent view of the city park.

At various times in the last seven years, this window had seemed almost enchanted, a window in a fairy tale. It had been the tower where Rapunzel had pined away for her lover, the glass case in which Snow White awaited her prince. Women waiting for the men who would rescue them, liberate them, marry them. Happily-ever-after was the theme; the analogy to her own life didn't escape her.

But today the window represented something entirely different. The tale it told was darker, denser, like a Greek myth. It stank of plots and betrayals and emotional treason and at the core of it was the question of power.

Who possessed it, who exercised it, who sought to keep it, and why?

Aline had run a criminal check on Jim Booth that had yielded nothing. But since his name graced the DOD memo, that was hardly surprising. The computer check on Paul Sapizzo revealed a lengthy record for petty thefts for which he'd done a total of maybe a year in the county jail. But then came the big one, armed robbery in Palm Beach, which had landed him at Raiford on a mandatory three years. She didn't know the warden or anyone else at Raiford who might be able to tell her how Sapizzo had gotten out after eighteen months. But she knew a woman on the parole board who owed her a favor, several favors, if she wanted to be technical about it. Louise Partelli wasn't going to be real happy about having a favor called in on a Saturday, but what the hell. If anyone could unearth the answer on Sapizzo, Louise could.

Aline looked up her Tallahassee number, punched it out on her private line. Busy. Teenagers, Louise had a house full of teenagers. Her son, in fact, had been picked up a year ago on Tango for DWI. Thanks to Aline's intervention, he'd gotten two hundred hours of community-service work and a stiff fine instead of thirty days in the tank where he'd belonged.

She tried the number again and this time Louise herself answered. She was open and friendly and assured Aline the call wasn't an intrusion at all. That didn't change even when Aline told her what she needed and asked her to look into it today. But an hour later her manner was cool and evasive. She couldn't find out anything, she said, not on a Saturday. If Aline could call her back on Monday . . .

"I need the information today, Louise."

"Everyone is out of town for the weekend."

"Look, it doesn't have anything to do with these homicides. It's for me and it won't go any further than us. I just want to know if a certain colonel in the air force pulled strings to get Sapizzo out early."

A hesitation, then: "Yes."

She waited for Louise to elaborate. When she didn't, Aline realized she intended to answer only the questions she was specifically asked and probably only in monosyllables. She'd run into this with other bureaucrats. One of the unwritten rules of bureaucracy seemed to be that you were permitted to impart information on topics you were otherwise forbidden to discuss if the other person knew the right questions to ask.

"Was the colonel's name Evan Nate?"

"Yes."

"Were you consulted?"

"No."

"Was anyone on the parole board consulted?"

"No."

"It came from the governor's office?"

"Yes."

"What does Nate want with Sapizzo?"

"I don't know."

Aline thought for a moment, then changed her tack. "Was anyone else involved in this decision besides the governor and Nate?"

"Yes."

It was like a treasure hunt in which the person who has hidden the treasure offers clues to the person who searches for it: you're hot, you're cold, you're warm. And right now she was warm. "Jim Booth?"

"No. Not that I know of. Look, Aline, I've really got to run."

"Please, Louise."

The silence coursed along the line that connected them.

"Louise?"

"I'm only going to say this once. Our esteemed governor went to law school many moons ago with Congressman Henry Sheen. Nice talking to you, Aline. Have a good weekend."

Aline stood there with the dead receiver in her hand, thinking. Then she called Meg Mallory and asked her to find whatever she could on Evan Nate and Henry Sheen and to go back as far as thirty-five years.

Meg whistled softly. "How soon do you need it, Aline?"

"As soon as you can get it. If I'm not at work, try me at home."

"Righto."

"And Meg, thanks, I really appreciate this."

"Your tax dollars at work, hon. Be talking to you."

Aline hung up, turning the names around in her head. Congress, the air force, the Department of Defense, the FBI. What next? The CIA? The NSA? The White House? God? Or maybe the aliens themselves were camped out in the heart of this labyrinth, having a good chuckle over it all.

"Hey, Al."

She looked up as Bernie rushed through the door. "Julie Ames's body was just discovered in her shop. I'll meet you out front."

Of course, she thought as she grabbed her purse. Of course there would be more victims. The true tale of power, after all, always came down to the power of life and death.

16

(1)

Margaret raised the door of the storage stall and poked her head out. Brilliant light filled her vision, light so white it swallowed the details of everything else.

Gradually, shapes materialized in the white, as if the primal soup of the world was only now solidifying. She could make out the low building directly across from her, a car parked in one of the stalls, and a family carrying boxes inside of it. Beyond them was another car, where two men were unloading Windsurfers from a truck.

She lowered the stall door to within six inches of the ground and walked back to the VW. She was famished. Her mouth tasted sour, she wanted to brush her teeth, her bladder ached, her head hurt. And that was only for starters.

After driving around for hours last night, she'd decided against calling Sam again and had returned here because it was the only place she felt safe. No windows, one door, three walls of solid concrete. But now it stirred a kind of claustrophobia in her; the stall was too much like a coffin. She craved fresh air, purpose. Yes, purpose most of all, a sense that she had seized control of her life, that she was thrusting toward a future shaped by *her* decisions, *her* actions. But she didn't know where to start, what place was safe.

The house, she thought. She would drive to the house in the woods. She would shower, eat, pack clothes. Beyond that, she didn't know. But at least now she was certain she could trust Sam. If he had intended to betray her, it would have happened last night or this morning. A stakeout at the stall, cops and feds surrounding the place, Treak urging her to surrender. Sure, she could see it. Treak talking to her through a megaphone or a P.A. system, the cops in full battle gear, choppers circling overhead. But it hadn't happened that way.

So she drove back through Pirate's Cove, past the clinic, up into the hills on the Old Post Road. As she neared the turnoff, as she slowed and downshifted, a white car nosed out onto the highway, as timid as a deer sniffing the air for the enemy. She saw two figures inside. Then the car swung out in front of her and Margaret barely resisted the urge to slam on the brakes, hurl open the door, and run. The car sped away, rounded a curve, vanished.

Lost tourists. Kids necking in the woods. She didn't believe it for a second. She drove past the turnoff, exited the Old Post as soon as she could, and wended her way south to the town of Tango, her eyes darting from the road to the rearview mirror. She bought toiletries at an Eckerd's Drug Store, a bag of groceries at Publix, three changes of clothes at K Mart. Then she drove north again to a motel on the east side of the Old Post where most of the guests were truckers. A place she and Sam had once stayed.

She paid cash for the room. The clerk could not have cared less who she was. But she didn't relax her guard until the chain on the door was fastened and the curtains were closed. Then she restored her humanity: food, shower, clean clothes.

Margaret removed the gun from her purse, flicked off the safety, sat at the edge of the bed. She flipped through the TV channels, hungry for news. She thought and planned and waited for dark, waited for whatever would happen next, waited because it was the one thing she did very, very well.

(2)

Aline watched as Bill Prentiss untwisted the length of wire at Julie Ames's throat, then eased it out of the bloody skin where it was embedded. It gave with a sharp, distinctive pop, flicking bits of soggy tissue that struck the front of Prentiss's shirt.

"Christ." He looked down at himself. The wire was pinched between the thumb and forefinger of his right hand and dangled like a broken fishing line. "I sometimes think it would be in my best interests to resign from this job and sell used cars."

"You wouldn't last six weeks." Frederick spoke around the unlit cigar stuck in a corner of his mouth. "Looks like wire from a mesh fence."

"A rusted fence." Prentiss pointed with a gloved finger at the top end of the wire where there was hardly any blood. "Her neck's broken, just like the shrink's." He dropped it in a clear plastic bag, labeled it, then motioned at two of the skeleton crew to take care of the body.

"Any other wounds?" Aline asked.

"I don't think so, but I won't know for sure until I do the autopsy."

Aline walked away from them, from the body, and moved around the crowded room with the restlessness of a traveler between flights at an airport. The air possessed a peculiar quality, a kind of queer vibration that suggested life. It was as if some essence of Julie's had escaped the suddenness of her death and been absorbed by the walls, the floor, even the scattered fortune-telling cards.

Next to a shattered vase that had contained a cluster of tiny yellow daisies she found one of the cards Julie had drawn for her. A man with a gun, the hunter. She picked it up, ran her finger over the smooth, cool surface, and slipped it in the pocket of her skirt. A reminder, a rabbit's foot, whatever.

The body had been discovered by one of Julie's employees, the elderly woman with the white hair who had waited on Aline. Mimi. Mimi, who was now in the front room, crying and trying to answer Bernie's questions. *Had Julie heard from her sister since her escape? Had Julie mentioned Margaret to Mimi? Had Julie spoken recently to Mr. Wickerd or Mr. Newman?* But Mimi's answers ("No" or "I don't know") told them nothing more than the body did.

The simplest conclusion was that Margaret had killed her sister. She was sick; she was bitter that Julie hadn't fought Pete about the commitment; she had come to her sister for help that Julie had refused to give: motives abounded. But no matter how Aline looked at it, Margaret murdering her sister just didn't fit.

The argument against all of this, the argument Frederick was no doubt mulling over this very second, was that crazy people didn't think or behave logically. But was Margaret crazy? What was crazy? Who defined it? A shrink? A court? Screw shrinks and courts, Aline thought.

The definition of crazy boiled down to some sort of mass consensus about what constituted normal behavior. It was not *normal* to pick your nose in public, to piss on the lawn, to copulate in public. It wasn't *normal* to steal, to kill, to eat your neighbor for breakfast. At least not in this country. But if you happened to live in a society where these things *were* normal, a place, perhaps, where people routinely communed with angels or aliens, then the rules of accepted behavior were drastically changed.

So where did that leave her? If Margaret hadn't killed her sister, then who had? Treak? Winthrop? Pete Wickerd? They were cut from the same mold, those three, but they wouldn't get their own hands dirty. They were more likely to hire someone else to do it, someone like Paul Sapizzo, ex-con, man in black, the colonel's lackey. The motive, then, would be to silence Margaret or to frame her or to make sure she was buried so deeply in the criminal justice system that she never saw the light of day.

Aline went outside to talk to Frederick. A crowd had already gathered at the end of the street. Several uniformed cops prevented them from venturing any closer, but the barricade hadn't stopped Special Agent Jones and two of his boys. They almost surrounded Frederick and Prentiss, like a posse rounding up bad guys.

The chief stabbed his unlit cigar toward the skeleton crew van, which stood just beyond them, its rear doors open, the stretcher inside. Prentiss's men waited off to one side for the dispute about Julie Ames's body to be settled.

Apparently the feds intended to claim this one, too, she thought, and stopped just short of the circle. "I'm afraid you don't have any choice," Jones told the chief in his most courteous voice. "This body is part of our investigation."

"He may not have a choice, but I do," Prentiss piped up. "I'm coroner of Tango County and this body's not going anywhere without the proper release forms. You have those forms, Mr. Jones?"

The fed's weathered face reflected acute discomfort, as if from a sudden attack of indigestion. "You don't seem to get the picture, Dr. Prentiss. The—"

"Do you have the goddamn forms or not?" Prentiss barked.

"Well, no, not with me, but—"

"Fine, when you have them, the body will be at the morgue." He gestured to his men. "Get her into the van."

Jones's two lackeys immediately stepped between Prentiss's men and the van, blocking their way. For seconds, no one moved or spoke. Then Frederick's voice cut through the silence, sharp and deadly. "Aline, go inside and call our contact at *Newsweek*'s Tango Bureau."

"You got it."

As she turned, Jones said, "I don't think that's necessary. We'll be at the morgue in thirty minutes with the release forms." Then he and his boys marched off through the barricade, the stretcher was loaded into the forensics van, and Prentiss climbed in with it.

Frederick and Aline watched as it moved off through the sunlight. "I guess Jones doesn't know that the closest *Newsweek* bureau is Miami, huh, Gene."

He chuckled and lit his cigar. "Too bad."

"I say we bring in a guy named Paul Sapizzo for questioning."

"The colonel's con?" He shook his head. "Not yet. The next move is theirs. We'll let them make it, then see where we stand. My guess is that Jones is going to back off on this one."

"How'd he find out?"

Frederick grinned through a cloud of smoke, slipped an arm around her shoulders, turned her toward their cars. "I called him. If you lead an enemy to believe you're cooperating, at least to a point, he tends to get careless."

"That sounds like one of Bernelli's Axioms." Which covered the prosaic to the exotic in a hundred succinct one-liners.

"It is. Number forty, I think."

She laughed. "Bernie would be honored. But how'd it make Jones careless?"

"Look, he's just following orders." Frederick puffed on his cigar with the relish of a man whose doctor had forbidden smoking. "He hadn't factored Julie Ames into the equation, but once he knew she'd been killed, he figured he'd better claim the body just to cover his ass."

"Should Bernie and I follow you to the hospital?"

"Yeah. Let's be sure that Julie Ames doesn't have a gizmo in her head."

(3)

Nate had spent yesterday at Homestead, attending to details that had been neglected in his absence. Nothing pressing, if he could overlook the urgent telephone calls from the two younger members of the committee and the reports every twelve hours from John Jones, who never had anything new to tell him.

We're doing our best, Colonel.

But their best hadn't yet found Margaret Wickerd, and the longer she was free, the clearer her memories would become. While it was likely that the electroshock had permanently destroyed some of those memories, he had no way of knowing which ones would be retained and that worried him. Worried him deeply.

So now he waited in a coffee shop for Nina Treak, who would spell out the hazards, the risks, the odds. Although he respected her work, he didn't like her personally. There were invariably moments in any conversation they had when he felt like one of her guinea pigs; moments when he knew she was measuring everything he said and did against some standardized norm of behavior. But at least she was on time; it was noon on the nose when she strode into the coffee shop.

As usual, she was dressed well, as if to compensate for her plumpness. She wore a navy blue suit with a white silk blouse and a strand of pearls; open-toed navy blue pumps; and carried a navy blue briefcase and purse. Nate wondered if she shopped for such an outfit in one fell swoop or if she, like his wife, shopped piecemeal. Whatever her method, he suspected she approached it with the same fanatical perfectionism that characterized her professional life.

He stood and they shook hands. "Nice to see you, Evan."

The familiarity chafed at him. But right from the beginning, she had addressed him by his first name, making it clear that she considered them equals. He didn't bother correcting it. "Thanks for coming, Nina. Did Tyler get off on his trip okay?"

"Oh, sure. And he left half a dozen numbers in the Caribbean where he could be reached. The break will do him good, but I had to call in a part-timer to take up the slack at the clinic." Her smile was brief but knowing. "But we're not here to talk about him, are we?" She brought out a file from her briefcase and set it on the table as she sat down. "Here's the technical report on her implant, Evan. It's more sophisticated and sensitive than the one Vance and I used on him and much too small to be detected on an X-ray. I assume that's how the coroner found Vance's?"

"I don't know."

"Well, it makes sense. What doesn't make sense is why he would X-ray a dead man's head to begin with, unless he'd died of a head wound."

"The point is that he did take X-rays."

"I assure you, Evan, that if anyone X-rays Margaret's head, there won't be anything to see."

"How long will it take for her to recover her full memory?"

"I can't predict that."

"Give me an educated guess."

"I don't think she'll ever recover fully."

"But you don't know for sure."

"Of course not. How can I? This is *experimental*, Evan. That means—"

"I know what experimental means," he snapped.

She gave a small sigh, rubbed her hands over her arms. "Look, let me put it this way. Based on the ECT treatments alone, she'll always have gaps in her memory. That's a given. When the implant is combined with ECT, the short-term amnesia could last as long as a year. That's what we've found with the control group."

But the control group was very small, ten patients scattered throughout other Whole Health clinics. "Those patients are being observed and treated by other doctors."

"But I did the implants, Evan. And I keep close tabs on their progress. I really think you're worrying needlessly. Who's ever going to believe a word she says after this? Besides, now that the FBI has her old house under surveillance, I feel very confident that she'll be found."

"If she's been staying there."

"If, hell. One of the things I've discovered from the control group is that they usually remember some vital detail from childhood. For Margaret, it's that house, I'm sure of it."

Nate wished he shared her confidence. But then, how could he? He had the full picture, knew exactly what was at risk; she didn't. For her, Margaret Wickerd was a delusional pa-

tient whose alleged experience had resulted in violence and
severe depression. She was a guinea pig who had received
an experimental implant that she had not been told about,
that she hadn't consented to. When the implant was electri-
cally stimulated, it reduced aggressive tendencies to mush
and, when combined with certain drugs, created a mind as
open to suggestion as a child's.

Suggestions, he thought, that possessed the quality of real
memories. But so far no one knew for sure whether the real
and the false would separate or whether they would continue
to intertwine. This uncertainty had always bothered Nate but
didn't seem to concern Treak. Since she didn't know the truth
about the cavern, this was all merely a fascinating foray for
her into the human psyche, into the creation of memory and
how it functioned. But, for him, it had become the center of
his life.

"Do you think this Mancino woman presents any threat
to us?" he asked, changing the subject.

"None at all."

"But she roomed with Margaret. She might know something."

"She might. But I think you're worrying needlessly,
Evan."

She was patronizing him and for a second he wanted very
much to grab her by her fat throat and squeeze. "It's my job
to worry. I want her placed under closer scrutiny until all of
this is resolved."

"I'm afraid that won't be possible. She's been released
from the clinic and is now living at a convent here in town."

The pattern, he thought. The pattern perpetuating itself.
"I should have been consulted before that decision was made,
Nina."

Her face hardened like bone. "If I consulted you before I
made every decision, I wouldn't have time to do my job. I
gave you my professional opinion about Jean and I stand by
it."

"Then let's hope you're right, Nina." Because if she
wasn't, she was going to join the list of casualties.

(4)

Record time, Aline thought. Only nineteen minutes had elapsed since the ambulance had left the crime scene and here was Prentiss, holding the X-rays up to the light. "I don't see anything, Gene."

"You're sure?" Aline asked.

"Positive. You could actually see the thing on Liscomb's X-ray. But there's nothing here."

The chief waved his cigar. "Then when shithead shows up with his papers, release the body to him, Bill."

Jones sailed into the hospital two minutes short of the half-hour deadline he'd promised. Aline was on the phone in the lobby when she saw him and turned her back so he wouldn't recognize her. He swept past with one of his men, grumbling about the stink in hospitals. She removed her hand from the mouthpiece.

"Okay, Meg, sorry. What'd you find?"

"Well, it's pretty typical biographical stuff. For the colonel, citations, awards, bombing missions; political successes and triumphs for Henry Sheen; appointments and whatnot for Booth."

"Is Booth DOD?"

"Was. Now he's a consultant in the private sector. I've got a list of the businesses he deals with. Heavy money people."

"Is there any obvious connection among these three guys, Meg? That's what I really need to know."

"That's the interesting part. They flew together in the very early days in Vietnam. Same squadron. Booth was the commander."

Three good ole boys up to no good. Yes, indeed, the picture was certainly getting clearer, she thought, and dropped another quarter into the phone to call Kincaid.

(5)

At 5:45, the shadows in the lot were thicker, denser. They seeped across the asphalt, claiming it, transforming it until its surface seemed slick with darkness. She hurried down the corridor, past several idling trucks, and stopped at the public phone near the ice machine. She called Sam. He picked up on the second ring, his voice clipped, tight. Sam waiting by the phone for her call: she could almost see him. Ached to see him.

"It's me."

"Maggie." Silence, then: "Sweet Christ, I thought something had happened."

"Meet me inside Lester's in three hours."

"Wait. Julie is—"

"I know. Three hours, Sam. Okay?"

"Yes. Yes, okay, three hours. Get there early and make sure I'm not followed. Let me go in first."

"Right."

Silence. Neither of them hung up. She knew he was gripping the phone as tightly as she was, reluctant to relinquish the connection. "Sam?"

"I'm here. Still here."

"I love you."

She thought she heard the air in his lungs breaking up and it hurt, Christ, how it hurt. She disconnected quickly. Ice churned through the machine to her right. One of the idling trucks started up, belching smoke. A door to one of the other rooms opened and a man emerged, scratching his belly and yawning.

Margaret turned away from the phone, dizzy with relief, with anticipation, dizzy with the need to see him, touch him, hold him. Three hours. That was all. When you had waited weeks, what were three more hours?

17

(1)

Do whatever you have to do to find her, Ryan, and if she's still on the island, get her off. I don't care how you do it. Just do it, then get in touch with me.

The chief's agenda was no more palatable to Kincaid now than it had been this morning on the jogging track. Although surveillance conducted in the bar of the Flamingo Hotel was preferable to the insurance variety, he still had doubts about whether it would lead him to Margaret Wickerd. Particularly when the individual under surveillance was John Jones.

His subject stood at the end of the bar nearest the door, under a Navajo rug that set the mood in the room's Southwest motif. He held a mug of dark ale as if it were a stage prop that contained colored water. He looked as Aline had described him, like an unemployed construction worker. But gone was the obligatory dark suit; this evening he sported casual clothes and seemed to be waiting for someone. Every time a person entered the bar, Jones glanced up expectantly, then sipped from his glass with a frown of disappointment.

"I still think Newman is the better choice," remarked Ferret, who was seated on the other side of the table. "I could talk to him. He trusts me. If he's heard from her, he'd tell me. Besides, Jones doesn't look bright enough to find his way home."

"Let's give him a little more time. I want to know who he's waiting for."

Ferret emitted a small, fussy sigh, slipped on his granny glasses, and turned back to the racing form he was studying. Kincaid glanced out the window, where a hotel bus belched passengers like a fish expelling eggs. They floated toward the hotel en masse, as if held together by invisible glue. At the end of the group was a woman walking with the aid of a cane.

"So what d'you know," Ferret said softly. "The lady with the cane is Helen Newman."

"I thought she was confined to a wheelchair."

"Not when she's out and about."

"What happened to her legs?"

"Car accident two and a half years ago. She was still in a wheelchair when she ran for circuit-court judge and, personally, I think it helped her win."

As she passed the window, Kincaid got a closer look at her. Makeup. Tailored black slacks. A sweater the same soft, pink as her lipstick. Granted, he was no expert on women, but Helen Newman looked like a lady dressed to meet a man. And her husband had been gone just—what? One day? Was that what Aline had said? Whatever. Helen Newman, circuit-court judge, didn't seem to be wasting any time getting on with her life.

Kincaid lost sight of her as she entered the lobby. But it somehow didn't surprise him when she appeared at the door of the bar or when Jones lifted his hand and she moved through the crowd and sat beside him.

"So," Ferret said, his lips pulling back from his sharp little teeth.

"Uh-huh," Kincaid replied, and wondered if Helen Newman fell under the column called *Pawns* or the one entitled *Players*.

From the pocket of his windbreaker, he brought out the camera Frederick had lent him. It was smaller than his hand, resembled an Instamatic, and was one of three in existence. The prototype had been developed by a whiz kid in the state narcotics unit in Tallahassee. It used regular 35-millimeter film and could be programmed like a computer for any number of complex tasks. At the moment, it was set for night photography, which Kincaid supposed was just fine for the dimly lit and smoky bar.

He gripped it in the palm of his hand and stretched out his arm until his hand reached the edge of the table. He snapped two quick shots of Jones and Helen, then pulled his arm back to his side.

"I figure that way back, you had a life as a spy," Ferret remarked with a roll of his eyes.

"And you were my faithful accomplice."

"Doubtful. I was probably the enemy who did you in and that's why this time around I'm obligated to help you. Karma, my friend. It's all karma. Which reminds me, I think I'll call Bino and see how we're doing at the races tonight. We're both due some good karma, don't you think?"

Kincaid laughed and Ferret darted off with the speed of the rodent he was named after.

(2)

You did this, Margaret thought, staring at the front of the house she no longer thought of as her own. The house where her husband lived. *You.*

She had left her car three blocks away, in the crowded parking lot of a convenience store. Now she stood at the edge of the pines across the street from the place she'd inhabited mostly on weekends, alone, when her real life had been lived.

It stood on stilts in a cul-de-sac at the end of the street and shared this quiet, affluent block with five other homes. Each place occupied four wooded acres and was built of pine and glass, like a ski chalet in Aspen. All but two were closed up until Thanksgiving, when the tourist season on Tango officially started, and would be sealed up again on Easter weekend, when the season officially ended.

On that day in April when she'd been hauled off, the street

had been as empty as it was now. She remembered that emptiness, the trees swaying in a pleasant breeze and Pete standing there in the driveway, staring after her, slapping a baseball cap against his open hand.

His Miata was in the driveway. A part of her was tempted to march up to the front door, ring the bell, stick the .38 in his face. *Start talking, Pete. Let's hear it, Pete. Let's hear your excuses.*

The porch light came on and she stepped back into the protection of the trees and hunkered down as Pete stepped out, locked the door, started down the steps. He didn't look much different than he had several nights ago when she'd watched him and Nina Treak leave the house: the snappy clothes, the blond hair that brushed his collar at the back, that smooth tan from the local tanning salon. This self-conscious look, she thought, started when he became Peter Wickerd, celebrity debunker.

Their first two years together had been good. They'd bought a refurbished warehouse in Coconut Grove where they'd lived and worked, she in her skylit studio on the second floor and Pete in his office across the hall. He was still wheeling and dealing in real estate then but joined the entertainment circuit on weekends. His magic shows were popular in resorts—Disney World, Vegas, Atlantic City, the Catskills, Aspen—and later expanded to include spots in the Caribbean.

By their third year together, he was moving away from stage magic and garnering something of a name for himself as a debunker of psychics. She no longer attended every function with him because it took her away from her own work too often. And that, she knew, was when the trouble in the marriage began.

No, that wasn't quite true. The trouble had been there all along. She wanted children and he hadn't. She didn't particularly like his friends and he couldn't stand hers. He expected her to put his work before her own. Basic differences, she thought, details she had hoped would change with time.

Pete strolled to his car, whistling softly to himself, the disjointed tune floating in the cool, still air with the clarity of an underwater sound. The Miata was equipped with security features that included an alarm, which he disengaged with a remote-control device. As long as she'd known him, he'd been security-minded and the propensity extended to everything. Especially the house. But unless he'd had the locks changed, the house wouldn't present a problem. One of the keys Hugh had given her fit the back door.

The Miata whispered down the drive. Don't hurry back, she thought, and moved quickly through the trees to the rear of the house. She waited a few minutes, just in case Pete had forgotten something, then darted out from the trees and up the steps. As she slipped the key into the lock, she remembered the trick of it: turn once to the right, then quickly to the left to shut off the security system.

The door swung inward. No sirens shrieked, no lights flashed, no fierce dog rushed her. She slipped inside, into the familiar air of rooms that she and Sam had boldly inhabited several weekends when Pete had been out of town debunking. She remembered, too, the breathless flush of their mutual passion, their insatiable hunger for each other.

During those weekends when she'd come home as a visiting patient, Pete had rarely been here. And when he was, they'd avoided each other, acting as politely as strangers who are forced to share the same space. The few times she'd broached the subject of a divorce, he'd refused to discuss it. *When you get better, Margaret*, he would say in his most patient and courteous voice, as though she were a young and stupid child.

She had slept in her studio with the door locked and he'd bunked downstairs in the bedroom. He'd never questioned these arrangements. But during one of her last weekends as a trustee, on a night when Pete had been drinking heavily, he'd come on to her and she'd pushed him away and he'd flown into a rage. He'd accused her of still seeing Sam (which she was) and threatened to have her privileges at the clinic revoked unless they resumed *conjugal relations*.

That phrase, uttered with Pete's weird formality, had struck her as funny and she'd started to laugh and then couldn't stop. Powerless against her ridicule, he'd left the house in a huff, only to exact his revenge a few weeks later. Pete carried grudges the way other people did dreams.

She hesitated at the door of the master bedroom, senses tightened, attuned for the sound of his car. But there was only the silence, a sharp, brittle thing that would break beneath the weight of a bird's song. Her eyes swept through the room: the neatly made king-size bed, the high-gloss black furniture, the little gizmos on the bureau that hailed from places like the Sharper Image. Margaret made a bee-line for the closet against the wall to her left, a walk-in his and hers, and was relieved to see that Pete hadn't removed her clothes.

She pulled a canvas bag from the upper shelf, then grabbed clothes and stuffed everything inside the bag. From a shoe-box in the corner, she retrieved nearly $1,700, the last of her stash. She pushed the remaining clothes close together, covering the gaps the missing items had left, then moved on to the bureau and the bathroom cabinets, collecting other items.

Her last stop was Pete's den. It was as tidy as every other room in the house, a comment on his housekeeper's skills and not on any trait of his. She booted up the IBM clone and searched the menu for the directory that held his journal. He was religious about his journal. It was in it that he confessed, analyzed, created, and made sense of his life. His entries were often mundane, but occasionally they were startling and insightful. She knew because she'd peeked when the journal had been a three-ring notebook that he kept in the nightstand drawer. But two years ago he'd switched to a computer. And since there was nothing in the menu that even hinted at a journal, she assumed it was tucked away in a hidden directory or coded with a password or both, a regular spy's network.

Maggie thought for a moment, then requested a global search for Pleiade.

Directory not found.
Lost Pleiade, she typed.
Password?
Wellness Clinic
Password?
Whole Health
Password?
Hidden One

The computer hummed and clicked, the screen blanked, and a menu appeared. It listed at least two dozen names of UFO investigators and researchers who Pete had taken on over the years. Her own name was included among them, a clear statement on where she fell within his scheme of things. She accessed her file and was surprised to find a chronology rather than a regular journal entry.

2/2	Maggie's abduction.
2/3 or 4	She contacts Sam Newman about light she saw and period of missing time. They drive out to site. Sam takes soil samples, photos etc.
2/4	Newman contacts Joe Mahoney, who visits site, then calls me. ''Got a quote for your fans, Pete?'' This is first I've heard about it; I was out of town.
2/5	I confront Maggie, incensed that she went to Newman and Mahoney first. She claims she was shaken up, didn't know who else to talk to.
2/10	Nightmares begin.
2/13	First hypnotic regression. I arrange & attend.
2/15	Maggie attends meeting of Newman's bozo group, refuses to drives BMW.

2/18	Second hypnotic regression. New-man arranges & I find out a week later when Maggie refuses to see hypnotist I set her up with in beginning.
2/21	Mahoney sends advance copy of *Saucer Slurs*. My attorney threatens to sue if newsletter is distributed on 2/23.
2/22	Mahoney's attorney says he'll withhold the newsletter from stands but not from subscribers.
2/23	M & I argue over her goddamn VW.
2/26	Julie & I meet for coffee. She thinks M has gone off deep end & holds me partially responsible.
2/27	M attends second bozo meeting.
3/2	Subscriber copy somehow gets to *A Current Affair*. They offer Maggie fifty grand for story. She refuses, but not out of deference to me. Idea of publicity horrifies her.
3/3	Call from Nate.
3/4	Nate & I meet. I tell him I'll consider his proposition. Meanwhile, I try to humor M. Her depression over miscarriage continues. Attends another bozo meeting.
3/6	Feature in *Miami Herald* appears. More crank calls, more arguments with M.
3/8	Yes to Nate.
3/10	Nate & I meet with Liscomb & Treak.
3/11	I suggest M seek psychiatric help. She leaves for house on Tango.
3/18	With no word at all from her in a week, I go to Tango. She is cold, unresponsive.

3/19	Piece in *Magician Times* ridicules me as debunker.
3/20	Second meeting with Liscomb & Treak.
3/23	M informs me she's filed for divorce.
3/24	Trip to convention in Vegas.
4/2	Return to crazy woman on porch. Goodbye, Maggie.

Blood pounded in her head. She stood so quickly the chair toppled. She experienced a swift, urgent compulsion to hurl the chair into the computer screen, to smash the photos on the walls, to damage the room, to *ruin* it. But her fear prevented it. Fear that he would return while she was in the midst of an adrenaline rage, that she would pull out the gun and blow him away. She turned off the computer and backed away, arms clutched to her waist as though a part of her believed her body would act without her consent, and fled from the house.

(3)

San Ignacio was the oldest church on the island and a cornerstone of Catholic life. For years, it had been more reliable than any of the local social services and, in the early eighties, had sheltered and fed more than five hundred Mariel refugees over an eighteen-month period.

This was made possible in part by the church's lucrative elementary school, which catered primarily to affluent Cuban and Anglo families on Tango. Judging from the size and lushness of the courtyard, these parishioners were very generous indeed. Aline thought.

The walks were cobbled, the gardens were meticulously tended, and the many small fountains were tiled in bright yellows and deep blues that whispered of ancient ties with Europe. At least a dozen cats roamed the grounds, hunting in the beds of impatiens, preening on mounds of grass, drinking from the tiled fountains. Several followed her right up to the front door of the convent, as if escorting her, and one marmalade cat strolled in with her.

The church had apparently made tremendous strides in the years since Aline had seen Audrey Hepburn in *The Nun's Story*. The woman at the front desk wore street clothes. Her short, graying hair wasn't covered. She didn't look to be suffering from sin or guilt or any of the Catholic edicts whose purpose had always escaped her.

"Hello, may I help you with something?" the woman asked pleasantly.

"I'm looking for Jean Mancino."

"Oh, Detective Scott. Hello." Dimples punctuated the corners of her mouth as she smiled and extended her hand. "I'm Sister Mary Catherine. I think Jean's still in the cafeteria. Supper was running late tonight, you know. Cook had a problem with the oven again. It seems we go for months where everything runs smoothly and then bang—" She slapped one palm against the other. "Everything goes at once."

"I have days like that all the time."

"The oven, the fan in the prayer room, the AC in the cafeteria. It's been a bad month." Sister Mary Catherine was rather portly but her bulk didn't slow her down. She moved at a swift clip through double oak doors and into a wide hall, chattering incessantly. Aline hurried alongside her and at the first pause, leaped in.

"You were friends with Jean's mother, right?"

"Oh, my, yes, years ago. In fact, I was Jean's teacher from kindergarten through third grade. Then her mother remarried and they moved and we didn't see as much of each other."

"Was that when she married the man Jean killed?"

Some of the sister's mirth hissed out of her. "Yes, that's right. Such a tragedy. For both of them." She brightened again. "But she's been doing wonderfully with us, both when she was visiting and since she was released. She works very hard wherever she's needed. And of course I think we're a good influence on her. I'm delighted that Dr. Treak consented to a temporary arrangement with Jean living here. We hope to make it permanent.''

''Has Jean talked to you at all about Margaret Wickerd?''

A small frown drew her brows closer together; they looped at odd angles over her clear hazel eyes. ''I'm afraid the recent incidents at the clinic have upset her more deeply than she's let on. And naturally, all this''—she waved a plump hand—''flying saucer business doesn't help things in the least.''

''So she's discussed it with you?''

''A little.''

Aline waited for her to go on, but she didn't. ''Discussed it in what context?''

''Oh, general things, you know.'' Her hand fluttered through the air again. ''Her concern about Margaret, how she's incapable of taking anyone's life, like that.'' She stopped outside another set of double doors and touched Aline's arm. ''You can't take anything Jean tells you too seriously, Detective Scott. She's given to, well, fanciful thinking. And I don't mean that in a derogatory sense.''

''Then how do you mean it?''

She fingered the crucifix she wore around her neck and gazed at a point just over Aline's left shoulder. Gazed intently. Aline nearly turned to see if anyone was standing behind her. An angel, a demon, God.

''I guess what I'm trying to say is that the line between what is real and what isn't often blurs in Jean's mind.'' Her eyes returned to Aline's face. ''If I told you, for instance, that I'd like to strangle the pope, you'd understand that it's just a figure of speech. But Jean might take it quite literally.''

Aline was under the impression that all good Catholics took things literally. The virgin birth. The host as the body of Christ. That God is always watching. That Satan is alive and well and living in Hackensack, New Jersey. But she kept her opinion to herself, and Sister Mary Catherine, bless her sweet old soul, smiled as though they had reached a mutual understanding and pushed through the double doors into the convent cafeteria.

(4)

Gone were the facial twitches, the nervousness, the frenetic energy. It was as if Jean the Lunatic no longer existed, Aline thought, and another woman now inhabited her body. This woman spoke softly, wore dark slacks with a pale blue pull-over sweater, and had her copper hair pulled back neatly with tortoiseshell combs. Her youthful innocence smacked of contradictions. Aline couldn't imagine this Jean killing her stepfather and chopping him up into little pieces.

They strolled through the courtyard, where the cool air was fragrant with jasmine, gardenias, the sweet lushness of damp earth. Jean talked about Sister Mary Catherine, the convent, the appeal of a cloistered life. To Aline, it sounded as though God would replace Thorazine and a weekly confession would be as good as a session with a shrink, but hey, whatever worked.

By the time they settled on a bench near one of the fountains, Jean still hadn't mentioned Margaret. She seemed content just to have someone to talk to about her plans, her hopes, her future. So Aline interrupted and asked her why she'd called.

"I have a paper to give you." She unzipped the large canvas purse in her lap and removed an 8 × 10 envelope. It was wrinkled and battered from being folded so many times and she clutched it as though it contained the secret of the universe. Perhaps, for her, it did. "These are from Dr. Winthrop's files. I knew I had to get you proof. My being a mental patient and all hardly makes me credible." She opened the envelope and handed Aline a letter dated April fourth of this year.

Dear Tyler:

   This is to confirm our conversation concerning Margaret Wickerd. You are to bill her monthly expenses to me personally. These shall include but are not limited to the monthly fee of $2,500 plus treatments, medication, and therapy. The fee shall not exceed $5,000 a month in any given month without written approval.

   The funds shall be paid by cashier's check and credited to Peter Wickerd's account. If you have any questions, don't hesitate to contact me.

                                                    Evan Nate

Well, well. So the government was footing Margaret's medical bills. "May I keep this?" Aline asked.

"That's why I took it. I don't want it."

"Why'd you go to all this trouble, Jean?"

Her mouth twitched, then fell still. "Because she's my friend."

The noble answer and probably true, but it wasn't the whole truth. "What haven't you told me, Jean?"

Her mouth twitched, stopped, twitched again. "Nothing." She drew herself up straighter and slung her purse over her shoulder. "Instead of accusing me of something, you could at least say thanks, you know. That's the least you could do." Visibly angry and hurt now, she got up and hurried away from the fountain. Aline went after her, caught her arm.

"Wait, Jean, I'm—"

She had a brief sensation of movement, of pressure exerted along the right side of her body, of the air shifting. Then she was sprawled on the ground, gasping for breath, the sheet of paper fluttering around her like a small, panicked bird whose wings had been clipped.

Jean rushed over to her, murmuring, "Oh, God, I'm sorry, I'm so sorry. Are you okay? You shouldn't have grabbed my arm like that. It scared me. It's not good when I get scared. Here, let me help you up. Oops, the letter, the goddamn letter."

She chased and caught it and crouched again. Aline rubbed her chest; it felt as if an ice pick were lodged in the center and it was an effort to speak. "How . . . what . . . ?"

"Tae kwon do." She brushed a strand of hair away from her forehead. "At one of the clinics I was in, it was part of our therapy, sandwiched in between aerobics and ballet. It's only supposed to be used for self-defense." She grasped Aline's elbow and pulled her to her feet. Her bones creaked and protested. Her chest ached. She took the letter from Jean and slipped it into the envelope. "Look, I appreciate what you've done, Jean. But I still think you haven't told me everything. When you feel like talking about it, give me a call."

As she handed Jean one of her business cards, a faint smile touched Jean's angelic face and seemed to glow like neon as Aline turned away.

18

(1)

Jones and Helen Newman didn't act like lovers, but Kincaid had the distinct impression that they were. The coyness in the way she laughed and spoke, Jones's attentiveness, the way he leaned toward her now and then as if to inhale the fragrance of her perfume: it was all there. The question was what it meant in the longer picture.

Jones got up several times while he and Helen were at the bar and went out into the lobby to use the phone. At 8:20, Helen finally rose from her stool, gave Jones's hand an intimate squeeze, and walked out of the bar. Kincaid watched her move through the double doors, no longer relying quite so heavily on her cane.

"I'll take her," Ferret said, already sliding out of the booth. He shrugged on a trench coat and flicked up the collar. A trench coat, for Christ's sake. It was too large on him and he had to fold back the hem of the sleeves so he could see his hands. He buttoned it to the throat and cinched it tightly at the waist, then grinned at Kincaid. "How do I look, Ryan?"

Like a man who has had a great night picking pockets, thought Kincaid. "You look fine, just fine. I'll check in with Bino if there's anything to report."

"Same here." Ferret worked a toothpick between his teeth. "Watch your back, amigo."

As Ferret followed Helen Newman out into the dark, Kincaid wondered how he would keep up with her. He always drove like a little old man, hunched over the steering wheel, his car stuck at thirty-five. He didn't have much time to dwell on it, though, because shortly afterward Jones left and Kincaid was right behind him.

The fed drove into the hills via the Old Post Road. He went west until he was beyond the Tango city limits, then turned east. Traffic was moderate and for most of the way Kincaid managed to keep at least two cars between them. Just outside the Cove city limits Jones swung into the lot of a small strip mall with the usual fixtures: a Publix grocery store, its slogan (WHERE SHOPPING IS A PLEASURE), visible on its huge sign; a drugstore; Video Biz; Radio Shack; and Book Emporium, the only bookstore on the island that carried the *South American Handbook*.

Jones parked; so did Kincaid. Jones went into the grocery store, emerged a few minutes later carrying a small brown paper bag, and walked over to a black van in the last row. As he knocked on its back door, Kincaid snapped several pictures of him. Then he locked the camera in the glove compartment.

At nine on the nose, Publix closed. Two minutes afterward the van backed up to leave and Jones was still inside. Here we go, Kincaid thought, and smiled.

(2)

Margaret watched the front of Lester's Bar & Grille from a wooded lot across the street. *Tick tock*, whispered the clock in her head. *Tick tock. Sam is late*. Unless he was already inside. But if he was, then his car would be in the lot and it wasn't. She had cruised through earlier just to be sure. Maybe he was driving a different car. His mother's car? Did old lady Newman leave a car on Tango while she was up north? Margaret couldn't recall their ever having talked about Sam's mother, but surely they had.

She rubbed her damp hands against her jeans. Rested her head against the seat. You wait, you bide your time, you don't take unnecessary risks, she thought. And for what? For this? To be hunted? To be blamed? To be framed? To wait at the edge of suspicion?

The door of Lester's opened and a couple came out holding hands, laughing, caught up with each other. Margaret looked away and watched a car headed toward her. It cruised past. *Tick tock*. Five more minutes, she thought. Then she would drive to the nearest phone and call him again. Five minutes, Sam, c'mon, c'mon.

Three minutes later, a maroon Volvo swung into the lot and stopped under a tree at the far corner of the lot; a man got out. Sam. It was Sam. Leather jacket. Jeans. Shoulders hunched against the chill. She began to ache all over but forced herself to wait.

He went into the bar and she sat through the departure of one car and the arrival of two others, each with a couple inside. None of them looked like cops, but she couldn't be sure. That was the point, though, wasn't it. There were no certainties now. No guarantees.

Margaret drove across the street, parked in the lot, headed for the rear door. She walked quickly but not too quickly, aware always of the weight of the gun in her purse. Despite the cool air, beads of perspiration gathered on her upper lip. Then she was opening the door, stepping inside the darkness, the smell of smoke, the noise of voices and "A Day in the Life" blasting from the jukebox.

Do tell, she thought. A Day in the Fucking Life of.

She thought of the times she and Sam had come here, a stolen hour, an afternoon, the two of them meeting like thieves. She clutched the memories against her as though they would protect her somehow, an amulet that would get her through the day.

Margaret picked him out of the crowd, the tall guy with the curly hair. Sam hated his hair. She wondered if Helen knew that, wondered just how much Helen knew about any of it. Maybe she and Pete had discussed it, trading information the way other people exchanged opinions or recipes. Maybe Helen, despite a decade of marriage, knew less about Sam than she did. Margaret rather liked that idea.

Sam walked over to an empty booth with a beer in hand, sat down facing the front door, his back to her. She kept her head bowed and moved toward him, her cheeks suddenly hot, feverish.

She slipped wordlessly into the booth and slid all the way to the wall. Sam, perched at the edge of the booth where he could keep an eye on the front door, didn't move. His blue eyes, eyes she could drown in, drank in the sight of her. His bottle was frozen midway to his mouth and when he set it down beer splashed over the sides. He moved so deftly and quickly into her side of the booth that it was as if he had always been there. He hugged her hard, his mouth against her neck, in her hair, whispering her name. Then he sat back, staring at her, smiling, his hands roaming her face, reading its bones, its lines, its stories.

"I didn't think you were coming," he said at last, his voice very, very soft, his hand gripping hers.

She felt an almost unbearable weight against the backs of her eyes and knew her senses couldn't support such weight very long. Her heart was already straining with the weight, hammering against her ribs, and she enclosed his hand in both of hers. You're real, Sam, she thought. Real.

"I was waiting to see if you'd been followed."

"I was careful." He kissed her and his hands slipped inside her jacket and over her breasts and her mouth opened against his and he breathed into her, filling her with the sound of her own name. Then he pulled back a little. "We'd better not stay here. The FBI has taken over the homicide investigation and the search for you. An agent named Jones, John Jones, came by Mom's place yesterday to ask me a few questions."

He talked—about what he'd pieced together, about what Hugh had discovered, about Pete—and he kept touching her.

One hand moved from her ribs to the side of her breast as if to define its shape, its contour, and the other slipped to the inside of her thigh. They were two figures hunched in a dark corner of a darkened booth, lovers who didn't have much time, and he was going to make her come without ever touching her skin.

"Don't, Sam, please."

But she heard the thick hoarseness of desire in her voice and so did he. "Let's get out of here," he said in the low, throaty tone she remembered so well, his body turned so that it formed a wall between her and the rest of the bar. Then his mouth was against hers again and he whispered that he wanted her, wanted to be inside her, and did she remember that day in the woods? Did she remember that day in the car when they'd left the fruit market? Did she remember . . . did she . . . did she . . .

His voice, the music, the pressure of his hand: it was like a teenage lust. She pulled back from him, her head pounding, and was astonished that nothing around her had changed. They were still in the booth, the air thick with music and voices and smoke, and now he was reaching for the bottle of beer, his face flushed, his voice odd, disjointed, as though they were trapped under a small glass dome where every sound echoed.

A shadow fell over them. She felt its weight, its substance and chill, its power to stoke the raw terror that hadn't been entirely absent since her escape. The inside of her mouth went instantly dry and a memory surfaced, whole and untouched, like a corpse that has been perfectly preserved at the bottom of the Arctic. A memory of Hugh.

Then the shadow moved, the shadow was on top of them. It belonged to a very tall man who was wearing a black leather jacket, slacks, a tie.

"I'm sorry for barging in like this," he said, standing right up against the edge of the table. "My name's Ryan Kincaid, Mr. Newman. We met at Ferret's a few years ago. There's a black van out in the parking lot with feds in it. One of them is a guy named John Jones who has taken over the investigation and—''

''I know who he is.'' Sam's voice was suddenly a stranger's voice, hard and dark. ''Where's the van? Front or back?''

''Back, but there are probably more men out front. There's a door through the kitchen that leads into a side alley. I think that's our best route.'' He looked at her then, turned his head and really looked at her. ''You and I are going to hold hands and head toward the flashing Pepsi sign. Mr. Newman, you follow us like the third wheel. If anyone comes in, don't glance toward the door. We'll stop briefly in the kitchen. Any questions?''

''Let's go,'' Sam said.

Kincaid gripped her hand tightly as they moved through the crowd. They passed the end of the bar, where a man on one of the twirling stools bit into a hard-boiled egg. From the jukebox, Mick Jagger bellowed ''Under My Thumb.'' Jimmy Stewart's benign face gazed down at her from a movie poster for Hitchcock's *Vertigo*. Yeah, she knew just how he'd felt.

Light intruded off to her left: the front door opening. She started to turn, to look, but Kincaid squeezed her hand. ''Don't.'' Then they were pushing through a set of double doors into the noisy clatter of Lester's kitchen, into the odor of chowder and seafood, bacon and burgers.

The room was nearly as large as the bar. An industrial-size stove and a long counter ran down the center of it, with another counter at one end and a small office and a pantry at the other. To the right of the pantry was a hall that angled off into darkness and above it was a bright red EXIT sign.

Four people hustled around, preparing sandwiches, chicken wings, and steamed clams, the staples of Lester's cuisine. Reggae music boomed from a transistor radio in the long window. They moved past the counter, the employees, through the sharp odor of something burning. Anxiety churned through her.

To come this far—

She cut the thought short and glanced at Sam, who was

bringing up the rear. His face was utterly white, as though he'd died and been embalmed. Sweat shone on his forehead. He managed a smile that was supposed to be reassuring but wasn't. A man with a tall chef's hat stopped them and Kincaid drew him off to the side, whispering urgently.

The chef glanced their way. Sam squeezed her hand. The chef nodded and Kincaid started toward them. She looked back as the double doors behind them swung open and a waitress strolled in, thumbing through a stack of orders. Behind her was a man in a coat and tie with fed written all over him.

In the instant that their eyes connected, everything else in the room dropped away. She and the fed stood alone in a cold, white space like enemies locked in the prelude of some ancient battle. His face was a pulsing light, a flawed moon. Then he shouted, "FBI, don't move!"

His voice crackled in the weird stillness and Sam suddenly lurched into her, shoving her roughly toward Kincaid. "Go!" he hissed, and she stumbled and Kincaid grabbed her hand and jerked her toward the dark hall and the glowing EXIT sign above it. In the seconds before Kincaid threw the door open, a shot rang out and she saw Sam falling back, back into the long counter. His name rose in a scream from someplace deep inside her, but it was too late. She was outside, Kincaid was pushing her into a white Saab, the car was now shooting up the alley, a pale bullet.

Seconds before they reached the end of it, the black van appeared, blocking their way. Its doors flew open and feds leaped out, their faces bright and flat in the wash of the Saab's headlights. Kincaid swerved around them, swung into the pines, and the feds opened fire.

The rear windshield shattered. Dark wind rushed through the car. The Saab shuddered and bounced across the floor of the woods. Her bones rattled like loose change. Another swerve and they were on pavement again, the van bearing down on them. Margaret scrambled over the seat, slivers of glass slicing into her hands, her knees. The gun was in her hand. She didn't remember digging it from her purse, but here it was, cold and heavy against her skin. So she steadied the gun, aimed at the advancing headlights, blew out the left one, and struck one of the front tires.

The van swung right, left, right in wide, careless arcs, tires shrieking. A bright, vivid image of Sam filled her head, Sam struck, Sam falling, and she squeezed the trigger again and again. Then the Saab leaned into an ascending curve and a moment later dived into the trees on the left. She watched as their branches sealed off the darkness behind them as surely as a boulder rolled into the entrance of a tomb.

(3)

When Kincaid was sure the van was no longer behind them, he stopped, killed the headlights, and turned around. He couldn't see her face, it was too dark, but he could hear her breathing. "Are you okay?"

"Yes." She climbed into the front seat. "But Sam—"

"Sam will be fine."

"Don't patronize me, Kincaid," she snapped. "I saw what happened. He was shot, he—"

"He pushed you out of the way and gave us the lead we needed, so let's not fuck it up." He cranked up the car, turned on the dim lights, and putted along in first gear.

Do whatever you have to do to find her, Ryan . . .

Done, Chief, she's found, now what? This wasn't what Frederick had in mind, but he couldn't change it now. So he drove steadily northward on back roads, dirt roads, and no roads at all, deeper and deeper into the wilderness in the cat's right ear. Neither of them spoke, which suited him just fine. He wasn't in the mood to answer questions or debate the moral issue of their abandoning Newman. Choices had been made and now they would live with them, good or bad, for better or for worse.

The problem wasn't where to go; it was getting there undetected, getting there before the needle on the gas gauge swung into the big red *E* and didn't swing back again.

He had already discounted the Super Cub as their ticket off the island; the feds would have the airport covered. The airport, the ferry, the bridge. Bye-bye, mainland. That left the open waters or the glades. But none of the boat-rental outfits stayed open after nine and it was well past that now. Bino might be able to procure a boat, but it would entail getting to a dock in the Saab, and by now the Saab was probably on a shit list.

That left the cabin. Ferret's cabin. He'd built the place years ago, his hedge against disaster: war, economic collapse, famine. He was ready for anything short of out-and-out nuclear devastation. It stood in the heart of ten acres of land in the Tango hills and backed up to the wilderness preserve. There was no electricity, no phone, and the water came from a well and smelled like rotten eggs. But the firewood would keep them warm for a month of nights like this one and there were sufficient provisions to see them through a very long time. Most of all, the cabin was safe and would buy them a little time.

. . . and if she's still on the island, get her off. I don't care how you do it. Just do it, then get in touch with me.

Easier said than done, *compadre*.

(4)

The temperature in the parking lot outside of Lester's Bar was now in the high forties, Nate guessed, about thirty degrees lower than what he found comfortable. But the chill was somehow fitting and he took a modicum of comfort in the fact that asshole Jones didn't look any more comfortable than he was.

"What's the prognosis on Newman?" Nate asked.

"I don't know, sir. He's in emergency surgery. Two of my

men are at the hospital and will be there for however long it takes for him to regain consciousness.''

"*If* he regains consciousness.''

"Uh, yes, sir.''

Nate's mind raced, weighing consequences. Even if Newman died, his death and the shooting were justifiable; he was aiding and abetting a fugitive who was armed and considered dangerous, a mental patient whose most recent victim had been her own sister. There might be problems with the local yokels, but nothing they couldn't deal with. Okay. Fine. They were covered with Newman.

"We've had an eye on him since he moved into his mother's place,'' Jones was saying. "The van's directional mike picked up a call last night from Mrs. Wickerd and another call from her tonight. They arranged to meet here.''

"Then how the hell did this other fellow get to Newman and the woman first?''

"I, uh, don't know, Colonel.''

He didn't know. Nate wondered how many battles like this had been lost to incompetence. "Who is this man?''

"He's a private eye. I don't know how he got involved in any of this.''

His voice had taken on a kind of whine that Nate found immensely irritating and he barely repressed an urge to knock his goddamn teeth down his goddamn throat. But in all fairness to Jones, he had only part of the story and couldn't possibly comprehend what was at stake. And yet even if he did, would it have made a difference? Nate doubted it. *Shit happens, Mr. President. You know how it is.*

He felt a sudden, terrible fatigue that seemed to press down against his shoulders with an almost unbearable weight, weakening the muscles in his legs until he thought his knees would buckle. He leaned into his car and watched the tow truck trundle out of the lot with the black VW bug attached to the back of it. Jones had run a make on every car in the lot, and the VW had come up with Margaret's name on it. Nate had no idea where she'd kept it. Another tow truck was taking care of the Volvo. Both cars would be searched thoroughly, but Nate wasn't holding his breath for answers.

"So does this dick have a name, Jones?"

"Ryan Kincaid, Colonel."

Kincaid. The man Sapizzo had shadowed. Jesus. "You know anything else about him?"

"Just that he's a pilot, Colonel, and—"

"A *pilot*? Is that what you just said, Jones? He's a fucking *pilot*?"

Jones winced; it deepened the creases in his weathered face. "The airport's covered, sir."

"That's good to hear, Jones, because if it wasn't, it'd be your ass. You got any idea how big this island is?"

"Not exactly, sir. Probably twelve by eight miles, something like that."

"Eleven by seven. At any rate, not very big as far as islands go, right, Jones?"

"Not very big at all."

Nate rolled onto the balls of his feet, leaned into Jones's personal space, and stabbed his thick index finger against the agent's chest. "Then let me suggest, Jones, that you get as many men as you think you'll need to comb every inch of this very fucking *tiny* island to find one woman and one man and that you do it immediately. When you find them, call me. There's to be no interference from the local cops. While you're at it, Jones, it might behoove you to pump your lady friend on additional information about her wayward husband. And this time make sure you ask her the right questions. Because we're running out of time. Have I made myself clear?"

"Yes, sir. Very."

"That's good, Jones. I hope we don't have to have another conversation like this."

"Uh, sir, there's one more thing. It seems that Kincaid lives with the detective who was investigating this case before we stepped into the picture."

The lady cop hired her boyfriend to poke around and the boyfriend found Mrs. Wickerd and now they were fugitives,

Nate thought. Perfect. ''Then if I were you, Jones, I would head straight over to the police department and find out what she knows.''

''I'll get on it right away, sir.''

On his way into the hills, Nate stopped at a pay phone and called Sapizzo. ''Your man in black routine has backfired, Paul. So you're going to set things right now and do it exactly as I tell you.''

''You bet, Colonel. Shoot.''

Nate explained, told Sapizzo to repeat the instructions, then said: ''Call me at the complex when you're finished.''

''You got it.''

No, he didn't have it. But, Christ willing, he would have Margaret Wickerd by morning and Kincaid and the lady cop would be out of the way.

Part Four

THE LOST PLEIADE

"When you get out there and you look at the infinity of time and the infinity of space . . . you begin to notice how small our earth actually is in comparison to the vastness of the universe. Statistically, there has to be an infinite number of other earths and an infinite number of other civilizations."
—Eugene A. Cernan,
        Commander of the *Apollo 17* mission

19

(1)

In the glare of the headlights, the cabin looked two-dimensional, a paper cutout pasted against the skin of the dark. "Who owns it?" Margaret asked.

"Ferret. Only his partner and I know about it. It's basic, but we'll be safe here for tonight."

"And what about tomorrow?" She turned toward him, her dark hair a wild tangle around her very pale face. "What then?"

"I don't know. My job is to get you off the island, but that's going to be difficult."

"Your job for who, Ryan?"

Good question. Frederick had made it clear from the start that Kincaid was on his own, and after what had happened at Lester's, he suspected he was very much on his own now. "Let's talk inside."

He turned off the engine, killed the headlights, and her face was hidden in darkness once more. They moved quickly and silently to the screened porch, night sounds crowding around them. The door to the screened porch was unlocked and the key to the front door was where it always was, taped to the underside of the rotting wicker rocker. Kincaid switched on his flashlight as they stepped inside, located the lanterns on the old wooden table, lit a pair, and handed her one.

The cabin consisted of a front room that also doubled as

253

a kitchen, a bedroom, and a small bathroom with a shower no larger than a closet. He knew the one-car garage out back held a 1968 Rambler, Ferret's emergency wheels. It might get them off the island, but probably not much farther, and that, Kincaid thought, was assuming that it would even start.

"There's food in the pantry if you're hungry. You can take the bedroom at the end of the hall. I'll bunk on the couch."

"How about hot coffee and a bite to eat?"

"Great."

While she puttered in the kitchen, Kincaid started a fire, then lit the gas water heater and dug out comforters and linen from the hallway closet. When he returned to the front room, the aroma of fresh coffee had chased off the musty, shuttered smell of the air. Margaret announced that the clam chowder would be ready shortly. Kincaid said he had to get some things from the car, zipped up his jacket, and stepped out into the cold again.

Stars stood out against the sky, bright and crisp and close enough to touch. Their light spilled over the pines that populated these woods, tall, scruffy Tango pines whose tops swayed in a gentle easterly breeze. The Saab looked diminished among them, the long survivor of some long-forgotten holocaust.

All that remained of the rear windshield were jagged peaks of glass. The lid of the trunk was pocked with dents from bullets. The sides were scratched and gouged from branches. The right front tire seemed to be losing air and the spare was flat. Overall, the damage wasn't as bad as he'd expected; everything could be repaired. But not tonight. Not tomorrow. If they were going anywhere, it would have to be in the Rambler.

He drove the Saab behind the cabin and parked it under the trees next to the garage. In the event the feds began an air search, the car would be less visible here. Beyond that, he didn't have the vaguest idea what the situation called for. What the hell was he supposed to do, anyway? Hide out here indefinitely? Call Frederick and inform him he'd found Margaret, but hey, there was a slight problem? Call Aline and hope she understood? *What?*

In his more than twenty years in this business, he'd never been in a position quite like this one. It was the oldest catch-22 in the book, damned if you do and damned if you don't.

He unlocked the trunk and unzipped the canvas bag he kept inside for emergencies. It contained a couple of changes of clothes, toiletries, odds and ends, and a Heckler & Koch P7-M13. He would have preferred a powerful rifle, but this automatic pistol wasn't a bad substitute. It held thirteen rounds, and unlike conventional single- or double-action automatic pistols, the P7 had a special cocking lever that comprised the entire front strap of the gun. When squeezed as the hand gripped the pistol, the lever caused the firing pin to be cocked and then released as the trigger was pulled. Unless the gun was properly held and the cocking lever pulled back, the gun wouldn't fire. This cocking feature made it awkward for shooters accustomed to more conventional handguns and had saved Kincaid's ass on more than one occasion.

He had fifteen rounds of ammo for this gun and another ten for the .38 in his shoulder holster. Enough to see them through a tight spot.

He unlocked the glove compartment, removed the camera, and stuck it into the bag.

He went back inside. Margaret had set bowls of chowder and mugs of coffee on the coffee table in front of the fire and was seated on the couch, smoking a cigarette and gazing into the fire. She glanced up as he dropped his bag at the side of the couch and settled on the floor across from her.

"I want you to know I didn't kill my sister, Ryan. I found her, but I didn't kill her. But it's possible that I killed Dr. Liscomb when he was trying to restrain me for treatment. I honestly don't remember. I didn't even realize Hugh was dead until I remembered where my VW was and found Sam's note."

"Maybe we should start with the things you *do* remember."

As she talked, firelight eddied across her features,

smoothing away the lines of fatigue at the corners of her eyes and mouth. He thought she was quite pretty, but beneath the prettiness she had the look of a woman who knows there is something terribly wrong with her life and isn't quite sure how to fix it. But she didn't look crazy. She didn't act crazy. She didn't talk crazy. There was, in fact, such an absence of weirdness about her that it made her claims tougher to dismiss.

Her recollection of what had happened to her that night eight months ago sounded like the typical abduction scenario. A lonely road, a bright light where there shouldn't have been any lights, then more than five hours of missing time, which she had gradually filled in before her commitment. Once the treatments had started, though, she'd lost some of those memories again.

"What did Sam tell you?"

Pain grew in her eyes at the mention of Newman. She sat back, clutching the mug of coffee, and pulled her legs up against her. "He said Hugh had been in touch with a guy named Ricky Ricardo who supposedly works for this Colonel Nate. He'd given Hugh information about the Lost Pleiade project, but Hugh was suspicious; he thought it might be part of some elaborate disinformation campaign.

"Sam also claims Pete never paid a penny out of his own pocket for my expenses at the clinic, that the colonel was billed directly because of an agreement he and Pete had made. Hugh didn't have proof, but I found proof tonight on Pete's computer." She told him about it, then slipped her fingers into the pocket of her jeans and brought out a plastic card. It looked like a credit card, but it was unmarked.

"I found this in my purse after I escaped. At first I thought it was the card patients use to charge purchases they make at the clinic drugstore and gift shop. But Hugh gave it to me before my escape. I think he may have gotten it from this Ricardo fellow."

She handed it to Kincaid. The magnetic strip on one side was half as wide as the card. "Did he say what it's for?"

"He said it opens the door to the Crystal Cavern. I think

I knew what it meant at the time, but I don't now. Is there anything by that name on Tango?''

Kincaid felt an odd tightness in his chest. ''Yes. A cavern less than two miles uphill from where your sighting took place. Years ago, it was mined for basalt, then it was expanded and became a weather research station, which it still is.''

But what if it wasn't just a weather station? Kincaid thought.

''You mean, people work in it?''

''As far as I know.''

''Would it be possible for us to get in?''

''If it is, we will. But let's get some sleep and then at first light I'll look at the Rambler in the garage and see what it'll take to get it moving.''

''I'd like to find out how Sam is.''

''I don't think you can do that without jeopardizing yourself.'' *And me.*

The intensity of her struggle burned briefly in the dark pools of her eyes. Then she nodded reluctantly, picked up her purse, walked down the hall to the bathroom. A palpable sadness lingered in the air through which she had passed.

(2)

Aline came to suddenly, blinking hard against the darkness, senses straining to detect whatever had awakened her.

But the lighthouse was utterly still; outside, only a shiver of wind skipped in from the Gulf. And yet both the skunk and the cat, positioned at opposite ends of the bed, were sitting up, alert, listening. Then Wolfe made a weird sound in his throat and suddenly jumped to the floor, followed a moment later by Unojo.

A car, she thought. They'd heard a car pull up to the front gate. But it was only four A.M. Kincaid rarely got home from the clinic before half-past six and there wasn't much traffic outside the lighthouse at this hour.

She slipped out of bed, looked around for jeans to pull on under her nightshirt but couldn't find them. Forget the jeans. She picked up her .38. At the bedroom doorway, a chill nipped at her bare feet. Granted, the lighthouse was drafty, but not like this.

A window was open somewhere.

She felt the burn of a hunch in her chest, flicked off the safety catch on the gun, and moved quickly down the hall, past unused rooms with windows sealed as tightly as some medieval virgin's chastity belt. *You couldn't pay me to stay alone in this place at night.* Uh-huh, thank you, Bernie.

She paused at the top of the spiral staircase, listening, certain someone was inside. She heard only the rumble of the icemaker in the freezer downstairs. That was it. But the sour taste of fear at the back of her throat, the dampness of her hands, the tenseness of her bones said that wasn't it. And yet she hesitated. At some level, she was certain that when she descended, she would find the creatures of Margaret Wickerd's nightmare swarming through her kitchen like busy ants. Were aliens impervious to guns? Did they bleed? Did they speak English?

She started down the staircase, praying that the old metal steps wouldn't creak or suddenly pull out of the wall. She reached the bottom and pressed up against the wall. The chill that eddied over her feet told her the sliding glass door to the atrium was open. Then she heard the rustle of papers in the kitchen.

She slipped around the corner and saw a figure hunched over her desk, going through one of the drawers. "There's a gun at your back, asshole, so raise your arms very slowly and turn around."

He raised his arms and turned, but not slowly. Instead, his body spun like a dancer's in a dizzying, graceful pivot that transformed him into a human dust devil, a giant dervish clutching the wooden desk chair. It slammed into her before she'd even squeezed the trigger, knocked the gun halfway across the room, and threw her back into the wall.

Then he was on her, hissing, "We goin' for a ride, bitch," and he jerked her to her feet by the hair. She screamed and slammed her elbow into his ribs. He kneed her in the small of the back, one hand clamped down over her mouth, the other twisting her left arm behind her until she thought she would pass out from the pain.

"We could sure have us some fun before the ride, though." He laughed and swirled his tongue in her ear and his hand dropped from her mouth and she gasped as he twisted her arm harder, higher. "No screamin', bitch." A switchblade appeared at the side of her face. " 'Less you want me to poke your pretty eyes out."

"No screaming," she whispered.

He spun her around by the left arm, touched the blade to her chin, his dark eyes boring into hers. "Nothin' personal. Got me a job to do, is all." The blade dropped lower, to her throat. The fingers of his other hand gripped her arm so tightly, she could feel their tips against her bones. "Soft skin." The blade nicked at the flesh on the underside of her jaw. "Bet your boyfriend sure likes that soft skin, huh."

A wall of sweat sprang across her back.

"Answer me, bitch."

"Yes," she rasped.

"Yes what?" The tip of the blade sank a little more deeply against her skin. "C'mon, bitch. Tell me what you like him to do."

"T-to . . . to . . ."

"Aw, the little lady's scared." The blade suddenly tore down the front of her nightshirt, tore so expertly and quickly that it didn't even graze her skin. He flicked the torn shirt open. "Bet he sucks good on these tits, huh."

Aw, Christ, no.

He drew the tip of the blade in a circle around her right nipple, then pinched it with his fingers. "That make you hot?" he whispered, leaning closer to her, so close she could smell the beer and smoke on his breath and see the fathomless black of his eyes. "You like that? Your boyfriend do it any better? Huh? Answer me, bitch!"

"N-no. No better."

He backed her up to a wall, let go of her arm, and held the knife at her throat as he thrust his hand between her legs. "He do this to you?"

"Yes." *Think fast, do something, don't just stand here.* "B-but not that hard."

He chuckled, slipped his hand inside her underwear, thrust his fingers inside her. Her dinner surged up her throat and lodged there; she could barely breathe. "This better, bitch?"

"Y-yes."

"You're not wet. Let's get these panties off." He pulled his hand out of her underwear and began to roll them over her hips.

"I'll do it."

The knife's pressure eased, as though he were considering it, then he stepped back, watching her and grinning as she rolled them down. She bent over and stepped out of them slowly.

Now, do it now.

Fist balled, Aline snapped up and caught him on the underside of his jaw. Pain blazed through her hand and radiated in hot flashes halfway up her arm. But he was falling back, back, astonishment frozen on his face. She slammed her foot into his crotch before he struck the floor, then dived for her gun. But he was already up, tearing into the hall, toward the open glass door, moving faster than anyone had a right to move.

She fired.

He kept running. She fired again, but he flew through the door and vanished into the dark beyond the atrium. Moments later, a car fired up. She slid the door shut, locked it, dropped a plank of wood in the track. She hurried to the front door, made sure the dead bolt was still engaged, and slid the chain lock into place as well. Then she backed away, trembling, her skin crawling, and ran around to the windows on the first floor, locking all of them.

When she was absolutely certain she was sealed up inside the lighthouse, she charged into the bathroom on the first floor, locked the door, and leaned into it. A sob burst from her mouth. *His hands on me. Sapizzo's hands. His fingers inside me.* She dropped the gun on the tank of the toilet, leaped into the shower, and stood under the spray, soaping herself again and again, until her cries subsided and there was no hot water left.

Sapizzo, you fuck, you're going to pay for this.

(3)

The peals of the phone bounced against the sealed silence in the lighthouse like a Ping-Pong ball. Aline, seated in the family room and wrapped up in a terry-cloth robe, stared at the phone and stroked Unojo, who had jumped into her lap.

She decided to let the machine get the call. It was probably Frederick again. He'd called half a dozen times last night, his voice thick with his usual urgency and blatant disregard for her days off. He could just wait for once in his goddamn life. She wasn't in the mood for him, for the department, for any of it. She intended to wait until Kincaid got home and then they would go after Sapizzo themselves.

"Hello? Detective Scott?"

She rose quickly and grabbed the receiver. "Gerald." The kid from the docks. "Kind of early for calls, isn't it?"

"Uh, yes, ma'am. I just wanted to let you know that Mr. Morales is back and I gave him your message. He said to meet him at Lester's at ten."

"This morning?"

"Yes, ma'am."

"Why'd you wait until now to call me, Gerald?"

"I just saw him a little while ago. I came in early to finish the billing and he was here. I got the impression that he may be going away for a while."

"Why didn't he call me himself?"

"I don't know, Detective Scott. I didn't ask him."

No, of course not. Gerald, like Sapizzo, was a good little foot soldier, a faithful minion who took orders and carried them out, right or wrong.

Like me? Is that what I am? She thanked him and as she hung up, she felt the lump swelling in her throat again.

(4)

The call came through on the phone in Nate's office in the complex. Sapizzo sounded hopped up, as though he'd been out drinking or screwing or both most of the night.

"The problem is, uh, taken care of, sir."

"*Very* good, Paul. You'll get a bonus for this one. What'd you do with her?"

"In the glades, sir. The gators will do the rest. You goin' to be back at the house today?"

"No. But stick close to the apartment. I may need you up here later."

"Got it, sir."

(5)

At 6:15, the phone in the lighthouse pealed again. Aline was certain it was Kincaid calling to ask if he should pick up any groceries on the way home, and she grabbed the receiver and said, "Yes, we need milk and coffee." *And I need you here, Ryan.*

"Correction," Bernie said. "You're going to need a massive dose of Valium. How soon can you get over here, Al?"

"Forget it. I'm off."

"Newman had emergency surgery last night and Bill says the prognosis looks pretty good, but he still hasn't regained consciousness."

"What're you talking about, Bernie?"

"Newman, Margaret Wickerd, and Ryan. He's in deep shit, Al. The—"

"Ryan's at work."

"No, he . . ." Bernie covered the phone with her hand, but Aline could hear Frederick's gruff voice in the background. Then Bernie whispered, "The chief's royally pissed. He says he called you a zillion times last night. See you in twenty minutes, Aline." She hung up.

Kincaid in deep shit, Newman in emergency surgery. Kincaid—hurt? Dead?

She sailed into the department seventeen minutes after Bernie's call. The dispatcher was on the phone, but she pointed an index finger at the ceiling and tossed a copy of the morning's *Tango Tribune* on the counter. Margaret Wickerd was the lead story.

Aline read the story as she climbed the stairs; Kincaid wasn't mentioned. Maybe Bernie was wrong. Maybe, if, suppose . . . Oh, Christ, she thought, and detoured into her office before heading down the hall to Frederick's. She called the apartment above Ferret's garage. "Yo," the little man said in a surprisingly chipper voice.

"Did you see Ryan last night?"

"Where're you calling from, Sweet Pea?"

"The secure line in my office."

"You positive it's secure?"

"Yes."

He hesitated, then said: "We met at the Flamingo to keep an eye on Jones and his boys, figuring they might lead us to Margaret Wickerd. Helen Newman met Jones in the bar. We got the impression there was something going on between them."

"A romantic something?"

"Right. So we hung around, and when she left, I followed her and Ryan waited to see what Jones was going to do. We were each going to call Bino if anything developed, but Bino never heard from him. Or from me. I sat at the end of Helen's street until midnight. She didn't leave and no one visited her, so I split. I figured nothing had panned out on Ryan's end, either. Then I saw the headlines this morning.''

''He's not mentioned in the story, Ferret.''

''True. But I just got off the phone with the chef at Lester's and it was Ryan, all right. The chef says it looked like Sam pushed Margaret out of the way and took the bullet intended for her. Bino went up to the hospital to see if we could get in to see him, but no go. Feds are posted at the door.''

''You have any idea where they went?''

''Off island if Ryan's got any sense.'' He dropped his voice a notch. ''And forgive me if I'm mistaken, Sweet Pea, but I believe your esteemed boss and Ryan arrived at some private deal concerning Margaret Wickerd. He didn't come right out and say it, but I could smell it on him.''

Yeah, she could, too. ''What about the Cub?''

''Nope. It's still at the airport. And besides, I think the feds have the airport sewn up.''

''Boat?''

''Doubtful. Our boat contacts are few and far between.''

Then he was still on the island. She tested this possibility against her knowledge of Kincaid and knew it was right. Stay hidden, plan, wait until dark.

''If I hear anything, Sweet Pea, I'll call. Bino and me, we'll be hanging around the hospital waiting for news about Sam.''

''Right. Thanks, Ferret.''

Gloom filled her as she hung up and began to tally the number of years Kincaid could spend at Raiford if he was caught. She figured fifteen to twenty with a good attorney, half that with gain time for good behavior and a sympathetic parole officer. His longest trip ever.

She would be gray by the time he was released. She would be living closest to whatever slammer he was in, visiting on weekends and holidays and remembering when she could have changed the outcome—or at least altered it somewhat—

by resigning from the department and risking her future on the uncertainty of self-employment. Something that simple.

Do you know the secret of the Lost Pleiade now, Ryan?

Did Helen Newman know?

Did Paul Sapizzo?

And what about Frederick?

She didn't bother knocking on the door to his office. She simply opened it and strolled in. Frederick was on the phone and slapped his index finger against his watch when he saw her. Bernie, seated on the couch, gave her a warning look that spoke tomes about what had transpired before she'd arrived, then pointed at Aline's bruised and slightly swollen right hand, her eyes asking what had happened. "Long story," Aline mouthed, and glanced toward Jones.

He stood at the window watching the sky lighten as if it was the most fascinating event he'd ever witnessed. She could guess at the chain of events that had led him here, with the colonel at the center of it all. Jones probably didn't know about Sapizzo, though, or about the order the colonel had given him to take her "for a ride." And she didn't intend to illuminate his ignorance. He was just one soulless foot soldier.

Aline walked back to the door, slammed it, and made a beeline for the coffeepot. She heard the receiver drop into the cradle, then Frederick's gruff voice sliced through the quiet. "Detective Scott, Special Agent Jones believes you may have information concerning the events at Lester's last night."

"I wasn't on duty last night."

Jones strolled toward her with the unhurried ease of a man who knows he holds three of the four aces in a deck. "This isn't about official business, Ms. Scott. It's about the private eye you live with, Ryan Kincaid."

"What about him?"

"Was he home last night?"

"Nope. He was working on a case."

"Oh?" Jones's brows shot up into bushy peaks. He reminded her of Snideley Whiplash just then, the cartoon villain of her youth who was forever tying helpless women to railroad tracks. "Would that be the case he's working on for you, Ms. Scott?"

She burst out laughing and looked at Frederick. "Did I ever tell you Ryan was working for me, Gene?" *C'mon, Gene, come clean, lay it on the line.*

"Not that I recall." Pushed into a corner, he defended her. "Like I told you earlier, Mr. Jones. They keep their cases quite separate."

"Ryan doesn't talk to me about his cases any more than Helen Newman discusses her court cases with you," she said, smiling sweetly. "And if you're accusing me of something, then spit it out. Don't stand there looking like you just swallowed your dick."

"That's enough!" Frederick barked, leaping to his feet, the blood vessel at his temple pulsing madly. "I won't have any—"

"You won't have what, Gene?" She turned on him with such vehemence, with such blatant disregard for the protocol the situation required, the protocol everyone *expected* her to follow, that Frederick's jaw dropped. "Tell me, please, I'm just dying to hear it."

"You're suspended," he spat.

"Wrong, I resign."

She slammed the door again on her way out, her anger so extreme that she was literally seeing red. It leaked from the walls, ran across the faded carpet in the hall, pulsed in the air like neon.

Bernie caught up with her before she reached the elevator, grabbed her elbow, spun her around. "What're you doing, Aline?"

Aline jerked her arm free, stabbed at the elevator button, and held out her badge. "Give that to Frederick. And this." She passed Bernie the envelope that contained the letter Jean Mancino had given her last night. "And tell him if he intends to let Ryan take the fall, he'd better think twice about it."

"You think I'm staying in this pisshole if you're not here?"

Bernie shook her head and darted into the elevator with Aline when the doors opened. "No way."

The doors shut and the elevator went down. "I need you here, Bernie. On my side. Please."

They stepped off the elevator at the same time, their strides perfectly synchronized as they moved in tandem past the dispatcher and toward the double doors. It was as if their neurological systems had suddenly merged. Their shoulders hunched in exactly the same way against the cold as they walked outside; their chins possessed identical, stubborn thrusts; their hands were jammed in their jacket pockets in precisely the same position. Each was utterly and completely aware of what the other was feeling.

This empathy, this strange and marvelous bond, had existed for more than thirty years.

They reached the curb. Cars whizzed past in the morning chill: commuters headed for work, people getting on with their lives. "Okay," Bernie finally said. "Okay, what do you want me to do?"

"Stall Jones. I need at least thirty minutes."

"Thirty minutes. You got it. What else?"

"I'll call you."

"Al, *ojo pelao*." She touched the corner of her right eye, pulling it down.

Keep your eyes open. "Count on it," she said, and hurried to her car.

20

(1)

At half-past seven on the nose, Nate stood at the edge of the tie-down area of the Tango Key airport. He wore jeans, a pullover sweater, his khaki aviator's cap, and a pair of aviator sunglasses. A chopper descended from the wide blue sky with the noisy bluster of a prehistoric bird, but what a marvelous machine it was, particularly in the hands of an accomplished pilot.

He downed the last of his coffee and strode out to the field, admiring the touchdown. As he climbed in, Henry Sheen grinned at him, Sheen wearing headphones, shades, and khaki like in the old days. "You know how long it's been since I've done this, Evan?" he shouted over the noise of the rotors.

"Too long," Nate replied with a laugh.

"Damn right. So where do we start? The Bureau pilots are covering the north end of the island."

"Not like we can cover it. Let's start at Lester's and work our way northward."

Something changed in Sheen's demeanor, something small that thinned his smile and made his nostrils flare. Then he flashed a thumbs-up and pushed the pitch control stick forward; the chopper began to rise. A flash of pain, Nate thought, that's all it was. Pain from the chemo, the cancer, pain that Sheen didn't want him to see. But as the ground fell away and the walls of blue sky rose up around them, he realized that for the first time in thirty-one years, he didn't know what Henry Sheen was thinking. And that frightened him more than the prospect of not finding Margaret Wickerd.

(2)

Aline heard the chopper before she saw it swoop out of the sky like some stone-age predator. Behind it was a second helicopter that was several hundred feet lower. They made tight, graceful arcs over the road, their powerful rotors beating the air so hard, she could feel the pressure of the noise in her head.

She knew they were scrutinizing the traffic on the road, searching for a white Saab, and she felt, suddenly, as though her life was under siege. She barely resisted the urge to slam her foot against the Honda's accelerator and race for the protection of the trees. Then they passed out of sight and she, gripping the steering wheel so hard her knuckles were white, drove a little faster to the next intersection and turned.

Her timing was perfect. Just as she pulled into the Newman driveway, Helen was coming out the front door, leaning on her cane. She wore a stylish red and navy blue shirtwaist with a red jacket, navy blue shoes, and a navy blue shoulder bag slung over her shoulder. Court attire, but not this early and not with her blonde hair loose, an ouzo river in the cool sunlight. Maybe a visit to her wounded hubby? Or breakfast with Jones before court?

"Morning, Mrs. Newman. Do you have a few minutes?"

"I'm afraid I don't." She fingered the gold heart that hung from a chain at her throat. The cluster of tiny diamonds on it caught the light, fracturing it. "I'm already late for an appointment."

"This won't take long." Aline stopped in front of her, blocking her way.

"I really can't, Detective Scott. How about sometime this afternoon? Around five-thirty."

"It can't wait."

"It'll have to." She stepped around Aline, who grabbed her arm. "Just what the hell do you—"

"We're going to have a little chat, Mrs. Newman. About what kind of information you've been feeding John Jones and why."

She pulled her arm free. Anger rippled across her features with the brightness of sunlight on aluminum. "You pull a stunt like that again and I'll have your badge yanked."

What fucking badge, Your Honor? "You're in no position to threaten me. I'm willing to concede my facts may be a little mixed up, so bear with me and feel free to correct me. The way I figure it, you've been feeding Jones information about your husband's abduction group. The experiences they've had, what the ETs look like, how they were treated, all of that. Specific details, particularly when it came to Margaret Wickerd's story. Then he passed the information on to Colonel Nate, who gave it to Vance Liscomb or Nina Treak, and then Margaret's so-called therapy was adjusted accordingly. Am I warm yet, Mrs. Newman?"

Helen's cane whistled through the cool blue air and Aline's hand, her injured hand, shot out, stopping a blow that was powerful and accurate enough to have broken her shoulder. She yanked the cane from Helen's hand, hurled it into the yard, and grabbed her by the front of her neat, crisp shirt-waist. Then she took a stab in the dark.

"You signed the commitment papers on Margaret, as a backup because Pete was afraid she might contest it. I want to know what's behind it."

"Take your hands off me, Detective Scott."

"Sure." As Aline released her, the gold chain around her neck snapped and the gold heart tumbled to the sidewalk.

"Look what you've done!" she shrieked, stooping to retrieve it. But Aline was faster. She scooped it up and turned it over in her hand, noting the inscription on the back.

"Oh. From John. What a shame." She dropped it and

covered it lightly with her shoe. "I probably can't crush those pretty diamonds, but I can sure screw them up."

Panic flooded Helen's eyes. She looked down at Aline's shoe, then up at her face. "Margaret deserved it." She spat the words. "So did Sam. They thought I didn't know. They thought I was blind. They thought . . . who knows what the hell they thought. It's all bullshit. She made up the whole story. She knew it was the one thing that would hold Sam. And it did, it did. Then John walked into my life and, yes, I told him things. I told him whatever he wanted to hear."

"Whose idea was it for you to sign those commitment papers?"

"Pete's." She tugged at her jacket, smoothed it. "He knew he was treading thin ice with that commitment because Margaret had filed for divorce. Pete wanted a backup. He wanted the divorce petition to disappear. So I accommodated him. Big deal."

"When did Jones enter the picture?"

"Not too long after that."

"How does the colonel fit?"

"I've never met the man."

"That's not what I asked."

Silence.

Aline pointed at her shoe. "Watch, Mrs. Newman."

"His arrangement was with Pete," she said quickly, perspiration beading on her face now. "About the payment for her treatment."

"Why's she such a threat to Nate?"

"I don't know."

"Give me an educated guess."

"I don't know enough to give you an educated guess."

"A bright lady like you? C'mon, you disappoint me."

"Maggie was . . . is . . . part of an experiment, that's all I know."

Aline moved her foot so that the heel of her shoe was now poised over the heart, the cluster of diamonds. "What kind of an experiment?"

"I don't know. I swear, I don't know. Nate is a big fish,

John's a little fish, and Maggie's in the way. It's about men playing spy games. The big boys have a secret and Maggie somehow stumbled into it, and beyond that, I . . . I don't know.'' Her voice broke. She covered her face with her hands and began to cry. ''It . . . it was never supposed to get so complicated. No one was . . . was supposed to get killed. Sam wasn't supposed to run off with her and get . . . get shot. . . .''

Uh-huh. And Kincaid wasn't supposed to get involved and she wasn't supposed to resign. Yeah. Shit happens.

She left the gold heart on the sidewalk and Helen Newman weeping into her hands.

(3)

When the helicopter swept in low over the pines, Margaret was halfway between the garage and the cabin, as visible as a monument on the midwestern plains. She dashed for the nearest clutch of trees, arms pumping at her sides, and dived into the thick shade, sprawling gracelessly through a bed of pine needles. She rolled, scrambled back until her spine pressed up against a trunk, and drew herself into a tight ball. A heartbeat later the helicopter looped into sight, a dark, menacing machine against which sunlight glinted.

The cabin was definitely visible. But no smoke issued from the chimney now, there were no cars in sight, and she hoped the pilot would write the place off as one more uninhabited winter home. She glanced toward the Saab, tucked safely within the folds of shade near the garage, and saw Kincaid beneath it, waiting as she waited for the helicopter to move on.

The choppers had been circling since dawn. They sometimes appeared in pairs, like insects mated for life, their movements so perfectly synchronized, they swooped and lifted at the same moments. But even when they were alone, they terrified her and a part of her died a little each time one appeared. It was as if she were awaiting execution while the hands of a loud but invisible clock marked the seconds to countdown.

As soon as the helicopter had moved on, Kincaid crawled out from under the Saab and she ran over to him. Without speaking, they went into the garage and resumed what they'd been doing before they'd been interrupted.

The Rambler was a pea-soup green covered with rust spots and bore a faded sticker on the back that said BE KIND TO FERRETS. It had a flat tire and a dead battery, so they had to push it out of the garage and into the shade. While she removed the Rambler's battery, Kincaid drove the Saab into the garage, removed its battery, and put it in the Rambler. The car sputtered to life belching clouds of greasy smoke, shuddering and shaking like a drunk in the throes of D.T.s. At this rate, the Rambler would hardly be inconspicuous on the highway. So Kincaid went to work under the hood, cleaning plugs, making adjustments, fine-tuning with the slow, meticulous skill of a surgeon.

Margaret, who knew nothing about cars, stood there feeling stupid and useless and nervously scanned the sky. When she couldn't stand it any longer, she studied the tools on the ground, picked up the one that looked best suited for the job, and sat on the ground by the flat tire.

"You ever done that before?" Kincaid asked peering around the edge of the hood.

"No."

She expected him to offer an instruction or two, like Pete or even Sam would do, or to say he'd get to it in a minute, but he didn't. She jacked up the car and popped off the rusted chrome rim. The shape, she thought, turning it around in her hands. The shape was like that of the room she'd been in that night, the room with the blinding lights, the soft, lubricious voice, the room where things had been done to her. She felt a hard pressure in the center of her skull, a memory struggling to escape, but just when she thought she could seize it, the noise of an approaching chopper tore through her concentration.

Margaret rolled under the Rambler from one side and Kincaid rolled under it from the other and they lay there hip to hip in the stink of gas and oil. She turned her head, cheek resting against her hand, and looked at him—grease streaked on his cheek, pine needles in his beard, sweat dimpling his brow. "Ryan, why're you really doing this?"

He looked at her. "I was hired to get—"

"No. I'm not talking about what you were *hired* to do. People are hired to do a lot of things, but that isn't it for you."

He rested his chin on his hands and gazed straight ahead. "Years ago in Nepal I was on a dirt road on the outskirts of a small village about fifteen thousand feet up in the Himalayas. I saw a light moving toward me. I guess it was two or three thousand feet up and maybe a quarter of a mile away. I figured it was a plane. But then it suddenly stopped, brightened, swooped down to five or six hundred feet, looped, shot straight up, and vanished. It lasted less than a minute. It wasn't a plane or a weather balloon or Venus or any of the other explanations that people like your husband come up with. I know what I saw. It was probably the most exhilarating fifty seconds of my entire life and influenced it more than I want to admit." He glanced at her, a wry smile lifting the corners of his mouth. "Does that answer your question?"

"Yes." She squeezed his arm. "Thanks for telling me."

"If there's anything in that cavern, Maggie, we're going to find it. Now, c'mon, let's finish up." With that, he rolled out from under the car.

.

(4)

Aline sat in the twilight of Lester's Bar & Grille nursing a tall glass of orange juice and nibbling at one of the house specialties, a ham and Swiss on rye. The hands on the clock over the jukebox now stood at 10:32. Morales, she thought, smelled like a no-show.

But in the event that he'd called and left her a message, she checked in with the bartender. When she told him who she was, he asked for ID and she passed him her license. He glanced at the picture, then at her, then at the picture again. She pegged him for an ex-county or state worker who had spent thirty years in a room without windows, shuffling papers and playing bureaucrat god. Some habits, she thought, you never outgrew. When he was satisfied that she was who she said she was, he slapped a white envelope down on the bar.

"Guy left this for you an hour ago."

"What'd he look like?"

"Light hair, maybe six feet, late thirties, just a guy."

Never trust a bartender for an accurate description of anyone. She walked back to the booth and tore open the envelope. Two things fell out: a neatly typed note and a plain plastic card with a magnetic strip on one side.

Regret that I can't stick around to fill in what you don't know. Paul Sapizzo can probably do that, but not willingly. Jean Mancino might be able to tell you a thing or two if you can keep her on course. At any rate, the card will get you through the cavern door when you're ready.

Sapizzo, Jean, a cavern door: abracadabra, presto chango, and just what the hell did she have here, anyway? Was Jean the woman Gerald had mentioned who had gone to see Morales several times?

Aline slipped the card into the zippered pocket of her jeans and stuffed the note in her purse. She had already decided to save Sapizzo until the last, so from the public phone she called the convent to make sure Jean was going to be there a while; Sister Mary Catherine said she was. Then she flipped through the phone book and found a listing for *Nate, Evan*. He lived out on Melaleuca Trail, a mostly dirt road that twisted through the island's citrus groves. If she remembered correctly, Kincaid had said that Sapizzo appeared to be taking care of the place and living in an apartment over the garage.

Hi, shithead. Remember me?

She left the bar humming softly to herself, the pain in her wrist not as bright or pervasive now. Outside, the sky was starting to cloud over and the air held a taste of rain. It had warmed to the mid-sixties and she stripped off her pullover and tossed it in the Honda's backseat.

From the trunk, she retrieved a canvas bag that was identical to the one Kincaid kept in the trunk of his Saab. It contained many of the same items, too, including a P7-M13. She loaded it when she was back in the car, put on her shoulder holster, pulled a lightweight windbreaker from the bag, and slipped it on.

Fifteen minutes later she was seated across from Jean Mancino in the convent cafeteria, amid the clatter of trays and the aroma of baked chicken. She looked as sweet and innocent as an angel, her copper hair pulled away from her face with tortoiseshell combs, her hands folded demurely in front of her. She was already firing questions at Aline about the article in the morning *Tribune*, but Aline cut her short. "Tell me about your visits to Ricardo Morales, Jean."

She began to twitch, to fidget, to look around.

"I want to help Margaret, Jean, but I need your help to do it. Please tell me what you know."

"I can help her myself. I don't need you."

"Margaret needs me and I need you."

Jean hesitated, twitching like a splayed frog, a dying fish. "She's my friend. Hugh was getting information from this Morales guy about things that concerned Maggie. He wouldn't talk to me about them." Twitch, twitch. "Neither would Maggie. They didn't want me to get into any trouble. So I went to Morales, but he wouldn't tell me anything. He told Hugh I'd gone to see him. Hugh got mad and told me I was meddling in things that weren't my business. He said if I didn't stop, he'd tell Liscomb or Treak. He threatened me, Detective Scott. *Me*. He was jealous of my friendship with

her. I know he was. I think that maybe he was in love with
her but wouldn't admit it to himself.''

"Did Morales give Hugh information about a cavern?''

"Yeah, right. Crystal Cavern. I took the convent car up
there one day, but I didn't find anything except an old hangar.''

"Why didn't you tell me all this stuff before, Jean?''

Her eyes filled with tears that fell as she twitched, as she
rubbed her hand across the back of her neck. "I . . . don't
know.''

"Is there anything else you haven't told me?''

Those wide, wounded eyes fixed on Aline's, eyes that
seemed to hold secrets so layered, so splintered, that a life-
time of therapy would be unable to retrieve them all. "No,''
she said softly. "There's nothing else.''

Aline didn't believe her. It must have shown on her face
because Jean, still twitching, stood quickly and hastened
away, her flowered skirt fluttering at her knees.

(5)

There was no warning, none at all. One moment they were
touching down near the terminal to refuel and the next, Sheen
muttered that he didn't feel well, turned his head to the side,
and puked. Nate cut the engine and helped him out of the
chopper. Sheen stumbled, fell to his knees on the tarmac,
and got sick again.

Nate somehow got him into the terminal restroom and was
now holding him by the shoulders as he hunched over one of
the sinks, coughing and splashing water onto his face. He
tried not to notice the specks of blood in the mucus Sheen
spat or how thin he felt under his hands, all bones and sharp
angles. He tried to ignore the odor of sickness that emanated
from the pores of Sheen's skin, the stink of decay, as though
he were rotting from the inside out.

"You don't have to hold me," Sheen murmured in a quavering voice as he straightened up. "It's okay now."

"Here, put this against your face." Nate pressed a wad of wet towels into his hands, but Sheen didn't seem to have the strength to lift his arms, so Nate wiped his face for him. "What's going on, Henry? Did you just have a chemo treatment or what?"

Sheen made a sound that was supposed to be laughter. "I had my last chemo two weeks ago."

"Then what—"

He pushed Nate's arm away gently and backed up to the wall. He leaned against it with visible relief, a man on dry land after weeks at sea. "Let's not kid ourselves, Evan. The odds of beating pancreatic cancer are piss poor. Hand me some more towels, will you?"

Nate yanked more towels from the dispenser. An ache throbbed at his temple. He had a sudden urge to weep, to press his hand over Sheen's mouth so he wouldn't have to hear the rest of this. He didn't want to know. He was terrified of knowing. Terrified for Sheen, terrified for himself.

Sheen wiped at his clothes with weak, pathetic motions. "The cancer's spread to my lungs, Evan."

Nate experienced a sharp, biting pain inside his chest, as if the lungs under discussion were his own. He groped for something to say, but his mind had gone utterly and completely blank and he realized there was nothing to say. It had all been said on their last fishing trip together, when Sheen had spelled things out in the calm, unhurried voice of a man who has glimpsed death's approach and prepared for it. His stash of Seconal would do the trick when the pain became unbearable. His financial affairs were in order. His wife and kids were well provided for. The only loose end was the Lost Pleiade.

"Jesus, Henry. How long have you known?"

"Since the day before we met on the ferry." He looked up then, his face wan, his eyes bright with pain, regret, sadness. "It's been an extraordinary five years, Evan, but maybe it's time to terminate the project. Destroy the records, seal the cavern, bury the whole goddamn thing.''

"If you and Booth hadn't insisted on bringing Treak and Liscomb into it, Henry, none of this would have happened. We didn't need them. We didn't need data on brainwashing and stemming aggression, we didn't—''

"We needed them to help justify the expense,'' Sheen snapped. "And that's all beside the point now. We both know that when I'm gone, you'll have Jimbo on your side and that's it. And he's so caught up in balancing the books, you can't count on him like we've been able to count on each other. The other two on the committee . . .'' He shrugged. "To them it's just another spy game, Evan. The whole thing will get fucked. Hell, it's fucked now. You know it, I know it, and we both know that's why I showed up here today. It's got to end, Evan.''

Seal the cavern, terminate the project, blow up Room 13. No way. "You're going to get some rest and then we'll talk about it.''

"We're talking about it now.'' Color flooded his cheeks, his eyes flashed, and he looked like the man in Nate's memory: Sheen the Dean, the man on the Hill whom you went to when you needed something done. "Don't you get it, Evan? Things have gone too far. Gotten too complicated. Jimbo's looking at dollars and cents and running scared. The—'' He started to cough, then hack, great wrenching hacks that sounded as if his lungs were blowing apart inside his chest. He doubled over, clutching himself at the waist until it passed.

"Let's get out of here, Henry.''

Sheen raised his head; he didn't look strong enough to speak, much less walk out under his own steam. Nate supported him until they were outside, then Sheen straightened up and insisted he could make it to the car unaided. Nate let go of his arm and Sheen, with puke on his clothes and his face the color of old butter, shuffled with quiet dignity beneath a graying sky.

But as soon as he was inside the car, he sank back against the seat and shut his eyes, his breath rattling in his chest like loose change in a cookie jar. "I'm taking you to the emergency room, Henry," Nate said.

Sheen lifted his head from the seat. "My flight leaves at ten tonight. Until then, the only room I'm going to is Room Thirteen, Evan. Now drive, will you? Just drive this heap and let the wind blow through. I love the smell of the wind. It reminds me of the things in my life that I did right."

He turned his face to the window and shut his eyes again. Nate's heart seized up with love for this man who was the brother he'd never had, a love that was all mixed up with flying and planes and war, with politics and secrets. He thought of himself standing alone against the committee, Sheen's vacant seat a silent reprimand, an invisible finger wagging at him from the grave, urging him to seal it up, bury it, let it go.

And then he drove, drove fast into the hills, into the scent of pine and green and approaching rain.

21

(1)

Thunder. A distant flash of lightning. The day darkening like a winter afternoon in Toronto or Minneapolis: This wasn't just some quickie shower on the way. This wouldn't be ten minutes of blinding rain, then bright clcar skies again. This, Aline thought as she peered through the Honda's windshield, was going to be a humdinger of a storm.

The sky sagged as if beneath the weight of the tremendous cumulus clouds that climbed through the waning light. Twenty thousand feet, thirty thousand, no telling how high they rose. It occurred to her that before she'd met Kincaid, clouds had simply been clouds, as indistinguishable from one another as yellow lollipops in a jar. Now they had names. Now she understood how they formed, how they behaved, and what each type meant to a pilot. Now she could tell the direction of the wind and estimate its velocity by watching clouds shift, dissolve, re-form. And it wasn't just clouds, she thought. Kincaid's perceptions had touched every facet of her world, enriching it, and so what if he was idiosyncratic? She could no longer imagine a life without him.

Fifteen to twenty years. Forget it. They would flee to Mexico with the cat, the skunk, the owl. They would settle in some charming seaside village where no one spoke English. She would bask in the sun, her skin would turn as brown as a peanut, and she wouldn't worry about skin cancer or bills or how things were supposed to be done. And when they were ready to leave, they would simply pick up and go.

A life on the run. The closer she got to Nate's house, the more attractive it looked.

It started to rain when she passed the first home on Melaleuca Trail, big, fat drops that smeared the dust on the front and back windows. Her wipers created dirty half-moons across the glass that reduced her visibility to about three feet. She slowed, downshifted into second, glanced in the rearview mirror. Headlights glimmered behind her. Someone who lived along the Trail, she thought, and dismissed it.

Nate's house stood alone at the end of the road. It looked ominous in the gloom, an enchanted castle at the edge of time. She made a U-turn in the cul-de-sac and cruised past slowly.

A gray van was parked in the driveway. A light burned in a window just above it, over the garage. There were no lights in the main house, at least none that she could see. But she wasn't going to take chances.

Aline parked in front of the house, slipped on her windbreaker, and put the P7 in one pocket, handcuffs in another. She got out with her canvas bag slung over a shoulder and rang the doorbell at the house first. When no one answered, she walked quickly toward the apartment over the garage, rain tapping the hood of her windbreaker.

Up the stairs. Punch the bell. Wait wait wait. *We could sure have us some fun before the ride.* . . . Yeah, well, fun's over, Sapizzo. She rang the bell again and stood off to one side, one hand on the gun in her pocket, the other clutching her canvas bag, her head bowed slightly.

"Yeah, okay, I'm coming, I'm coming," Sapizzo shouted. The door opened. "Well, hey, you're not the mailman."

"Nope." She looked up, grinning, the gun aimed at his crotch. He was wearing a short terry-cloth robe and was rubbing his wet hair with a towel. "I'm the bitch from the lighthouse. Now move back into the house or my first shot makes you a soprano."

His arms lifted slowly and he fixed his eyes on the gun. "Now just a goddamn—"

Aline swung the canvas bag, swung it hard. It slammed into his face and he stumbled back into the hall, arms pinwheeling, blood leaking from his nose. She kicked the door shut, astonished at how good she felt, then dropped the bag and advanced toward him with the gun cocked. He was sprawled on the floor, his hands at his nose. "That was for this morning, Sapizzo." She fired a shot to the right of his head and it exploded against the wall, spewing plaster. He jerked his legs up against his body and looked at her like she was crazy. Hell, maybe she was. "And that's just to remind you that cooperation is your best ticket out of here in one piece. We understand each other?"

"You crazy bitch," he hissed, his fingers standing against the floor now like the legs of a pair of large and very nasty spiders. "What the fuck you doin'?"

"Teaching you some manners. Scoot back nice and slow to that couch." A long couch with a solid pine base. "Now cuff your hand to the armrest." She tossed him the cuffs and he did exactly what she told him to do. "First question. Where was my little ride suppose to end?"

"Six feet under."

"And that order came from the colonel?"

He wiped the back of his hand across his nose, smearing blood across his cheek. "Yeah."

"And he also ordered you to kill Vance Liscomb and Hugh Franks."

"I don't know shit about that."

She fired at the floor an inch from his right foot.

"I swear!" he shrieked. "I don't know about that. I don't know who killed them."

It was difficult not to believe a man who would probably lick the floor if you told him to. "What's in the cavern?"

"I dunno. I swear. My card don't get me past the hangar. But twelve people work down there."

"Including a man named Ricardo Morales?"

"Yeah, yeah, he works there. In the computer room with Bullwinkle. He don't like some of the shit goin' down."

"What does Margaret Wickerd know that's such a threat to the colonel?"

"I think she saw somethin' she wasn't 'sposed to see and she's got this gizmo in her nose that one of them shrinks stuck up in there, some weird shit that makes her, like, real mellow, okay? She's . . . she's an experiment and she's not the only one. There're others, in other states, looney patients. And the colonel, he keeps tabs on some of these UFO groups, okay? That's part of what they do down there in the cavern with their computers. They . . . they listen, they spy, they plant lies in the whole UFO network, they . . ."

"Manipulate?"

Sapizzo's elevator finally reached the top floor and a light winked on in his eyes. "Yeah, yeah, that's exactly what they do. That's part of it."

"Is the colonel there now?"

"I'm not sure. He and his buddy Sheen was goin' to join the chopper search. Don't know if they did or not."

"What kind of security does this place have?"

He told her about the security and the layout and how many people would be on duty today. Within the parameters of what he knew, he gave her the answers to whatever she asked, singing the way cons usually sang, as though the sweet clarity of the lyrics would save them.

When he had nothing more to tell her, she went into the bedroom to get the keys to the van. There were two packed bags on the bed and the dresser drawers were empty. It looked like this loyal foot soldier knew he'd screwed up bad when he'd failed to snatch her and had decided to hit the road.

"I got news for you, Sapizzo," she said as she returned to the front room. "The only place you're going is back to prison. But I think I'll let you sit awhile before they pick you up. Enjoy what's left of your freedom."

She left him handcuffed to the couch with his nose already swollen and turning a soft shade of purple and his vocal cords crackling as he hurled obscenities at her back.

The noise of the rain swallowed his voice as soon as she was outside. She unlocked the van, tossed her bag into the passenger seat, then drove her Honda into the trees across the road from the house. She hoofed it back to the driveway and climbed behind the wheel of the van.

And what a fine van it was: leather captain's chairs in front, tinted windows covered by miniature Levolor blinds, a dashboard that belonged in the cockpit of a 767. The middle seats had been removed and the floor was piled high with camping gear.

Things were certainly starting to look up, she thought, and flicked the key in the ignition, put the van into gear, and let her roll.

(2)

Margaret wasn't sure what she'd expected, but she knew it wasn't this. How could this be a weather research station?

The tall chain-link fence that marked the government property didn't look sturdy enough to survive a strong wind. The padlock on the old gate was already broken, so they drove to within a quarter of a mile of the hangar, then ditched the Rambler in the trees and continued the rest of the way on foot.

Rain poured over them. Trees rustled and swayed in gusts of wind that blew in from the east. When they were within a thousand feet of the front of the building, the trees suddenly ended and they stopped.

"There must be some sort of perimeter security that starts just beyond this point," Kincaid said. "The trees here have been cleared out."

"How do we get past it?"

"It depends on the type of sensor. But the safest bet is probably over the roof, then we drop down in front of the door."

"You going to tell me you have wings under that poncho, Ryan?"

He laughed. "I wish. C'mon, let's find a tree to climb."

They veered left, following the line of trees to the eastern side of the building, which was less than a hundred yards from the lip of the cliff. Here, a line of mushroom trees— *banyans*, she thought, suddenly remembering their name— formed a wall of green that broke up the wind. Their roots had long since pushed up through the soil, creating a thick network like a miniature interstate that would eventually burst through the hangar wall. The branches had been trimmed recently, but over the years the wind had pushed the tops of the trees in toward the building.

"The second one," Kincaid said, pointing.

"Let's try it."

Despite the rain and her awkwardness, the tree wasn't difficult to climb. There were dozens of footholds and the branches were thick and strong. But the higher they went, the worst the wind became, shrieking in off the Atlantic with the fury of a bitch in heat. It slapped at the leaves and snapped smaller branches against her knuckles and cheeks.

When Kincaid was slightly above the height of the hangar roof, he stopped, looked down at her, and shouted, "Right here." He adjusted the canvas pouch at his waist, slipped his weapon inside his poncho, then mounted the branch as though it were a horse. He swung his legs up, leaned forward, and inched along the branch, pushing with his feet. He looked like a giant snake. Less than a minute later the branch snapped back and he was on the roof, motioning for her to follow.

She climbed another three feet, mounted the branch as he had done, and made the mistake of looking down. A wave of dizziness washed over her, a sourness surged in her throat, and she squeezed her eyes shut. *Jesus, I can't do this, I don't know how, if I fall . . .*

Kincaid shouted something; his voice sounded frail and distant. She opened her eyes, forced herself to lean forward, to bring up her legs as he had done, and yes, okay, it would

be okay if she didn't look down. But as she crept forward,
her body suddenly slipped to the right and she flipped over.
A scream clawed its way up her throat and died at the tip of
her tongue. She hadn't fallen; she was clinging to the underside of the branch, water dripping into her face, the wind
swinging her back and forth like a hammock. She moved
hand over hand, pushing herself along with her feet, the muscles in her arms screaming for respite.

The branch dipped with the abruptness of a dowser's rod
and adrenaline coursed through her. She dropped her head
back and saw an upside-down Kincaid perched at the edge
of the roof to catch her, Kincaid shouting, ''C'mon, c'mon,
c'mon,'' as though it were a relay race. In a burst of reckless
speed, she scrambled the last foot and a half, he grabbed her
around the waist, and she let her legs swing down and released the branch.

They stumbled, she fell to her knees, and she didn't move.
Then laughter shoved up from someplace deep inside her and
exploded from her mouth. Kincaid grasped her elbow, pulled
her up, and they moved across the slope of the roof to the
front of the hangar.

Margaret spotted the camera first, a dark shape huddled
under the eaves. It moved slowly from side to side, scanning
the area in front of the hangar. Kincaid flattened out on his
stomach and emptied two shots into the neck of the lens.

''There's a narrow ledge just under the eaves. As you ease
your way over the side, let your feet swing toward it and use
it to push away from the hangar as you fall. Don't tense up.
Keep your legs loose and just drop.''

She nodded, moved to the edge of the roof, turned so she
was facing him. She slipped slowly over the side, her feet
grappling to find the ledge as she repeated his instructions
silently to herself. Then she was swinging, dropping, her
arms straight up over her head, the ground rushing to greet
her. She landed on both feet, but it felt as though she had
jarred loose every major organ inside her. She scampered
toward the hangar's metal door and pulled the SmartCard—
or whatever she should call it now—from her pocket.

Moments later, Kincaid dropped to the ground with the certainty of a cat that knows it still has nine lives ahead of it. She found the slot for the card, inserted it, and the door whispered open.

(3)

Sheen was seated on the couch in Nate's office, clutching a mug of hot tea as he went through some of the month's reports. A blanket was wrapped around his shoulders and he hadn't had a coughing spell since they'd left the airport. He looked better, but that wasn't saying much.

"How about a bite to eat, Henry? I can get one of the men to fix you something."

He shook his head without glancing up. "Don't feel much like eating."

"You feel like taking a walk? *To Room 13, old buddy? To the place that makes it all worthwhile?*"

"In a minute, Evan."

The phone rang. Nate hoped it was Jones with good news, but it was Bullwinkle in the computer room. "Sir, camera one went on the fritz a few minutes ago and camera two is starting to act up. You want me to send someone topside to take a look at them?"

"Any activity in the perimeter security?"

"Nope, nothing."

"Then wait until the storm passes. And tell Dole to put in a requisition for cameras that are impervious to electrical storms."

"Dole's off for the week, sir."

"Tell Morales to do it."

"He's off, too."

The whole goddamn staff was out to lunch. "Then you do it, Bullwinkle," he snapped.

"Right away, sir."

"And make sure the cameras aren't Japanese."

"I will. And, uh, sir? You know that septic tank problem I mentioned this morning?"

Nate squeezed the bridge of his nose. "Deal with it. That's what you're paid for." He slammed down the receiver.

Sheen clicked his tongue against his teeth; a malicious glee danced in his eyes. "Your blood pressure, Evan."

"You sound like my wife."

"Jimbo's going to shit when he sees these figures."

Nate ran his palm over his bald head as he paced across the room and back again. "Then I'll change the figures."

"Look, there'll be other projects for you that—"

"Cut the crap, Henry." The sound of his own voice astonished him; it was razor-sharp and very, very soft. His hand covered the small black box hooked at his belt. His thumb stroked it, caressed it. "We both know there won't ever be anything else like this. It was supposed to be a ten-year project and it's been five. Give me the other five years. Convince Jimbo. He still listens to you. It takes time to run experiments, to analyze data, to monitor the progress of the whole thing, Henry. Five years. And don't tell me the money isn't there. I know it is."

Sheen set his mug of tea on the coffee table with a sigh and rubbed his hands over his face. "Evan, this isn't the same world that it was five years ago. No Berlin Wall, no Soviet Union, no cold war, no space race. The boom's over, the economy is fucked, banks are closing every day, and I know guys in the Pentagon who're shitting bricks about their own job security."

"Spare me the nightly news report."

"You're missing the goddamn point, Evan. In a climate like this, you can't justify millions to produce more stealth bombers. You can't justify a star-wars defense system. And you can't justify a mind-control experiment that may or may not blow apart tomorrow."

"It's not going to blow up. There're some minor problems, yes, but any project has problems. The—"

"*Minor* problems?" Sheen exploded with laughter. "My

friend, I'm afraid that Margaret Wickerd is more than just a minor problem. But Margaret aside, Evan, the bottom line is that in today's political climate, how're we going to use what we've learned? What're the practical applications? Just who the hell are we going to brainwash?''

He didn't understand, Nate thought. It wasn't just about brainwashing. It was about manipulation of public opinion. It was about involvement in the birth of a new pattern and monitoring how that pattern built momentum and perpetuated itself. A unique type of alien had been introduced into the collective consciousness. Didn't Sheen understand that if they could do it with a goddamn alien, they could do it with virtually anything? A political candidate, a product, a religion—the possibilities were limitless. ''You don't get it.'' Somehow, that was all he could say. That Sheen didn't get it. Christ.

''No, *you* don't get it. It's too late, Evan. Ole Jimbo Booth thinks you consider this project your private playground, and that's a quote,'' Sheen said. '' 'Evan's private playground.' So yesterday afternoon he called an emergency meeting of the committee—''

''He can't do—''

''Sure he can. Four's a quota. And three out of four voted to pull the plug on funds, Evan. That means you and your people have two weeks to dismantle everything and then this sucker''—he opened his arms wide—''will be sealed.''

That word, *sealed*, bounced around inside Nate's skull like a tight, hard ball. He stared at Sheen, at his open arms, and was only dimly aware that he'd reached inside the middle desk drawer, that his fingers had closed around his service revolver. Its appearance was almost as much of a surprise to Nate as it was to Sheen, who pressed back against the couch, his arms dropping to his sides like lead weights.

''Jesus, Evan,'' he whispered.

''No one's going to take this away from me, Henry. I can't let that happen. Stand up.''

''You don't want to do this, Evan.''

"Stand up!" he barked. "We're going to Room Thirteen for a ride."

Sheen pushed to his feet and stood there like a man who believed that the rest of his life had been reduced to a matter of minutes.

(4)

Kincaid turned off the light in the elevator as it descended. The darkness might give them an edge in the event that the doors opened to people. But it was like being sealed up in a coffin that was plunging toward some bottomless grave. His ears popped, his gut lifted into his throat, he thought he was going to puke.

Then the elevator slowed, stopped, and the doors whispered open. A hall. Dimly lit and as empty as the moon. He stepped out, the P7 tight in his hand, Margaret hugging his back. A door to his right was ajar, light spilling through it and into the hall. As he advanced toward it, he sensed the weight of the earth above him and wondered how far down they were. A hundred feet? Two hundred?

They reached the door and took up positions on either side of it. Kincaid nudged it open wider with his shoe. A man the size of a small house was seated on a stool in front of a counter filled with electronic equipment. His blubber melted over the sides of the stool, rendering it nearly invisible. His back was to them. He was fiddling with dials on a CD player, adjusting the volume of music that was soft, unobtrusive, but loud enough to cover the squeak of his damp shoes against the floor.

Kincaid got to within a foot of the guy before he turned. His mouth literally fell open, his jowls quivered, and the half-eaten candy bar in his hand dropped to the floor as he raised his arms.

"You make a move, you're dead."

"No problem, man."

"How many people are in the complex?"

"Six. No, seven."

"Where's Colonel Nate?"

"Level two. In his office with Mr. Sheen."

"Congressman Sheen?"

"Yes."

"Where's everyone else?"

"Carruthers is on duty in Room Thirteen, level two. The others are on level three, checking out a problem with one of the septic tanks."

"It takes three guys to check out a septic tank?"

"It's a big tank with a big leak and it may have seeped into one of the pools we use for drinking water and the sprinkler system."

"And that's it?"

"Yes."

"How do I find the colonel's office?"

"First door to your right as you step off the elevator."

"What's your name?"

"Vic. They call me Bullwinkle."

"Pick up your candy bar, Bullwinkle."

"Excuse me?"

"Your candy bar."

"Oh." He tried to laugh. "Right."

As he stooped to retrieve it, Kincaid hit him over the head with his gun. He slumped off the stool, blubber quivering. "Nighty-night, Bullwinkle."

"Catch, Ryan." Margaret tossed him a roll of silver duct tape and they wrapped Bullwinkle up like a chocolate bar.

(5)

Aline had stopped once to buy gas and to call Bernie. But she wasn't in, so she'd phoned Bill Prentiss at the hospital and told him where to find Paul Sapizzo. He said he'd relay the information to Frederick—discreetly—and asked where she was headed. She had replied she didn't know and said she'd be in touch. She now regretted the lie; she had the uneasy feeling that she was going to need help before this was finished.

A lot of help.

She was parked alongside a green Rambler. Even without the BE KIND TO FERRETS bumper sticker, she would have known to whom the car belonged. Ferret used to drive it years ago when she'd met him. She thought he'd sold it. Kincaid obviously knew a few things about Ferret that she did not and the reverse was apparently true as well. Perhaps Ferret had known all along where Kincaid was hidden and had elected not to tell her because he, like Kincaid, didn't want to compromise her job.

What fucking job?

She slammed the van into gear and drove through the trees until the hangar was in sight. No cars. No people. Nothing around at all. The place looked as deserted as it always had. She stopped just short of the metal door, slipped on the windbreaker's hood, and kept her head bowed as she climbed down.

Morales's plastic card fit; the door slid open and she drove into the hangar. She parked next to a red Porsche Carrera, then stripped off her windbreaker. As she turned to toss it into the rear of the van, a lump of blankets lifted up from the lengthening shadows like a corpse rising from the dead and began to speak in the voice of Jean Mancino.

22

"Don't be mad at me, Detective Scott. Please. I had to come. I followed you in the convent car to that house in the woods and then I . . . I saw you toss your bag in the van, so I climbed in and hid . . . Well, you know where I hid. I'll do anything you say, just don't tell me to leave, okay?"

Aline's initial astonishment and fury gave way to incredulity. Hadn't she just been thinking of the help she might need and didn't have? Granted, she hadn't expected it to arrive disguised as Jean Mancino, but, hey, Jean was functional and she'd had plenty of practice following orders.

"You don't even know what I'm doing here, Jean."

"You're here because of Maggie. Please let me help."

"You do exactly what I tell you or you're gone."

Her head bobbed enthusiastically.

"Okay, climb up here. Let's go over a couple of things."

She scrambled into the passenger seat like a grateful pet. "Margaret and the man you know as Ray Rourke are down in this complex somewhere. We're going to find them and whatever the colonel's got stashed away. I don't suppose you know how to shoot a gun, do you?"

"Don't you have a knife? I'm really good with knives."

Yeah, I bet you are. "No, I don't have a knife." Aline ejected the cartridges from the .38, gave her a quick lesson in its safety and use, then handed her the gun and decided she should probably have her own head examined. "Any questions?"

Jean lifted the gun with both hands, aimed at something beyond the windshield, and sighted down the barrel with the ease of an old pro. "I don't think so."

"One more thing. Don't ever aim it at anyone unless you intend to shoot it."

"Right."

"Let's go," Aline said, and hoped she wouldn't regret it.

(2)

The deeper they descended into the complex, the sharper Margaret's perceptions became. It was as if she had been born somewhere within these dimly lit corridors, in this tight, eerie silence, and was only returning to her natural element, like a fish to water.

When the elevator stopped, Kincaid stepped out first, like before. She worked off her damp shoes and socks as she waited. She could smell the political power in this air, a weighted, heady scent like that first whiff of damp loam in an autumn woods. A colonel and a congressman, two men with a secret who had excised a part of her life as though it was no more important than a slice of apple pie.

Surprise, boys. I'm here to collect.

Margaret moved down the corridor to the open door of Nate's office. She paused briefly, listening, heard nothing, and swung into the room. Kincaid was kneeling next to the couch, peering into what looked like an air-conditioning duct. A very large duct. Above his head, high on the wall, a red light pulsed. "What is it?" she whispered.

He stabbed his index finger at the light. "I think that means we're in deep shit, but for some reason the colonel decided an intruder wasn't as important as getting to wherever this leads. He and his buddy didn't leave that long ago, either. The mug of tea on the table is still warm. You game?''

She leaned over his shoulder and peered into the hole. Before she could reply, an alarm started to wail, a high-pitched sound that throbbed against the air like a tremendous heart jammed in adrenaline overdrive. She pushed her hands against Kincaid's back. "Move, just move!''

He ducked into the hole and she squeezed in behind him, Alice in pursuit of the elusive white rabbit.

(3)

Aline heard the wail seconds before the elevator reached the first level of the complex; it sounded as though the gates of hell had been flung open. Then the elevator door began to slide back and she glimpsed two men hovering outside, men with faces even a mother couldn't love, and she slammed the heel of her hand against the *Close* button.

One of the men shouted and grabbed on to the edge of the door with fingers like thick stumps and tried to wedge his body into the space to keep the door open. Aline whacked his knuckles with her gun, but the fingers didn't vanish. He had a hip and one leg inside the elevator when her arm jerked up and she squeezed the P7's trigger.

Nothing happened. The tricky grip, the cocking lever, pull the goddamn thing back. Jean let out a sudden, sharp cry, a battle cry, and her leg flew out, a weapon so accurate and precise that the man's body exploded away from the door and he fell back, back, and the door shut and the elevator started down again.

"You've got to teach me that trick,'' Aline murmured.

Jean was hunched forward like a Neanderthal, hands against her thighs, breathing hard, her copper hair wild. "Good trick,'' she said. "A real good trick.'' She straightened, flicked the Stop switch, and the elevator ground to a halt. "You can do it with hands, too, you know." She wiggled her hands in Aline's face, the right still clutching the .38. "These hands broke Dr. Liscomb's neck."

I'm fucked. She and this fruitcake were going to shoot it out in an elevator two hundred feet underground. But there was nothing menacing about Jean's posture. Her gun was aimed at the floor. Keep her talking, Aline thought. "Why Liscomb?"

"He and Hugh were arguing and I was watching from the supply closet through the crack in the door, and I saw him slit Hugh's throat, saw it, saw the blood, heard Hugh gasping for breath, and you can't just let something like that go by, so I flew out of that closet and broke his fat ugly neck. Maggie was trying to get off the table. He'd gagged her and put her in a jacket and zapped her without any medication and I got her off the table and told her to run like hell and she ran. Then I got the syringe and jabbed it into his neck. He was still alive, paralyzed but alive. I just don't see how that was wrong, Detective Scott, do you?"

As if they were chatting over tea and crumpets at a polo game. Aline's head pounded. *Jean, the wild card.* When she spoke, her voice sounded strangled, disembodied. "No, it wasn't wrong, Jean. You were protecting Maggie."

"That's right. I was. And then I had to even the score with her sister because what she did to Maggie wasn't right, and I was going to set Pete straight, too, but there wasn't time. Someone has to put things right in the world, otherwise bastards like my stepfather just keep on hurting people. Bullies, Detective Scott. I hate bullies. And I think this colonel is a bully, don't you?"

Bullies, uh-huh, she had to agree with her about bullies. "Absolutely." Whatever you say, Jean. "So let's go find him."

"Aren't you going to arrest me?" Her mouth twitched into a half-smile, as though the idea of Aline even attempting an arrest amused her.

"I resigned. I'm not in the cop business anymore."

"Oh." She frowned, as though this both puzzled and disappointed her, and Aline tensed in anticipation of a blow from Jean's powerful hands. But she released the *Stop* switch and the elevator started moving again. Aline felt giddy with relief and decided this was enough to make her believe in God and guardian angels. "Well, I just wanted you to know the truth."

Honor among lunatics. "I'm, uh, glad you did."

The elevator slowed and Aline held her hand poised above the *Close* button. But the door opened to a corridor that was utterly empty. The terrible wail assaulted them as they stepped out. Aline tried to remember what Sapizzo had told her about the layout of the complex. Left or right to the main cavern? Just go, she thought, and started down the left corridor with Jean hugging her back.

(4)

Tunnel or air duct: it was open to debate, Kincaid thought. The passage was barely four feet high and maybe three feet wide, which forced them to move like crippled ducks. But they didn't need flashlights; the luminous stuff that flecked the natural rock walls and that had given the cavern its name emitted enough of a glow to let them see where they were going.

It wasn't crystal but a tiny organism with a Latin name he could never remember, much less pronounce, whose entire purpose in life was to adhere to the rock and feed off moss and lichen until it had matured enough to reproduce. The glow actually came from the waste the organism exuded. Luminous shit. Mine it, package and market it, and it would probably outsell flashlights.

The tunnel curved, then forked. They stopped and dropped to their knees; the wail of the alarm was muted now, as distant as the surface of the world, Kincaid thought, and glanced at Margaret. "You call it. Right or left?"

She hesitated, rolling her lower lip between her teeth. "Right."

"Right it is."

A hundred feet in the passageway began to slope downward, juts of rock broke up the smoothness of the walls, and the ceiling had dropped to less than two feet, forcing them to crawl. "Wrong choice," she said. "Let's—"

The sound of a gunshot cut her off. It exploded through the tunnel with all the subtlety of a July Fourth celebration and was still echoing when it was followed by a second shot.

Suddenly the air leaped to life, a rushing tide of noise and movement as bats poured through the tunnel.

Margaret screamed and threw her arms over her head to protect her face. Kincaid hurled himself to the ground, whipped the hood of his poncho over his head, and propelled himself forward with his feet, trying to remain as flat as he could. He shouted for Margaret to move, to cover her head with her raincoat, then a bat struck him in the cheek, silencing him.

The ceiling dropped another six inches, making it impossible for him to sit up even if he wanted to. Bats fluttered and shrieked and clung to the walls, blocking off the glow from the rocks. He rolled onto his side and dug frantically in the canvas pouch at his waist.

C'mon, where is it, there, quick, aim it, go go go, he thought. A flame shot out of the butane lighter in his hand and leaped at a dark mass on the wall. The air instantly filled with the stink of charcoaled flesh. Bats squealed, wings beating wildly, and Kincaid spun like a dial, flicking the lighter again and again and again. Margaret scrambled past him, swimming through the erratic spill of firelight, and he skittered along behind her like a snake, the lighter nearly spent and the bats still squealing.

The floor dipped more steeply but so did the tunnel's ceiling. Only inches remained between it and his head and there appeared to be nothing but solid rock and bats around him. He squeezed up against the wall in front of him, still flicking the lighter, the squealing so pervasive that it seemed to be emanating from inside his own head. An ignominious death, suffocation by bats two hundred feet underground: Bubbles of panic broke against the surface of his awareness. Then he felt air against his cheek—*cool* air, *fresh* air. He flopped over on his stomach and dug his fingers into the crack where it was coming from. Dirt crumbled and fell away, exposing an opening large enough to wiggle through.

He shouted at Margaret and she dived through headfirst. The bats, sensing the fresher air, swooped down and Kincaid stabbed the lighter at them, the miserable little flame hissing and flickering, as he jammed his feet into the hole and squirmed. He expected to touch solid ground. Instead, his shoes slid around on a smooth, slick surface, like wet metal, and suddenly he was sliding down it on his belly, grappling for something to clutch, to seize.

A moment later he was knee deep in water that reeked of raw sewage. He couldn't see a damn thing, it was too black, and Margaret was shouting, "Over here, Ryan, over here!"

The big septic tank with a big leak. Gagging on the stench, he pushed through the water and realized it was rising.

Rising fast.

(5)

One moment she and Jean were running through a long, narrow corridor, and the next moment a dark mass filled the air in front of them. Bats. Hundreds of them. Spooked by the shriek of the alarm or by something else, they converged in a thick cloud, their ultrasonic cries like the chatter of machine-gun fire amplified by the walls of the tunnel.

Aline dived for the ground and curled up in a tight ball, her face smashed against her thighs, her arms wrapped around her head, and rolled until she struck the nearest wall. Bats slammed into her from every side, attached themselves to her clothes, sank their talons and little sharp teeth into her skin. She tore them away and pummeled them with her fists, her panic so extreme it effaced all sense of where she was.

Then it was over. The bats had flown on to wherever they were going and the alarm had stopped, as though the two events were connected. Aline lifted her head. The silence, abrupt and deep and terrifying, grabbed at her like a malevolent ghost. She sat up, her body smarting in a dozen places, her hands bleeding, her heart racing and leaping as she slapped the ground, feeling for her gun, her flashlight, her canvas bag.

''Jean?''

Nothing.

She stood slowly, her back against the cool, concrete wall. She said Jean's name again, louder this time, and moved away from the wall. She stumbled over something—her bag, it was her bag—and scooped it up. Lights suddenly blinked on along either side of the tunnel, tiny dim glows like aisle lights in a theatre.

She heard a whirring noise and dropped her head back. Sprinklers spun on the ceiling, but nothing came out of them.

Now the lights began to blink.

It was as if this place were alive, possessed of consciousness, and its neurological wiring had gone berserk. She didn't want to know what might be next—the ground under her feet trembling or rising, the walls breathing, a voice speaking to her from the depths of the cavern, some weird hallucination conjured from the heart of the place. She was afraid to know and she started running. Her shoes slapped the floor of the corridor, her bag knocked against her hip, her breath balled in her throat like food she could neither swallow nor spit out.

A low hum rippled through the tunnel. It was as if hundreds of tuning forks had been struck at once and they all resounded at the same pitch, middle C. She shouted Kincaid's name. The humming grew louder and the blinking lights angled uphill and she followed them until they simply stopped.

She stood at the edge of what seemed to be a vast, impenetrable darkness—the mythical underworld of the ancient

Greeks, the border between life and death, or just the lip of a cliff, no telling. But the hum radiated from the center of this darkness, and as it increased in volume, its pitch flew up the musical scale to a note high enough to shatter crystal, eardrums, china.

Water that reeked of raw sewage now flew from the sprinklers behind her, pounding her back, and she clambered down the slope knocking loose rocks and dirt. She stumbled at the bottom and dropped to her knees. She pressed her hands over her ears, her very bones seeming to vibrate, as if to adjust themselves to the pitch.

A glow burned from the middle of the darkness, the sky at sunrise or sunset, and it spread and brightened, punctuated by black gaps. The glow assumed a shape. A part of her knew what it was, knew what she was seeing, but the rest of her went empty and dark and slack, as though she'd been injected with a drug that anesthetized the vital connections between her brain and her body but left her conscious, aware.

The disk was as round as a Lifesaver and rested on a concrete surface. It was perhaps eight feet across and seven feet high. Light radiated from the bottom of it and from its middle, which was broken up by dozens of small, circular portholes. A door stood open at the side of it, a gaping mouth. Silhouetted inside it were Jean and a man, locked together as if in some strange and exotic dance. The light stabbed through the wild nimbus of Jean's hair as she clung to the man like a spider. Then they stumbled back through the door.

Aline leaped up and charged toward the platform. But the door slid shut before she reached it and the humming escalated and moments later, the disk began to rise.

(6)

Kincaid had climbed onto a low mound above the depression where the sewage had gathered, but the stuff was rising so rapidly, it was already leaking around his shoes again. He barely noticed it. He was staring at the platform in the middle of the cavern.

It was the kind that might hold a band at an outdoor concert, but there were no musicians on this sucker, no guitars, no drums, no piano, just a disk that was pale blue or silver and rising. Books, movies, stories told and retold when he was a kid, a strange light in a Himalayan sky. Folklore, myth, your basic bullshit, and yet it was right here in front of him and he couldn't move, couldn't wrench his eyes away.

But his hands remembered what they were supposed to do. They lifted the camera to his eye, his palm wiped frantically at the muck on the lens, and the motor drive whirred. Then something flashed into his peripheral vision and he lowered the camera and gaped.

Aline, frozen in the spill of pumpkin light. Aline, here.

He stumbled away from the mound shouting her name, but his voice didn't carry over the earsplitting hum. He fired his gun into the air, once, twice, three times, and her head snapped around and she started toward him.

(7)

The woman—*the loon, this is Jean the loon*—was unconscious when Nate dropped her on the floor next to Sheen. He left her there and leaned into Sheen's face. "We're going for a ride, Henry. We'll visit Jimbo. Won't he love it? The canceled project coming right to him." He laughed, but Sheen seemed oblivious.

Sheen, in fact, just sat there, clutching his bleeding shoulder and slumping against the wall where Nate had deposited him. His lips moved, but no words came out. His eyes bulged in their sockets as if from some internal pressure, but they were unfocused, glazed. Nate hadn't meant to shoot him, he really hadn't, but Sheen had gone for his goddamn gun back there in the tunnel. Now it was too late. For Sheen, for the woman, for all of them.

Nate's hand dropped away from the black box hooked at his belt and he squeezed into the seat at the console. Relief hissed through him, relief and a kind of peace. Mine, he thought, running his hands lightly over the console. Mine.

Never mind that it was manmade, built over a two-year period before the Lost Pleiade had become his project. Never mind that the technology that made it fly was strictly of this planet. He didn't care. It was his.

"We'll scare the Commies shitless," Booth had boasted. *"We'll let the word leak out slowly."* But somewhere along the way that idea had changed, transmuted, become this other, larger plan to create and manipulate a pattern. And then everything had changed, the world had changed, the Cold War had ended and the Soviet Union had crumbled.

Nate pulled the black box from his belt. His fingers played a coded sequence that opened the heavy metal door at the entrance to the cavern. He intended to fly the disk through it. It had arrived through this door swathed in black plastic on the back of a flatbed truck, and it had left through this same goddamn door on many nights, hovering like the real thing, rising like the real thing, sighted by people like Margaret Wickerd and claimed to be the real thing.

So tonight it would be the real McCoy again. He would fly it out over the water, out over the Tango bridge toward Key West, and then he would do what people were always saying a UFO should do. He would drop in for dinner at the White House.

(8)

Margaret had seen Kincaid stop, had seen the other woman, but she had kept on running toward the mouth of the cavern. Now she stopped, watching as the disk lifted toward the ceiling, its glow melting over the walls and spilling onto her skin. She stood transfixed just short of the rising door, mesmerized by the disk's beauty, its strange magnificence. Gears shifted in her memory; doors slammed open; images filled her. She remembered that night.

It erupted through the layers of false memories they had implanted: how she had been grabbed out in the woods, drugged, brought here to this complex, and taken to a white room within that disk. She remembered the lights, the voice, the images of beings that had flashed around her in the room, holograms, she thought, or something else, but not real, definitely not real. Had Treak done the implant? Liscomb? Did it matter now?

And this thing in front of her, it was what she had seen in the woods. And now she could imagine the man inside, a man no more alien than she who was making the disk rise, dip, hover above the rising water like some futuristic ark. Then it pitched from side to side like a spinning top losing momentum. Its lights blinked off and on. Its glow faded, brightened, faded again. The humming leaped an octave higher into a shrill and terrible keening, the sound of a sentient being seized by agony, trapped in it, as though the disk itself were alive and aware that it was falling, that it was dying.

Margaret spun and charged up the gravel slope behind Kincaid and the woman. She didn't know who the woman was or where she'd come from, but it didn't matter. She ran as she had never run in her life and barreled through the mouth of the cavern seconds before the disk struck the platform. The explosion hurled a ball of fire and smoke that shot out behind her and lit up the wet twilight like a sun going nova. She stumbled over the rocks and raced away from the hangar, her bare feet pounding the ground.

(9)

Birds, Aline heard birds, and then the air was thick with
them. They lifted in dark, noisy clouds from treetops, wings
beating the twilight in a blind, white panic. And then she felt
what the birds had already sensed, a rumbling deep in the
earth, the eruption of gas lines, electrical circuits, fuel
pumps. Aline hurled herself to the ground, pulling Kincaid
with her.

He landed on top of her just as the first explosion decimated the hangar and blew off the eastern edge of the hill,
altering the shape of the island forever. It jettisoned debris
more than a hundred feet into a flaming sky, ignited an av-
alanche of rocks and trees from which dust would still be
rising at dawn, and was felt at the south end of Tango Key.

The second and third explosions toppled banyans and
gumbo-limbos that were more than a century old, snapped
pines like matchsticks, and flung a ball of fire whose heat
was so intense that it burned an eighty-foot path through the
wet foliage of the wilderness preserve before it flew over the
side of the cliff and plunged into the Gulf below.

Aline braced herself for more explosions. But there was
only the muted thunder of falling rocks and, more distantly,
the sirens of police cars, ambulances, fire trucks. The greasy
stink of smoke and charred ruins mixed with the damp smell
of the earlier downpour. Just beyond her, tongues of flames
crackled through low bushes that were still dry enough to
burn, but not for long.

Kincaid rolled away from her, helped her sit up. Firelight
touched his forehead, his nose, his beard; the rest of his face
was cast in shadow. He looked, she thought, like a man who
wasn't sure whether he'd witnessed the impossible or an elaborate hoax. She knew the feeling, all right, and hugged him
fiercely until he pulled back.

"Christ, Aline, what the hell are you doing here?"

She pointed at the camera around his neck. "Did
you . . ."

He nodded, his eyes gleaming, then he pulled a leather-bound book from inside his jacket. "Nate's journal. I took it when we were in his office down there."

"Ryan?"

Margaret Wickerd emerged from the trees and Kincaid stood, helped Aline to her feet, and made the introductions. It was oddly fitting, she thought, to meet her now, like this, in the ruin of the Lost Pleiade. As if by mutual consent, the three of them started toward the road and the noise of the approaching sirens, asking questions and answering them, sometimes all talking at once and sometimes saying nothing at all. The stink of the sewage in the cavern, of the smoke in the air, clung to them long after they'd reached the road.

(10)

The small army of police cars, fire trucks, and ambulances screeched to a halt around them, encircling them. Kincaid saw Frederick leap out of the lead cruiser. He marched toward them through the glare of the headlights, moving like a man who had swallowed a box of lit cigars. Kincaid ignored him and answered the squeeze of Aline's hand.

"Hey," she said, "when do you want to leave for Chile?"

"You're the one with the job."

"I resigned. I think I'd like to go look for that ghost ship on Chiloé."

Resigned. She had resigned. He started to laugh. "And afterward?"

"I kind of like the idea of the lighthouse as an office."

"You'd better have a good explanation for this," Frederick roared, his face bright red.

"Mind your manners, Gene. This is Margaret Wickerd. How's Sam?"

Frederick managed a weak smile at Margaret, then

jammed an unlit cigar in his mouth. ''He'll recover. But you may not, Ryan. Now start talking.''

Kincaid handed him the journal and the camera. ''Those say it all, Gene. Now excuse us.''

They brushed past Frederick with an arm around each other's waists and started down the road, both of them glancing now and then at the sky. And there, high above the trees to his left, stood a small, bright light as motionless as a star. But as he watched, it began to move as the light in Nepal had moved so many years ago. It glided, it rose, it swooped downward in a quick, graceful loop. Then it shot straight up until it vanished and only a pale moon remained, hanging above the trees like a pearl, round and perfect and filled with promise.

About the Author

Alison Drake lives in South Florida. She is the author of *Tango Key*, *Fevered*, *Black Moon*, and *Lagoon*. She also writes mystery novels under the name of T. J. MacGregor.

The T. J MacGregor series continues as St. James and McCleary join forces again.